PRAISE

"A delightful novel about fate, second chances, and how our worst moments are only the gateways to the best moments to come. When you're finished, you'll be writing your own reverse bucket list to check off."

—JODI PICOULT, #1 *New York Times* BESTSELLING AUTHOR

"Nora's remarkable transformation is a testament to the power of second chances. Her quest to conquer her past and fulfill her reverse bucket list is bright with warm humor and poignant moments that will make you laugh, cry, and cheer for her all at once. With richly developed characters and a plot that keeps the pages turning, this novel is a captivating exploration of what it means to truly live. *Nice Work, Nora November* is a delightful reminder that no matter how bleak the past, the future is filled with endless possibilities. A must-read for anyone seeking inspiration and the joy of second chances."

—SUSAN WIGGS, #1 *New York Times* BESTSELLING AUTHOR

"Wonderful! Nora's amazing journey is fresh and heartwarming. This book is a keeper for sure!"

—SUSAN MALLERY, #1 *New York Times* BESTSELLING AUTHOR

"A touching, heartfelt story you won't want to miss! London will have you making your own reverse bucket list."

—LAURA GRIFFIN, *New York Times* BESTSELLING AUTHOR

"I love a gal with a list, and Nora November makes hers in reverse! With equal measure of heft and humor, this clever novel is brimming with inspiration, tenderness, hope, and heart. If you're looking for a feel-good story that will bring cheers and groans, laughter and tears, look no further than *Nice Work, Nora November*. It is a triumph to the dreamer, to the nonconformist, to the one who dares to take control and change her life."

—LORI NELSON SPIELMAN, *New York Times* BESTSELLING AUTHOR OF *The Life List*

"What if you had a near death experience and decided to create a 'reverse' bucket list of the simple things we sometimes take for granted? In Julia London's new book, she makes readers understand the fragility of life, the power of self-discovery, and how important it is to take control of your own life. A thought-provoking, delightful read."

—REA FREY, #1 BESTSELLING AUTHOR OF *Don't Forget Me* AND *The Other Year*

"A poignant, beautiful, and surprising novel. Julia London's writing is heartwarming and true."

—LIA LOUIS, INTERNATIONAL BESTSELLING AUTHOR

"A book that tackles serious issues, complicated families, a heroine who fails again and again . . . and somehow remains utterly charming throughout. The perfect blend of women's fiction and romantic comedy."

—KRISTAN HIGGINS, *New York Times* BESTSELLING AUTHOR

"*Nice Work, Nora November* is a sparkling, spirited, emotionally engaging story of self-discovery and reinvention. I loved it."

—JAYNE ANN KRENTZ, *New York Times* BESTSELLING AUTHOR

"A story brimming with hope, humor, and heart. I rooted for Nora November from the very first page, and so will you."

—TERI WILSON, *USA TODAY* BESTSELLING AUTHOR

"Nora is a character you are immediately rooting for—her story is funny, moving, and carries an important message about being true to yourself and finding your own happiness. Witty, warm, and wise—a wonderful read."

—DEBBIE JOHNSON, AWARD-WINNING AUTHOR OF *Jenny James Is Not a Disaster*

"Quirky, loveable Nora grabbed me from the beginning, and I couldn't let go—or stop rooting for her—until the very last page. Julia takes you on a heartwarming story of finding yourself, starting over, and forgiveness. I love all the heart Nora has and her perseverance to keep going and hoping even when everything falls apart. She's a modern-day, genuine heroine, and I adore her! Worth every second of reading!"

—JENNIFER MOORMAN, BESTSELLING AUTHOR OF *The Magic All Around*

Nice Work,
Nora November

JULIA LONDON

Nice Work, Nora November

Published by Harper Muse, an imprint of HarperCollins Focus LLC.

Library of Congress Cataloging-in-Publication Data

Names: London, Julia, author.

Title: Nice work, Nora November / Julia London.
Description: Nashville : Harper Muse, 2024. | Summary: "Now that Nora is not dead, only one question remains: what does she want to do with her life?"--Provided by publisher.
Identifiers: LCCN 2023057548 (print) | LCCN 2023057549 (ebook) |
ISBN 9781400245734 (paperback) | ISBN 9781400245741 (e-pub) |
ISBN 9781400245758
Subjects: LCGFT: Novels.
Classification: LCC PS3562.O48745 N53 2024 (print) |
LCC PS3562.O48745 (ebook) | DDC 813/.54--dc23/eng/20231218
LC record available at https://lccn.loc.gov/2023057548
LC ebook record available at https://lccn.loc.gov/2023057549
Printed in the United States of America

24 25 26 27 28 LBC 6 5 4 3 2

Who looks outside, dreams; who looks inside, awakes.

—CARL JUNG

Chapter 1

L*ater, people would ask her what it was like.*

"Death?" Nora would ask casually, as if she were a frequent traveler to this other realm with a return ticket. "Nothing like you could ever imagine." Which she knew wasn't terribly illuminating, but it was the best she could do. It was beyond her ability to account for her near-death experience. How could she adequately describe finding herself wedged into the frayed seam between life and death, neither alive nor dead, like some philosophical riddle on a college entrance exam?

Her response was inevitably followed by a pause in which the listener would politely wait for her to imagine for them. But that was all she had the words for. "You kind of had to be there," she'd say.

She hated when people said that.

She didn't want to be coy, but that extraordinary event was too precious, and too complicated, to try to put into words. It separated her new, improved life from the life she'd had in the Before, and it was deeply personal. Dying, then coming back to life, had altered her at the cellular level. She felt reimagined and reinvigorated, capable of things she'd never even contemplated, like rock climbing and trigonometry. Not that she intended to tackle either of those things—at least she didn't think so; it was simply knowing that she could. How hard could anything be after surviving death? Her optimism was as high as if she'd been shot through with vats of B12 and Pacific sunsets.

She had no idea how she'd shown up at death's door or how she'd died. And yet, the facts were irrefutable—she'd been clinically dead, having spent several minutes underwater.

The November family was not particularly religious except when it served a purpose . . . like when an important client invited them to Easter church services and her father made them all attend. Still, Nora was familiar with the traditional symbols and had expected pearly gates and cherubs with lutes flitting around her. At the very least, the angel Gabriel checking in newcomers. Or Lucifer ushering the ones who'd found themselves at the wrong entrance into the fiery pits of hell. But when she died, there was nothing to suggest that she'd entered another realm.

Early in her legal career, she'd represented a family whose car had been hit by a casket. A truck was carrying several of the company's best sellers when the chain holding them on the back of a flatbed broke. The caskets bounced off and onto the highway, piling up like a giant version of the game Jenga. In preparation for that case, Nora had seen so many caskets that it was inevitable she would think about being stuck in one and planted six feet deep in the ground for all eternity. Not unreasonably, given the dimensions of your average casket, she'd imagined cold and lonely, dark and cramped.

It was a great surprise, therefore, to discover that death was, in fact, deliciously warm, like the first spring day after a long winter or the warmth she remembered feeling in her grandmother's kitchen.

It wasn't dark either—she'd found herself lying in a field bathed in soft gold light, the color of dusk on an autumn evening. Not the light of the sun, exactly, but something richer, soaking into her like cream on cake.

Nor had she anticipated beautiful, ethereal birdsong. It reminded her of childhood summers she'd spent at the family ranch in the Hill Country, where she'd wake every morning to the chirping and singing of mockingbirds. She'd loved their chatter.

Her father had not. *"What is making all that racket?"* he'd bellow. Then one morning a man in a blue work shirt and stained trucker hat pulled up in a pickup truck hauling a strange-looking cylindrical thing. *"This will get rid of the birds, the neighbors, and anything else you don't want,"* he'd said and patted it like it was a dog. It turned out to be a cannon, which he and Dad gleefully fired, the massive *boom* reverberating through the hills like a Revolutionary cavalry. In the kitchen, two empty glasses shimmied right off the edge of the counter and shattered on the tile floor.

The mockingbirds didn't come back. Neither did the squirrels.

On the day she died, Nora thought maybe the mockingbirds were in that golden field with her. They sounded better than a symphony, the only thing she knew to compare it to . . . but even that description trivialized what she heard.

The sensations—the warmth, the light, the sound—had put her in a state of perfect tranquility, and while she'd understood she was most likely dead, she couldn't grasp *why* she was dead.

She'd sat up, feeling certain that the precipitating event to one's death would stick out in memory, right up there with weddings and births and heartbreak. Or, at the very least, there would be a clue nearby. Like the twisted metal of a car. Or a gun.

There was nothing.

She noticed she was wearing her favorite dress, the one she'd worn to her she-passed-the-bar-exam party her parents had thrown for her at the Headliners Club in Austin. It was pale blue with off-the-shoulder straps and a sparkling skirt over tulle.

That night was the one time in her life she'd felt like a princess—beautiful and enchanting and proud and unreachable.

If she had to be dead, she was happy that at least she was stylish about it.

Her joy—and it *was* joy—felt like champagne bubbling in her veins. She glittered in the same way she had when she fell in love for the first time with dreamy Ramon Toledo in the ninth grade, but on a supernova level. She felt pure and unfiltered, free of every single burden she'd ever felt in her entire life, floating away from all the worries that had been her constant companions through thirty-one years of living. It was an extraordinary amalgam of orgasm and Christmas morning and a baby's laugh all rolled into one.

She marveled at the spectacular view around her—the field of gold, the deep green of a distant tree line. And just ahead, a lush, verdant garden where the light seemed a little brighter, beckoning her.

She began to move, but a dog's bark stopped her—and not just any bark. She turned to see a shaggy black-and-white dog racing toward her, and her heart immediately swelled. "Roxie?" The word was more of a croak because something was lodged in her throat. She tried again, but nothing would come. She was overcome with happiness—this was the dog she'd raised from a pup, her constant companion, her best friend during those periods in her life when no one else would be, who'd crossed the rainbow bridge when she was in college. Roxie leapt into her arms and began to lick her face. Nora could feel the solid weight of Roxie's body against her, could feel the wet slurp of her tongue against her cheek. She buried her face in Roxie's fur. She smelled like flowers.

Death was fantastic! Everything around her was bursting with color, the air was crisp and clean, she was beautiful, and Roxie was here. When had she ever felt such peace?

She looked toward the garden again and felt an urgent need to get there. The mechanics of movement required no effort—she glided along. Roxie led the way, trotting ahead, then circling back to make sure Nora was coming.

When they reached the garden, her dog disappeared into one of the deep rows, her snout to the ground. Nora could barely absorb all the beauty in that garden. The shrubs were kaleidoscope shades of green, the fruit trees as tall as buildings. A patch of peonies as big as dinner plates intruded onto the path, bursting with colors she'd never seen in life. She wanted to feel every velvety vine and silky petal. She wanted to drink the heady scent of floral and clover. She wanted to bathe in the petals of perfect flowers and eat the fruits that hung ripe for the plucking.

A contented hum filtered into her conscience. She glided deeper into the garden in search of the source and spotted a being standing amid tomato plants that grew like trees. Roxie trotted right up to the being, and it said, "Hello, Roxie, hello, old girl. I wondered where you'd got off to."

Nora's heart immediately climbed to her throat. "Grandpa?"

Grandpa turned and smiled. It really was him, her beloved grandfather, gone from her life too soon. "Well, hello, Nora," he said cheerfully. "I wasn't expecting you yet."

A swift and deep rush of love washed over her—she'd always loved her maternal grandfather best of all, had missed him so much it hurt. But she'd forgotten until that moment what it felt like to love him. Safe. Weightless and free to be exactly who she was. He'd always protected her, advised her, listened to her. No one had ever made her feel quite so loved as he had.

Grandpa looked good. Ageless. A perfect specimen of a grandfather. He was wearing his typical spacious denims with the cavernous pockets. He'd always kept surprises in those pockets for Nora and her younger sister, Lacey: A robin's egg. Seeds. Hard candy. He had his familiar red wagon by his side, his ratty sun hat atop his head. Once, she'd gifted him with a new sun hat. He'd hung it proudly in the mudroom, but he never wore it—he preferred his old sun hat for working in the garden.

Nora tried again to speak and croaked, "Grandpa! I'm dead!" She must be, if she was here with Grandpa. But she wasn't certain if he understood what was happening and felt it was important to explain why she was here.

"Well, you look beautiful. Come over here and give me a hand, will you?"

Paradise. That's where she was. She was with Grandpa and Roxie in a stunning garden, and it was absolute paradise.

Grandpa turned back to the tomato plants and cut a tomato as big as a volleyball from the vine and placed it in his wagon. He cut another one and bit into it, juice dripping down his chin. "That's good." He held up the tomato for her to take a bite. The burst of flavor in her mouth was so shockingly delicious that she never wanted to eat anything else ever again.

"I've got an excellent crop," Grandpa said proudly. He cut two more from the vine and put them in his red wagon. "It's the compost. You get some great compost here." He moved down the path.

She grabbed the wagon handle, trailing behind him like she always had during those summers spent with her grandparents at the ranch. She'd follow him for hours, pulling the red wagon and saying aloud every thought that popped into her mind, no matter how trivial. He never tired of her. When she asked if she could be in the rodeo when she grew up (because her sister said she couldn't), Grandpa said she could be anything she wanted to be in the whole entire world. When she pondered if she wanted to be Mandy Grant's friend anymore because Mandy had told Kelly, who told Sariah, who told Nora that Mandy thought Nora's hair was cut like a boy's, Grandpa said she could be friends with whomever she pleased, but that he didn't think a haircut was something to end a friendship over. The point being, he listened.

As she followed him now, Nora noticed the light near the back of the garden seemed to be expanding onto the path they were on. It was getting brighter, turning from gold to pale yellow to almost white. It reminded her of a veil—something shimmering and beautiful was behind that bright light. "Is that a lake?"

"Don't look back there, kid. Look at this squash." Grandpa held up a yellow squash the size and shape of a baseball bat like he was the Lion King holding his cub. He put it in the wagon. "You like salad, Nora?"

"I *love* salad." She stated this with an enthusiasm she'd never felt about salad.

"You know what the secret is to a good salad?"

The secret to a good salad was the dessert that came after, but she gave it her best guess. "Dressing?"

"Nah, dressing is superficial—you pour it on top to make it look good. A good salad is about the ingredients underneath the dressing. You gotta have the right mix of flavors. Too much of one thing throws the whole salad off. Not enough of another thing, it's boring. Do you understand?"

She understood the words, but they seemed to be dripping with meaning she couldn't grasp.

Grandpa produced a perfect watermelon crescent. He bit into it, then handed it to her to taste. "Do you remember what I told you makes for a good watermelon?"

"Lots of water," she said automatically.

Grandpa smiled proudly.

It was weird that she could remember some things with vivid clarity, but other things were murkier. Like how she'd gotten here.

A movement caught her eye—a stately Black gentleman dressed in a lab coat was standing beneath some orange trees. Jesus? But that didn't seem right because Nora was pretty sure Jesus wouldn't be there for her. He'd have nuns and other devout people he needed to greet. Still, she had a feeling she knew who the man was, but his identity slipped out of reach.

She turned back to the man who had shaped her life. The surge of love she felt for him was so great that she could barely physically contain it. But then something hard clamped down on her chest, making it difficult to breathe. She sensed her grandfather was about to slip away. Her euphoria began to sink under the weight of fear he wouldn't take her with him. "Grandpa, I'm so sorry—"

"Earthly concerns have no place here, Nora. They go in the compost bin. Come on, bring the wagon."

She tried to swallow, but the fear of losing him was stuck in her throat, choking her. She followed Grandpa, glancing over her shoulder at the shimmering white light again. She was desperate to stay here with him, where she was safe and loved.

"Don't look there, sweetie. Now, what are you growing in your garden? Did you tend my plot?"

When Grandma died, Grandpa sold the ranch and moved into senior living in Austin, where he got himself a plot in a community garden. Nora had solemnly promised that if anything ever happened to him, she'd take care of it.

A different sensation flooded her, hot and potent. Oh, she knew that feeling—it was shame, and it stung like the devil. She looked around for Roxie, needing her support. Roxie was gone.

"I never went, Grandpa." Her voice had grown shaky and coarse. She tried to clear her throat again, but that *thing*. It tasted bitter, like a big ball of regret.

The man in the lab coat was suddenly beside her. He put a hand on her arm and smiled kindly. "Just breathe."

Nora ignored him. "I didn't go, Grandpa. I didn't—"

"That's okay, Nora." Grandpa's smile sent a shock of warmth and forgiveness through her. "Look at these." They'd come upon a rosebush in full bloom, each flower at peak. "See how each petal is perfectly shaped and placed? And yet each one is unique. Magnificent, aren't they? Reminds me of the exhibit we talked about seeing at the Laguna Gloria art museum. Did you get to see it?"

"No." She felt small and plodding. Images and thoughts flew at her, scenes from her life, bits and pieces of the mundane mixed with terrible upheaval. Her thoughts were racing through all the things she'd meant to do but never had. The list of things left undone sailed past her like a flock of swallows. There were so many.

Grandpa gave her a reassuring smile. "You're a good girl, Nora. But you must believe in yourself." Love radiated from him, wrapping around her and holding her close, banishing her shame. She turned, trying to see the bright light, but she couldn't turn her head enough—something was blocking her.

"Just breathe," the man in the lab coat whispered.

Everything started to go all *Alice in Wonderland*. The bright light was fading away, sucking up all the warmth as it went. Grandpa's love was fading. Everything was turning cold.

"Nora? Listen to me now."

She felt heavier. Distressed. She looked down—her beautiful dress had turned to gray cotton. She was slowly slipping into a dark hole that felt like the death she would have expected. Was she going to *really* die now? "Grandpa?" She tried to reach for him, but her arms were useless. She was desperate to hang on to the one person she felt had truly loved her. To the only person in her life who seemed to understand who she was.

"It will be all right, kid. This is the season to grow your garden. Plant what you need to make a good salad. Throw some nuts in there! Have a little fun!"

Nora couldn't breathe. She didn't want to go back to whatever had been before. "I want to stay!"

"Not now, sweetie." Grandpa's voice was even farther away. "You left too many things undone."

She tried to ask what, but her throat felt clogged. Grandpa was moving down the path with surprising speed. He whistled, and Roxie trotted out from between two bushes to join him. Nora was still gripping the wagon. "Wait!" she screamed.

But it was too late—everything had faded, and she had the sensation of falling into a dark, inky nothing. Hell, probably—what else could it be?

She fell and she fell and she fell for what seemed a very long time.

And then she woke up.

Chapter 2

N*ora! Can you hear me?"*

The voice sounded like it was underwater. Nora tried to respond, but it felt as if someone had shoved a fiery poker down her gullet.

"Oh my God, oh my God! Nora! Can you hear me?"

She recognized her sister's voice and turned her head slightly. It took a great effort to open her eyes, and when she did, Lacey was looming over her. She was wearing a dark suit with a white shirt buttoned to the very top. Her shoulder-length blonde hair looked uncombed, and there were shadows under her eyes. Nora knew instinctively she was the cause, and sadness began to throb at her temples. She felt alone in her grief, even though it was evident there were others nearby.

"It's going to take a minute for the medicine to kick in. Her throat will be raw," said a male voice.

"Blink if you can hear me," Lacey loudly commanded.

Nora blinked. Everything about her hurt. She tried to lift her head to see where she was, but it was excruciatingly painful. Something was beeping nearby, each sound a stabbing pain in her brain. *Beep. Beep. Beep.*

"Hey, kiddo."

She felt a big hand on her arm. Gus! Good ol' Cousin Gus. What was he doing here? Where *was* here?

"Are you okay?" All six foot three of him tried to smile, but it was a lopsided attempt, like he couldn't decide whether to commit to it fully. A thought whispered through Nora's head that it was hard for Gus to smile, and her sorrow ratcheted up.

"Do you remember what happened?" Lacey asked. "Blink once for yes, twice for no."

"Lacey, for God's sake, give her a minute."

That voice was unmistakably her mother's. Nora couldn't see her, but she felt the touch of cold fingers on her forehead. Did she have a fever? Was she sick? Was that what happened? She had a jagged recollection of some new virus going around.

"Nora." Her father's face was suddenly looming over her, his brow wrinkled with concern. She had to be on the cusp of dying, because her father never took time off from work. His salt-and-pepper hair was neatly combed, his face clean-shaven, his suit impeccable. Was *this* her real death? How was she to know? Death was so disorganized!

"I've got it all under control," her father said. But he looked slightly annoyed, and Nora could only surmise that she wasn't dying properly.

Lacey nudged Dad out of the way. "How do you feel?"

Confused. Detached from herself, like an astronaut untethered and weightless in space. Different in ways she couldn't make sense of. She didn't feel like she was in the right body. Her thoughts were racing in an endless loop, cleaving to straggling bits of euphoria while a new well of sadness slowly filled her chest.

What had happened to her? Was she dying or not, and who did she see about that? "Where am I?" Her bed suddenly lurched into motion, her head and torso rising. She squeezed her eyes shut and hoped she wouldn't vomit. When the bed stopped moving, she drew a shaky breath, forced a swallow against the burn in her throat, and slowly opened her eyes.

Her family was gathered around the bed. Dad, arms folded. Mom, a compact in her hand as if she was doing a little touch-up while she waited for Nora to wake up. Lacey. Gus.

It felt like there was something or someone in that room with them. Not a person, exactly, but a presence. Grandpa? Tears immediately filled her eyes. She'd lost him once, had found his lifeless body on his kitchen floor. But she'd found him again, in the garden, his old self radiating love, filling her with indescribable joy. She couldn't bear to lose him again.

"Nora, honey, you're in Austin, in a hospital," her mother said carefully. Her hair looked redder since the last time Nora had seen her. When was that? She was too thin, her cheekbones so sharp that Nora had once told Lacey they ought to come with a warning. "We had you transported from the coast."

The coast. The Texas coast? "What happened?"

"A miracle, Nora. A miracle happened." Lacey's voice was full of relief. "If that couple hadn't been there—"

"Lacey." Her father's tone was curt. He put a hand on Lacey's shoulder. "Let her recover before you give her all the gory details."

Gory? Maybe a car wreck? No wonder it felt like something was terribly wrong with her body.

"You had a bad accident, honey." Her mother leaned over to stroke her brow and tuck some of her hair behind her ear. "It was a terrible surfing accident. They say you were underwater for a long time."

A surfing accident? That would not have been Nora's first guess. Flotsam of memories floated back to her. Lots of very cold water. Goose bumps on her skin. A glimpse of a gray sky being swallowed by water. Raw, icy fear.

"You never should have been on that beach," her father said.

His disapproving tone put her squarely back in her childhood.

"The beach was closed. The hotel staff never should have taken you out there." He was pacing at the foot of her bed now, impatiently or angrily. It was hard to know with him.

"You've been through hell," Gus said. "Do you want to talk about it? Because I—"

"Thank you, Gus," her father said crisply. "Can we all take a breath here? Nora is fine. She's come out of it. You heard the doctor—she's young and healthy and should recover, so let's stop acting like she's about to kick the bucket."

Ah, so she wasn't on her way out but on her way back in, complete with a gaping hole in her memory about what had happened to her. Her brain felt full of debris, which was a bit overwhelming and explained why panic was chainsawing its way through her jumble of emotions. She needed to tell them that she'd been with Grandpa, but she couldn't gather the words. At least she thought she had been with him, but . . . Wait. Was it possible she'd dreamed everything? No! It had been so real. She could still taste the tomato. How high was her fever? Didn't people hallucinate with high fevers?

The door swung open, and a smiling nurse walked in. "Welcome back, Nora," she said, as if Nora had just hopped off a train that had pulled into the depot. "Dr. Umaru will be right back." She pressed two fingers to Nora's wrist.

"How long?" Nora asked hoarsely. "How long have I—"

"You've been on a ventilator," Lacey said. "Do you know the odds of getting off a ventilator?"

She did not.

"A week," her mother said. "The longest week of my life. Oh, Nora, you had us so frightened. I am so glad you're with us."

The door opened and a Black man wearing a lab coat, thick glasses, and a stethoscope sailed into the room. "There you are!" he said cheerily.

A jolt of recognition tore through her. "You were there," Nora managed. "In the garden."

"What's that?" He leaned over and studied her face. "I'm Dr. Umaru. I'm going to check a few things if that's okay." He put his stethoscope to her chest. "Those lungs are sounding a lot better. Can you wiggle your toes for me?"

She tried, but her feet were wooden. Any feeling of weightlessness had evaporated—she was like an immovable heavy bag of sand sinking into the mattress.

"Is she going to be brain damaged?" her mother asked anxiously. "Can you tell?"

"Let's give your daughter some time to fully wake up," Dr. Umaru said. He smiled at Nora and patted her arm. "You're going to have a lot of questions, I'm sure, Ms. November, but for now, just know that you were underwater for several minutes and were clinically dead when you were rescued. Your heart had stopped. But you're a fighter, Ms. November, and with the efforts of the first responders who got your heart going again, here you are. You're pretty banged up and you're going to require some physical rehabilitation, which is normal in these circumstances. Our social worker will be by later today to help—"

"We've got it taken care of, thanks," her father said dismissively.

Dr. Umaru glanced impatiently at her dad but turned a smile to Nora. "First things first, however. Let's get your strength back and make sure you don't develop pneumonia. If you keep progressing, we'll have you out of here before long. Follow this pen with your eyes, please," he said and held up an ink pen. As he moved it back and forth, he shone a light in her eyes. "All right. You get some rest, and we'll talk a little later. Good to have you back." He wished everyone a good day and went out of the room.

When the door swung shut behind him, her family started talking at once. They were laughing, making remarks Nora didn't quite get. But she understood they were relieved she was alive, and she wanted to laugh too. Only she feared her laugh would lean more to the hysterical, what with the panic slipping under the covers with her. Something had happened to her that went well beyond this hospital room. She'd drowned? It was clear that drowning had broken her physically, but it was more than that. Much bigger than that. She couldn't explain this painful resurrection she was having, other than oddly, it was a good painful resurrection. Panic notwithstanding.

She felt something wet on her cheeks, sliding into her hair. Tears. For Grandpa, for Roxie. For all the things she'd left undone. For herself. Tears of happiness. Of elation at being alive. Tears of sorrow. She would have wiped them away, but she didn't have the energy to lift her arm.

"Are you okay?" Lacey wiped away the tears for her.

"I miss Grandpa so much."

Lacey gave her a funny look. "I miss him too."

"Lace . . . I *died*," she whispered. "I died, and Grandpa was there, and so was Roxie."

"Roxie? Our dog? Where?"

"Good Lord." Her mother sounded tense. "Nora, that was a dream. It's the drugs they give you. When my sister had cancer, they gave her so many drugs that half the time she thought she was in Houston getting ready to play golf. You remember that, don't you, Gus?"

Gus's face darkened. His mother had died of that cancer.

"Roxie's been gone for years. I don't know why you'd dream about her," her mother continued, sounding exasperated and alarmed at the same time. "But that's all it was, honey, just a dumb dream."

Dumb? "No, it was amazing, Mom. I don't know how to even describe it. Grandpa was there. We talked." Nora's heart constricted painfully. There'd been so much more she'd needed to say to him. "He wants me to grow a garden."

"This is beginning to sound a little *Wizard of Oz*-y," Lacey said. "You didn't happen to see a tin man and a lion, did you?" She chuckled at her joke.

Didn't they understand what she was saying? "The doctor was there too. The one who was just here."

"Oh my God, it *is* brain damage," her mother whispered loudly to her dad.

"Don't be ridiculous," her father said. "Hallucinations are a common side effect of heavy sedation."

"I think it's kind of cool," Gus said.

Nora felt an odd sensation, like she was being cleaved in two—the weight of her family and who she'd been before she died was separating from the extraordinary moments she'd spent with Grandpa. Everything about her felt out of place. She belonged in that garden. Not here.

"I'm going to step out and call Cynthia and let her know you're okay," her mother said with a thin smile.

"Mom!" Lacey said, but her mother was walking out the door, already on the phone to her best friend, Nora's father hanging over her shoulder, probably asking how long he had to stay.

Exhaustion began to weigh Nora down. Her regrets and vague anxieties of things left undone continued to flit through her fluffy clouds of exuberance.

Inexplicably, one memory popped into her head, front and center. Of a man she'd met months ago in a corner store. They'd been caught up in an attempted robbery. She couldn't remember his name, but she could still see his face so clearly, and the scarf he wore around his neck. She remembered how she'd made him laugh. The connection had been instant, a preternatural tether between them. Like he was the first beam of sunshine to break a cloudy sky, pulling her attention to warmth and light.

What happened to him? She'd meant to call him, had written his phone number on the back of her hand at the time, but she never did. Why hadn't she? Why hadn't she done anything she'd meant to do?

Her head was throbbing now, making it hard to see. The beeping seemed louder. "My head," she moaned. "That beeping is killing me."

"I'll call the nurse," Lacey said.

"Is there anything I can get you?" Gus asked, looking worried.

"A tomato." It wasn't a joke—she wanted to taste that tomato again. She wanted to go back to the safety of the garden.

But first things first, the doctor had said. What was first?

"Grow your garden."

The words floated back to her on a whisper, instantly soothing.

Also, maybe she should get a dog.

Chapter 3

Nora's *recovery, both physical and mental, was dis*jointed and progressed slowly. Nothing in the After—as in, after the accident—felt the same as it had in the Before. Not her body, not her thoughts, not even the world around her. She felt fundamentally changed, which was both exhilarating and urgent—like she was speeding down a highway to something new and exciting, but the engine was on fire and she had to get there before her car exploded.

Some things were more vivid than before, like the feel of sunshine on her skin and the smell of the bouquets of flowers that arrived from friends of the family and office staff to wish her well. She'd been moved to a physical rehabilitation facility, secured for her at a high cost, her father made sure she understood. The patients were mostly geriatric, and no matter how much room freshener they sprayed, the smell of Bengay and bleach lingered. Dad said it was the best facility for "this kind of thing" in Central Texas. Lacey said it was the best facility because it was out of sight of family friends and clients.

Nora didn't care. The only thing she cared about was discovering how different everything seemed on this side of death. Some things felt much duller than they had in the Before. Such as time—she never knew what time it was and couldn't make herself care. At first, her sense of which world she was inhabiting had needed constant readjusting. Her dreams were filled with magic carpet rides and strangers and big tomatoes and crazy cloud art that was hard to distinguish from reality. Sometimes she thought she was in Grandpa's garden, only to wake up and realize she was in a rehab center.

But mostly, steadily, assuredly, she felt increasingly cheerful. Shiny and new. Her experience had rubbed off all the tarnish to reveal the real her, and she was gleaming, just like she gleamed as a girl when she'd been full of life and wonder and dreams of being a pirate or a pop star, because anything had seemed possible. Before she knew that people judged you for the way you looked, or where you came from, or for your dreams. Before life had begun to chip away at her.

She had a psychiatrist now; her parents had assumed Nora would need help with the emotional trauma she'd suffered from dying and coming back to life, so they'd retained Dr. Beth Cass, a middle-aged woman with long silvery blonde hair and lots of bangle bracelets.

Dr. Cass was unabashedly thrilled about treating a client who'd had a near-death experience. According to her, having wonky senses was to be expected. *"Your entire perspective on life and death has shifted dramatically while everyone else's has stayed the same. You're a butterfly emerging from a cocoon."*

Nora loved that description and imagined herself in full bright-winged glory, emerging.

Dr. Cass said it was so interesting to work with someone who had experienced a different dimension. Nora said she would not recommend near-death as a dimension, as it left a lot of questions in its wake. Dr. Cass said sure, but wasn't it more interesting to answer those questions than to know everything there was to know? And wasn't Nora lucky?

That's what everyone said—she was *so lucky* for having survived death. She was certainly lucky. But it was more than that—it was rejuvenating. *Lucky* sounded like she'd won a few rounds of bingo, whereas *rejuvenated* sounded like true transformation. She woke up every day bursting with an eagerness to be released from rehab so that she could sort out the new life she was determined to have, buoyed by her newfound optimism. She wasn't quite sure what that would look like, as she couldn't fully recall her life in the Before, but she knew she wanted to be a better person. She would read more books. Volunteer somewhere. Tap into herself to make . . . something!

What did she want to do with her life? She had to think about that. The Before was like a blanket of fog that covered part of her brain. Dr. Cass said that the fog would lift eventually as they did a little digging underneath and delved deeper into her past. She said Nora had arrived at rehab pretty beat up, and it wasn't every day a person drowned and came back to life, and *whoo-boy*, wouldn't it be strange if Nora *didn't* need time to recover from her near-death experience?

The physical therapists had reassembled her piece by piece, Humpty-Dumpty style. Now all that was left of her to finish healing was a slowly fading bruise on her face and her busted ankle. *"Water has the force of a sledgehammer,"* said one of the therapists. *"Get hit by one good wave and—boom—broken ankle."* The orthopedist said it was probably the safety cord on the surfboard that had twisted her up. He said it would be easy to figure out by looking at the surfboard, but no one ever found it.

In the mornings, after breakfast, she would hobble to the small inner courtyard where patients came to smoke. She liked to sit and listen to the birdsong and remember Grandpa's awesome garden and let the sun sink into her skin. She'd never been much of a garden sitter in the Before. Frankly, she wasn't sure what she'd been, other than a little boring and lacking motivation. She didn't want to be that anymore. She wanted to be the woman who went to museum meet-ups and met friends for drinks and ran along the Lady Bird Lake trail so she could say hi to all the dogs. But she didn't know where to start.

Once, she'd asked an elderly woman sitting on a bench next to her if she would do anything differently if she had a chance to start over.

"You bet. I would have divorced my husband long before he died."

"Oh," Nora had said. She was thinking that maybe she'd wanted to be an astronaut or a librarian or something.

Nora was not bothered by the fractured memories of her life that had begun to come back, popping up like champagne corks, usually apropos of nothing, reminding her that the Before hadn't always been easy. She'd been a little melancholy at times. Dr. Cass was right, and she was a little curious as to why. But for the time being, she tucked those fragments of memories away and carried on with the general sense of joie de vivre she'd felt since she'd come to in the hospital.

Like, one morning, when she was still in the hospital, a nurse was changing the dressing on a wound in Nora's side that she had no idea how she got, and she had the philosophically startling thought that if you found yourself trying to justify the life you lived in the Before, maybe you should take a hard look at that sooner rather than later. This, from someone whose most recent deep thoughts had more to do with what they would serve for dinner and why her left wrist itched.

Lately, her most cogent thinking was about Grandpa's garden. How did he get that tomato to taste so perfect? She missed him so much that her bones ached. Which was only slightly better pain than the searing blame she leveled at herself every time she remembered she hadn't gone to see him when she said she would, and he'd ended up dead and alone on a cold tile floor. Despite her shiny new feelings, she still loathed herself for that.

At long last, her body was deemed well enough to release her back into the wild. She was excited to be going home after weeks in this place.

Her mother was sending a car for her. "The traffic to Georgetown is ridiculous," she'd said.

"Mom! Really?" Nora's disappointment had been swift and deep.

"What? You don't want me to drive in that mess, I hope."

"I thought . . . I was hoping we could talk about . . . everything."

"Like what?" her mother had asked.

Like what? Epiphanies galore. About her path going forward. About how an NDE felt.

"Whatever it is, you can tell me later," her mother added before Nora could respond.

"Right. Sure," Nora had said brightly. "It's just that it's been a long recovery—"

"Please don't lay a guilt trip on me, Nora."

Nora recoiled. "No, no, that's not what I meant. I don't want to do that."

But she did want to do that. It hurt that her mother wouldn't brave traffic to be here on what Nora considered to be a momentous day. Alas, Nora remembered that she was used to disappointment. Unfortunately, it was typical of Roberta November to pretend that mothering was an abstract construct and not something she needed to actively participate in. Even when Nora and Lacey were kids, she'd used nannies as a proxy for motherly love.

Nora collected her few things from the bathroom. It was a little jarring to look at herself in the mirror these days. She looked different. Thinner. Her jumbled emotions made her feel like she was looking into a mirror with a crack in it—it felt like the halves of her didn't quite match up.

She stared at the powder-pink ensemble her mother had brought her—a track suit made of indestructible velour that hung loosely on her frame. It was cut with a wide leg that sported jaunty baby-blue stripes down the sides. Her mother had purchased a size large because it was better to "err on the side of caution."

"But I've lost so much weight," Nora had pointed out.

"Really?" Her rail-thin mother had casually studied her frame as if to confirm that.

Yes, really. A sudden surge of anger caught Nora off guard. As much attention as her mother had paid to her weight over the years, how could she miss that Nora's stomach had hollowed out? That it had taken a drowning for her daughter to end up with the body she'd always wanted her to have? It was enraging to be considerably smaller than she had been before the accident, and yet her mother still couldn't seem to really *see* her.

As for herself? She felt surprisingly blah about a flat stomach. She was realizing that skinny had never been her goal. Why, then, was it her mother's goal for her? Nora had just blindly accepted that she ought to be smaller because her mother said so, which, in retrospect, seemed a little passive on her part. But the new her had more important things to think about—like the haze lingering over her memory.

An ad suddenly blared out from the TV in her room, startling her. Nora had turned it on for the weather, which thus far the station had refused to give. *"If you've been hurt in an accident, call 444–4444. At November and Sons, Austin's premiere personal injury firm, we treat you like family."*

The timing of that ad could not have been worse. It happened that *she* was a November, blood-bound to the esteemed

November and Sons law firm, a practicing personal injury attorney. Not the son, obviously. That had been Nathan, her twin brother who'd died of SIDS when they were nine months old. Her father, who had started the family law firm with his father, never changed the name. Hope springs eternal, she guessed.

During her time here, Nora had managed to avoid thinking about how much she hated her job, but a memory hauled off and punched her, startling her. *Wake up!* She didn't just hate her job; she hated the whole practice of law. At the thought of going back to that sterile, air-chilled abyss, bile rose in the back of her throat. She didn't belong in that job any more than she belonged in this track suit—it was not her. She was, at least on the inside, more free spirit than lawyer, more guppy than shark.

Still, she was not going to let that ad ruin her happiness. She had survived death and rehab and was finally going home. She would worry about what else she had to survive later.

She finished packing and checked the bathroom once more. The paper bag with her prescription medicines—some new to her, some not—was sitting on the edge of the sink. Anti-inflammatories, antidepressants, antibiotics, antianxiety, antitoxin. *Anti, anti, anti.* It had always struck her as ironic that the drugs that actually helped her feel better could sound so negative.

She leaned over to pick it up and had to brace herself against the sink. Another side effect of her NDE was a buzzy sensation in her head from time to time. It reminded her of the white snow that occasionally rippled across her grandparents' TV. This fuzziness came and went without any discernible pattern, showing up to muddy her thoughts when she least expected it. Dr. Cass said it would "probably clear up on its own" the stronger she got.

Her phone pinged; she dug it out of her jacket pocket. Your driver is approaching your location, the screen said.

Nora picked up the paper bag and shoved it into her larger bag, then slung that over her shoulder. She was getting the hell out of here.

On her way out, she said goodbye to the attendants at the desk, then clomped down the long hallway in her new therapeutic boot.

The suited driver standing next to the town car at the curb opened the car door for her. "Ms. November?"

"That's me!" Or rather, a facsimile of the Ms. November she'd once been. The new Nora, so to speak. But she figured it was probably best not to attempt to explain it all to this guy.

When they were on the road, Nora asked, "We're headed for the Grant apartments on East Riverside, right?"

"Yes, ma'am."

Nora didn't trust her mother. *"I wish you'd agree to come stay with your father and me,"* her mother had complained this week over video chat, her preferred method of communication now.

Nora would rather be a troll living under a bridge than stay so much as a night at her parents' house in the swanky neighborhood of Rob Roy. All she wanted to do was lie on her couch and flip channels and eat something that wasn't half-baked chicken and mixed vegetables from a can. She needed time in her own space to regroup, to piece together what everything that had happened meant for her now. Once she figured that out, she would reenter the family sphere and resume her role as a November and Sons dutiful daughter at work and in society.

A sharp stab of pain in her head punctuated that thought, like her body was telling her it was dead set against that. Well, so was her heart. She'd signed a lease on a new life, and she didn't want the old one. But what, exactly, was her new life? She felt so new and different, but she was still struggling to figure out how to *be* new and different. She needed time to think.

They had reached the river when Nora's mother called. "How close are you?" she asked impatiently. "We're waiting."

Nora's antenna popped up. "Who is 'we'?"

"Your sister and me, of course."

"Is that all?" Nora asked. "I don't want any surprises, Mom."

"Who else could you possibly expect? You live like a monk. Why do you always assume the worst?"

"Because I always assume the worst?" Nora asked as more of a point of clarification.

"Oh, Nora," her mother said with a heavy sigh, as if the disappointments were already starting to pile up again. "No one is here. And besides, your place is so small. You should have accepted your father's offer to buy you that loft near Zilker Park. I don't know anyone on this side of town, and there are all those homeless people."

Nora glanced heavenward, seeking strength from a nebulous god who never granted it. "I'll be there in a few minutes," she said, ending the conversation.

The driver deposited her at her apartment building, and Nora Frankensteined her way to her apartment, a hard slog in her therapeutic boot. At her door, she knocked twice before opening it.

"Surprise!" shouted a single voice, and Nora's heart was suddenly beating out of her chest. She wasn't ready. She looked like she'd been roaming the wilderness—her skin was blotchy; there was a patch on her neck that itched something awful; she was wearing one old Ugg to match her boot. There ought to be a checkout manual for families, things you should do for your loved one straight out of rehab, starting with: no surprises. She felt wildly irritated that she was about to be pushed into something she didn't ask for or want, and her immediate instinct was to flee, to pogo right on out of there—

But it was only Lacey looking back at her. "What?" her sister asked.

Nora tried to see past her. "Anyone else?"

Her mother's head popped into view in the narrow entry. "I told you, me and Lacey."

"And me, Mrs. November."

"And James," her mother added.

James? Her legal assistant? Nora shared an office suite with him, but his presence here did not compute.

"You're acting weird," Lacey said disapprovingly.

The remark snapped like a rubber band against Nora's wrist. Funny how ingrained habits filled in the holes in her brain at the drop of a hat. She immediately understood that she was not acting like a November, a family in which you learned early on to be happy no matter how you felt. She forced a smile. "Sorry. Just . . . ready to be home."

Lacey grinned, pleased that Nora was playing her part, and pulled her inside.

Whoa. Talk about stepping into an alternate universe. One foot into her apartment and she was immediately thrust back into the Before. Her head felt foggy as she tried to fit herself back into the world that existed inside these walls. It was definitely her apartment, with its view of the parking lot, two bedrooms, two baths. The same exterior brick wall, the same small galley kitchen she rarely used. The sofa and two armchairs that looked like they ought to be in a museum, selected by a friend of the family who was famous for designing houses in West Lake Hills. Near the windows, an expensive dining table where Nora sometimes worked from home and on which she occasionally ironed a piece of clothing.

She took another cautious step into the Before like she was stepping into a dark back alley. "James is here?"

"He came by to drop off some paperwork for you, and I asked him to stay."

"No rush on the paperwork," James added magnanimously from the living room.

"What about Hannah?" Nora asked, referring to Lacey's girlfriend.

"She's at work."

"Dad?"

"He's tied up in court," Mom said and toyed with her earring.

Mom was covering for him. Dad couldn't be bothered to call her, much less be here when she came home. "Gus?"

"Couldn't make it."

Something felt off, in her, around her—she didn't like the way any of this felt. It was not the cheerful *I'm so shiny and new!* she'd felt in rehab. This felt heavier. Colorless. This wasn't her; this was someone else's life that she adamantly did not want. "But he was invited, right?"

"For heaven's sake, Nora." Her mother took her firmly by the elbow and forced her into her apartment. "Can you just enjoy the effort that went into welcoming you home?"

She would really like to do that, but the puzzle pieces of her brain weren't fitting together properly.

"We're all really glad you're back," James said, appearing before her. He adjusted his trendy eyeglasses and swept a thick lock of hair that always fell over one eye, exciting both male and female staff alike. "I am, for sure."

"Let me take your bag." Lacey grabbed it off Nora's shoulder and disappeared down the hall.

"You really don't look too bad," James said. "I mean, considering. I was expecting much worse. Your dad said you were pretty messed up, but you've only got the one bruise that I can see." He gestured at the faint mural of yellow and green across her cheekbone and temple.

He leaned closer and whispered, "You're coming back to the office, right? Because Candice has been a bitch. I have so much to tell you."

Nora felt a world away from her job as an attorney, and as much as she enjoyed office gossip, that too. An actual world away. A galaxy. A solar system. She tried to imagine herself walking into the office and the buzz started up, vibrating unpleasantly against her inner ear.

"Earth to Nora," James said.

"Present. Sort of." She smiled. She could not possibly convey how surreal her Before life felt to her now—as if someone had rearranged all the furniture of her memory. Except that everything was exactly where she'd left it. It was an unnerving dichotomy—she couldn't see how she fit into this picture. Was it even possible? It didn't *feel* possible.

"Look!" Lacey threw her arm around Nora's shoulder and pulled her to the dining table. "Recognize anything?" She pointed to the food on the table.

Beef cubes and tiny potatoes, chicken skewers, little cups of shrimp cocktail. And there in the middle, a sheet cake with something written on it. Nora leaned forward to have a closer look. "Does that say . . . 'Turn around, don't drown'?"

"Oh my God," James muttered under his breath.

"What?" Lacey asked. "It's a joke. Too soon?" She genuinely seemed unsure.

But Nora wasn't looking at the cake—she remembered what had been on this table, the things she'd left here. Important things. Her case files, bills that needed to be paid, her checkbook. And more. "Where are my things?"

"What things?"

The buzz in her head was making it hard for her to think. "The things I'd left on the table. Right here." She pointed at the cake. Her stomach was suddenly doing some uncomfortable flips—she had to put a hand on the table to steady herself. What was it about her things that seemed so urgent? "I had everything organized."

"I didn't un-organize. I tidied up, that's all. Your apartment was a mess. Honestly, I don't know how you lived like that. Anyway, I boxed it all up and put it in your closet."

Lacey's response provoked a surprising burst of anxiety. That was something Lacey would have done in the Before, taking care of everything whether Nora wanted her to or not. But Nora wasn't that woman anymore, and it was starting to panic her a little that she didn't know who she was, exactly. But she didn't belong here. Where did she belong, then? *"Grow your garden,"* Grandpa had said. But grow what?

"Come on, do you recognize any of the food?" Lacey was beaming again. "It's from Chef Borgia's restaurant. Your favorite place!"

Chef Borgia. At an End SIDS fundraiser last year, for the charity her father had founded in memory of her twin, Nathan, Nora had bid three thousand dollars during the auction for a private lesson from the popular TV chef. But she'd never arranged for the lesson. She suddenly realized that was one of the regrets that had flown at her in Grandpa's garden. She'd forever wanted to learn to cook, to be able to make something other than box macaroni, and that had been the perfect opportunity to learn from the best. Why had she let it slip through her fingers?

The disorienting buzz in her head was tinny now, ringing in her ears.

"The teriyaki chicken is to die for," Lacey was saying, but she sounded far away.

Whatever had kept Nora from taking that lesson was hovering just there, right beyond the veil, but she couldn't quite see it.

"Aren't you going to try it?"

Like a robot, Nora picked up a skewer of chicken. Apparently she was still a people pleaser—good to know. She took a bite. "Delicious!"

"This might be the best chicken I ever had," James said. He leaned over to take another skewer, and when he did, Nora caught sight of a shadow behind him. *Grandpa?*

She hadn't told anyone about the Grandpa shadows. She'd first noticed them in rehab, just fleeting shadows that felt like Grandpa was near. No one would believe her, and besides, she was a little worried she was seeing things. Was it normal that she liked it? It made her feel close to Grandpa and reminded her of how amazing she'd felt in his garden, how an eddy of love had swirled around her. She'd felt so safe and protected. She'd *fit* there.

She remembered the time Grandpa had taken her and Gus fishing when she was about six years old. Grandpa had shown them how to put worms on their hooks and how to throw the line. But Nora couldn't hook the worms—she hated the thought of touching them, much less spearing them. *"I'm sorry,"* she'd said to Grandpa as he baited her hook.

"For what?" he asked with an easy smile. *"For being a girl who cares about living things? Be proud of that, kiddo."*

Grandpa. That was where Nora fit. With him. In his garden. Where she could be proud of who she was, no matter what.

"Don't let me eat it all," James said. "Aren't you going to try some, Mrs. November?"

"No, thank you," her mother said, stabbing a single bite of pineapple with a toothpick and carrying it to the window.

The shadow passed Nora's vision again, and when she looked, she saw the small corpse of a plant on her sill. It looked so dry that if someone touched a leaf, it would crumble into ash. Her modus operandi when it came to plants had been to put them in her window with grand plans for nourishing them. But then she'd forget to water, or she'd overfeed or something, and they would die.

But after being in Grandpa's heavenly garden, seeing the dead plant made her feel nostalgic and unsteady. And she was overcome by a terrible, deep shame for having failed to look after his garden here. "My plant died."

Mom shrugged. "Get another one."

Grief thickened in Nora's throat. A familiar sensation she didn't like crept along her spine—emotions hovering just below the surface, ready and eager to fully consume her at a trigger's notice. All that time in rehab, Nora had felt mostly really good. Hopeful. Excited. But then—*bam*—along came her old apartment and a dead plant to knock her on her ass.

"When will you be back in the office?" James asked. He'd heaped a plate with more of Chef Borgia's food.

She rubbed her forehead and swallowed against a swell of nausea. "I'm not sure." She put down her plate. "I've been thinking . . . I want to make some changes."

Lacey looked at her blankly. Her mother glanced at her watch.

"Like what?" James asked.

"I . . . I don't know," she said uncertainly. "But I had this really profound experience, and I want to start over."

"Really?" Lacey sounded a bit skeptical, and Nora couldn't blame her. She wasn't exactly known for her follow-through. She had a vague memory of canceling on Lacey at the last minute a few times. Including once when she'd promised to lend a hand with a fundraiser for Lacey's school, leaving Lacey in the lurch.

"What does that mean, 'start over'?" James asked.

"Good question. I don't actually know. Yet," Nora said. She must sound like a lunatic to them. "But I have a second chance, and I want to take advantage of it. I want to do better. I want to be my authentic self."

"You're authentic, Nora," her mother said impatiently, missing the point. "Now, I'm sorry, but I have to run." She leaned in to kiss Nora's cheek.

"Now?" Nora asked. "I want to explain—"

"You don't need to explain anything to me, sweetheart. I'm just so glad you're home and everything can get back to normal."

"Have you tried the potatoes?" Lacey asked. "They are so good."

Her family wasn't listening. And James, who had seemed somewhat interested, was now trying the potatoes.

So Nora tried more of the food, tried to be part of the party, but she began to get a headache, which was a common occurrence since her NDE. Lacey cut the cake and put a thick slab on a plate. "I'll clean up," she said. "You should go rest."

The sun had begun its slide from the city sky when Nora walked into her room. No one had tidied up here. Her clothes were still tossed on a chair and the bed. Two drawers of the bureau stood open, like she'd been searching for something. There were papers and shoes scattered across the floor, and there, through the open door to her very messy closet, on a shelf, she could see her box of things from the dining room with her name scrawled across the side in Lacey's handwriting.

She turned her back on the box and walked across the room. She slid down onto the floor and rested her back against the bed. She just needed a minute. To settle into reality.

"Nora? Can I come in?"

Her eyes flew open. How long had she been sitting here? "Sure, James."

He sank down on the floor next to her and handed her a piece of cake with the letters *OW* on it.

"Cake, my favorite food group."

"I had to grab a piece before Lacey ate it all," James said.

Nora took a bite. She expected to sink into chocolate ecstasy because, heaven knew, she liked a good piece of cake. But that dark, gooey goodness tasted like paper. She tried another bite. Still tasted like paper.

James drew up his knees and wrapped his arms around them. "Don't hate me, but I have to ask—how's your head?"

"My head?" She touched her hair. It felt like straw. "What do you mean?"

James pressed his lips together.

"Wait . . . are you asking if I have brain damage?" she asked incredulously.

"I'm not! I mean, I'm only sort of asking. Okay, yes, I'm asking. But only because there's a betting pool at the office."

Nora gaped at him. "People are betting if I have brain damage?"

"Of course not, Nora," he said, sounding offended. "Everyone already assumes it. The bet is how many days you'll last before your dad fires you because of it."

Nora gasped. And then she laughed. "That is abhorrent." And yet it sounded like something that would definitely happen at November and Sons. Sharks, all of them. She shoved the cake back at James.

He took the plate. "I agree. But really, how are you?"

She narrowed her gaze on him. "How much money have you got riding on my brain?"

He clucked his tongue at her. "I was not allowed to bet because I work with you every day. And besides, you're my best work friend and I've missed you." He pressed his hand to his heart.

James was her only friend at work. Or pretty much anywhere else. Another piece of the puzzle clicked into place. "It feels like someone took a leaf blower and blasted it inside my head, but my brain is fine for the most part. My memory is still missing some chunks. Like, I remember taking the week off and going out of town . . . but I can't remember the accident."

"That doesn't sound good."

"Right? Sometimes it's weird, because I feel like my old self, but I also feel like I'm living in an alternate universe. And I keep thinking about my grandpa." The pang of sorrow hit her again, squarely in the chest. Missing him hurt. "I saw him, you know."

"No way," James said.

"I swear it." She shifted around to face him. "He was so real, James. I could *feel* him. He talked to me. He reminded me of things I never did. Like . . . a cooking lesson," she said. "I won a private cooking lesson from Chef Borgia at the End SIDS silent auction, and I never scheduled it. I'd love to learn to cook. And I never went to see the art exhibit Grandpa told me about at Laguna Gloria—"

"Love that place."

"And you know what else? I even thought about the guy from the corner store robbery."

James was nodding up until that point. "Wait . . . what guy?"

Nora couldn't believe he didn't know who she was talking about. "The corner store robbery, remember?"

"I remember you were in a store when some guy tried to rob it. That guy?"

"No, no—another hostage. He had dark brown hair and clear blue eyes." She remembered his handsome face perfectly. Bits and pieces of memory about him were coming back. "It was cold and wet that night, and he wore a hand-knitted scarf wrapped around his neck." She knew it was hand-knitted because the stitches were so uneven. "I must have told you."

"You did not." James was appraising her through a squint, like maybe he thought this was the brain damage talking.

But oddly, this was one thing she was completely sure about. "We . . . we had this connection." The spark had been instant. "We hit it off."

"Wait—you hit on some guy during a robbery?"

"I didn't hit on him. I made him laugh while we were being held hostage." They'd stood together watching the robbery unfold and he'd said it was weird how you met people when you least expected it, and she'd said it was weird that the robber was dressed like Darth Vader.

"Well, *that* sounds totally normal, Nora." James playfully nudged her with his shoulder, then glanced at his watch. He hopped to his feet and picked up the plate of cake. "I would love to stay and hear more about how you picked up a guy during a robbery, but I've got a date. Let me know when you're coming back to work. I've been using your office and I'll need to move a few things. By the way, I'm glad you're not brain damaged. That place is hard enough as it is." He gave her a thumbs-up before he disappeared into the hall.

That place *was* hard. Nora knew it was; she could feel it in her bones. But an army of ants was running through her brain, so many thoughts and memories vying for attention. She had to pull herself together, had to figure out who or what she was now that she'd come back from the dead.

Then she'd think about just how hard that place was and what she was going to do about it.

Chapter 4

N*ora slept so deeply that her brain decided to turn the* craziness of her NDE up a notch and take her through some bizarre dreams, replete with talking dolphins that dragged her farther and farther from shore, and then a skydive where her parachute wouldn't open with an ocean below her. And there was the corner store guy, wordlessly and valiantly trying to make a raft from his hand-knitted scarf.

Then she dreamed she was wearing the same beautiful blue dress she'd worn in death. She was trying to return to Grandpa's garden but somehow ended up on a boat that Ruth Bader Ginsburg was steering. When the boat started taking on water, she woke with a gasp, practically bolting upright.

Nope—no boat. She was in her apartment. These were the same walls, the same sounds of traffic outside, the same loudly ticking wall clock in her bathroom. The only difference was her. She could feel herself bloom into this new space in her head as bright sunlight streamed through her window. She felt happy. She felt at peace with herself. And she had an enthusiasm for daylight she'd never felt in the Before. Quite the contrast from the groggy dread of the day she used to feel.

She got up and hobbled into the kitchen on her bum ankle, brewed some coffee, and pulled the cake out of the fridge. She took a fork and ate directly from the box like a heathen. As she mindlessly shoved cake into her mouth, her gaze fell on a tourist brochure, the sort typically available in hotel lobbies, tacked to a small bulletin board next to her fridge. It was for the Laguna Gloria art museum, listing the exhibits Grandpa had urged her to visit there.

It suddenly hit her, the cause of the weird dichotomy she was feeling—she was firmly living in the After in her head, but her body and her life were firmly entrenched in the Before. Everything about her apartment encapsulated the snow globe she'd lived in most of her adult life: work and family, family and work, and nothing in between. *Be a good daughter. Be a November. Doesn't matter how you feel. Doesn't matter what you want. What matters is that you are a November.*

But Nora remembered she'd always wanted more for herself. She'd wanted to know how to cook, for one. Her mother had employed personal chefs all her life, but when Nora watched a cooking show or was at a friend's house where a mom was making dinner, it had always appealed to her. She wanted to know how to do that.

She'd wanted to pursue art and to be an athlete. She'd wanted to be Lacey's best friend and be supportive of Gus. She'd wanted a different job and to help Grandpa in his garden. And she'd wanted—*desperately* wanted—to call the corner store guy.

She'd done exactly zero of those things. Zero! What had stopped her? That she'd been in a funk? Numb to herself? Swimming through the doldrums? Dispirited, pessimistic, heartsore, gloomy, and blue?

"Also known as depressed," she muttered. Fine—she could admit it now. Her motivation had been hindered by periodic bouts of clinical depression. Days of feeling like her body was filled with lead and suffocating under the weight of it. Days when depression gripped her in a vise and wouldn't allow her to generate the slightest bit of energy. She'd lacked confidence in almost everything she did because everything she did felt wrong. She'd felt empty and useless and like an abject failure. Thirty-one-year-olds were supposed to handle their business, but her life had felt completely out of her control.

And then somehow, in the aftermath of a terrible accident, her confidence had been unearthed. It was raw and unused, but it was there. She could feel it in her heart. She believed she could do *all* the things. Right now.

But how did she go about transforming from the person she'd been into the person she felt she was at her core? That kid who'd followed Grandpa around, who'd wanted to try everything, to be everything. What she needed was a manual for shedding the skin of the woman who hadn't managed to try or to be anything but what other people wanted of her. She needed a checklist.

"A bucket list," she said aloud. Lots of people made them, lists of things they wanted to do before they died. Except in her case, the list was of things she wanted to accomplish *after* she'd died. *Because* she'd died. "A reverse bucket list!" She dropped her fork into the box. Yes! There was nothing stopping her—she'd make a reverse bucket list and uncover the person at her core.

One summer when she was eight or nine years old, she had written a play. It was a retelling of Robin Hood, where Robin Hood was a girl. She'd forced Lacey and Gus to perform in it, and with the help of tables set on their sides to become a forest, and jackets and towels repurposed as costumes, they had staged the entire production for Grandma and Grandpa. When it was over (probably at long last), her grandparents had applauded and cheered, and Nora, Lacey, and Gus had taken their bows. Grandpa had wrapped one arm around Nora's shoulders and said, *"You're a natural, kid. You've got what it takes."*

That was what she was trying to reach—she'd lost what was natural about her. But she had to believe she still had what it took to get it back.

First, she had to annihilate the stifling Before in this apartment and create the After to match what she felt inside.

Nora limped back to her room. She looked around, not sure what she was after. She went to her walk-in closet and stared at the clothes there, at the designer bags arranged along one shelf. Bags that cost more than one month's rent. She didn't like them—some were impractical, many too showy. It was a habit her mother had instilled in her as a teen—the bag made the woman. And if you have money, you show it.

Not in Nora's After. She would start by creating the version of herself that lived in her head. The Nora she liked, who didn't care about designer bags. The Nora she desperately wanted to be. She would wear flowy clothes instead of dark suits because she *liked* clothes with room and comfort and color. She would get rid of those purses. She would cut her hair so she couldn't wear a severe bun anymore and get some running shoes and eat cake straight from the box. She would be friendly and vivacious and great at parties, and she would always know the right thing to say. That was the woman she believed the little girl Nora meant to be when she grew up—the bohemian adventurer with a passion for sports and surrounded by friends. Not the dull, listless, buttoned-up Nora she'd become.

She could still be that woman, couldn't she? Sure she could. She'd just have to work at it. She'd have to dig, as Dr. Cass liked to say. Start from scratch if she had to.

She dug through her boring clothes looking for something that didn't wholly represent the Before and came upon the blue dress she wore in Grandpa's garden.

She pulled it out of her closet and tried it on. It hung loosely on her, but she admired herself in the mirror, recalling how she'd felt wearing it.

But then she noticed the dark stain on the hem, and a memory slipped into her thoughts like a tiny garden snake. It was suddenly five years ago, at the party her parents had thrown her for passing the Texas bar exam.

The party was everything she could have imagined. Towering vases of pink dahlias and chrysanthemums in the center of every cloth-covered table. An open bar and two serving stations where staff in white coats shaved off healthy portions of roast beef and heaped scalloped potatoes on plates. Two additional self-serve buffets, one piled with shrimp cocktail and caviar canapes, and the other holding slices of cake, key lime pie, and crème brûlée.

"This is crazy," Lacey had said. "This looks like the bar mitzvah Dad would have given his Jewish son if he were Jewish and had a son. Don't be surprised if they lift you in a chair later."

"If they do, I'm up for it." Nora had been giggly from the champagne and excitement. She'd never been the belle of the ball and had been happy to bask in the sparkle of all the congratulations and good wishes. It felt good. She could get used to this.

The place was packed; her father had invited the firm's partners and senior leadership. Half of Austin's movers and shakers were there, including the dean of her law school and the provost, both of whom were beyond grateful for Dad's generous donations.

Lacey had come with a stunning brunette. She and Dad had fought about her date before the party—Dad didn't want her to bring "that woman," and Lacey, who was very good at sticking to her guns, said she wouldn't come if she couldn't bring whomever she pleased. She'd won the battle that night.

Waiters wended through the crowd, handing out drinks and hors d'oeuvres. Gus was there, hovering near the appetizer table, a sweaty glass in his hand that matched the sweat on his brow. He beamed at Nora. "You did it, Nora," he said. "You're such a badass."

She *had* done it. She was proud of herself. But the smell of alcohol on Gus's breath had left her with the dull feeling that disaster was lurking. "Slow down," she'd whispered. "We haven't even had dinner yet."

"Oh, this is my last one." They both knew it wasn't. Gus had what her parents called "an issue."

Grandma and Grandpa were there too. Grandpa wore a tuxedo he'd pulled from his closet, a 1970s special with a ruffled shirt and a leisure suit vibe. Grandma wore a navy mother-of-the-bride two-piece gown, with a top that provided ample coverage and a skirt with an elastic waist. Grandpa had gone around the room, introducing himself to people. "That's my granddaughter," he'd say, pointing at Nora and rising up on his toes with pride. Grandma and Grandpa had the best time of anyone, garnering lots of applause by doing a "boogie" they used to do back in the day.

Nora had known most of the November and Sons law partners since she was a girl, when her mother would force her and Lacey to wear dresses and put bows in their hair and parade them through the office. They'd asked her what kind of law she wanted to practice. Environmental law, she'd said, because if she was going to practice law, she had visions of saving the rainforests and stopping the polar ice cap melt.

When it was time for the supper, her father directed her to a big table at the head of the room. She laughed and said it looked like she'd just gotten married. She reached her hand out for Gus, but her father stopped her. Gus and Lacey's date were not invited to sit at the head table. Nora remembered the helpless look she and Lacey exchanged. They knew better than to argue—Dad had the attitude of a general, and it was better to go along to get along.

Gus said it was fine and wandered back to the bar, bumping into two chairs on his way.

Supper was served, but Nora had lost her appetite—a ball of nerves had taken root in the pit of her stomach, a common feeling when her father was around. And then, before the plates were cleared, her father stood up, inviting everyone to lift their glasses. "A toast to my daughter Nora, who required only two attempts to pass the bar."

Everyone chuckled and applauded politely. Nora instantly felt queasy with anticipation.

Her father looked at her and said, "I am proud of you." The week before, he'd said she'd humiliated him by failing the first time.

Her father turned back to the guests. "Ladies and gentlemen, I am pleased to announce that the future of November and Sons is set."

Nora's stomach dropped. *What the hell?* She'd been very clear that she was not going to work at the family firm. He'd insisted she be a lawyer—fine, she was a lawyer. But she wanted something different from personal injury law. She wanted something different from *law*. She wanted to be a journalist, out in the world. A war correspondent, a travel writer, but, as usual, she compromised her desires for the sake of peace.

"To Nora, my eventual successor. And November and Sons' newest senior attorney."

An anemic smattering of applause followed. Nora's mother frantically gestured at her to stand up. Reluctantly, Nora did, but her brain had been knocked off its merry-go-round. She felt like she'd been smacked, stunned into voicelessness. Who took a lawyer fresh off the bar exam and made her a senior attorney?

One of the partners, Richard Seinz, asked that very question in shorthand: "What?"

"Under my tutelage, of course," her father said, as if that explained everything. As if it was no big deal.

But it *was* a big deal, and there was a rumbling in the crowd, the swell of a few voices going from a whisper to a hot protest. Nora pressed a hand to her stomach. It was beginning to churn with the humiliation she sensed was coming. "Dad . . . I'm going into environmental law, remember?"

He held up a finger. "You and I will talk later."

"Wait a minute, David." Richard was on his feet. He'd been with November and Sons longer than anyone. His face was turning an unhealthy shade of purple. "We haven't talked about this."

"Listen, everyone, it's just a title. Of course she'll need experience, and I will see that she gets it. Come on, Rich, do you honestly believe I'm going to pass November and Sons on to anyone other than my own flesh and blood? My father and I started that firm, and when he died, I made it what it is today. It's a legacy I intend for my family to keep. I need her to learn from me, to get up to speed as quickly as possible."

"But, Dad, I—"

"Not now, Nora," he said sharply, as if she were a child interrupting his important speech. And like a child, she felt herself shrink into a dark corner of her soul.

Richard started to say something else, but a sudden crash startled everyone. Nora's heart fell when she spotted Gus on the floor, the shrimp cocktail on top of him. He was trying to get up, but his feet kept slipping in the mess. "I'm so sorry," he said. "I must have bumped into the table."

"Get him out of here," her father growled.

Nora did. Her father called after her—clearly he'd meant a bouncer—but she had to get out of there too. Her chest was burning with shame and fury, and she was breathing too hard, only a step away from a paper bag and her head between her knees. It was supposed to have been her night. Her moment to bask in the glory of having completed three grueling years of law school and finally passing the hideous bar exam. She'd realized too late that none of this was to celebrate her—it had all been about a power grab she didn't fully understand.

Gus had gained his feet by the time she reached him. He towered over everyone, his mop of dark brown hair unkempt, his shirt open at the collar. Cocktail sauce was everywhere—on him, on the floor, on her dress.

His bottom lip began to quiver. "I'm sorry, Nora."

"It's okay, Gus." It wasn't okay, but what could she say?

"It just hit me. I was doing fine, and then it hit me," he said pleadingly.

Funny, she thought, standing in her bedroom now—the same thing had happened to her. She was doing fine, and then life—and death—had just hit her.

Nora looked at the stain on the hem of her blue dress. She'd been living in the November snow globe for so long that she'd become desensitized to how suffocating it was. But then she'd almost died, the globe had shattered, and now all the things she'd wanted to be were vying for her attention. She wanted to be happy. To be the Nora who wasn't beaten down by the fear of failure and the need to keep the peace.

She clawed the dress off her body and threw it aside with the force of the memory of the ghost of her from another life. But that ghost was at the bottom of the Gulf of Mexico. That Nora had left some baggage, sure, some brain junk she didn't know what to do with yet, but *this* Nora, the new Nora, was not going back to hell.

She went back to the kitchen and found pen and paper.

Reverse Bucket List (in no particular order):
Learn to cook
Grandpa's garden
Corner store guy (??)
Make art
Be a better sister to Lacey
Support Gus
Play basketball
Get a new job

She studied her list. For a reverse bucket list, it seemed somewhat . . . lame? Maybe she ought to have loftier goals, like seeing the Seven Wonders of the World or building schools in underprivileged communities. Maybe the loftier stuff would come later, but for now, these were eight unanswered desires she'd lost along the way that she could feel pressing against her edges, changing the shape of her.

She looked at the cheap bank calendar on her bulletin board. She had two weeks, max, before she was expected back at work. Dread blossomed in her. She sincerely believed that where drowning hadn't killed her, her job might. She wasn't cut out for the work. She didn't have the guts or the drive to score a kill. She didn't have the fortitude to stand up to her father's withering criticism. She was nothing but a disappointment and a failure every day. She wished she could quit right this moment, but she didn't have a lot of money saved, and medical bills and past-due notices were filling up her mailbox. The smart thing would be to get another job before she quit.

She had only a couple of weeks to put the wheels in motion to change her life. It felt to her as if everything, including her sanity, was riding on it.

She needed to get started.

Chapter 5

A *few days later, Nora decided that living in the After* was awesome.

Her mother continued to use video calls as a substitute for in-person mothering, limiting her time to one daily phone call on her way to tennis, back from lunch, or in the dressing room while shopping. She always excused her absence from Nora's life by saying she was just too busy. "The annual End SIDS fundraiser has gotten so big, I may need to bring on staff," she'd complain. "I think we might be able to get Lyle Lovett to play this year. Wouldn't that be a feather in our cap? Are you taking your medicine?"

"Yes," Nora would say, impatient to get off the phone. She was busy transforming her space from the Before into the After.

She started with her furniture. She made a few calls, found a charity that would pick up the couch, the chairs, and that terribly formal dining room table. She gave away the china she rarely used to someone she found on the apartment's neighbor app. Most of the dead plants were given a proper burial—she couldn't look at them without feeling massive guilt—but she wasn't ready to let go of a dead tomato plant Grandpa had given her. She could remember that sunny morning when he'd proudly handed her the pot. *"This is for you, kid."* It was such a small thing, but he always had a way of making her feel so special. A gift only because he was thinking of her, not because he was obligated by an event like a birthday.

She cleaned out every nook and cranny and deposited anything that belonged to the Before into a trash can or a donation pile.

In her closet, she didn't touch the box with her name on it but worked around it. It looked heavy, like it held too much of the Before that she wasn't ready to tackle. She'd deal with it later.

She took down all her handbags and boxed them up to be shipped off to an online luxury goods store that would sell them for her. She would get back only a fraction of what the bags were worth, but she didn't care. Anything would be a help with her bills.

Her clothes were a dismay. She'd never really noticed, but she'd dressed like storm clouds in the Before—everything she owned seemed to be black, gray, or navy. She threw all that gloom into a bag and took it to a nearby consignment shop. Then she popped into the thrift store next door to pick up a couple of gently used pieces.

She went to the library and checked out self-help books about the courage to change and steps for living in the moment instead of the past. She made an appointment at a hair salon. Not the trendy one where she had her caramel-colored hair highlighted because her mother said it made it look less brassy. But a more affordable salon with rock music playing in the background and a stylist who had all the colors of the rainbow in his hair. She asked him to lop off twelve inches of the ghost of Nora's hair.

"Did you say *ghost*?" the stylist asked.

"Just cut," Nora said. Now she was sporting a new shaggy shoulder-length lob that she loved. It was carefree and perfect for someone determined to live in the moment.

By the end of the week, she had her first postrelease appointment with Dr. Cass.

She really liked Dr. Cass. During her rehab, Dr. Cass had coaxed her to talk about many things she'd buried deep down over the years.

She met Nora in her office wearing a giant turquoise squash blossom necklace that was hard to look away from. "Hey! You look great, Nora. Love the jeans and the rainbow T-shirt. And the hair! Va-va-va-voom!"

"Thanks," Nora said. "I'm so . . . comfortable." She'd been dressing like an uptight November for so long that she'd forgotten how comfortable cotton and Lycra could be.

"How's your ankle?"

"Getting better every day. I should be out of the boot next week."

They sat in armchairs facing each other. "So tell me, now that you're home, how are you feeling about things?"

Nora eagerly scooched forward in her seat. "Surprisingly good. I feel like I'm still me, but so different. And I'm excited."

"Tell me about that."

"Remember I told you about the regrets I had for things I meant to do and never did?" Dr. Cass nodded. "I'm going to do them—I made a reverse bucket list of all the things I want to do after I died."

Dr. Cass gasped with delight. "That's brilliant! People who experience NDEs often come back feeling that things were left undone and have a renewed and invigorated purpose in life."

"That's *exactly* how I'm feeling."

"Well, this is a perfect opportunity. Let's talk about your list."

Nora pulled the paper from her purse and showed it to her. Dr. Cass pointed to Lacey's name. "Your sister?"

Nora nodded. "She's always been there for me, but I haven't always been there for her." And just like that, she felt tense. "I want to do better." Which sounded too vague and simplistic.

She wasn't sure Lacey even cared if she was a better sister. Nora had tried calling her more than once since she'd been home, but it always rolled to voice mail. Her sister was a middle school principal and insanely busy, and maybe that's all it was . . . But Nora was beginning to recall just how difficult she'd made life for Lacey in the Before. It mortified her.

"Why do you think you weren't there for her?" Dr. Cass asked.

The tension settled painfully at the top of her head. "Because—" She was horrified when a sob she hadn't even known was there suddenly erupted. Dr. Cass nodded encouragingly. "Because my depression, it . . . it disfigured our relationship," she managed to get out. "It changed us."

"Can you say more about that?" Dr. Cass asked gently.

Another sob escaped. "I used to be the big sister Lacey looked up to. Until life became too much for me. There were days that staying in bed sounded a whole lot better than helping her move. But I'd promised her, and she was stuck without my help." Nora swallowed down another sob. "It wasn't the only time I wasn't there for her. She couldn't trust me to be her sister. She couldn't trust me not to disappear."

"That must have been very difficult for you both. But it was not your fault, Nora. Depression robs us of our ability to function in ways we generally consider normal. Was it the same with Gus?"

Nora's head began to throb behind one eye. She rubbed hard at her brow. "Not exactly. He's my cousin. He's an alcoholic and struggles with sobriety." He'd been to treatment twice. Before the last stint, Gus had reached out to Nora, needing her. Nora promised him that she'd come by, but she hadn't made it. Gus ended up drinking so much that he'd wandered outside wearing only his boxers. He'd tried to fight an old man who wanted to help him, and the cops had picked him up. He'd gone first to a hospital to detox, then to a treatment facility. "And I didn't help him. I *couldn't* help him."

"Did you think you were responsible for Gus's drinking?" Dr. Cass asked. "Wasn't that a choice Gus made?"

"Yes . . . but I should have helped him," she said quietly. "I could at least have been present. Been someone he could lean on."

Her dad had arranged Gus's treatment, but not without complaint. "That's the Levinson in him," he'd said dismissively, referring to Gus's father. "A bunch of losers. And this one is making us look like trash."

Nora had been horrified at her dad's lack of empathy. "He's sick," she'd exclaimed.

Her father had rolled his eyes. "There's nothing wrong with him that putting down the bottle won't cure."

Gus's life had been hard. His father died in a car wreck when he was fifteen. When he was twenty, his mother—Nora's maternal aunt—died from cancer. The Novembers were all the family that Gus had, and Nora had let him down. She hadn't had the strength to be there for him when he'd needed her most, because she couldn't be there for herself.

She tried in vain to will away her guilt, but the only thing she willed was more tears.

Dr. Cass handed her a box of tissues. "We will talk more about this," she said soothingly. "But for now, let's keeping looking at your list. What's this?" she asked, pointing to *Corner store guy*.

Nora's face turned hot. What was the matter with her? She couldn't seem to regulate her emotions anymore. In those hours Nora had spent with the corner store guy, locked in a storeroom, the world had seemed bursting with hope and possibilities. "That . . . that was a missed opportunity." And a colossal, gaping hole of regret.

She gave Dr. Cass a watered-down version of the story. A robbery, a hostage situation, sitting all night with a man she really came to like. "Anyway, I wrote his number on my hand. But I must have washed it off. And now I can't remember his name." The one good thing to happen to her in years, and she'd, what, just let it slip away? She avoided Dr. Cass's gaze. "It's one of the things I lost in the NDE." Maybe. But the truth was that after the robbery, Nora had fallen into a black hole of depression, the can't-get-out-of-bed variety. Maybe she'd forgotten his name then.

"My goodness! That must have been traumatic for you."

Nora nodded.

"With trauma like that, sometimes details can be buried," Dr. Cass said. "You remember what he looks like and the emotional connection you felt, but the name is lost. It will eventually come back to you, just like your surfing accident will. Still, without his name, it's going to be a real challenge to find him, isn't it? You'll have to be creative, and that's the best kind of challenge to have. What's this?" She pointed to *Get a new job*.

"I, ah . . . I never wanted to be a lawyer, so . . ." She shrugged. She didn't know how to put into words that she, a grown woman, had been afraid to cross her father at a critical time in her life. She'd needed something from him: His approval. His respect. His love. Parents were supposed to love their children, but Nora was apparently unlovable. She'd spent so much of her life trying to be worthy of his affection, waiting for him to see her and understand her.

"Very interesting," Dr. Cass said. "That's a lot of school and training to be something you never wanted to be."

"Wasn't it?" What a waste of years of her life. She used to rationalize it by thinking she'd drawn the short straw. Her brother, Nathan, had died as a baby, and Lacey made it clear early on that she was gay, therefore making herself an unsuitable substitute for dear old Dad. Which left Nora. Eager to please, malleable, chicken-shit Nora, who was too afraid to stand up to the man who'd tyrannized her all her life.

She suddenly remembered being eleven years old. Her mother had signed her up for ice-skating. But Nora wanted to play basketball—Grandpa had loved basketball and she'd spent many evenings curled into his side as he explained the rules of the game. At dinner that night she'd announced quite innocently that she wanted to be a basketball player when she grew up. Her father had brought his fist down on the table, rattling glasses and plates, and told her never to say that again. "I can't think of anything more graceless. You will be a lawyer, like your father, like your grandfather. You will carry on the November name. That's it."

She could remember feeling like it was a matter of life and death to stake her place in this world as a basketball player. She'd been on the verge of tears, but her father hated crying more than almost anything. "I want to play basketball!" She'd felt afraid and brave in the same breath. She was planting her flag, and she was ready to fight off anyone who tried to take it.

Her father laughed at her. "Don't be ridiculous," he said. And she'd crumbled, just like she always did.

"What would you do if you didn't practice law?" Dr. Cass asked curiously, drawing her back into the present.

Nora swallowed. She'd spent a few weeks blissfully free of her father and didn't want thoughts of him to ruin things now. "I'm thinking about that. Maybe something in the arts. Or something completely different, like volunteering at Greenpeace." No, that wasn't it—she wasn't going to volunteer at Greenpeace. "I mean that I would like to be useful somewhere. To someone."

"Exciting!" Dr. Cass said. "Your list is brilliant, Nora. I can't wait to talk more about it. Unfortunately, that's our time today." She stood up.

Nora stood up too.

Dr. Cass grasped Nora's shoulders. "You know what's great? You're alive, Nora November. You. Are. *Alive.* You get to do things you very nearly lost the opportunity to ever do. Who gets that chance? *You* do. Make the most of it." She dropped her hands. "Same time next week?"

Make the most of it. Yes, that's what she had to do. She had to find a way to do the things she'd left undone, face the painful trip to Grandpa's garden, figure out how to reach Lacey and Gus, and . . . and find the corner store guy.

Somewhere there was a record of that robbery. Someone had taken down his full name. Surely someone somewhere could remember what she couldn't.

Chapter 6

TEN MONTHS AGO

The night was wet and the sort of bitter cold that slipped into your marrow and would not leave without a long soak in a steaming hot bath.

Nora was exhausted, she was hungry, and she was in desperate need of a glass of wine. She'd had a terrible court case that day, a real heartbreaker. It was a car accident, and the defendant was a pizza delivery guy who'd tried to slide through a yellow light with his young son in the back seat. The light had turned red before he made it through, and the other driver—her client—had T-boned him. Her client's blood alcohol was over the limit, but that didn't matter in this civil lawsuit. The pizza driver had been at fault for running the red light.

Nora imagined his son, earphones canceling out the world, his gaze on his phone screen. Now he was paralyzed from the waist down. She couldn't stop the anguish imagining that boy's life now. How difficult the road ahead would be for him and his family as he learned to negotiate life in a wheelchair. Of course, he could go on to have a very productive life, but the getting there would be the test.

When the jury found for the plaintiff, she watched the pizza man's shoulders slump with the weight of his responsibility—a son who would need a lifetime of care because of his mistake, and on top of that, he owed the other driver damages for running a red light.

When the verdict in favor of their client was reached, it felt to Nora as if no one from November and Sons cared about that little boy except her. As they exited the courtroom, John Rodriguez, her cocounsel, high-fived their client. He turned to Nora to do the same, but dropped his hand and asked incredulously, "Nora . . . are you crying?"

"What? No!" She hastily wiped a tear from her cheek. This corner of the law was a tough business, and sometimes it felt as if her heart wasn't big enough to contain all the sorrows of these cases. It wasn't fair—one decision could alter a person's life forever, and too many times, the November law firm feasted on that mistake. No matter which side she represented, she felt dirty participating in what was often a heartbreaking process.

She declined the offer of drinks with the excuse she had an early day tomorrow, and frankly, John and the client seemed relieved she wasn't going. She dragged herself back to the office, and after spending some time staring blankly at the wall, she decided to go home.

James had popped in. "Congress Avenue is closed for a protest at the capitol if you're thinking of going that way. And there's a wreck on Lamar if you're thinking of going that way."

Nora groaned. "Should I spend the night here?"

"Would not recommend," James said. "Have a good night. And try to cheer up—the dude was reckless. He ran a red light with his kid in the back seat."

Yes, but . . . people made mistakes. They just did. The only person she knew who didn't believe in honest mistakes was her father. And she lived in fear of making one in his presence because he treated her like he treated defendants—with no mercy.

She decided to take a walk, hoping the cold would perk her up.

By the time she reached the corner store, she was a frozen Popsicle and it was starting to mist. She went inside to warm up and grab something to eat.

The man behind the counter didn't even glance up when she walked in. She wandered down the aisle to the selection of "fresh" foods and crowded into the narrow space beside a man in an overcoat and a scarf wrapped around the lower half of his face. She perused a paltry selection of wilted, prepackaged salads. The egg in the only Cobb salad left looked a little suspicious, but not as suspicious as the four Caesar salads with anchovies. Who thought anchovies on salads was a good idea for a fast-food operation? Nora reached for the Cobb salad at the same moment the man did. She looked up into a pair of lovely eyes that reminded her of patches of bright blue sky.

"It's the last Cobb salad," she said.

"I know. I'm being chivalrous by taking it, because I can't in good conscience let you eat this garbage."

Nora smiled for the first time that day. Maybe that week. Maybe that month. "I'm fine with garbage. I eat a lot of it. It's a palate thing with me—very unsophisticated."

His smile lifted his brows, and he pulled his scarf down to reveal a shadow of a beard. "Same here. That's why I left the better garbage for you—the last slice of pepperoni," he said, using his chin to indicate a point behind her. She turned to see a slice still sitting under a heat lamp, oil pooling on it. Nora wrinkled her nose.

"On second thought, don't eat that," he said and held out the container with the Cobb salad to her. "Here. It's yours. But if I were you, I'd leave off the egg."

They both looked down at the salad. Up close, it was even more suspect. "Am I crazy, or did this look a lot better a minute ago?"

"You are not crazy. You know what really looks good? The hot dogs—shriveled to perfection."

Nora laughed. At least she thought she did—but at the same moment someone screamed.

"They're not *that* bad," he said, and they looked to the front of the store where a commotion was erupting. Someone was waving a gun around. The store cat, which was resting on the top of a stack of water bottles, looked bored by the gun, even though the robber waved it right in front of its face.

Nora's heart skipped a few beats. "Hey," she whispered, her voice shaking a little, "is that . . . Darth Vader?"

"Um . . . yeah," the guy said, his gaze locked on the gun.

Everything seemed to slow to a crawl around them. Nora had always wondered what kind of person she would be in an emergency. This was definitely an emergency, but she didn't feel like she was going to pass out, which was what she assumed she'd have done. Weirdly, she thought she might be the one to race to danger, which was definitely not something she would have believed about herself.

"No one move!" Darth Vader roared and swung the gun around, pointing it down the aisle at them.

The guy at the counter said, "Dude, that's not even real."

Darth Vader took offense. He pointed the gun at the ceiling and fired. The cat leapt off its perch and bolted for the back of the store. The man behind the counter raised his hands. "I don't want any trouble."

Nora, who apparently was not going to race into danger after all, couldn't seem to make her feet move. Neither could the guy—they stood paralyzed, watching disaster unfold before them.

"Then hand over what you've got."

"Can't. The drawer is locked."

"Don't tell me it's locked unless you want everyone in here to die!"

"That's not good," the guy next to her muttered.

"What do you want me to say? It's locked and I can't open it."

"What do you mean, you can't?" Darth sounded as if he thought the clerk was pranking him and pointed the gun at his forehead.

"Well, this has escalated quickly," the guy muttered to Nora, holding his arm across her body as if to shield her. Nora slowly put down the salad.

Darth Vader swung the gun toward them again. "All of you, in the back."

Glass crashed somewhere and an older woman in a puffy coat darted past them to the back. But Nora and the guy froze.

Darth pointed his gun at the guy. "You."

"Me?"

"You and her, in the back!"

"Okay," he said, holding up his hands. He turned to Nora. "I think we should go to the back."

Nora's heart had climbed to her throat. "What if he shoots us back there?"

"What if he shoots us here?"

"Good point." Nora feared that if she turned her back, she'd be dead. But standing there didn't seem to be a better option. So she forced herself to turn, to make her legs move, and walked, the guy behind her and Darth Vader on their heels. She could hear his heavy breathing and felt as if she were floating above herself, watching this catastrophe unfold. Her panic was making her light-headed. They hurried into a small storeroom, where a woman was crouched next to a mop bucket filled with dirty water.

Darth shut the door behind them and plunged them into darkness—the only light was the dim fluorescent light filtering in through the small square window in the door. The woman began to whimper. They heard something being dragged across the floor, then pushed against the door. Nora felt like she was floating in space—it was all so surreal.

Light suddenly flooded the supply closet.

The guy had groped around until he found the switch. He took one look at the woman and walked over to her, crouching down. "You're okay. Take a deep breath and release it slowly."

"We're going to die."

"I don't think so. He just wants some money. Breathe." The guy sat with her a minute, then looked up at Nora. "You okay?"

Was she okay? This was the type of thing that should have had her on the floor. But she felt incomprehensibly sturdy. So unlike her normal operating procedure. She nodded.

"Well, this is . . . something."

"Do you think there's any chance we're dreaming?"

"Pretty sure I didn't dream the gun."

Nora glanced up at the window in the door. She looked around and spotted a milk crate, pulled it over, and stood on top of it so she could see.

"What's happening?" he asked.

Darth was talking with his hands. "I'm not sure, but I think they're arguing."

The woman began to frantically murmur Hail Marys. The man got up and edged in next to Nora, and together—their arms pressed against each other—they peered out the narrow window. His scent, spicy and sweet, filled her head. She thought she could even hear his heart beating. Or maybe that was hers. It was all so very strange, because whatever was happening, Nora could summon no hysteria. She was more aware of the man beside her than the actual danger they were in and didn't feel much fear, her faithful companion. It was like she was watching an absurd play. She briefly wondered what it would be like to die in a hail of gunfire. Would it hurt? But like the guy, she was beginning to believe Darth didn't have it in him to shoot. He seemed to want to plead his way through the robbery.

They watched for a few moments until Nora couldn't help herself. She said, "Luke . . . *I am your father,*" in her best Darth Vader voice.

The man's blue eyes locked on hers with shock. But then he tried to swallow down a giggle. So did Nora. A moment later, they were laughing like two kids at a solemn church service.

"What is the matter with you?" the woman hissed. "We could be killed at any moment."

"One of us should probably call the police," Nora suggested.

"I'm calling my husband," the woman said and yanked her phone from her purse.

The guy pulled his phone from the pocket of his overcoat. "My guess is that later, Darth will list not taking our phones as one of his biggest blunders. What's happening now?"

Nora peered out the window. "The cat is back. He's on the top shelf near the chips."

"I meant with the robbery."

"Oh." The clerk had come out from behind the counter, his hands up. He went to the door—at least Nora thought he did, but she couldn't see—and then they heard the unmistakable sound of the metal door coming down to cover the storefront. "Oh."

"What?" the woman cried.

"He pulled down the garage door thing. We're stuck."

"Yeah, hello. I'm at a corner store and it's being robbed. The man locked us in the back room and is arguing with the clerk," the guy said into the phone. "He's got a gun."

He looked up; his gaze met Nora's. "We're customers . . . Three. Um . . . hold on." He lowered the phone. "What's the cross street?"

The woman answered, but Nora didn't hear what she said—she was fascinated with Darth Vader. She tried to picture his preparation for this. Had he planned to rob the corner store and thought that a striking costume was his best bet for staying anonymous? Or did he put on the costume and think, *Yeah, I should rob a corner store*? Maybe the latter, because he was pacing now, as if he had no idea what he was doing. "He's so bad at this," she mused. "Part of me wants to go out there and help him out."

"Are you crazy?" the woman nearly shouted.

It was not an unfair question, as Nora wasn't sure herself. "Not officially. But it's hard to watch someone flail about like that."

The guy glanced warily at her.

"I'm *not* going out there," she reassured them. "I'm just saying." But how would it feel to step into the maw of real danger? Would she like the adrenaline surge? Probably not, since elevators speeding to the top of tall buildings gave her heart palpitations. Was it normal to wonder such things in the middle of a crisis?

"I see," the guy said into the phone. "Okay . . . right. Right. No, no, we are . . . well, we are at the moment."

"We are what?" the woman begged.

"Okay, thanks. Yes, this number." He clicked off the phone and slid it into his pocket.

"What did they say? Is someone coming to help us?"

As if on cue, they heard sirens.

"Yes, they are coming to help us . . . but apparently we're in a bit of a hostage situation."

"Looks pretty much like a full-blown hostage situation to me," Nora said.

The woman started whimpering again. The guy stepped up beside Nora, and they peered out into the store. The cat was asleep. The clerk had gone back behind the counter and was smoking a cigarette. Darth was still pacing.

"He's got to be sweltering in that helmet and mask," the guy mused.

"What do you think his endgame is?" Nora asked. "Ransom?"

"Unclear," the guy said thoughtfully. "Maybe we should make ourselves comfortable." He stepped back and held out his hand in a gentlemanly manner to help Nora down from the crate.

"Thanks." He had kind eyes. There was a warmth to them that she didn't often see in others. And she felt weirdly safe with him. "You know what I wish?"

"That you'd never come into this corner store?"

"Definitely that. But also that I'd held on to that salad."

"I don't know," he said as he arranged two crates for them to sit on. "That could have added to the problem. We'll have to make do with Starbursts." He pointed to the shelves behind her; she turned to see two boxes of Starbursts neatly stacked.

"Starbursts are my favorite! My grandpa was right—he always said there is a silver lining to any situation, and there you go."

"I like your grandpa. What's your name?"

"Nora. Yours?"

"Jack." He smiled. "What's your name?" he asked the woman.

She sniffed. She clutched her purse even tighter to her body. "Juanita."

"Juanita, would you like some Starbursts?" He reached around Nora for a box and ripped it open. Packages of Starbursts tumbled to the floor. Jack picked up several and held some out to Nora. "You look like a pink Starburst girl."

That delighted her, because she was. "I love the pink ones."

They sat side by side on the crates, eating Starbursts like grapes. Every so often, she or Jack would get up to peer out the window to see what was going on. Jack reported that the clerk and Darth were involved in a serious but less argue-y conversation. A few moments later Nora said that Darth had taken off his mask and was on the phone. "His hair is sandy blond."

"No way," Jack said. "I would not have guessed Darth to be blond."

Juanita, finally convinced they were not going to die, called her sister. As she talked about the latest thing someone's son had done, she sorted her Starbursts into piles of red, orange, yellow, and pink. The pink ones she tossed to Nora.

Nora and Jack talked about anything that came to mind. "Like, why Darth Vader?" Nora asked as she unwrapped another pink Starburst. "Why not Chewbacca?"

"I'd go for Yoda," Jack said.

"Princess Leia," Juanita said. "But then you could see my face."

"Princess Leia is the most popular Star Wars character," Nora said with an absence of any proof other than her gut. "I mean, I think."

"Nope," Jack said, shaking his head. "Luke Skywalker."

"No way," Nora said. "Han Solo would come before Luke Skywalker."

"You're both wrong," Juanita piped up. "Lando Calrissian is the favorite."

They went on to rate Star Wars characters in descending order of likability.

From there, they somehow got on the topic of the weirdest things that had ever happened to them. "I was once mistaken for Ryan Reynolds, the actor," Jack said. He was leaning against the stack of milk crates, his legs long and crossed at the ankles, his hands behind his head, looking a little smug at the comparison.

"He was filming a movie here and, like, this woman was convinced I was him and would not take no for an answer. So I signed an autograph."

"You don't look anything like Ryan Reynolds," Juanita opined.

Jack shrugged. "She thought so." He looked at Nora. "What about you?"

She didn't even have to think about it. "I saw the ghost of a very happy dog in the middle of the Madewell store in the Domain."

"No way," Jack said.

"One hundred percent," she said. "I was holding up a jacket to myself in the mirror, and this small white dog with a curved tail trotted past behind me. I looked all over the store for him to pet . . . but there was no dog."

"Were you high or something?" Juanita asked.

She was obviously giving off a different sort of vibe to Juanita than Jack. "Nope."

"I believe it," Jack said. "I believe anything is possible."

That delighted Nora. She used to believe that too.

As they talked, Nora could feel the sparkle in her growing. The warmth in Jack's eyes drew her in, and when he reached for a Starburst and his fingers brushed her hand, or his knee pressed against hers, a thousand little shivers of sensation shot through her.

It was staggering, really—she'd felt so hollow inside since her grandpa had died, devoid of any feelings. She'd forgotten what an emotional connection felt like. And now she couldn't stop looking at him, this miracle man in a corner store.

Juanita returned her full attention to her phone call, and Nora and Jack named three things that were giant pet peeves about living in Austin, both listing robbery at a corner store before you've had a chance to buy a soggy salad right at the top, followed by how hard it was to meet people, and, of course, traffic. They ranked Halloween candy and then positive traits they liked in a partner. Nora was privately thrilled that they had almost the same list. They played rock paper scissors for the lone bottle of water in the storeroom, only to discover that Juanita had helped herself to it as she had discussed her brother's latest girlfriend with her sister.

Eventually they heard a lot of noise and hopped up to see what was happening. The metal door had been raised from the entrance and the police were taking a distraught Darth away without incident. The clerk watched with a bored expression, smoking another cigarette. The cat stood up and stretched, then hopped down and strutted in front of one of the police officers all the way to the storeroom. When the officer announced herself and opened the door, the cat went to the litter box, tucked in beneath the shelving. The officer looked at all the Starburst wrappers, neatly piled into a pyramid. "So . . . I guess everyone is all right?"

They said they were fine. Nora was better than fine. She was glittering from the inside out, high from the connection. She didn't want the night to end—she imagined they would pull a cot into the storeroom, and they would live on salad and Starbursts and Monster drinks, and the cat would come to visit, and they would talk about everything and laugh and maybe kiss and even more. Just the two of them like that. No need for the outside world at all.

"I need you all to wait here for the crime unit," the officer said. "They're running a little behind after the protests. Plus, you don't want to go out in this."

The three of them looked past her to the windows. A deluge of cold rain was coming down.

Jack and Nora glanced at each other as the officer walked away. "Well, Nora, this has been a pretty wild night."

"The wildest," she agreed. It felt as if there were a million things to say, so many she didn't know where to begin. Because she'd thought that was the end, of course. The cavalry had come; the bad guy had been arrested.

But it was not nearly the end.

Chapter 7

Jake. Jack. Maybe John?

Nora was trying to dredge up the corner store guy's name as she made her way to the police station to get a copy of the incident report.

She'd planned to tackle Grandpa's garden this afternoon, but for two days it had rained on and off. Instead, she'd gone to Goodwill and bought some pots and pans. She'd never owned more than an omelet pan. She'd tried to make arrangements with Chef Borgia to take the private lesson but learned he was on sabbatical to Italy this year. So she signed up for a class at the Saucepot Kitchen Classroom instead.

Then she'd tried to get hold of Lacey and got a single text back. Sorry, it's exam week. Super busy. Call u soon.

It seemed to Nora that her sister was avoiding her. And that hurt in a way Nora wasn't used to feeling—it burned. She didn't understand the reason for what felt like rejection. She attempted to get Gus on the phone too, but his phone rang and rang. She figured he was at work.

She continued her purge of the Before—she packaged up her flat iron, her Nespresso coffee maker with the ridiculously expensive pods, and her Amazon Alexa and took them to recycling.

She'd also scoured the internet for a mention of the robbery in the local papers. Despite the hostage situation, it hadn't made any sort of news at all, except for a single paragraph in the online edition of the *Austin-American Statesman*. The paragraph said only that the situation had been "resolved without incident." No mention of Darth Vader or hostages.

But there had to be a police report.

At the substation, the female officer standing behind the plexiglass chewed gum obnoxiously as Nora explained she was looking for information about a particular incident.

"You want a report, you gotta fill out a request online."

"Oh, I . . . I'm not really asking officially, just asking if anyone remembers. Really, I only need a name. I was hoping whoever responded to the robbery could help me."

The cop stared at her for a long moment like she thought she was being punked. "You think any of us remembers a single incident, much less someone's name? Can you at least give me a name of a responding officer?"

Nora shook her head.

The cop sighed wearily into a bubble of gum, let it pop, and drew it back into her mouth. "You're wasting my time."

Obviously, Nora realized. But the idea had sounded so reasonable in her head. "Sorry," she said. "I thought maybe since it was a hostage situation it would stand out. The thing is, it was harrowing, and I just want to find the person who was with me." She did not add that he was the one person in a very long time she'd felt she could really talk to.

The officer propped her elbows on the metal counter and leaned forward. "Do you know how many robberies and hostage situations and general situations we respond to in a year? No? How about a quarter? Or a month?" She paused, forcing Nora to give another humiliating shake of her head. "You can't even say what day it was. You even sound a little unsure about the month. You gotta know *something*, lady. They should have given you an incident report number. A phone number to call. Are you telling me they didn't give you anything?"

"I'm not saying that. But I've had a lot of stuff happen since then, and—"

"Yeah, we've all had a lot of stuff happen." She snorted. "Come back when you can remember the date."

Frustrated, Nora walked outside. She'd truly imagined that the cops were still talking about it. *Remember that night at the corner store? Boy, was he a nut job.*

The corner store! Why hadn't she thought of it before? Someone there would remember that horrible night.

••••••

Nora almost laughed with relief when she stepped inside the corner store and saw the same wiry guy behind the counter. His cat was perched high on a shelf behind him, its tail swishing lazily as it eyed Nora.

This, she decided, was a good omen. She grinned at the man behind the counter. "Hi! Remember me?"

The clerk stared at her blankly.

"From the night of the robbery."

"Which one?"

"Oh, wow . . . more than one? The, ah . . . the hostage situation?"

He propped a foot on the counter. "No, don't remember you."

Nora was slightly offended. She wasn't *that* unremarkable. "I'm trying to find the guy who was locked up with me and the other woman. Maybe you remember him? Tall? Wearing a scarf?"

He snorted. "Don't remember anyone."

Her impatience was ratcheting up. "Come on . . . we were here for hours."

He shrugged. "What do you want with him?"

"I want to say thank you." And a whole lot more that she didn't have to share with him. Mostly she wanted to say she was sorry for not calling. To explain how that night, and those hours with him, had meant more to her than she could put into words. How he'd made her feel alive again. And how she'd fallen into a dark hole afterward from which she couldn't escape.

Someone joined her at the counter, thereby forming a queue. The clerk motioned her out of the way. A man put a soggy sandwich and a Monster drink on the counter. There was a brief exchange about an Astros baseball game while the man paid. As he walked out the door, Nora stepped up to the counter again. "I thought maybe he was a regular."

"Who, that guy?" the clerk asked, looking at the back of the man who'd bought the sandwich.

What was his problem? "No . . . the guy from the hostage situation."

The clerk had the gall to look perturbed. "Look, lady, people come in and out. I don't pay attention; I just ring them up. I don't remember you. I don't remember him."

Okay, rude. Frustration percolated as Nora walked to the door. Why was she always the one to walk away empty-handed? Because she was a coward, afraid of confrontation. Well, she was different now. She paused at the door and looked back at the clerk. "You're such a prick."

She was as startled by her words as he was, judging by the way his mouth fell open. She never called anyone out. For anything.

But she had to admit, calling him out felt pretty damn good.

She didn't feel the sting of dejection until she was in her car and well down the road, when she began to wonder if this search for the corner store guy was a pipe dream. She remembered his beguiling smile and imagined him cheering her on. *You can do it! Keep looking! I'm here! And yeah, that guy is* such *a prick!*

She managed a small smile. Okay—giving up and letting dejection turn to despair was something she would have done in the Before. But this was the After, and Nora sat up a little straighter. It was hard as hell to reinvent herself, but she believed the corner store guy was worth it.

She'd keep looking. She'd go home and fill out the online request that would go into some police department bureaucratic black hole. And, ugh, there was always social media.

And as the light turned green, a thought whispered into Nora's head. *There was a protest at the capitol that night. Start there.*

Chapter 8

Jack

T*ony Patricelli died at 8:52 a.m. with his parents, his* siblings, and a couple of ex-girlfriends at his side. His passing was peaceful, mainly because he'd been pumped full of morphine to ease the pain of his bone cancer. He drew one last rattled breath, and that, as they say, was that.

Jack Moriarity had known from the beginning that his line of work—hospice and palliative nursing—would be hard. But he hadn't anticipated it would be *this* hard.

His interest in the field had begun the summer he was fifteen, when his single mother had slowly wasted away from cancer. When chemo and radiation hadn't worked, she'd decided to let nature take its course. And Jack, her only child, had spent that summer lying on the bed with her, looking through old photos and videos, eating licorice, and talking about the future.

It hadn't been his idea to talk about the future—even to his fifteen-year-old brain, it had seemed unnecessarily cruel to imagine a life without her. But his mother had insisted. She said that death was part of life, and all anyone really needed to pass from one realm to the other was someone to hold their hand.

He held her hand all the way to the end. And to this day, he couldn't abide the smell of licorice.

His mother had arranged for Jack to go live with her maternal aunt in California, who, as far as Jack knew, was the only family his mother had. He'd never known his father—his mother had said he wasn't important. Jack thought he could have been really important, especially that summer. But whatever. He went to live with Aunt Patricia.

Aunt Patricia wasn't bad. Though he never felt any affection from her, she took her duty seriously. She made sure he was provided for and had a college fund. Who could blame her lack of enthusiasm? People didn't get to seventy years old and hope to take in a teenager. But he could look back now and see how much he'd needed a little love. A hug, a pat on the head. Something. He'd lost his mom, had never known his dad. He'd moved around a lot as a kid, his mother always exchanging one bad job for another. He never knew where he belonged.

After he graduated from high school, he decided he belonged back in Austin. He said goodbye to Aunt Patricia, and she packed him peanut butter and jelly sandwiches for the drive.

He attended a small college and dated some. Nothing serious, not until he met Brandy when he was twenty-two. He was instantly smitten with her long blonde hair and tanned legs and fell head over heels in love. He'd never felt something so intensely. It lodged in his chest, swelled with every breath he took. He thought Brandy felt the same. She twined their names in calligraphy and fantasized about them living by the sea and saving turtles.

It had been only a few weeks when he felt her pulling away from him. She finally admitted it. She said he was too "clingy."

Clingy?

Jack was mortified by this pronouncement. She ended their short, flaming affair, and he suffered the loss deeply. He added the fear of being "clingy" to his insecurities.

After Brandy, after his mother, he was afraid of needing anyone again. He was even more afraid of losing anyone again. *"You can't love someone without the constant fear of losing them, can you?"* a girl at a party had asked him one night when they were both nursing beers, both on the losing ends of breakups.

Her question had resonated uncomfortably in him.

But life moved on. When he completed his education and specialized training and passed his boards, he was 100 percent sure of his calling. He believed that helping people transition from this world to the next was a necessary and unique skill.

By the time patients reached Sanctum House, where he worked, they had usually accepted the inevitable, had cycled through their stages of grief. But not everyone had someone to hold their hand all the way to the end. And because of staffing shortages, Jack had been holding a lot of hands in the last year or so. It was getting to him.

On his first day of work, Sandra, the head of nursing, had taken him around. She was a large woman who wore pink Crocs and faded scrubs bedecked with cartoon animals. She'd been at Sanctum House for twenty years. She'd said, "Let me tell you something, Jackie—take this job for what it is, and it will be much easier on you."

"Um . . ."

"I mean, don't get emotionally involved. Look around—all these souls we're caring for? Here today and gone tomorrow. Accept that, and it will make this job a lot easier on you mentally." She'd tapped herself in the head as she spoke. "Trust me, I know what I'm talking about."

He had no doubt that she did. And he worked hard not to get emotionally involved. For the most part, he was successful.

And yet . . . *and yet.*

He understood that patients came to Sanctum House to die. He'd studied end stages of life, had probably read more about death and dying than your average priest. And still, he struggled to absorb the losses. Especially when it was someone like Tony Patricelli.

Tony was only forty-one. Eight years older than Jack.

Tony was funny. Boisterous. A real bro. He told wild stories about women he and Jack both knew didn't exist. He flirted shamelessly with female nurses and doctors and tried to hustle any man who walked into his room. Sometimes, after his shift, Jack would hang around to play *Call of Duty* with him.

Tony never talked about dying. He talked like he was about to go on vacation, like he'd be back in a few weeks or months. Tony wasn't the first patient Jack had nursed who preferred not to acknowledge the inevitable—so Jack thought about it for him. Tony's death was one he'd tried to prepare for, and he truly believed he was ready for the end when it came. But he wasn't.

Everything felt so temporary. *Here today, gone tomorrow.* What was the point of it all?

After the funeral home picked up Tony's body, Sandra found Jack in the medicine closet, his back against the wall, his eyes closed, swallowing hard against tears. That was another thing you learned early on—don't cry, don't mourn, because there is always someone else who needs you to hold their hand.

"Okay, Jackie." She took the clipboard from his hands. "Take the afternoon." When Jack didn't move, she nodded at the door. "Go on. Get out of here."

"That's not necessary," Jack had lied.

"Like hell it isn't. Look, we've all been there. Just take off, clear your head, and come back when you're ready. We can live without you for a day or two." She'd patted his cheek. "But we can't live without you for long. Get outside and hear the birds and see the trees or, I don't know, kiss a girl."

He'd gotten into his car and started driving with no destination in mind. He wondered where Tony was now. If he was alone, if he was afraid. If loved ones were there to greet him when he passed. He wondered if Tony knew how much Jack would miss him.

All that wondering unwittingly took Jack to the place he often ended up when he lost a patient: the Goodfellow Community Garden.

As improbable as it was, Jack had a garden here. *"Man, how old are you, anyway?"* his best friend, Byron, had asked him. *"Never had a bro who liked to putter around a garden like a retiree,"* he'd joked.

The plot had been bequeathed to Jack by Mr. Ronald Hauser, a former patient. At the time of Mr. Hauser's death, Jack had not been happy with the gift of a garden. It was too much responsibility—what was he supposed to do with it in the middle of his busy life? He'd told Mr. Hauser's children that they should keep it, but he could tell by the way his son kept looking at his watch and his daughter kept glancing at her phone that they didn't want it either. Their father's death had been a long and slow one, and they were ready to move on. They'd insisted their father wanted him to have it. They'd taken care of the paperwork.

It was a bit unsettling to think that Mr. Hauser's children could so easily dispose of something that had meant so much to him. But Mr. Hauser's desires and joys had gone home with him and had not become the desires and joys of his children. The plot was Jack's.

Toward the end, before Mr. Hauser was heavily sedated, he'd begged his kids to take him to see the garden one last time. But he'd been too frail to leave the facility, so at last his daughter had gone for him. She'd walked around with her iPhone, giving her dad a remote tour. Mr. Hauser didn't say anything as Jack held up the iPad so he could see. The old man had a vague smile on his face, squinting at times, his brows rising with surprise at others. When his daughter was done, Mr. Hauser had nodded and closed his eyes.

Jack had been the new owner of the garden plot a month or so before curiosity got the better of him and he went to have a look. He'd come after a long day at work, tired and grumpy. But the moment he stepped through the gates, he felt an immediate change in the air. In the middle of a crowded city, it was cleaner and brighter here. He could practically feel the budding life in the forty garden plots vibrating inside him. Maybe it was all the green, or maybe it was the electromagnetic field of the earth—who knew?—but something was suddenly moving in him and through him.

Mr. Hauser had written out detailed instructions when he'd still been able. Tomato plants went in the ground after the last frost. Cabbage should be planted in the heat of summer to harvest in fall. Bee balms must have full sun, so plant them on the west side of the plot.

The first few times Jack had come to this little patch of paradise, he'd been alarmed by his peculiar need to cry—he could hardly stop himself. He was ashamed of it—his shoulder was the one onto which others cried. But this was the one place he could let go of his emotions. Only a few birds and God to see him. Well. And the old lady who sat in a rusted wheelchair and watched her companion work a plot.

Jack soon discovered that work in the garden was therapeutic. It was good to thrust his hands in the dirt, breathe sweet garden air, have the cycle of life confirmed again and again.

Thankfully, there was no one around the day Tony died. Jack sagged onto his knees in the middle of the plot. A lone tear tipped from the corner of his eye and slid down his face. He hoped Tony was in a better place and free of pain.

Godspeed, Tony.

He unlocked his supply locker and took out a spade. He started turning the earth, preparing it for new life.

Chapter 9

Nora *was making progress on her transformation, but* she wasn't anywhere near where she wanted to be, and she was increasingly aware she was running out of time before the need to eat and pay bills would force her back to work. A few days ago, she'd gotten a call from a debt collector for a credit card bill she had failed to pay in the Before. She was mortified—she'd always kept her finances in good shape. She was afraid to look at how much she owed. Especially with medical bills starting to come in.

But Dad might force her back to work before bankruptcy did. His communication with her since the accident had been very limited. On the one hand, she felt miserably insignificant that he didn't seem to care how she was. On the other hand, she was relieved to be free from the weight of his criticism. How was it possible to want his attention and loathe it at the same time? She could never seem to stop wanting his approval. But he never had it to give.

Yesterday he'd finally reached out to her. Not to check on her, which one might assume, given the ordeal she'd been through. But to complain that he needed her in the office as soon as possible.

He was insistent and overbearing, and Nora knew she couldn't put him off much longer.

But today the skies had cleared and she was headed to Grandpa's garden. She expected the trip to be hard, mostly because the guilt she carried was so pervasive and heavy. She'd not only broken her promise to look after the plot when he was gone, but even before that, she couldn't seem to muster the energy to visit him. Her mother had told her she needed to snap out of her "funk." That was the euphemism for depression in the November family.

Nora stopped at a big-box hardware store and picked up a spade and a shovel. She would need more than that, but she didn't want to arrive empty-handed like she had no clue what she was doing. To be fair, she didn't have a clue what she was doing, but she was hoping some of Grandpa's garden tutoring would come back to her.

From there, the drive to the Goodfellow Community Garden was unpardonably short, hardly enough time to give herself a much-needed pep talk before she pulled into the parking lot.

High stone walls surrounded the garden. Entrance was gained through an ornate iron gate. The two acres of land had once belonged to an old Austin estate before it was broken up for development. Nora remembered Grandpa telling her that this part of the estate had housed the stables.

Through the gate, she could see bursts of color among the green plants that were beginning to unfurl. Her heart began a staccato beat in her chest. A shadow crossed over the sun, and she instinctively looked up. Grandpa was not there, of course. She had been seeing his shadow less and less. Still, she hoped for it every day.

A trickle of perspiration slid down her temple despite the cool temperatures. *What the hell?* Could she not walk into a community garden without having an episode? She thought she'd rid herself of that unpleasant occurrence of the Before—

panic attacks. When they first started happening, she tended to get them in court. But in the last few months before the accident, they'd started happening at weird times and places, without any obvious reason. She'd be getting ready for work and feel her heart rate suddenly skyrocket. Or she'd be sitting second chair in a trial and imagine the first chair suddenly taken ill and her hands would get clammy, her heart would race, and she'd have to excuse herself.

The unmistakable signs of an attack were painting in at her edges now, slipping in under her nails and shooting white hot through her veins and into her chest. She had to move before it paralyzed her. She shoved against the gate, but it was rusted and didn't budge. She slammed her body against it, and it swung open with an alarmingly loud squeak, announcing to one and all that at long last, the ne'er-do-well granddaughter had arrived.

Fortunately, only a couple of people were present, and they didn't seem to notice her.

Nora took several deep breaths. She remembered what Grandpa used to say when she would get overwhelmed. *"Listen to the birds,"* he said. *"You ever hear a more optimistic sound in your life? That's God saying good morning to you. That sound is telling you everything is going to be all right."*

Nora listened to the birds for several moments, the sound of their chatter reminding her of the utter joy she'd felt in Grandpa's celestial garden. It really was a very optimistic sound. *You know what else is optimistic, Nora? Your reverse bucket list.* She had to keep her eye on the prize. So when her heart had calmed, she picked up her shovel and spade and stepped inside and shut the gate behind her.

The community garden was as lovely as she remembered. She noticed the dark purple ranunculus and a lemon tree in full bloom, its boughs spreading prettily over two lucky plots.

She could see the tender shoots of vegetable plants, the start of vines trained to poles and lattices. Bluebonnets were beginning to peek up in small patches. The air smelled sweet, and the constant noise of the city seemed to fade away as Nora moved along a crushed granite path. Some of the plots had plaques denoting awards won, like Best Floral or Best Use of Space. All awarded by the board of the Goodfellow Community Garden.

But the deeper she went, the more dread built. She could hear Grandpa whispering to grow her garden, to put some color in her salad.

His plot was near the back. She couldn't see it yet, and she hung on to a hope that it had somehow survived her neglect since Grandpa died almost a year ago. One time at the ranch, they'd had a prolonged hard freeze that looked to have killed the roses. But the bushes had come back more beautiful than before.

No such luck today. When she reached Grandpa's plot, she swallowed down a swell of nauseating dismay. What had once been a tidy, beautiful urban garden was now a tangle of weeds and dried-out stalks. Even his chair had rusted and toppled over. Grandpa would die all over again if he saw this garden.

Her raging disappointment with herself, she was sorry to note, felt as familiar as a pair of old house shoes. It was a wrecking ball to her psyche—the light seemed to change around her and her head began to pound at the temples, the buzz deafening. She pressed a damp hand against the churning of her belly.

She dropped her tools and made herself step onto Grandpa's plot. Her foot sank down into the detritus all the way up to her ankle. One particularly showy weed brushed her knee, and she bent over and yanked it out of the earth.

She reached for another weed, but this one would not come free. She wrapped both hands around the stalk and yanked—it broke at ground level, the roots sunk deep. That infuriated her. The weed was mocking her, reminding her that there was nothing she could do to fix this terrible mess, that she'd let her grandfather down, that she'd broken her promise to do the one thing for the one person who had ever loved her exactly as she was, and she abhorred herself for it.

The ghost of Nora wanted to give in to defeat, but this was one way the new Nora was different—she wasn't going down without a fight . . . her near panic-attacking notwithstanding. She whirled around to grab the spade to get that weed out of her garden but was distracted by the sight of an elderly woman barreling down the path toward her in a wheelchair with a wheel so wobbly, it looked as if it might fly off at any moment. The woman wasn't using her arms to propel her; she was using her feet. The wet crushed granite was making her progress difficult, so she suddenly surged out of the chair and marched forward.

Nora froze, uncertain what to do.

The woman's silver hair was wrapped in a tight ballet bun at her crown. She wore flannel palazzo pants and a worn motorcycle jacket. And her expression was murderous. "How dare you," she growled when she reached the edge of Grandpa's plot.

Nora looked behind her to see if the woman was perhaps addressing someone else, but there was no one there. "I'm sorry?"

"You've got some gall showing up here now, you Lolly-come-lately."

Nora was stunned. "I'm sorry, ma'am, but I think you've mistaken—"

"I most certainly have not! I know who you are. He was my friend! Maybe even my best friend! Besides Walter, obviously." She jerked a thumb over her shoulder. In the next plot over, a slight man was casually raking. "He waited for you."

Confused, Nora asked, "Walter?"

"Jim! Every week he said, 'Oh, my granddaughter is going to come. She promised she'd come,'" she said with a mocking tone. "But you didn't, did you?"

Oh gosh. *Jim.* James Brian Carpenter, her grandfather. Bile began to crawl up Nora's throat. That terrible sledgehammer of grief struck her in the gut, making her feel nauseous. "You knew Grandpa?"

"I just said that. Good Lord, he worried about you. Now why would you let an old man worry like that?"

"How . . . I mean, what makes you think that?"

The woman glared like she thought Nora was being intentionally stupid. "Because he told me. He worried that you needed a break from your job because it was eating you up. He worried that you weren't taking care of yourself. All he wanted was to see you, and look what happened!"

Nora couldn't listen to this, because there was no room in her for more soul-crushing guilt and self-loathing.

"One day he was out here and announced to us all that his granddaughter was going to come visit, and oh, was that old man excited. But you didn't show up and he dropped dead of a heart attack. *That's* what happened."

It was worse than that. Nora hadn't come, hadn't been able to fight through another dark day. And two days later, when she finally did go to see him, she'd found him dead on the floor of his kitchen, his body cold and stiff, his skin mottled. She could recall every moment of that day like it had happened this morning. She had knocked several times on his door, pressing her ear to it to listen for movement—Grandpa was always home that time of day to listen to the news and weather. A resident passing by said they hadn't seen him for a couple of days.

Nora frantically dug a key out of her bag and opened the door to his apartment. She could feel death in the apartment before she ever saw him—the air was stiff and lifeless. "Grandpa?" She'd dropped her designer bag and walked in, checking his bedroom first, seeing the neatly made bed, and then the bathroom. His TV was off, his remote placed carefully beside the paper's crossword puzzle.

Nora moved on to the kitchen and saw his bare feet sticking out from behind the bar. Her scream stuck in her throat and came out as a roar as she ran around to him. He was wearing his pajamas. A coffee cup lay shattered, and brown liquid had spilled and stained the floor. He looked like death, but the possibility that he was dead was too far out of reach for her. She grabbed his shirt by the collar and tried to shake him awake, shrieking his name between sobs. She'd wept as she'd scrambled for a phone, then screamed at 911 to send someone now. She kept trying to rouse him, begging him, as the unthinkable snaked its way like a serpent into her heart, biting off pieces bit by bit.

When the first responders arrived, they did what they could but eventually put a sheet over him. A police officer asked her to wait in the living room. She stood stiff and disbelieving, her fingers clenching and unclenching, her breath shallow and raw, her heart aching.

They said he'd been there about a day or so. Which meant she could have saved him if she'd found a way to come when she'd promised she would. Which meant, in that twisted way grief has of destroying us, that she'd killed him.

Without warning, she whirled around and vomited the contents of her breakfast into the weeds.

"Holy crap!" the old woman yelped.

Nora braced her hands against her knees, dragging deep breaths into her lungs to keep from having a heart attack or vomiting again. She despised herself for her failure, and now her worst fears were confirmed: She hadn't hidden anything from Grandpa. He knew how hard her life had become, how the law firm was making mincemeat of her. He died knowing that she was drowning in despair and that she wasn't coming. That no one was coming.

"Are you sick?"

"Not like you think," Nora managed on a gasp of air.

The woman bent over so she could peer into her face. "Are you having a panic attack?"

Nora didn't answer because a big glob of tears erupted from her, spilling down her face.

"Good grief." The woman reached into a pocket and handed Nora an embroidered linen handkerchief, the sort Nora's grandmother used to wash and iron and fold into triangles for Grandpa's suits. "Why is your generation so weepy about every little thing? How bad is it?"

"Oh," Nora said and sucked in another breath, fighting another swell of nausea. "On a scale of one to ten, I'm at want-to-die."

"That's ridiculous," the woman insisted. "When anyone says they want to die, what they really mean is, they want to live, but they don't know how."

Nora choked on another sob.

"Stop that." The woman straightened up. "I wasn't asserting cause and effect. But I can't help but be mad that you didn't show up for your grandfather. Do you have any idea how much he loved you girls? Oh my God, stop crying."

A bony hand landed on her shoulder and squeezed. It felt almost comforting. Still, it took everything Nora had in her to make herself straighten up and not collapse to the ground. "You're right, ma'am—I was horrible. I didn't do half the things I said I would. I—" The tears exploded again, sliding down her cheeks, coming out of her eyes, her nose, her mouth. She had let

Grandpa down, over and over, in the worst ways. He had loved her so much, and all she could do was screw up.

"Stop crying, girlie. There's no crying in theater."

"I think you mean baseball."

"I mean theater."

"Gracious, what'd you do?" A man in a wide-brimmed hat—Walter—had appeared. "Leave the girl alone."

"I didn't do anything, Walter," the woman said. "Go check your precious Venus flytraps." She sighed. "The man wins an award for Best Exotic and suddenly he's a master gardener." She woodenly patted Nora's arm. "Look, I'm sorry I upset you. Walter says I talk too much, and I'm not one to sugarcoat anything. But Jim was my friend, and I miss him, and I guess I needed someone to blame."

"Well, I blame me too, so get in line," Nora said weakly.

The woman looked her over. "Jim was right about one thing—you're a mess. Much worse shape than I pictured."

Nora put her hands on her waist and drew another shaky breath. "I'm not sure how to take that." She couldn't banish the image of Grandpa's lifeless body or how she'd clung to it.

"Come here," the woman said and gripped Nora by the elbow and guided her over to the rusted metal chair. She bent down and righted it, made Nora sit in it, then told her to stay put. She went and got her wheelchair and rolled it up next to Nora and took a seat.

Nora wiped her face with the handkerchief, then looked at the woman. "May I ask who you are?"

"I should have said. I'm Catherine Henry."

Nora nodded.

"You've heard the name?"

"I'm sorry, but Grandpa never—"

"I mean, you've heard the name, generally speaking?"

Generally speaking, she had not. She shook her head.

Catherine Henry muttered under her breath, "What is wrong with this country? Don't they teach art anymore? I was a Broadway star back in the day. A *big* Broadway star. Jim knew who I was, but of course he did—he loved Broadway. What about closer to home? I headlined at Esther's Follies for a few years. That must ring some bells."

Esther's Follies was a long-standing vaudeville comedy theater in town. Nora had never been, but it was true that Grandpa loved a good rowdy show with lots of dancing and music.

"He saw some of my performances. At least he pretended he did. And he didn't mind me talking about my glory days. Not like Walter." She cast a dark side-eye in the direction of the man who'd gone back to his rake.

"Is Walter your husband?"

"Oh my God, no. My husband died twenty years ago. Liver disease. Didn't even know he had it until he got a strange pain in his side. The next thing I know, they're telling us he's only got a few weeks. No, Walter and I've been friends for fifty years, since we were wide-eyed theater students in New York."

Nora blew her nose. "You met my grandfather here?"

"Yep. I like to come down to the gardens while Walter works in our plot. Gives me something to do to keep my mind off my troubles. Jim missed you and the other one something fierce."

"Lacey," Nora said. "I'm Nora."

"I could tell by looking at you that you were the lawyer. You have that skinny, hard look about you."

Nora wasn't quite sure how to take that either. "Well, the skinny is a recent development. But I feel like the hard look has been around awhile."

The lady almost smiled. "He sure had high hopes for you. Always talking about what a great lawyer you were and how you could do some good in the world if your boss would let you."

More tears leaked from her—Grandpa would say she was excellent at anything she did. He once called her high school failing grade in physics a "launching pad to greatness."

"How?" she'd demanded, dismayed by the grade and fearing the criticism she'd get from her father.

"There's nowhere but up, and if I know anything about you, I know that you're only going up."

"Now, don't get me wrong, he loved the other one too," the lady said. "But he said she was self-sufficient."

"Yeah . . . but me, not so much, right?"

"Well, he worried more about you. You know, now that I'm looking at you, I don't see the lawyer so much. I see skinny and a little lost." She leaned forward to peer at her. "I'll be completely honest, Nora. I'm disappointed after the big buildup Jim gave you."

Not as disappointed as Nora was. She couldn't help a tremulous smile. "Well, thanks for your honesty, I guess."

"You owe it to your grandfather to bring this garden back to life, you know."

Why did this old woman think she was here? Tears erupted again, and she leaned over, folded her arms across her knees, and tried to stop them.

"Good Lord, there you go again. I'm just saying, after you let him down, you should make it up to him. I can help you. For starters, you need to clean out this plot." She leaned forward and put her hand on Nora's knee. "Don't cry, honey. There's nothing here that can't be fixed. You have to want to fix it, though. Jim always said that happiness was born of usefulness. He had a lot of sayings like that. Anyway, you could be very useful here and get yourself happy. Get the weeds out before doing anything else. You can't grow the good stuff when the life is choked out by weeds."

What was it with old people and their garden metaphors? Was this woman channeling Grandpa? *Was* she Grandpa? Had Nora completely lost her mind? Entirely possible. She sniffed. "Thank you, Miss Henry. I appreciate your . . . insight."

"Call me Catherine. Now, go home, and when you come back, you're going to need a hat."

Yes. A hat. Grandpa was never without his battered sun hat.

"Catherine, leave her alone," Walter called down the path.

Catherine muttered under her breath again. She began to back down the path, pushing with her feet, her gaze on Nora.

Nora sat still for a long time before she put her things away in Grandpa's footlocker with the spare key he'd given her ages ago. She looked around at the wild plot and pictured him puttering around. She missed him so very much.

She sank down to the ground and then slowly leaned back until she was lying on her back among the dead plants and weeds, staring at a fat white cloud floating across an azure sky. *Oh, Grandpa, I'm so sorry. I'm trying. I really am.*

She was trying so hard to make the After work because she *needed* it to work. It was harder than she'd thought it would be—she hadn't been able to completely rid herself of that weird sensation of her skin not fitting properly. And her emotions were all over the map. She longed for that slice of heaven that was Grandpa's celestial garden. She longed to feel that warmth of love wash over her again, to feel his arms around her, holding her safe.

A memory floated back of Gus, Lacey, and her, lying beside Grandpa on a blanket in the middle of a field. They were looking at cloud shapes, calling out what they saw. Gus only saw chickens.

Nora later told Grandpa that day was one of the best days of her entire summer.

"Well, that's the thing, sweetheart. Joy is found in the simplest things," he'd said. *"You never have to look too far for a little shot of it."*

Maybe that was what was wrong with her, Nora mused. Maybe she'd been looking too far for a little shot of it. Maybe she needed to try harder to figure out why joy was so hard for her to see in life. And maybe Grandpa's garden was the simple thing that could bring her joy and really make her new life different from the Before.

The new Nora found the strength to get up. She left her ghost lying in the overgrown plot to rot with the weeds. The new Nora had work to do.

Chapter 10

The day Nora was to return to work arrived on a sled of trepidation that crashed through the front door and flooded her apartment. The anxiety she'd managed to stave off lately—with a few notable exceptions—was back with a vengeance.

She would have been quite happy to never darken the door of November and Sons again . . . but reality was a bitch. With her usual bills and rent, plus the medical bills that were piling up (thanks to her trip to the coast, bills from a hospital her insurance deemed "out of network" were twice as costly) and her dad's increasingly reproachful texts, she had no choice but to return. For now.

She felt like she was walking into a prison, presenting herself to do her time. No one, save James, would be happy to see her. She'd never fit in there, had always felt like a tiny island far from the office shore.

Her father had leapfrogged her over everyone to install her into a coveted position in a swank corner office for having done nothing more than pass the bar exam. "On your second attempt," as he so often liked to remind her. But she knew how the staff viewed her: the owner's kid without even a fraction of the experience most of them had and even less finesse. She was the walking definition of nepotism, and if there was any doubt, she'd heard the daddy jokes over the last few years.

After the night of her disastrous pass-the-bar party, Nora had insisted to her father that she was going into environmental law. He'd responded with a smirk. Which turned out to be a prescient smirk—she couldn't get an interview. On the rare occasion she did, she was told the field was highly competitive and they'd get back to her, but no one ever did.

At one interview, she'd told them she'd start anywhere. In the mailroom, if necessary. One of the partners had walked her out. At the elevator door, she'd said, *"Do yourself a favor. Capitalize on your name and go to work for your father."*

That's when it had clicked—potential employers saw no reason to give her a position and spend their resources training her when they assumed she would likely end up at November and Sons anyway.

Her lack of success at finding a job had emboldened her dad. He'd showered her with promises. He'd said he'd never show her favoritism, that he would treat her like any other lawyer. That those who were concerned about nepotism would be proved wrong.

But they weren't wrong, and her father didn't treat her like any other lawyer—he gave her high-profile cases that she was not prepared to take, told her exactly what to do, and left nothing to her judgment. At case review meetings, he would expect her to present, then pick apart everything she said, leaving her self-confidence in tatters.

In the two weeks leading up to her accident, she hadn't been sleeping well. She'd been wandering around her apartment at night, worrying about her work and the state of the world in general. About the state of *her*. She'd even told her parents that it didn't feel as if her mind was firing on all cylinders.

"How could it with all the carbs you eat?" her mother had said.

Just before she left on vacation to the coast, she'd had a case settlement meeting for a client who'd been injured at a refinery and fractured his hip. The man was in his fifties, had four kids, and was out of work for weeks. November and Sons was suing the company for damages on his behalf—the pockets of the oil and gas industry were notoriously deep. November and Sons maintained that the man's injuries were such that he'd probably never work again.

Before the meeting began, an attorney for the defendant pulled Nora aside and showed her footage of her client riding a motorcycle, picking up debris in his yard, and then going out for a jog. Nora understood that if they didn't settle, a trial would expose her client exaggerating the seriousness of his injury. She explained to her client that a judge or jury would not see his physical improvement as miraculous but more likely would conclude he'd made a fraudulent claim, and she convinced him to settle for less than the firm had been expecting to get.

She remembered walking into the case review meeting afterward, so tired that she'd bumped into another staff member on her way in. "Wow," he said. "You look like you've been on a bender."

"Sorry," Nora had muttered, lacking the energy to disabuse him of that idea. She sat at the table and looked down and happened to notice a coffee stain on the lapel of her light gray jacket. When had that happened?

When it came time for her to present the settlement results, her father had listened expressionless. When she'd finished explaining what had transpired, he asked, "How do you feel about the settlement?"

Nora had been his daughter for thirty-one years and knew a trick question when she heard one. But she never could seem to think fast enough. "Um . . ."

"If you don't have an opinion, which is a problem in and of itself, let me give you mine. You were too quick to settle. The amount you agreed to means we lose money on this case."

"I did the calculation and—"

"I'm talking," he snapped. "We were prepared to go to trial, Nora. Do you think someone's doctored video would stop us?"

Anxiety was radiating up into her brain, making it hard to think. "It wasn't doctored."

"Oh, so you're our new video expert? Because we have several, and I'm sure they would have found a way to prove the video was doctored or filmed at such an angle as to be misleading."

What he was suggesting was impossible. "The video was—"

"Not only have you let our client down, but you've also let this firm down."

"Wait . . . you haven't seen the evidence."

"Just admit that you blew it. Now all the other attorneys in here are going to have to bill more hours so that we can still meet our quarterly projections." He'd looked around the room. "You can thank her later."

Nora sat down. She could feel herself disappearing . . . fading into nothingness.

Later that afternoon her father walked into her office and perched on the table, all smiles. "I think you learned a valuable lesson today."

"Yeah," she said. "That no matter what I do, you'll find fault."

He'd chuckled. "I'm hard on you because I must be. If you're going to be in any shape to lead this firm one day, you need to be prepared. Those people are never going to respect you if I don't push you."

"Dad." Tears burned the back of her eyes. "They are never going to respect me because *you* don't respect me."

He didn't deny it. He'd probably assumed she would thank him for his tough-love tutelage. "You're too sensitive. Stop moping and clean yourself up. You look terrible."

She'd felt absolutely shattered. Nothing was ever right about her. She was one big walking mistake.

Well.

That was the Before. This was the After. Not only was she determined to get a new job as soon as possible, she was determined to learn how to never feel like a mistake again. She would start her transformation by walking into that office with confidence and surprising them all.

••••••

Confidence was not something Nora knew anything about, so she had to fake it. She kept her head high as she walked through the doors of November and Sons, sailing through cube nation in her therapeutic boot with a smile on her face, making eye contact with everyone she passed. They had never seen her exude confidence. And she couldn't be sure she was exuding it right.

But she remembered what Grandpa taught her many years ago, when she'd had to change softball teams after a reshuffling of the summer league. Nora had been scared to join a new team, scared the girls wouldn't like her. *"You go in with confidence,"* Grandpa said. *"Say hi to everyone. And then give them some of this."* He'd handed her a brown paper bag.

Nora looked inside. *"Bubble gum?"*

"That's right. All great baseball players chew bubble gum. You introduce yourself, offer them a piece of bubble gum, and then you walk through that dugout like you invented the game. Now, go get 'em, Tiger."

She didn't have any bubble gum today, but she remembered doing what Grandpa had suggested that day and walking confidently through the dugout. And she'd found friends.

"Hey, Randy!" she called, startling a lawyer she'd worked with only once. "Felicia, hi! When is the baby due?"

Kevin Strothers, a new partner, came out of his office. "Kev," she said, pointing at him. "What's up?"

Everyone stared at her with a mix of alarm and fascination. In the Before, she would dart past them, head down, avoiding conversation.

She recalled how once, in her second year on the job, James had talked her into attending an after-work happy hour. *"You never participate in anything, Nora. People talk,"* he'd said.

That's because she knew how they felt about her. But she took James's advice and went. She didn't say much; she didn't get the jokes about office life they were flinging around. At one point, she went to the bar to buy a round—she'd at least had enough sense to do that. She was standing next to a massive man, hoping the bartender would notice her, when she heard her name. Two of the firm's attorneys were standing on the other side of the man. And they were talking about her.

"It's like, seriously, Nora, law school 101—be prepared to present," the woman said. "Like, how hard is it? We do it every day."

She'd known immediately they were talking about a case review meeting earlier that week. Everything Nora had said about the case, her father picked apart. Contrary to what they thought, she got it. She just sucked at it.

"She's an Eeyore," the man said.

"A what?"

"You know, the sad donkey. Always down in the dumps about something."

There was a silence.

"Winnie-the-Pooh?"

"Sorry, Yulang, I haven't read that classic in a very long time. And anyway, what does she have to be down in the dumps about?

She sucks as a lawyer, and yet she'll run this firm one day. Cry me a river."

Nora winced with sympathy for the woman she'd been in the Before, trapped in the November snow globe.

But this was the After, and she was not an Eeyore; she was a . . . well, she didn't know what she was—yet—but she was not a sad donkey.

When James spotted her, he hopped up from his desk and followed her into her office.

"Hey, James. Thank you for vacating my office."

"I didn't have a choice. That weasel Brandon from HR came by and made me. Speaking of choices, that skirt is a brave one. And what did you do to your hair?"

"Like it?" she asked, raking her fingers through her hair. She glanced down at her ankle-length skirt with the splashy yellow and white flowers on a navy background. She'd spotted it in the window of the thrift shop. She'd gone in and bought this skirt, a couple of tops, and a pair of combat boots. She was wearing one on her left foot.

She twisted one way, making the hem flare out. "I like this skirt. It's comfy and it covers the therapeutic boot." She twisted again, but when she did, her gaze landed on a pot of succulents on the windowsill. The leaves had wilted and were draped over the sides of the pot like wet linens laid out to dry. The center plant, which looked like a fat cabbage, had turned yellow.

The shame of another dead plant crawled across Nora's skin.

"Nora!" Her father strode into the room, all smiles. He was tall and trim, wearing a bespoke suit. She could remember a time when he'd put her up on his broad shoulders to see the floats at the Fourth of July parade. How proud she'd been of her handsome, strong dad way back then.

"Good morning, sweetie." He held out his arms for a hug.

Sweetie? That was new. He never called her anything but Nora. "Hi, Dad." She cautiously walked into his arms, and he managed a loose embrace. He was not an affectionate man.

He dropped his arms and stepped back, still smiling. He looked pleased to see her, which was terribly unsettling, because Nora knew the hammer would eventually fall. "That's quite a haircut." His gaze drifted to her outfit and the smile disappeared. "What are you wearing?"

She glanced down. "I've decided to wear more color."

And just like that, his brown eyes turned cold. "You look like you're on your way to a folk dance."

This was the first her father had seen her since she'd come home from rehab, and the only thing he could say was that he didn't like her clothes. "I wish!" She smiled.

David November's heavy sigh was disturbingly familiar. "We have some cases that need your immediate attention. The bus company case has languished since your accident. You need to choose a lawyer to assist you and prepare for the deposition."

The new Nora jauntily saluted him, surprising herself. "Aye, aye, Captain." What was the matter with her? Her father was not a jovial man, and she'd certainly never been known for making things light around the office.

True to form, his face darkened. "Why are you acting like this?"

"Like what?" Not like her usual obsequious self? She wished she knew the answer, but she could only offer that she'd been completely rearranged and this was her now. And she liked her now. "I guess because I had an NDE. Who knew it could be so invigorating?"

"A what?"

"A near-death experience."

"Don't say that," he said sharply. "You had an accident. You don't need to dramatize it."

"True. It was pretty dramatic all on its own." Wow, the new Nora was on fire today.

Her father's expression turned darker. Once, when she was in college, he'd been upset with her for a semester of grades that were average. He'd demanded to know if she knew what a higher education like hers cost per semester. She didn't know, because her parents had always said she was not to think of it, that she was to concentrate on her grades. She'd said, *"More than a Maserati?"*

He'd slapped her across the face.

For the record, she'd been right. Each semester cost more than a Maserati, but less than a Lamborghini. Gus had done the research for her.

Today's answer did not satisfy her dad either, and he shifted so close to her that she hardly had room to breathe. She could see a tiny fleck of toothpaste in the corner of his mouth, the beginning of what looked like a sty in his left eye. "Sweetie?"

Ick. She really did not like this new *sweetie* business.

"I know you had a bad experience. But it's over. You're a senior attorney at November and Sons law firm and on track to be partner by the end of the year. You need to show some decorum, snap out of this Daffy Duck routine, and get back to normal."

So if she wore a floral skirt to work and was perky, she was daffy. Got it. He wanted normal? But he'd always insisted on exceptional. He wanted a superhero in a cape who was demure and polite and a size 4, and if she could morph into her brother, Nathan, while she was at it, even better. "I'm just being myself, Dad."

He snorted disdainfully. "You're playing a victim, and I don't need victims in my firm. Never wear anything like that skirt into this office again. And do something with your hair. We have a dress code. At least have the decency to give the illusion of strength."

Ooh, there it was, the thing that had haunted her in the Before. She would never be able to give him what he wanted—he wanted a man. He wanted a son.

Nora wanted Nathan too. So many times in her life she'd felt herself missing him, wondering what life would have been like had he lived. Would they have been close? Shared a secret language? Would he have protected her, or her him? Would he have borne the brunt of criticism from their father so she was spared? Or would he have been like dear old Dad and found fault with her?

Her dad turned and stalked out, pausing to bark at James, "Don't you have work to do?"

James and Nora stood unmoving, breaths held, waiting to see if he returned for one last verbal blow. He didn't, and James slowly turned to her with a wide-eyed stare. "Like . . . are you okay?"

Astonishingly, she was. She felt weirdly exuberant, like she'd solved a puzzle for a big cash prize. She slid her foot out from beneath her skirt. "What do you think he'd say about this?"

James slapped a hand over his mouth at the sight of her combat boot. "Girl . . ."

"It's the same height as the therapeutic boot. It makes for a more comfortable walk. Stop staring at me like I've lost it."

"But, like, *have* you?"

She laughed. "Honestly? I'm not sure. I'd better get to work."

"I can't stop seeing the flowers on your skirt." He started for the door.

"Hey, James? The office pool . . . who has me going out early?"

James paused at the door. "Kevin. He said you wouldn't be back, and if you did make it back, you wouldn't last a full day."

Kevin had worked with her on the church van case. Four kids had died in a rollover. She'd not been able to get the four children out of her mind. To be fair, at the time she'd been thinking about children, wanting them, even though there was so much hopelessness in the world and no one had magically appeared to have them with.

Okay, so, yes, she'd had her Eeyore moments. But the world seemed much brighter today. She felt stronger. She felt like she was beginning to figure out how to control her life. All she had to do was find a job that didn't involve so much death and dismemberment.

She looked again at the succulents. She picked up the pot and brought it to her desk and poured a little water in it. There was a garden shop near her apartment. She'd pop in there after work and see if they had any suggestion for how to resurrect nearly dead cactuses.

Chapter 11

The *oddly named Stinking Iris Garden Shop had a faded* stenciled sign in the window that said "All Things for Garden and Household Plants." A tiny bell over the door tinkled, signaling Nora's entry.

The shop was long and narrow, stuffed to the rafters with gardening tools and greenery, plants and lights and gloves, wheelbarrows and hanging baskets and pruners. A chemical floral scent tickled her nose, reminding her of the mix Grandpa used to spray on his flowers to keep the bugs away. The shop felt muggy; the air-conditioning was struggling to keep up.

She came to a halt beneath a tangle of hanging baskets. "Hello? Is anyone here?"

There was a rustling toward the back of the shop, and then a man appeared in the doorway to a back room. He was as broad as he was tall and filled the entire threshold. He was wearing a green leather apron, some rubber boots, a knit beanie, and sported a beard that hung halfway down his chest. "Yes?"

"I was wondering if you could help me." Nora held up the pot of dying plants. "They've lost their oomph."

"Their what?" He looked at the pot she was holding. Then at her. His face morphed into a frown, and he suddenly strode forward, his hand out for her pot. Nora was so startled that she hastily shoved it into his hands. He held it up in front of him, eyeing it critically as he turned the pot one way and then the other, examining it.

"I, ah . . . I think they might be dead, but I'm not sure."

He turned before she could think of an answer and went to the back room with her pot.

Nora was momentarily rooted by surprise. But she quickly followed him.

He took her pot to a table, yanked open a drawer, and bent over it, rummaging around so roughly that metal things were clanging.

"I had an accident, so I was out of my office for a while, and when I came back, they looked like this."

He had nothing to say to that. Then again, he was still in the drawer, muttering to himself, until at last he held up what looked like tiny pruning shears. "Haworthia is desperately hard to kill, and yet you've almost managed to do it."

"I hope not. I'm so sorry, but I—"

"I'm going to prune away the rot and we'll see what we've got." He began to work on the plant like it was a delicate sculpture, cutting off leaves that were limp and lacking fullness. They fell to the table, a little pile around the perimeter of the pot. When he was done, the five plants that made up the pot were trimmed down to their centers. He gingerly nudged what was left with his pinkie, then grunted, gave her a stern look, and stalked off across the room.

He returned with a bottle. "A teaspoon in a cup of water twice a week for three weeks. No more, no less. Make sure the pot drains. And for God's sake, don't leave it alone. Can you commit yourself to this pot for three weeks? Yes or no? Because if you can't, I'll keep it here and look after it for you."

She couldn't help her smile. "Yes." This man clearly hadn't meant to be amusing, but she had to admire someone who took plants so seriously.

"Where's this garden of yours?"

"How . . . how do you know I have a garden?"

He squinted at her. "Because you're in a garden store, miss. It's not in some desperately hot backyard where you pay a poor immigrant to look after it, I hope."

"No, it's . . ." She swallowed. "It's in a community garden."

"Oh." He looked abruptly interested. "And what do you grow there?"

A very good question—it had been so long that she didn't know. And whatever had been there was certainly dead now. "Some, um . . . tomatoes? And squash, I believe. Hydrangeas, maybe?"

The shopkeeper tilted his head curiously, probably unable to understand how she didn't know what she grew.

"I . . ." She rubbed her nape. "I had this accident, and . . . well, never mind that. It needs work."

"Mm." He looked at the plant. "What else can I do for you?"

He could show her how to revive Grandpa's garden. But Nora shook her head. "How much do I owe you?"

He waved his hand at her. "Take it. I'm doing the poor thing a service. Just do as I said. And promise you'll care for your garden and not leave it to rot. Commit to it."

"Well, now I'm brimming with confidence," she muttered.

Her head was starting to hurt. She rubbed her temple. "The thing is, I don't know if I can salvage it. It was my grandpa's garden. He died, and then I . . ." Then she'd what? He'd died and she had what? A sour feeling spread in her belly. There was something else she wanted to say, but the words hid from her, buried under her sorrow. "I don't know if I can bring it back to life."

The man looked at her with concern. "Of course you can. Nature seeks to heal what is broken."

A tender shoot of hope broke through the piles of thoughts and feelings she'd been collecting for the last few years, piles she still needed to sort and put away, feelings she needed to find words to express. She had the crazy idea that maybe this man understood what she didn't understand herself. Had Grandpa led her here? No, that was impossible. But maybe. She held out her hand. "I'm Nora."

He took her hand in his beefy one. "Nick."

"There is one other thing." She pulled the dead tomato plant from her bag. The one that had died in her apartment while she'd been rehabilitating. It was encased in a Ziploc tomb now.

Nick winced when he saw the carcass.

"Grandpa gave it to me last year."

"But it died because, what . . . your accident?"

Not exactly. Because she'd often felt as if she was treading in a soup of persistent malaise and couldn't touch the bottom. Because she could hardly take care of herself after Grandpa died, much less this plant. "I hoped maybe it wasn't totally dead. Maybe I could plant the roots in his garden."

"Give it here. It could be diseased. You don't want to add a disease to your garden." He took the bag from her. He walked to a rack with a display of a variety of seeds, carefully searched through them, then tossed a packet at her that she missed and had to bend down to pick up. "Try that." He disappeared in the back. When he returned, he didn't have her dead tomato plant; he had a tray with little pots for seedlings and a bag of soil and a jar with something in it that looked like ground sage.

"I plant the seeds in that?"

"I suppose you could toss them out the window and wait for Johnny Appleseed to come along, but you'd have better luck if you planted them." He went behind the counter and came back with a pamphlet. It had a picture of a tomato on the front. "Read this front to back. Don't skip a single word, do you hear?"

She heard him, all right. "Yes. Thank you."

"And this." He thrust the jar at her. "It's nothing but worthless tomato dust from your grandpa's gift to you. But sprinkle it in with your seeds for good luck."

Gratitude sparked in Nora's heart. "That's perfect."

"It's not perfect; it's probably an exercise in futility. But gardening is often more about hope than skill."

Nora liked this guy.

"You'll be needing to carry a few things when you go to your garden, so you might as well get a proper tote," Nick said and took a green and white one from a rack. "Come back when you're ready to plant. And you'll need a garden guide, so better find one."

"Can't you guide me?"

"Absolutely not."

And yet somehow she knew that she'd be back and he'd guide her. She had the comforting idea that Grandpa had steered her to Nick for that very reason. *Thanks, Grandpa.*

She left his shop with some garden tools all neatly placed in her new garden tote and went home to germinate the pods like a proper gardener.

Chapter 12

Jack

Christine Livingston tried very hard to die at home with her four kids, but the pain management had proven too much for her husband and her mother. For the last two weeks of her life, Christine had been at Sanctum House.

Her singular goal before dying was to make sure her kids were set to go on without her. That meant dictating letters to be sealed until some future date, having private meetings with the spouses of her grown kids, and, in the case of her youngest, still in high school, making a dental appointment that had been neglected. Christine told Jack that she wasn't leaving this earth without a fight and firmly believed that her damaged heart was determined to go on.

When her heart began to lose its determination, she still fiercely maintained she would not leave until she knew they'd all be okay without her.

As if they could ever be okay without her.

Had she finally been convinced they would survive, or had the fight become too much? And where was Christine now? Did she have a to-do list in the afterlife? She struck Jack as someone who needed goals to thrive.

He was thinking about all of this at his garden plot on a blustery Sunday afternoon. He was weeding a raised bed, ostensibly getting it ready to plant some annuals, but really, he needed the task for his hands. Life was hard and unfair. Why would someone like Christine, in the prime of her life, with so much yet to do, be the one with a heart too weak to hold all the love she had to give?

And why would someone like him, with a strong heart, have no one to love?

Love had never been his luck. It wasn't that he hadn't tried for it, because he had. After Brandy, he'd dated a few women, but none of them ever amounted to more than a handful of dates. Were his standards too high? Was he too fearful of another woman delivering a body blow?

Byron's girlfriend, Tracy, was intent on setting him up with one of her friends, but Tracy had never introduced him to anyone who was his type.

Not that Jack had a firm handle on his type by any stretch. He only knew when it wasn't working. He thought about the woman he met in the corner store the night it was robbed. Her name was Nora, and he couldn't have asked for better in that situation.

Nora had appeared from thin air, reaching for the same salad as him, her hair the same color as the toffee candy Sandra brought to work. And she had some amazing crystalline green eyes.

Nora had had the same reaction to the ordeal that he'd had, which he figured was at least one way to know if someone had potential. And somehow Nora had made him laugh about the absurdity of it all.

He'd felt the thrum of attraction for the several hours they spent talking until Darth was taken into custody. The deluge of rain had closed some streets and forced water rescues from others, so the crime unit was slow to respond. He and Nora had sat cross-legged on flats of water in the aisle eating from cans of chili as they waited their turn to give statements to the police.

The bodega cat was in her lap. "What do you think?" she'd asked. "Was this fate? Or bad luck?"

Fate, he'd thought immediately. "Are they different?"

"Gosh, I hope so. Earlier today, when I asked the universe if this day could possibly get any worse, I didn't expect it to respond with a hold-my-beer routine."

"But it could have been worse, right?"

She looked up from stroking the cat. "How?"

"For starters, we had a bathroom," he reminded her. "Imagine an all-nighter without one. Especially when you started feeling queasy from the Starbursts."

"Yikes. Excellent point."

"And we didn't have to drink mop water."

"But we came pretty close." She dug her plastic spoon into the chili can he held. "What would you say was the worst thing to happen to you before tonight?"

He didn't have to think twice—the memory lived every day in his thoughts. "My mom dying from cancer when I was fifteen. And then being sent across the country to live with an aunt I'd only met once or twice."

"Oh." Nora paused, her spoon in the can. "I'm sorry."

He waved her off. "No need." He never knew what to say to offers of sympathy. It had been traumatic, but it had also been so long ago. It had a hazy, otherworldly feel to it now.

She swallowed and removed her spoon without any chili. "My grandpa died recently."

"That sucks."

"Yeah." She glanced up, and her eyes had the sheen of tears.

"Hey," he said and put a hand on her arm. "You don't have to talk about it."

"Thank you," she said gratefully. "I wish I *could* talk about it, you know? I miss him so much." Her voice cracked a little, and she pushed a long lock of hair from her face that had fallen out of her bun.

Jack caressed her arm. "I get it. The loss gets easier in some ways, but in other ways, it gets worse."

She nodded and ran a finger under one eye. But she looked up and smiled, recovering. "Honestly? The first thing I thought of was the day my dad stabbed my basketball to death."

"Excuse me?"

"Crazy, right?"

So crazy he didn't believe it. "For real? On purpose? With a knife?"

"For real. On purpose, and with a very big knife."

"Why?"

She shrugged and resumed stroking the cat. "He didn't believe girls should play masculine sports. Especially basketball."

"Wow." So at least one Neanderthal still roamed the earth.

"I freaked you out," she said. "That sounds totally deranged, right?"

"Totally."

She laughed and shrugged a little.

"What's the best thing that ever happened to you?" he asked. "Please tell me you won an NBA championship or something."

"I wish!" In what he assumed was her Marlon Brando voice, she said, "*I coulda been a contender!* But the best thing?" She looked at him, and there was a new shine in her eyes. "Meeting new friends in the weirdest places."

A glittery swirl of pleasure wrapped around him. He took her hand, laced his fingers through hers. "Same here. So . . . bad luck? Or fate?"

Her smile sparkled. "Oh, it's fate."

Yep, that night still ranked as one of the more amazing things that had ever happened to him.

He and Nora didn't have paper, and both their phones were dead because they'd used them to look up YouTube videos of the dumbest things people did. He wrote his name and his number on her hand. Nora wrote her name and number on the back of a receipt. He lost the bit of paper with her number like a chump. But she'd had his, and for the longest time he waited and hoped she would call, convinced she'd felt the connection as strongly as he had. But she never did call. She probably assumed he'd ghosted her. Nothing could be further from the truth—he'd racked his brain trying to find a piece of memory that would help him find her number but had come up short.

If he dwelled on it, he could get maudlin. He took his spade and began to turn the dirt. Earth to earth, dust to dust.

"Excuse me!"

He glanced over his shoulder. It was a woman he'd often seen in here. Elderly, usually sitting in a wheelchair under the shade of a tree. But here she came, rolling her way down the gravel path toward him by digging her heels into the ground to propel her chair forward. Jack came to his feet. She'd piled her hair on top of her head like she often did, wore leopard-print earmuffs, and was dressed in a fur stole and thick, utilitarian sweatpants.

She rolled right up to his plot and peered up at him. "Goodness, young man, are you crying?"

"What? No," he said and hastily brushed his hand across his face. He hadn't even realized a few tears had fallen. "Perspiration."

"It's sixty degrees. I don't perspire when it's sixty degrees." She pulled her stole tighter around her neck, which, on closer inspection, looked more faux than fur. Two plots over, Jack spotted the thin, wiry man who was always with her, trimming some ornamental trees.

"I wondered when you were coming back," the lady said.

This remark confused him. He thought back to the times he'd seen her and couldn't remember them ever speaking. "Pardon?"

"Why haven't you introduced yourself? We all know each other in here."

"Oh. Sorry, it didn't occur to me."

"Hmm." She casually eyed him up and down. "So what's your story?"

"My story?"

"Your story. Like, why are you here? This was Hauser's plot. He never mentioned a son."

What was she after? "I'm not his son, but he left it to me."

"Obviously, but why are you here? Mr. Starr in Plot Six, he came to get away from his wife. She was a harpy, to hear him tell it. But she's dead now and his kids made him go to assisted living. I heard he was living on popcorn until he nearly burned his building down."

Jack blinked.

"Plot Two, that's Eileen with her two awful twins. Good Lord, don't get me started."

He made a mental note not to get her started.

"And then there is Plot Nine, just abandoned like it's worthless dirt." She pointed.

Jack looked in that direction. A plot near the back wall was overgrown with weeds. "What happened there?"

"I'll tell you what happened. She should have been here a long time ago. But that's what's wrong with America; everyone is too busy to take care of things. Now she's going to have to start from scratch."

Jack looked at the offending plot again. He wished he could have a crack at it. He liked the idea of starting fresh in a garden, building from seedlings up. Everything dies, but there is always something new growing.

"She thinks her husband is having an affair, you know."

Jack winced. "Maybe that's why it's in such a state."

"Not Plot Nine, Plot Two. The twins! He stays out all hours, takes calls outside. I told her those were classic signs of infidelity and she needed to hire a private detective. What do you think?"

Think? Impossible. He couldn't even keep up. "I think . . . you don't miss much."

"Well, I don't. I like knowing what's going on in our little community. I see it all."

That remark made his neck prickle with unease.

"We all look out for each other, you know. You never said what your story is. Don't think I didn't notice."

There was no danger of him thinking that. "My story isn't very interesting. Mr. Hauser left me this plot. I'm not really into gardening, but I like it here."

"Well, you're right—that's not very interesting. But that's how most stories start."

He didn't think most started by having a plot bequeathed to them by a former patient. "What's your story?"

She snorted. "You don't know who I am?"

"Sorry, no. Should I?"

She leaned forward and pierced him with her pale blue eyes. "Catherine Henry?"

He searched his mental data banks for anyone named Catherine Henry.

She sighed loudly as if he were being intentionally obtuse. "Broadway? Catherine Henry, star of productions such as *A Chorus Line*, *Rent*, *Follies*, and *No, No, Nanette!* And I headlined at Esther's Follies!" She suddenly stood up from her chair and did a step-ball-change to the right and then to the left, with jazz hands.

"Oh, wow," Jack said. "That's . . . that's surprising."

"Why?"

"Because of your chair. Most people in a wheelchair can't dance."

"Says you. Where there is a will, there is always a way to dance. Anyway, this was abandoned outside the gates. I like to use it while Walter works on our garden. You wouldn't believe how much time he spends on those prizewinning Venus flytraps."

"I see."

"You know what I see? That you don't see anything. You're too sad or depressed or something."

Because she saw everything. He smiled faintly.

She sat in the chair again and it rolled backward. She heel-toed her way closer to him. "I think you could use more joy in your life."

Jack couldn't help it—he laughed.

"What's funny?"

"I don't know. You don't even know my name and you're telling me what I need."

"Okay. What's your name?"

"Jack. Jack Moriarity."

"Pleased to meet you, Jack, Jack Moriarity. Now that we've got that out of the way, you need more joy in your life. Tell me I'm wrong."

This woman was a trip. "Okay, you're not wrong. But who doesn't?"

Catherine Henry suddenly smiled, and it was a lovely, warm smile. "I think we're going to be friends, Jack Moriarity. I was like you once, you know. I'd lost the lead role in *Fiddler on the Roof* to Bette Midler."

"You . . . what?"

"I couldn't pick myself up off the floor. What did she have that I didn't?" Catherine Henry settled back into her wheelchair that was not a wheelchair and launched into a tale about a brush with depression while he turned the earth and listened.

She was very entertaining.

He realized, after he'd said goodbye and left the community garden for the afternoon, that after he'd met Catherine Henry, former star of the stage, he hadn't thought about his job again.

Chapter 13

It was embarrassingly clear that Nora's newly minted confidence needed some tweaking—her attempts to be part of the gang at work were not landing. And then there was the conversation with Colton Morris from accounting in the break room that had left her feeling unsettled.

"Soooo," he'd said as he'd poured an obscene amount of sugar in his coffee, "you're a surfer."

"Not anymore." Nora chuckled at her joke. That was different about her—she could laugh at herself . . . sort of. She hadn't tested the limits of jocularity yet.

"But, like . . . why were you surfing?"

A sudden memory rushed back of her standing on the beach, the wind whipping her hair. She remembered how cold and wet the sand was beneath her bare feet, how she'd shivered in the freezing temperatures. But there were pieces of her memory she still couldn't quite grasp. What was it? She suddenly felt lightheaded, like she needed to sit down.

"Seems weird to me," Colton continued. "Never knew any female surfers."

"I am offended on behalf of female surfers, Colton. There are lots of them. I was surfing because I wanted to try it." But as she spoke, the fizziness turned thick in her head. She felt off-kilter—she'd wanted to try surfing? Since when?

"You just, what, suited up and got a board? Without taking lessons?"

The buzz erupted in Nora's chest and spread to her extremities. She was *not* going to pass out. "Actually, I don't remember anything about the accident," she said. And when she tried, some invisible vise squeezed her brain. But she wasn't going to tell him that.

"Interesting," Colton said dubiously. He'd wandered off, but later Nora heard him telling someone that "you don't just get on a surfboard without some training."

Was he right? Would she ever know? It was incredibly frustrating that she couldn't remember what had happened to her.

Colton's skepticism made her loathe this place even more. She had to keep her focus on her reverse bucket list or she'd lose hope, because so far, her job search had yielded exactly zero opportunities. She'd sent her updated résumé to a dozen different job listings, most that sought experience in different corners of the law. Unfortunately, the only thing she was qualified for was personal injury.

She'd also posted on a website called "Lost and Found in the ATX" that was devoted to helping Austinites find missed connections. The website fed the posts out to social media. Nora hoped the corner store guy might see himself on at least one of those platforms. But so far, her post had only fourteen likes. She thought she'd been so clever too—she'd used one of her better photos and styled the page like the old-school missed connection ads that would show up on Craigslist: You: tall guy with blue eyes in beanie and handmade scarf. Me: trench coat. Together in the corner store when it was robbed and then held hostage in the storeroom by Darth Vader. Sorry I never called. Would love to meet up and explain.

Every day she checked. Every day, nothing. It was disheartening.

She'd also seeded her little pots, which Nick's pamphlet said would produce shoots in five days. But so far, nothing. Incompetence seemed to be her middle name.

Lacey still was not calling her back. She'd been sending curt texts in response to Nora's calls. Can't talk now, talk soon. Or Rushing out the door call u ltr.

At least that was a response—Gus hadn't been picking up or acknowledging her texts. But this morning she finally got lucky and Gus picked up.

"Gus!" she cried with relief. "I've been trying to get ahold of you."

"Oh. What for?" He sounded groggy.

"I was hoping we could hang out."

"Hang out?" He repeated the words like they were a language he didn't understand.

"Maybe go to a movie or something?"

On the other end of the line, she thought she heard a disbelieving snort.

"What?" she asked.

"Nothing. I'm . . . I'm busy. I mean, I'd love to go, but . . . I'll have to try to fit it into my schedule."

Since when did Gus have trouble finding time in his schedule? "What, you mean your job?"

"This is the busy time of the year."

She didn't know cell phone sales had a busy season. Gus was brushing her off, and her disappointment felt crushing. What did she expect? That he would suddenly make time for her when she'd never managed to make time for him? "Can you look at your calendar and maybe figure out a time we could get together?"

"Sure." He sniffed. "Listen, can I call you back? I've got another call."

He didn't have another call. She wasn't sure what to say. "Right. Talk soon," she said. She clicked off, dismayed.

The ghost of Nora would have pulled down the blinds and sunk into despair, but the new Nora was going to keep trying.

Gus and Lacey had always been sympathetic to her struggle with depression. But it was difficult for them to understand how the disease could affect her to the point that she just wasn't very good at being a person. Things that seemed so simple—like showing up when she said she would—could turn into a massive slippery hill she couldn't seem to climb.

She had to prove to them that she was truly different now. That she could be a part of their lives. That she could be fun (working on it) and trustworthy (give her a chance). That she was not despondent; she was happy (mostly?).

She tried Lacey again on her way out the door and left a message. "Lacey? It's me. You still haven't called me back. Which means I'm going to show up without an invitation. If that's something you wish to avoid, then you'd better call me back." She clicked off and tossed her phone into her purse. She headed for work, feeling the pain of their division but determined to fix it.

James was waiting in her office when she arrived. She strode in and set down her garden tote, which she was now carrying as a handbag.

James looked at it, then at her. "Really?"

"I'm telling you, these totes are perfect for the home and office. And I have all my bags on consignment." So far she'd made a whopping one hundred bucks.

"What?" James sounded horrified.

"Who's out of the betting pool today?" Nora asked, changing the subject.

"Melissa from Admin and Ted Franklin."

"Ted?" Nora was stung. "But he's so nice."

"He would have won a grand. Anyway, the case review meeting starts in ten minutes. I hope you looked at the bus file, because it's on the agenda," James said.

He was referring to a case where a charter bus had slid off a rain-slicked road. If by "looked at" James meant skimming it while inhaling a bag of chips, then yes, she had.

Nora made a quick cup of tea, then walked down the corridor to the executive conference room with the long, oval-shaped cherrywood table, surrounded by thickly padded executive chairs.

Her seat was always next to her father. She'd once suggested that she should sit against the wall like the staff lawyers since she was still rather new to the firm. Her father had snapped at her, *"You're not a staff lawyer. You're going to inherit this firm, so start acting like it."*

Stupid Nora had thought she was acting like it by being respectful of the experience in that room.

"Good morning, everyone!" she said sunnily as she entered, persevering in her quest to be the Nora she'd always wanted to be. No one responded. Her father's expression closed. He probably saw greeting coworkers with enthusiasm as weak.

She took her seat beside him and arranged her files and cup of tea in front of her, acutely aware of his hawklike gaze. In the Before, she would have come in feeling inadequate and tense, and would have sunk into a vat of self-doubt as the meeting wore on. But today she felt uncharacteristically indignant. Why was it so hard to like her? She finally turned her head to look at him. "What?"

"I think you know."

There was always plenty about her to disappoint dear old Dad—it was easier to accept that than try to guess what it could be.

The weekly meeting proceeded as usual. The man-eating sharks in the room reviewed cases where a personal injury may or may not have been severe but had all the necessary ingredients to win Big Money. None of the staff attorneys wanted to do these briefings—no matter how good they were, fault would be found. It was a particularly evil game they played at November and Sons.

Forty minutes in, Nora thought she was going to skate through and mentally sighed with relief. No one even looked at her until the bus case rolled to the top of the list. It was typical fare for November and Sons, a slam dunk, an easy win. The small charter bus company had been hired to collect some wealthy teens from summer camp and drive them back to Austin. Nora knew they were wealthy because she recognized some of the family names—the parents had dined at her parents' bimonthly Sunday night suppers. The bus had slid off a road and into a ditch, and some of the kids had been mildly injured, although nothing worse than a broken wrist.

The parents were suing the bus company for damages. According to the police report, there was evidence that the kids' rowdiness might have contributed to the accident. In other words, they'd distracted the driver. But that didn't matter at November and Sons—it only mattered that you win.

Her father said, "We'll hear from Nora."

Well, hell. The ancient, familiar thrumming began in her chest. It was her old companion, fear of failure, that ever-present confidence blaster that mixed with her blood and her breath. She sat up. She cleared her throat. She reminded herself that the ghost of Nora was dead—or at least in the throes of death, as Nora was working on a complete burial but wasn't there yet. At any rate, today the new Nora was in charge. "I'll let Andrea give the briefing. I've decided to give her first chair on this one."

Andrea Silver's head snapped up so fast, it was a wonder it didn't bounce right off her neck and out the window. She gave Nora a murderous glare. "Thank you," she said and opened her file.

When Andrea had finished her review and had offered her assessment of damages, David November shifted his gaze to Nora. "What do you think?"

She thought she hated these meetings. She thought she was through allowing these meetings to nauseate her with anxiety and self-loathing. She clicked her pen a couple of times. All eyes were on her, and the quake got worse. But she refused to play the part of the old Nora, jittery and queasy, second-guessing every word she said. No matter how hard she had to fight, she would not allow that Nora to be resurrected.

She looked her father directly in the eye and said, "It's not complicated. The driver had an accident. Kids said they were hurt, but they weren't, not really. Nevertheless, their parents are suing for damages and it sounds like Andrea has evaluated the suit and assessed those damages using our guidelines." Wasn't that the way these things went? She glanced around the table for approval, but none was forthcoming.

"So," her dad said smoothly, "your professional assessment is . . . what?" His voice was low and deadly, and the little army of fearful ants scrambled in her, rallying to make her sweat.

"*My* professional assessment? Mine is that we should not pursue this case. It's ambulance chasing." Holy hell, did she really just say that? "But I know that's probably not a popular opinion."

The room grew deathly quiet, and every employee locked in on David November.

He slowly leaned back in his chair and drummed his fingers against the table in a dull *rat-a-tat-tat* while he considered her, delaying his response because he liked to watch people squirm. Especially her. In the Before, this was the point at which Nora's insides would turn to mush and she'd perspire and stumble over her words. Astonishingly, the new Nora rallied. Her fear gave way to annoyance. *Why the power trip, Dad?*

Her father looked at her like he wished she were anyone else. Preferably Nathan, but really, anyone else.

And the feeling was entirely mutual.

"Perhaps we ought to make Andrea a senior attorney," he said. "She'd be a good one."

Her father wasn't used to her talking back. He calmly returned his attention to the meeting and carried on as if nothing had happened, curtly correcting what Andrea had wrong about her assumptions.

Nora was aware of the slight tremble in her. But oddly, it felt like this time, the fear was forging some long overdue mettle.

When the meeting was over, her father commanded Nora to stay put. He closed the door behind the last person and turned to look at her, his arms akimbo, his expression thunderous. "Just what was that little display?"

She curled her fingers into a tight fist to steady herself—her rage was pounding at the door, demanding to be let out, ready to smash any fear and maybe even smash his face. "Well, *Dad*, Andrea is better prepared on this case than I am. I thought she did well."

His expression morphed from thunderous to surprised to infuriated. He took two long strides toward her and she stepped back, bumping into the table, her pulse racing with anger and terror at once. "That should have been your assessment, Nora. It should have been *you*."

She'd been hearing some form of that refrain all her life.

"I'm done waiting for you to get over the accident. I want you up to speed on the bus case by Monday morning. Do I make myself clear?"

She could feel the corners of her mouth tip up in an ill-advised wry smile. "You always do."

His breathing turned a little ragged. David November hadn't struck her in a very long time, but sometimes she wished he'd go ahead and do it, because the anticipation of the blow she always expected had to be so much worse than the actual thing. How embarrassing it was to be thirty-one and feel eight years old every time he walked into a room.

At the thought of that, a surge of courage—or rage—electrified her. Nora lifted her chin. "Do it, Dad. If you want to hit me, just do it."

His jaw clenched. He didn't hit her. But he didn't deny he wanted to. He composed himself, ran his hand over his head. "Are you okay, sweetie?"

Ugh, that word again. "I'm fine."

"Should I call Dr. Cass?"

"What? No!" The suggestion that she needed help angered her. She was standing up for herself. Could he not see that? Or did he see it clearly and want to undermine her confidence?

He nodded slowly. Smugly. "Then let's get back to work," he said. "Maybe leave early today and get some rest." He gave her a brief, blistering scowl as he exited the conference room.

Nora watched him move down the hall. Her knees were shaking, and it was possible she might throw up . . . but the new Nora had just done something that the ghost of Nora had never been able to do—she'd stood up to her dad. And it felt awesome. Empowering. She was not so foolish as to think she would go unpunished for it—he would find a way to humiliate her when the time was right—but she didn't care. Right now she felt like King Kong.

She glanced at her watch. "Yikes," she muttered. She had fifteen things to do before the end of the day. She didn't want to be late for her first cooking class.

Chapter 14

Lacey texted back as Nora was about to leave for her cooking class. So sorry I've been MIA. Super busy! Hope all is well and you don't need anything urgent. Talk soon. xoxo

She hoped Nora didn't need anything urgent? Still riding the high of standing up to Dad, Nora was ready to take on Lacey's avoidance too. If the mountain wouldn't come to Muhammad . . . she was stopping by Lacey's house after cooking class.

The chef's studio was on Springdale Road above a Caribbean restaurant. The music was blaring, the *thump, thump, thump* keeping time as she walked up the narrow staircase.

At the end of the hall was a door and a neat little plaque on the wall that announced the Saucepot Kitchen Classroom. Nora opened the door and peeked her head inside.

"Come in!" A woman in a chef's coat gestured her inside. "Don't be shy."

The room was dominated by a large metal table that stretched the length of the room and ended at a bank of windows overlooking the street. Pots and pans hung overhead, and on one side of the table, people were seated on the metal stools. On the opposite wall, behind the chef, were eight cooktops. At each seat was a set of mixing bowls, utensils, and a folded kitchen towel. Plates and serving bowls were stacked neatly at the end of the table.

"Take a seat, hon," the chef said.

Nora's pulse quickened. The ghost of Nora may have been too awkward and anxious to meet new people, but the new Nora was too eager. She waved. "Hello, everyone!"

She got a few mumbles and no direct eye contact in return.

She slid onto a metal stool next to the stacked plates and surreptitiously checked out her classmates. Two men she assumed were a couple—one had his hand around the other's shoulders as they looked over the course notebook together. Two older women she assumed were *not* a couple but possibly sisters given their identical tightly wound gray curls. A young man who wore a knit cap low over his brow and his greasy long dark hair. And next to Nora, a woman with a girl who looked to be about twelve years old. She was wearing Air Jordans. Nora would know those kicks anywhere—they'd been all the rage when she'd played basketball as a teen.

The girl must have felt Nora looking at her because she slowly turned her head to scowl with contempt before turning her gaze back to her phone.

"I think this is everyone," the chef said, consulting a paper. "All right! My name is Bernice Williams, and I will be your chef instructor for this course. Now, at each place, you'll find a notebook with the recipes we'll be covering in this class, along with a kitchen towel, mixing bowls, and utensils, all of which are property of this class. But the apron is complimentary and yours to take home. Please bring it to class with you. You may unfold them now and put them on."

Everyone dutifully unfolded the red cloth aprons embroidered with a saucepot and put them on. Nora felt almost euphoric, surrounded by bottles of oil and spices and a bowl piled with heads of garlic, lemons, zucchini, eggplants, and tomatoes. After years of wishing, she was finally doing it—she would learn to cook.

She couldn't help herself. "This is kind of cool, right?" she whispered to the girl as she tied her apron strings at her waist.

The girl ignored her.

"Do you like to cook?" she asked.

"No."

The girl responded loudly enough that the chef looked at her, but the girl's attention had already slid back to her phone.

Bernice charmingly promised that they would be well on their way to being excellent cooks at the end of the six-week class. When she asked everyone to open their notebooks, the girl's mother took her phone and deposited it in her purse. The girl sighed loudly, propped her chin in her hand, and stared straight ahead, expending a lot of energy in the work of active disinterest.

"To begin, we will review Italian cooking techniques. Tonight we're making a garlic sauce to put on sautéed eggplant. The sauce is also suitable for other vegetables, such as potatoes or zucchini, and it's very easy to make. Anyone could do it. A trained seal could do it."

The class laughed, but the girl looked dubiously at Nora.

Bernice held up a long purple vegetable. "Does anyone know what this is?"

"Japanese eggplant," one of the older women said.

"Correct. The taste of this variety is milder and the skin softer than the eggplant you may be accustomed to seeing in the markets. You can sauté, steam, or roast this vegetable, which makes it perfect for the urban dweller."

Nora was an urban dweller. She made a mental note to plant some in her garden.

"We'll begin by sautéing the eggplant. Who among us has not sautéed eggplant?"

Nora's hand shot up.

"Oh my God," the girl said contemptuously and angled her body away from Nora.

Bernice handed out cutting boards and big knives. She demonstrated how to cut the eggplant, first slicing it down the middle, then cutting the halves into chunks. She invited everyone to take their eggplant and do the same, and the class began to chop with a vengeance. Even the girl was chopping. Her pieces were more uniform and smaller than Nora's.

Nora meant to compliment her, but when she turned, she was distracted by a shadow of movement at her feet. She glanced down as a basketball rolled out from beneath the girl's stool and touched Nora's foot. *Willow* was written across it in big silver letters.

A painful memory pierced Nora's glee for a moment. She bent down to get the basketball at the same moment the girl snatched it from Nora's reach.

"Is that yours?" Nora asked.

"Duh."

"You like basketball?"

Willow stared at Nora like she was an imbecile, which, okay, her question was stupidly rhetorical. "I like basketball too."

The girl rolled her eyes and returned her basketball to its place beneath her stool.

"Okay, have we all chopped our eggplants?" Bernice asked. "Now we'll salt the pieces. Does anyone know why we salt the eggplant?"

The guy with the knit hat said, "To pull out the moisture and some of the bitterness."

"Very good! Perhaps you should be teaching this class." Everyone laughed except Willow.

They salted their pieces and patted them dry with paper towels, then took their cutting boards to the cooktops where Bernice had set up woks. She showed them the correct amount of oil to add to the pan. Too much and the eggplant was oily. Not enough and the eggplant wouldn't taste right. "The last thing anyone wants is mushy eggplant," Bernice gravely informed them.

As they cooked, she moved down the row, observing. She leaned over Nora's shoulder and said, "Goodness, those are some big pieces. Cut pieces about one inch in size next time. Stir more vigorously, hon."

"Got it," Nora said. As Bernice moved away, Nora smiled at the girl.

"Your eggplant looks like chunks of barf," Willow observed.

"Willow!" Over the top of her daughter's head, the girl's mom gave Nora the universal head shake of parental disappointment.

"It does, sort of." Nora stirred harder. "So anyway, I loved basketball when I was your age. I always thought I'd be a pretty good point guard."

"Because you sucked at shooting?"

Nora's mood was sliding from euphoric to short on air, and not just because Willow was spot-on. Because she'd loved basketball until she wasn't allowed to love it. She'd never talked about that night of the basketball slaughter to anyone but the corner store guy. Funny how she could feel so safe with someone after a few short hours. It had been the perfect alchemy of mental and physical attraction.

"Great job, everyone," Bernice announced. "Please plate your eggplant and return to your prep area."

Bernice handed out whisks and explained the proper amount of peanut oil, soy sauce, and ginger to whisk together. She showed them how to peel and chop garlic and scallions, then instructed them to add those to the liquid. She gave her advice on using garlic and said that spices will make or break the simplest or most complex dish.

Nora managed to whisk some of her concoction onto the metal table.

"You suck at cooking too," Willow said.

Willow was warming up to her. "I know, *hello*, that's why I'm here. What's your excuse?"

"My mom made me. *Hello*," she said, mimicking Nora.

They returned to the stovetops to cook the sauce. When the scallions and garlic were properly translucent, they poured the sauce over their eggplant pieces.

The time had come for a taste test. They were all given forks and lined up to move down the row and sample the dishes. Most everyone gave compliments. Bernice gave constructive feedback. Willow gave sharp criticism, offering a loud opinion on every dish—too salty, too mushy, just gross. And when she came to Nora's, the last one, she took one bite and made a face. "Your chunks are too hard. And it's too garlicky. And something else tastes nasty."

"Willow Faye! Will you please stop being so rude?" her mother implored. She also tasted Nora's dish and made a valiant effort to keep from spitting it out. The others barely dipped their forks into the dish.

Bernice was last. She very carefully put a bite in her mouth. "Oh!" She coughed. "The eggplant is not cooked through, hon. Plus, I think you got a little happy with the garlic. Did you follow the instructions?"

She was failing already? "Yes, I think so." She looked at her book. "The butter and oil, the three tablespoons of garlic—"

"Oh dear. T-s-p means teaspoons."

Nora looked at the recipe. *Tsp.* "Oh." How could she be so bad at this right out of the gate? She felt hot with embarrassment and ineptitude. The ghost of Nora wanted to slink out of the kitchen and never return. So did the new Nora, but she was too humiliated, especially in front of Willow. What a loser she would be if she left. So she gamely tried to muster as much courage as she could in order to stay.

Bernice gave her a motherly pat on the back. "New to the kitchen? Don't you worry, hon. We'll turn you into a cook."

Sure, just like law school had turned her into a "lawyer."

As they packed up their leftovers, Bernice said they would continue their tour of Italian cuisine next week and learn how to make pasta.

Great! What could possibly go wrong?

Nora tried not to be completely deflated by her abysmal first outing as she walked out of class behind Willow, who had her ball tucked under her arm.

The moment they were on the sidewalk, Willow began to dribble. Her mother paused to put Willow's apron in her bag and noticed Nora. "She'd be on the court all day if I let her."

Nora could remember feeling like that. She ate, slept, and dreamed basketball. "Don't you like basketball?" she asked Willow's mother.

"I do. But I'm a single mother of three and don't have time to be at the Y every day after school and on weekends, you know?"

Nora did know. "I'm Nora, by the way."

"Tanya," her mother said. "Willow, please stop."

"Hey, Willow?" Nora dropped her garden tote and apron onto the sidewalk. "May I try?"

Willow looked at her mother, who gave her an impatient nod. Willow passed the ball so hard that it forced Nora back a step. Nora turned the ball in her hands. It had been years since she'd picked up a ball. She began to dribble. She was tentative for a moment, but then began to dribble like she was on a court. She passed the ball back and forth between her hands in a crossover pattern. She remembered how to dribble the ball low in a square, to pass it in front and behind her, then between her legs.

This was something she could do. With a laugh of surprise, she passed the ball back to Willow. The girl caught the ball easily but stared at Nora, wide-eyed.

"Thankfully I don't suck at dribbling," she said cheerfully. "See you next week!" She picked up her bag and apron and headed for her car.

Time to tackle another item on the reverse bucket list, because Nora had just rediscovered her inner athlete. She was going to play basketball. Somewhere, somehow, she was getting back on the court.

Chapter 15

When *Nora pulled up outside of Lacey's neat bungalow* in Hyde Park, she spotted only a single light on in the house. She could hear faint music as she stepped onto the porch and knocked on the door. No one came. She knocked louder.

The door suddenly swung open, and Lacey stood there with frizzy hair in an old Foo Fighters T-shirt and baggy gym shorts. She looked quite unlike her usual, very put-together self. "Nora?" she said, her voice full of surprise. She looked past Nora to the street as if she expected someone else, then at Nora again. "Wow, you cut your hair. It looks great. It's so good to see you. I've been meaning to call, but I'm so busy, and anyway, Mom says you're struggling to get back into the swing of things, so I didn't." The words were rushing out of her.

"Why did she say that? I'm not struggling," Nora said.

"Whatever," Lacey said with a wave of her hand. "Come in." She opened the door wider.

Nora stepped into the living room, which was in disarray. This was not the way Lacey usually lived—she was organized, very particular about neatness, and very proud of the renovations she'd done to this house.

"You want something to drink?" Lacey dragged her fingers through her hair as she turned toward the kitchen. Lacey was two years younger than Nora, but she'd always acted more like a big sister. She was confident and competent in all the ways that Nora wasn't. Seeing her this on edge was jarring.

"Some wine?" she asked as Nora followed her into the kitchen.

"No, thanks."

"Oh, sorry. Are you not allowed to drink with . . . everything?"

Allowed and *everything* were a couple of curious word choices. "What do you mean? Wait . . . is Mom still saying I'm brain damaged? Have you been talking about me?"

"Not talking about you. Just . . . checking in, I guess. She said you've been doing some weird things and that you're taking a lot of medicine."

"Well, FYI, I'm allowed to drink. And I'm down to just a couple of prescriptions. But it so happens I'm not drinking these days because I'm not ready to return to any state of oblivion. And I cut my hair. Is that suddenly weird?"

"It's really cute, by the way. Not drinking is probably a good idea too, what with the medicine. You don't mind if I have some bourbon, do you?" She was already pouring it into a glass.

Nora slid onto a barstool. There were papers stacked on the end of the bar and dishes stacked on the kitchen table, as if Lacey had been cleaning out cabinets and drawers.

"I'm a little shocked you're here," Lacey said and took a healthy swig of her drink.

Her surprise pricked at Nora and, naturally, powered up the old guilt engine. They'd drifted apart in their adult years. Different lives, different hours, different parts of town. Different headspaces. Honestly, Nora had done more drifting than her sister. As far as Nora knew, Lacey had never suffered from depression. "I warned you I'd come by if you didn't call me."

"Yeah, well, you always say you're going to do something and then . . ." She fluttered her fingers in the air.

Another gut punch. It wasn't that she hadn't wanted to, but she'd get busy and life happened and . . . She wanted to prove to Lacey that she wasn't that Nora anymore. "Lace? I'm sorry I was such a workaholic in the Before."

Lacey frowned. "In what?"

"In the Before, as in before I died and came back to life. Now I'm in the After. And I'm strangely sensitive to things in a way I wasn't before—like how much I miss my sister." Desperately so, she realized as she gazed at her sister's flawless complexion. She would give anything to have back the friendship they'd had as girls. They'd played together, traded clothes and makeup, teased Gus. Clung to each other when Dad was at his worst.

Lacey put down her glass. "Huh."

"Tell me everything. How's work?"

"Work?" Lacey groaned. "Diversity and equity training of staff and faculty is going to eat my lunch." She began to explain to Nora the new standards her school had adopted for training and impossible timelines and confusing contracts and so many other things that Nora didn't try to follow. She'd always appreciated that Lacey was a no-nonsense kind of woman who could get the hardest things done with élan. Lacey was really the son her father never had, and yet he'd called her a feminazi. He was so wrong about Lacey—she wasn't a radical feminist. She was passionate about life and lived it fully.

But the thing Nora most admired about Lacey was that, for whatever reason, she'd always been able to stand up to their father's withering criticisms, whereas Nora crumbled.

She thought back to the summer she was fifteen. Her parents had rented a villa in Cancún to see and be seen by all the wealthy Texans vacationing there—Important People who would think the Novembers were Somebody. She and Lacey were expected to be on their best behavior and attend every freaking pool or beach party to which their parents managed to wrangle an invitation. Her mother was a pro when it came to social climbing.

The day came when thirteen-year-old Lacey would not put on the bikini Mom insisted she wear and donned her favorite board shorts instead. Dad got so angry with her disobedience, her willful insistence on looking like "a dyke," that he'd sent Lacey back to Austin for the rest of the summer in the company of Leda, the nanny Lacey and Nora despised. Leda liked to pinch them in the soft flesh of their underarms if they didn't behave.

Nora would never forget Lacey defiantly marching to the car, her backpack slung over her shoulder with her anime graphic novels—Dad hated those too—still wearing her board shorts. She once told Nora she wore them every day until Leda managed to nab them and throw them away.

Life hadn't been easy for Lacey. When she officially came out to their parents, Nora had supported her as best she could, but her best wasn't nearly good enough. There were terrible battles during which their father would accuse Lacey of being a deviant, of being sick in the head. Their mother would say Lacey needed help, that it wasn't natural. Lacey fought back, challenging their beliefs as best she could, while Nora faded into the background. She'd been mired in her own teenage misery at the time and hadn't been much of an advocate, too easily cowed by her father's admonishments to shut up, uncertain of what to say. She wished she'd been a better sister then and in so many ways since then. It remained to be seen if Lacey would allow her to make up for that now.

"Anyway," Lacey said with another heavy sigh. "What's new with you?"

"Well . . . Gus finally picked up. He said it was his busy season," she said with a self-conscious laugh. "I didn't know that was even a thing in cell phone sales."

Lacey frowned. "Cell phone sales? Nora . . . Gus hasn't had a job in weeks."

A soft buzz erupted in Nora's chest. "But he said . . . What does that mean?"

"What does that always mean? He's drinking again."

"What?" Nora pressed her fingertips to her temples. How had she missed it? "I didn't know."

"Yeah, well, now you do," Lacey said, sounding slightly annoyed.

"I wish you'd told me—"

"Sorry," she said curtly. "I can't be everyone's personal assistant. Anyway, you had your own drama, remember? You thought it was a good idea to take a little vacation, and then you almost died and spent weeks in hospitals and rehabs, and now we're all supposed to pretend it didn't happen."

She sounded angry, and every word was a slice across Nora's heart. Before her accident, she'd been suffering a depressive episode. It was hard for someone as enthusiastic for life as Lacey to grasp how crippling depression could be. How it could pin you down, make it impossible to move or pick up a phone or eat or bathe or anything else. Nora felt utterly worthless during those periods. "I'm not pretending. I'm so sorry to hear about Gus," she said softly. "Have you seen him?"

Lacey shook her head and took another deep swallow of bourbon. "I can't take him on right now, okay? Between work and Hannah and your accident—"

"Hannah? What about Hannah? Where is she?"

Lacey's face fell. "We broke up."

Nora gasped. "When? Why?"

"A couple of weeks ago. She . . ." Lacey rubbed her face. "I don't know, honestly. She thinks I'm not emotionally available or something. That I'm always solving someone else's problems instead of my own." She picked up her bourbon glass. "Not the first time I've heard that, to be honest," she added miserably and polished off what remained in the glass before filling it again. "She packed her bags and left, and now I'm sorting out her stuff," she said, indicating the clutter in the kitchen.

"Oh my God, Lacey . . . I'm so sorry."

Lacey shrugged. "Shit happens."

Compassion mushroomed in Nora. She loved Lacey and wanted her to be happy. *Really* happy. "Are you okay?" She got off her stool and came around the bar to hug her sister, but Lacey sidestepped her.

"I'm fine," she said, quite unconvincingly. "Or I will be. I always am, aren't I? Heaven knows someone has to be in this family."

Nora reached for her sister's hand, but Lacey ignored that too. The rejection was painful, and deserved. "Listen, Lace . . . I know we didn't have the closest relationship in the Before, but I love you. I want us to be closer. I want us to have a relationship where we can talk about anything."

Lacey said nothing.

"What?" Nora pressed.

"I mean . . . great. That's great. But honestly? I just don't have the bandwidth to deal with your issues right now, Nora."

Another ghastly stab into Nora's heart. "Yikes." She tried to laugh it off, but how many times had Lacey called Nora in the Before to make plans, only to have Nora bail at the last minute, her day too dark to get off the couch? "That's a little harsh. I know I haven't been there for you like you've always been there for me, but—"

"I didn't say that. You've been there for me."

"No, I haven't. You've always been able to stand up to Mom and Dad, and I never could. I wish I'd had the strength to be more helpful to you."

"What are you talking about?"

"So many times, Lacey. Going way back. Like when you came out to Mom and Dad."

Lacey looked confused. "What could you have done? Dad was being an ass, as usual, but look at what you did do. You got my journal and my Spurs hoodie that Dad hated and said made me look like a drug dealer. You hid them before he could stab them or burn them or whatever. You were there for me in the only reasonable way you could be."

"But I—"

"Hey." Lacey held up her hand. "You couldn't have saved me. No one could have. You know who he is and you know he hates who I am."

The tears began to burn behind Nora's eyes and her compassion for Lacey surged. "I love who you are," she said softly. "I always have. I just wish I'd had the courage to say it then, and when you got the award for administrator of the year that I missed, and when—"

"Don't do that to yourself," Lacey said. "Don't. You were there for me, but we were a dysfunctional family, and it was impossible for two girls to know what to do about it, and let's be honest, two girls grew into women who still don't know."

It was a disquieting, ugly truth—they'd spent so much of their life swimming upstream.

"It wasn't until we were grown that I knew I couldn't count on you."

Nora blinked. "Oh."

Lacey shrugged. "Don't look so surprised. You know you disappeared. You stopped caring what was going on with me. I only heard from you when you needed me. Which, to be honest, was a lot, Nora. A *lot*. There was always some problem that you needed me to fix, and frankly, I'm tired of having to fix things for you and everyone else."

The buzz started again, climbing up to settle in Nora's head. Nora had asked a lot of her, that was true. She had a vague memory of literally crying over a beer on her couch while Lacey rubbed her back. She gripped the edge of the bar. "I was depressed—"

"Right. You were depressed, and Gus is an alcoholic, and Dad's an asshole, and my job is intense . . . and now this thing with Hannah." She sighed, dragged her fingers through her hair. "I feel like I'm Atlas holding up the world sometimes. I need a break, so . . ." She shrugged and turned toward the sink.

In the Before, Nora would have promised to do better and then wouldn't. But tonight she had a dull fear she might never get Lacey back. She didn't hope for better—she was committed to it. Her relationship with her sister was completely up to her now, and that was only fair. "I get it."

"Don't get me wrong—I love you, Nora. I never would have recovered if we'd lost you. *Never.* I'm so thankful you're still here."

"Understood," Nora said. "But you need me to be a better sister. *I* need me to be a better sister. I'm asking you to give me a chance."

"Sure," Lacey said, but her tone suggested she'd heard it all before. "I'm happy you're feeling so good right now, and I sincerely hope it sticks this time."

Ouch. She knew what Lacey meant. In the Before, she would feel great for a while. She'd be present. And then she wouldn't, because sadness was in her marrow. "You know, in the Before, there were days so bad that I would wake up just so I could go to bed again. I know it was bad. I know I was a burden to you—Don't deny it," she said quickly when Lacey opened her mouth. "But I swear I am changing. I feel so different now."

"Maybe so," Lacey said with a shrug. "You had a really scary experience, and you want to change things. I get it. But seriously,

Nora—what makes this time different?" She poured more bourbon. "Honestly? I don't trust you. There, I said it."

Nora tried to shake off the weight of her grief for the sake of her sister. "Okay, fair. But I've been working hard to change into the me I want to be. I've been molting and shedding all the stuff in my life that makes me unhappy. Like my hair."

Lacey smiled a little. "I hope that means you got rid of that floral twin set that made you look like someone's spinster aunt, because that made *me* unhappy."

"As a matter of fact, I did," Nora said. "And I took all my designer bags and clothes to consignment. And I'm getting rid of my job."

Lacey's mouth gaped. "I don't believe you."

"Believe it," Nora said emphatically. "I mean . . . that's the plan, anyway. I have some past-due bills and medical bills and rent to pay, but I am actively looking for a new opportunity, as they say. It's on my reverse bucket list."

"Your what?"

"I made a bucket list after I died. So . . . in reverse."

Lacey laughed. "What's on the list?"

"Grandpa's garden. I'm going to bring it back. And be a better sister and cousin to you and Gus. Make art. Learn how to cook. I had my first class tonight. And, Lacey, there was a kid there, a girl—she had a basketball, obviously totally into it. Anyway, she let me have her ball, and I couldn't believe how well I could still dribble. My old coach would be so proud. I'm going to play basketball again."

"That's fabulous. You were the club's star player, after all. Until Mom deliberately signed you up for that ballet class at the same time." She suddenly laughed. "Oh my God, did you hate ballet."

"You would too, if you were the gangliest kid in class."

"All because a November doesn't play a masculine sport like basketball," Lacey added. *"Too manly,"* she added, mimicking their father's voice.

Dad had sneered at Nora when she'd come home with a basketball. *"Are you a lesbian? Do you like girls?"* Nora had been fourteen—she'd liked everyone. "I'm sorry he said that, Lace."

Lacey waved a hand. "Par for the course. Listen, I understood way, way back that Dad was a dick. Anyway, I remember Grandpa taking you up to the YMCA in Pflugerville so you could play."

"Until Dad found out and murdered my basketball."

They both laughed as if it were perfectly natural for a father to stab his kid's basketball. But the memory made Nora a little fizzy with rage. She'd begged him not to do it, had fallen to her knees crying and begging, but he'd been so angry she'd gone behind his back that he'd been a little frothy at the mouth.

She remembered something else too. Lacey had crawled into bed with her that night and wrapped her arms around her. Nora ached with love for her sister. She would give anything to be that comfort to Lacey . . . if her sister would let her.

"What else is on your reverse bucket list?" Lacey asked.

Nora dragged herself out of her memories. "The corner store guy."

"The who?"

"Did I seriously tell no one about him?" She reminded her sister of the hostage situation, which Lacey remembered. But she didn't know about the corner store guy, so Nora filled her in. She told her about her search and posting on the "Lost and Found in the ATX" page.

"I love this," Lacey said, her enthusiasm returning. "Have you boosted the post?"

As Nora's social media experience in the Before had been limited to a personal Facebook page where she'd last posted more than two years ago, she didn't know what Lacey meant. "What's a boost?"

"Here's what you do," Lacey said and explained how to get more eyes on the post. They spent the rest of the evening eating chips out of a bag and strategizing how to widen the search.

When Nora stood to go, Lacey asked her what was next on her reverse bucket list.

"Art," she said, smiling. "Gus and I are going to take an art class. He just doesn't know it yet."

Lacey rolled her eyes. "Good luck with that." Like she thought it was impossible.

But nothing was impossible. Nora had to believe that.

Chapter 16

Jack

M*r. Calamari had died at half past one the day before,* his extended family gathered around like vultures at a kill. Jack couldn't help the macabre comparison, maybe because the entire family was big—big bellies, big laughs, big feelings.

Pauline, another nurse, said she heard Mr. Calamari was a mobster. Jack didn't generally put much stock in the things Pauline said—she tended to state opinions as stone-cold facts—but then, even Sandra said she didn't like to go into his room because she was afraid of who might be there. *"Never know when contact with the mob is going to come back and haunt you,"* she'd said ominously.

Jack was off today. He was at the garden, mixing some plant food with a vengeance, based on a recipe Mr. Hauser had left behind. He had no tears—Guy Calamari was one of those rare patients Jack had from time to time whose death, as shameful as it was to admit, couldn't come soon enough. Calamari had called Jack a dick, said Pauline's ass could feed a nation. He told his wife he was sick of her hanging around and told his oldest son that he wasn't leaving him a bloody dime.

And still his teary-eyed family came, asking if he needed anything. What he needed, he said, was a gin and tonic. What he wanted was for them to shut the hell up; all their *yap, yap, yap* was driving him crazy. He said they were the reason he was dying, that they'd essentially killed him.

Once, as Jack was hooking up a saline drip to Mr. Calamari's beefy, tattooed arm, he asked Jack if he had family. Jack shook his head.

"Lucky you. Family is nothing but a pain in the ass."

Jack could have said he'd always wanted a family and, as a kid, asked Santa for one. And that as a man, he held out hope that he'd have one of his own eventually. He could have said that he hadn't given up.

But he didn't say anything because he'd learned that everyone comes to death on their own terms. Often, by the time people got to hospice, they were in so much pain or trapped in bodies that no longer functioned that they welcomed the peace and an end to the suffering. But some people came angry and confused, fearful and combative. Mr. Calamari belonged in that group. He felt wronged, like life owed him more than a mere sixty-four years. Tell that to the six-year-old who'd died from brain cancer last week.

Calamari's last act had been to yank his hand free of his daughter's grip even though he was unconscious. Jack reported this remarkable fact to Sandra. They both knew that in the final stages, patients weren't generally aware of hand-holding. But somehow Calamari had sensed one last opportunity to be a jerk and had taken it.

Jack finished mixing his plant food and was digging some holes for his new plantings—he was going to try green beans on the advice of Byron's mom—when he heard the familiar rattle of Catherine's wheelchair on the crushed granite path.

"Who'd you lose today?"

"A guy whose time had definitely come," he said. "How's your day?"

"Fine, I guess." She sighed and looked away.

This was not the Catherine Henry Jack had come to know and appreciate. She was generally full of news, gossip about the other plots, advice about who to vote for in the upcoming mayoral election, and sartorial critique of his gardening clothes. Jack dug another hole. "What's up?"

"Hmm?" She shifted her gaze to him again. "Nothing. I've got a lot on my mind."

"Like?"

"Like . . . life, kid. Bet you hear enough of that at your job. Bet people looking death in the face want to unburden themselves before they kick off."

Jack put the seedling into the ground and lightly tamped dirt around it. "Some do. Some don't. Depends on the person."

"Well, I believe if you've got something to say, say it. Better when you're alive and kicking and can do something about it." She rubbed her forehead and sighed again.

Jack stood up and brushed dirt from his knees. "Have you got something you want to say, Catherine?"

"You don't care. And there's no point—we're sunk."

"First of all, I wouldn't ask if I didn't care," he said and, without thinking, pulled up the lap rug she'd draped across her knees before it slipped off onto her feet. "And second, who's sunk?"

"It's a long story. Hey . . ." She peered up at him curiously. "You want to get out of here and do something fun?"

"Like what?"

"You'll see. I'll give you the address and you can meet me. I want it to be a surprise."

He eyed her suspiciously. "You and surprise are not two things I think should be in the same room."

"Come on, Jack. What are you afraid of?" She waggled her brows at him.

He had to admit he was intrigued. If anyone could surprise him, it just might be Catherine Henry. Besides, he had nothing going on for the rest of the day, and anything was better than going back to his apartment to dwell on Mr. Calamari. "Okay."

She obviously hadn't expected him to agree and grinned. "Walter? Walter! Come type in our address or whatever it is you do with the phones for our friend here."

••••••

Later, Jack paused in the middle of the sidewalk and looked again at the address Walter had given him. He was north of the Triangle, in a cluster of old buildings surrounding a parking lot. A closed warehouse was on one side, next to it a small, dilapidated theater with a marquee (blank), a ticket window (shades drawn), and some empty display case windows in the middle. At the other end, a twelve-unit brick apartment building faced the theater. Faded curtains billowed out of one of the windows. Some had boxes attached filled with fake flowers. The doors were painted a variety of colors, and the brick was crumbling on the west corner.

Was he surprised? Yes, he was.

He opened the door of the theater. The air-conditioning unit was making a terrible racket overhead, and he was immediately hit with a musty scent of dusty carpets and mildew. There were a few people inside milling about in dancewear—women in leotards and knee-length jersey skirts, men in black sweats. But most notably, they were all senior citizens. Maybe the theater had been repurposed as some sort of senior day care center.

He spotted Catherine near the entrance to the auditorium. She was wearing a dance leotard and a zip-up hoodie. She had sweater socks on her legs, straight out of the '80s fitness craze.

Her face lit with pleasure when she saw him. "You came. I didn't know if you would."

"I did. But where exactly did I come to?"

"This," she said, casting her arm out, "is the Triangle Theater."

He looked around. "A senior center of some type?"

"Excuse me? No, Jack, it is a theater. We are thespians! A dance class is starting soon."

"A dance class?" He smiled. He might have even smirked at the idea of these old cats dancing around.

"Is that funny?" Catherine snapped.

"No. It's . . ." He was fighting the urge to laugh. "It's great." He looked down to avoid her blazing look, and his gaze landed on her shoes. Tap shoes.

"Have you ever tap-danced, Jack?"

The laugh he'd been holding burst out of him. "Um . . . no."

"It's excellent for the brain, you know. You repeat complex steps and then do them in reverse. It's also great for balance. Not to mention it's a social art. What social art do you enjoy, Jack?"

"I don't know what a social art is."

"A social art is something that requires interaction with others. For example, one tap dancer often taps out a rhythm for another to follow." She leaned forward, into his personal space. "Social."

"Okay," he said and held up his hands, palms out. "I apologize. Tap dancing is not funny."

"It most certainly is not, which you'll see for yourself in a few minutes."

He would? Jack ran his hand through his hair and glanced at his watch. "I don't know—"

"Oh, I see." Catherine folded her arms as other thespians filed into the auditorium. "You're too good to watch us tap-dance."

Man, someone had a bee in her bonnet. "That's not true."

"You're acting like it is."

"I'm not acting like anything."

"Your body language says it all. That's fine, Jack. Why don't you run back to all that death and—"

He threw up his hands. "Fine, okay, I'll watch."

Catherine grinned triumphantly.

The auditorium was small—maybe three hundred seats in total. Most were covered in pleather, splitting from overuse. He followed her down a worn center aisle to the stage. There was a distinct, old-folks-home smell, like disinfectant had been used in abundance. Or Bengay had been applied too liberally. The stage was scarred and needed to be refinished. The curtains had faded to a Pepto-Bismol pink and were dotted with what he guessed were moth holes.

"This place needs work," he said.

"Tell me about it," Catherine agreed.

The others had gone up onstage. A man in tap shoes, tights, a white T-shirt, and a sweater jauntily tied around his shoulders walked around, positioning them, spacing them evenly apart.

"Where should I sit?" Jack asked.

"What do you mean, 'sit'? You're going to dance, aren't you?"

The idea was so absurd that Jack laughed. Catherine didn't. Jack stared at her. "What the hell, Catherine? Did you really ask me here to see if you could get me to tap-dance?"

"No, I asked you here to see the theater. But while you're here, I don't see why you won't give it a go. It's fun."

He could not believe he'd fallen for her "surprise." "I am not going to tap-dance. I don't dance."

She shrugged, and Jack had a glimpse of a twenty-year-old Catherine, who probably had known how to shrug and force horny young men to their knees with want. "Chicken."

"I'm not chicken. But I know my limits."

"Bok, bok, bok."

He sighed. "I hope you won't take this the wrong way, but you can be super annoying."

"Like that's news. You don't get to seventy-six years old and not understand a thing or two about yourself, pumpkin. Are you going to take the class or not?"

"All right, my darlings. We're starting small," the man in the sweater announced. "We'll begin with some simple toe-toe, heel-heel. Meredith, did you practice like I asked? Or am I doomed to spend the entire lesson correcting you?"

"Shut up, Jerry," a woman—presumably Meredith—said.

"Toe-toe, heel-heel. Can we do that?"

"Of course we can do that," a man said gruffly. "We're all veterans of the stage, Jerry."

"Here's your chance to dance with stage veterans," Catherine said.

Jack looked again at the stage. They had begun the toe-toe, heel-heel. More than one watched the feet of their neighbors. One of the women on the front row went rogue and began tapping out a different rhythm until Jerry forced her to stop. None of the seniors were taking it too seriously, judging by all the laughing and smiling.

It did look sort of fun.

"Catherine? Are you going to join the class or not?" Jerry asked. "Chop-chop. And if your boy toy is going to join us, get him up here. You can stuff him on the back row."

"Well, boy toy?" Catherine asked.

In a moment of sheer insanity, Jack said, "Okay, fine."

He followed her up onstage and was placed in the back row, where, he quickly discovered, all novices were placed. Catherine went to the front.

"Places, everyone!" Jerry shouted, unnecessarily loud. "Follow my lead!"

Jack tried to follow his lead: toe drop, heel drop, toe-heel, toe-heel, slide to the right, slide to the left, then heel touch—"Big step! Big step!" Jerry shouted and dropped into a curtsy toe touch. The group applauded themselves.

"Again!" Jerry said grandly and wove in and out of the three lines of dancers as he called out the moves. He paused behind Jack and said, "Your shapely legs are as flexible as four-by-fours, my good man." He startled Jack by putting his hands on his hips and pushing them forward. "Hips tucked. Weight centered over your feet, shoulders over your hips. My name is Jerry, by the way, should you need any private lessons."

Jerry walked to the front of the stage. "Are you ready to put this to music?"

The group roared that they were.

Jerry exited stage left, and in the next moment, "Uptown Funk" featuring Bruno Mars nearly blasted them off the stage.

They had to be kidding.

Oh, but Jerry was not kidding. He reappeared, clapping the beat. "Let's go again, and please, try not to move like a zombie apocalypse. One, two, three!"

Jack missed the first step and stumbled around, but he found his footing by keeping his eyes glued to the feet of the woman in front of him as Bruno blared from the speakers.

By the end of the lesson, Jack was panting along with the people on either side of him, laughing like he hadn't laughed in ages. It turned out that all he had to lose were his inhibitions and maybe a small piece of his dignity.

At the end of it, he informed Catherine that while he had enjoyed himself, he would not be hoodwinked into tap dancing again.

"Well, that works out for both of us because I really need you and your hammer," she said.

"What makes you think I have a hammer?"

"You look like the type."

He looked around that run-down little theater. What the hell had he gotten himself into? "I have a hammer, so I guess I am that type."

Catherine smiled. "How fortuitous."

How fortuitous indeed.

Chapter 17

Saturday morning was punctuated with the foghorn blare of Nora's phone. She grabbed it to shut it up and saw it was a video call from her mother. With a groan, she tapped the button to answer.

"Good morning," her mother chirped. She brought the phone closer to her eye. "I really wish you hadn't cut your hair."

Nora put her hand to her head.

"I'm calling to remind you of dinner Sunday evening. I've told everyone you'll be back."

As if she needed to be reminded. Sunday dinners were something her mother had done for years without fail. Even though Nora had been on approved Sunday dinner leave while recovering, her mother consistently reminded her of them, listing the illustrious dinner guests she'd missed. Roberta and David November—Bastions of Rob Roy mansions, Pillars of a Select Society of Rich White People living on the shores of Lake Austin—held sacrosanct twice-monthly dinner parties for their wealthy clients and friends. Attendance was mandatory for anyone with the last name of November except in cases of life or death. Which, Nora supposed, she'd tried and, predictably, failed.

In the Before, even at her lowest point, she'd attended. She didn't have the energy to put up the fight necessary to keep her mother off her back. Now she still had no desire to go, but without a firm excuse, she knew it was easier to go along to get along.

There would be enough fireworks in the family when she quit her job.

"Six sharp. And for God's sake, please don't wear anything from that thrift store. And do something with your hair."

"Should I also lose ten pounds?"

"You've done remarkably well keeping the weight off since the accident. You look great. Other than the hair, which may be because you haven't styled it. And the clothes, of course."

Given a platform, Nora's mother could single-handedly set the progress toward body positivity back fifty years. *Nothing is as good as skinny feels* had been a quote on a little plaque her mother had kept in her kitchen until it mysteriously disappeared. Lacey and Nora had taken it behind the house and smashed it with rocks one blistering hot summer afternoon.

"You're getting out and not moping around your apartment today, I hope."

That was her mother's way of asking if she was depressed. The vagueness of her question, her arm's length from the truth, hurt. In the Before, her mother's distance had made Nora feel unworthy of her concern. Now it aggravated her. Her mother never looked for a way to support Nora—she looked for a way to find fault or avoid her at her low points.

Nora remembered a time when her mother had put her and Lacey in matching red velvet dresses for a Christmas party. Nora had gone outside to see a neighbor's new puppy, and she'd come back with muddied paw prints on the skirt. Her mother had hauled her into the bathroom to try to clean her up. *"Why do you always find a way to hurt me?"* she'd demanded hotly. Nora had been six years old.

"Why do you automatically assume I'm moping around?" she asked her mother curtly. "I've been very busy."

"With what?"

Nora glanced at her laptop, still on the side of the bed where she'd left it last night. Every day after work she scoured the employment websites and law firm postings for jobs and sent off résumés. And when she wasn't trying to find a new job, she was boosting her post about the corner store guy and spreading the search onto other social media sites. She'd posted on all of them, even making a cringeworthy video for TikTok in which she tried to sound cute and adorable but came off looking like an excitable cat lady—but without the cat.

She'd tried to get Gus on the phone again, but her calls rolled to voice mail. So she texted him a link to her TikTok. What do you think?

An hour later, he responded. You're weird. I love you, man.

She was so happy for a response that she instantly texted back. I'm going to come see you. I have something exciting planned.

Gus didn't respond to that text, but he read it.

"A million and one different things," she said pertly. "Hey, Mom, didn't Grandpa plant some calla lilies at your house?"

"Did he?" Her mother tapped a finger against her bottom lip. "Maybe near the pool. Why?"

"Because they were Grandma's favorite and I want to plant some in his garden. I think he'd like that."

"Why do you talk about him like he's alive? That worries me. And I hope you're not ruining your skin with all that time in the sun."

Nora sighed. God forbid she get a little too much sun and bring even more shame to the November family.

"I have to run. Dad and I are playing in a tennis tournament this afternoon. Don't forget about dinner tomorrow—our friends are anxious to see you."

"To see how skinny I am?"

"Claudia will be so jealous," her mother said gleefully. "Oh, I almost forgot. We're announcing your father's award."

"What award?"

"Didn't I tell you? He's getting an award for all the work he's done to fund SIDS research." She glanced off for a moment. "It's a special man who responds to the death of his baby boy in such a way. He's raised more money for End SIDS than anyone."

"Oh. Wow," Nora said faintly. What a wonderful accolade. How lucky for Nathan that, thirty years later, their father was still more interested in him than her.

"Don't be late," her mother said.

"I never am. Bye, Mom." She clicked off and then, in a surprise to herself, hurled her phone across the room.

••••••

She dressed in another thrift store outfit—a long jersey skirt, a battered sun hat, an old denim jacket over an Austin City Limits T-shirt, and her combat boots. She really liked those boots.

She looked forward to her first stop of the day—Dr. Cass.

Dr. Cass inquired after Nora's health, confirmed she was taking her medicine and sleeping, and asked about her progress toward her reverse bucket list. Nora reported it all. Her conversation with Lacey, her confrontation with her father, the mess she'd found at Grandpa's garden. "It was so bad," she said. "Dead and overgrown. Look at my hands." She held up hands scratched and raw from pulling weeds. "And this woman showed up and told me I was a horrible person for not coming to see Grandpa."

"Oh my! That's not true."

"Yes, it is," she said flatly. "If I'd gone when I promised—" The image of him lying on the kitchen floor, cold and lifeless, roared to life. She doubled over and covered her face with her hands. The memory never got easier—the regret was always right there, wanting to choke her. If she'd gone when he expected her, if she'd been there, she could have called an ambulance. "I'm sorry," she said through gasps for air. "Emotions keep exploding in me when I least expect it."

"I know it must feel like your emotions are racing out of control. But really, you're peeling the layers. Your life wasn't a particularly happy one before you drowned, right? To be happy in this new life, you must keep digging to discover the real you and why you couldn't be the real you before. I think you're doing great," Dr. Cass said. "Let's keep going with this—how are you feeling about everything in general?"

"I think good, mostly." She did feel good . . . but there were also moments she felt in over her head. "And hopeful. But I still get buzzy, and these emotions that keep coming at me from nowhere are so frustrating. I had panic attacks before, but this feels different. Like I'm on the verge of vertigo. I feel great, and then I don't. I feel confident, and then I don't."

"You're experiencing classic fire hose."

"Classic what?"

"Think about your NDE and the trauma to your brain. You were clinically dead for a few minutes. You were in a coma. You went to rehab to heal your body, and all that time, your brain was on bed rest. So now you're reentering your life after a significant traumatic event, and with a new reverse bucket list you're tackling. But the world is overstimulating. With the noise and movement and expectations from your job and your family, on top of your expectations for yourself, and then feelings you've kept buried for years are bubbling up—it's like you're being blasted with a fire hose while you try to piece your life together."

Yikes. Hearing it laid out like that made her want to crawl in bed. "That sounds horrifying."

"Transformation after trauma isn't easy. It takes a lot of work. Don't judge yourself for setbacks. You get a blast of emotion and revelation, and your brain adjusts, and you try again. But eventually everything will fall into place."

"I'm afraid I've spent so much of my life trying to fit into someone else's idea of me that I won't know when the pieces are all in place."

Dr. Cass smiled. "Really? Because you've made yourself a road map with your reverse bucket list, haven't you? You already know what pieces need to be in place for you to be happy. For example, you said you were looking for a new job?"

Nora nodded. "I've been sending out résumés."

"Wonderful." Dr. Cass smiled brightly. "Have you thought about starting your own practice?"

That was so out of reach that Nora laughed. "I have medical bills and rent—I need a steady income."

Dr. Cass kept smiling.

"I wouldn't even know how."

Dr. Cass's expression didn't change.

"I mean, that's not something you up and do without a lot of preparation."

"No doubt. But you don't know how to cook either, and you're learning that skill."

A solo law practice was a vastly different animal than a cooking class.

"Oops, that's our time," Dr. Cass said. "By the way, Nora . . . I'm really proud of you."

Something in Nora's chest puffed up instantly. No one ever said that to her. Moreover, she'd never said it to herself. And she really wanted to be able to say it to herself.

Chapter 18

Gus lived in a dicey part of town where rent was notoriously cheap. His apartment was in a three-story complex built around a greenish-tinted pool and a playground where beer bottles, used condoms, and cigarette butts were scattered about. Nora walked past doors littered with kid toys and shoes. A used diaper was lying on the stairs as if the kid had slipped right out of it. One door had some potted plants neatly arranged to the side, which she appreciated. So did a cat—it was curled up asleep in one of the pots.

Gus's door was beat up, like someone had tried to break in. A bag of trash sat beneath his living room window.

It was shameful that she couldn't recall the last time she'd been to Gus's apartment. She knocked on the door and could hear some shuffling, something being moved. A moment later, the door cracked open, and she could see half of Gus's unshaven face. He opened it a little wider. "Nora? What are you doing here?"

"I texted you last night and said I was coming over, remember?"

He dragged his fingers through his greasy hair. "Yeah, but I didn't think you'd actually come."

Another small kick to the gut. "May I come in?"

"Inside?"

She hated that he sounded so incredulous. "No judgment, I promise."

He glanced uneasily over his shoulder. "Okay," he said reluctantly.

When she stepped over the threshold, her eyes watered with the pungent back-alley smell of alcohol and unwashed body. Gus's hair was disheveled, his shirt stained, his sweatpants dirty. His apartment was a mess—Big Gulp cups and empty fast-food wrappers littered the battered coffee table. Clothes and more trash were strewn about on the floor, and everywhere she looked, there was a bottle or can of some sort.

Gus rubbed his face with his hands as if he were trying to rub off his state of being. "I'm sorry. I'm so sorry. I've tried, Nora, I really have tried—"

Nora turned and wrapped her arms around him. He sagged into her arms, a giant man trying to curl against her. She could hear her father's voice in her head—*"Just a dumb drunk like your father."*

"Hey." She gripped Gus's meaty shoulders. "It's okay." She stepped over an empty pizza box as she moved into his apartment, trying not to wrinkle her nose.

"Pretty bad, right?" he asked sheepishly.

"Well . . . it's not good, Gus."

He sighed.

"I've got a great idea."

"What's the idea? Rehab? Is this another intervention?"

An uncomfortable spasm of remorse ran down her spine. About three years ago, she'd picked him up under the pretense of getting some dinner but had driven him to her parents' house instead. Her mother had convinced her to do it, had said they only wanted to talk to Gus about his inability to keep a job. But to Nora's surprise, they'd had a whole team assembled to cart him off to rehab.

Once he was out of sight, he was out of mind for her parents. And her mother had used her—she knew Gus would come if Nora asked him.

The feeling turned to a low buzz in her chest; Nora sank down onto the arm of his grimy couch.

"Are you okay?" Gus asked, sounding a bit desperate. "I know it's pretty gross—"

"This is not an intervention, Gus. The only thing behind this visit is that I love you and I know I haven't been here when you needed me. For the record, I didn't know what Mom and Dad had planned that day. Mom said she wanted to talk. If I'd known, I never would have taken you there. Not like that."

"Nora . . . it's okay." He managed a smile. "I never blamed you. I didn't blame anyone. I mean, I needed it. I'm thankful to Aunt Roberta for trying to help me. But . . . I guess I'm too broken."

"You're not broken."

He smiled sadly. "We both know I am. It doesn't take a genius to guess why you haven't been around."

The buzz intensified. "Huh?"

He gestured to his apartment. "It's easy to drive me to an intervention. It's harder to hang out with a loser."

"Gus! That's not true."

"Yeah, it is."

He didn't sound angry, he sounded . . . indifferent. That hurt more, because he was right—in the Before, she couldn't handle his problems on top of her own. She'd ignored him. "I'm sorry, Gus," she said softly. "I sort of had my own demons."

He nodded. "Depression."

She shrugged. "It made me pretty useless."

"But it was more than that. You're ashamed of me."

"No," she said immediately, shaking her head . . . but that was a lie too. She loved Gus. And she'd been ashamed of him. But how could she be ashamed of him when she couldn't even help herself? She felt as if she'd betrayed her beloved cousin, and that left her feeling demoralized. How could she?

A moment in their shared history stood out. Lacey had won an award for an after-school arts program she'd created at her campus. Nora, her mother and father, Grandpa, and Gus had attended the presentation. And Nora, in her tailored suit and tightly bound hair, had sat on the other side of her father so that she wouldn't have to sit next to a lumbering, disheveled Gus, with his greasy hair, scuffed shoes, and a button-up dress shirt with the elbows nearly worn through. She hadn't wanted to be associated with him. And she didn't want to have to hear her father's disapproval, his biting remarks.

It disgusted her that she'd treated Gus the way her father so often treated her.

But what was truly amazing was that Gus had never been ashamed of her, even during those periods she struggled to get off her couch.

"So this isn't an intervention?" he asked, pulling her back to the moment.

"Nope. I came to invite you out."

"Not your mom's Sunday dinner," he said. "She already told me she didn't have room for me. Which, you know, is code for I'm not welcome."

It was appalling that her mother could behave so dreadfully toward her only nephew, but what else was new? "I would never invite you to the torture that is Sunday dinner. I was thinking of a painting class."

A beat or two passed as he took that in. "Seriously? Like one of those paint party places?"

She nodded.

"Why?"

"I thought it was something we could do together."

He looked dubious. Trust, she was learning, was a hard thing to get back once it was lost.

"Gus . . . this may sound a little nuts, but I feel really different now. Maybe I wasn't great at hanging out in the past, but I want to change that."

He grimaced. "I don't know. I don't know if painting is my thing."

"You won't know unless you try. Say yes, Gus. Please. If you say yes, I'll help you clean up." She stood up, put down her bag, and crossed to the bar that separated his kitchen from his living area. She began to pick up empty bottles.

"Let me do that," Gus said and grabbed a trash can as he pushed Nora out of the way, obviously embarrassed by the number of bottles.

"You're going to say yes, right?" she pressed him. "I've found a couple of places. We could go as soon as next week. And then . . . maybe we could go to an AA meeting? You used to like them."

His bottom lip trembled slightly. "Okay," he said softly.

"Okay?" The buzz began to ease. Nora hugged him again.

Gus said she needed to calm down. Nora said she couldn't, she was too excited. Gus rolled his eyes, but he was smiling.

Later, when Nora left with three bags of trash, she knew that Gus needed more from her than a painting class. But at least this was a start of being there for him.

Chapter 19

Jack

R*alph and Doris Haines were married seventy-six years.* Doris had Alzheimer's, and as her mind gave way to that terrible disease, she didn't know her husband any longer. She was rarely even awake. That didn't stop Ralph from shuffling in on his walker every day to sit with her and hold her hand. Sometimes Doris would speak. Most of what she said was nonsensical to Jack, but Ralph always answered.

Just before her death, Doris opened her eyes and looked up. A rapturous, joyous smile filled her face. "Kenny?" she croaked. And then her eyes slid shut.

A half hour later, she was gone.

Ralph finally let go of her hand. He folded it across her belly, patted it, then took out a faded handkerchief and wiped his eyes. "That disease," he said. "I thought it had stolen the best of her. But the best of her was still in there."

Kenny, Ralph said, was the son they'd lost in the Vietnam War. Like so many others who had died in Jack's care, the vision of a predeceased loved one was the last thing Doris had seen before she'd shuffled off this mortal coil. While science debated what the visions really were, Jack thought that remarkable phenomenon was what surviving family members needed most. The belief that a loved one was waiting on the other side brought enormous comfort to them.

He'd come to the garden today, not with grief but with awe. He would never forget the look on Doris's face when she saw her son, or what Ralph had said about the best of his wife. Jack wished for someone to be that devoted to him. He wanted a love that would sustain him through the worst of times, through disease and strife and disaster, and at the end, for someone who knew he was still in there, no matter what. He wanted someone who would be impatient with him in long checkout lines, and watch movies with him that didn't live up to the hype, and appreciate lazy Sunday mornings and walking the dog and wine tastings and dinner parties and football. Was that asking too much?

The only trouble was, he wasn't interested in anyone. The closest he'd come to an interest in the last year was Nora, from the corner store. What had happened to her, anyway? He recalled them standing under the awning in front of the corner store, waiting for the crime scene unit to arrive and watching the rain turn the street into a river that cars shouldn't attempt to drive through. They took bets as to which cars would go for it. They agreed that they were too smart or too cowardly to attempt it, and that the "turn around, don't drown" campaign had been seared into their fearful consciences as children.

Jack asked if she could remember her greatest childhood fear.

"I had two," she said. "Quicksand and razors in apples at Halloween."

He laughed. "Have you ever seen quicksand?"

"Never. But in fifth grade, Cressida Talley said she had a sister who was sucked into it and disappeared, so for weeks I was on the lookout for it everywhere I went, sure I would be swallowed up."

"What about a razor in Halloween apples?"

"Never got an apple in my bag." She laughed. "Wouldn't it be totally obvious if an apple had a razor in it?" She shook her head. "What about you?"

"Easy. Spontaneous combustion. My mom told me about it."

"Your mom?" Nora laughed.

"Turns out, it was her greatest fear too," Jack said. "We spent an entire summer afraid of getting hot on the off chance we would simultaneously combust. I think I wore my Ninja Turtle flame-retardant pajamas every day."

She'd smiled up at him, her eyes glittering in the light of streetlamps. "Prepared for an emergency. I like that."

Jack had been so sure Nora would call him after that night. Why hadn't she? He would really like to know the answer to that—heaven knew he'd waited long enough, hoping she might guess that he'd lost her number and reach out.

He was ready to plant some squash. He borrowed a wagon at the garden entrance and trundled his seedlings to his plot.

The first thing he did was check on the tomatoes he'd planted. He thought maybe he'd planted them too early, but one plant had taken the assignment and run with it, already producing three small but perfect tomatoes. He'd tilled a row for the squash during his last visit, and after he planted them, he had some cleanup and weeding to do. This garden had become his part-time job.

Byron had been exasperated when Jack canceled loose plans earlier this week to check on his plot. *"Dude, you're all plants and dead people."*

"Nearly *dead people,"* he'd corrected him.

Byron's complaint wasn't entirely fair—they'd squeezed in a baseball game last weekend. And he'd helped Clark, another buddy, move. He'd picked up a couple of extra shifts and gone out after work with Sandra and Pauline for drinks. He was busy.

He was even busier now because he'd gotten roped into making some cosmetic repairs at the Triangle Theater. In fact, he was headed there today. Where did the weekend go?

* * * * * *

He found Catherine in a foul mood, stomping around the faded lobby. She immediately put him to work shoring up the old ticket box, but then proceeded to bark orders until Jack told her—politely—that he was doing this as a favor to her, and if she would rather he come back another time, he would. But he was not putting up with that.

Catherine was instantly contrite and heaved a sigh that carried the weight of the world in it. "I'm sorry, Jack. I'm a little upset, that's all. These repairs should have been done a long time ago, but we didn't have the money."

"Who is we?" he asked curiously as he nailed planks to the side of the ticket box.

"Us. The thespians."

"Sounds like a traveling show." He grinned at Catherine, expecting her to laugh with him.

But she was glaring back at him with an expression that said he was downright dumb. "Who do you think lives there?" She pointed in the direction of the old apartment building at the end of the parking lot.

"People without a lot of money?"

Her expression turned thunderous. "That building has been home to stage performers for years."

"Wait—you all *live* here?"

"Where did you think we lived?"

"I don't know—I never thought about it."

Catherine explained to Jack that she and her husband, Douglas, and Walter and a couple of others had scraped together the money to buy the property and existing structures years ago. Walter, Jack learned, was not a driver or an award-winning gardener by trade—he'd been a set designer on Broadway. The others were dancers, actors, and even a costume designer—some with Broadway experience, some with local experience, all of them with careers in theater.

"It's our own damn fault," Catherine said angrily. She threw her fuzzy purple scarf around her neck in dramatic fashion. "I used to keep on top of things, but when Douglas died, I lost my way."

"Maybe you should sit—"

"Don't treat me like an invalid!" And then she promptly sat down on the one folding chair in the lobby, leaned over, and buried her face in her hands.

"Catherine!"

"You don't understand how broke we are," she moaned. "All I have is Social Security because Douglas left some debts I didn't know about. I live like a pauper."

"Oh," Jack said, wincing.

"Get that pity off your face. I found my peace with it, I really did," she insisted. "Until that asshole with the gold rings on his fingers showed up and tried to evict us."

"What? Who?"

Catherine winced. "We're a smidge behind on our taxes."

"What's a smidge?"

"Thousands. There's a lien on the property. The guy who bought the lien wants to build luxury apartments here. He said it's an up-and-coming part of town," Catherine said bitterly.

That didn't sound like something that could be fixed by spiffing up the place. "Have you thought about selling?" Jack asked.

"For God's sake, Jack. We're all living on fixed incomes. Where are we going to go?"

"Family?"

"Those who could live with family have already left. The rest of us have no place to go." She sat up. "We've got a different idea. We're going to fundraise to pay the arrears before he evicts us."

Jack instantly imagined them selling baked goods and knitted scarves on the street corner. He glanced up to the stained ceiling where gold paint was chipping off. He thought of the rotting floor in the theater—he suspected a water leak somewhere. And the bathrooms that needed to be overhauled, the stage curtains that looked more fire hazard than functional. "That's a lot of cookies, Catherine."

"Cookies! Have you always been this dumb? We're staging *A Streetcar Named Desire*."

"Oh." He perked up. "I get it. You'll get some actors to donate their time?"

She squinted at him. "*We're* performers! Stage veterans! Right now we are debating whether it should be a musical—because of course Martin wants to sing. And Meredith thinks she will play Blanche DuBois, but that will happen only over my dead body."

"Wait." Jack put a hand up as he tried to picture a geriatric musical. It seemed a bit of a stretch with the odd little clique of dance class participants he'd seen so far. And could they really bring in enough money to pay thousands in back taxes? Surely there was a better option. Maybe the city or a nonprofit could help. "How long do you have?" he asked.

"Sixty days. We'll be needing help with set design," Catherine said slyly.

Sixty days? Jack looked at the ticket box that was currently in the process of a slow disintegration. "Just curious . . . did you con me into doing a few repairs around here with the hope I would build a set?"

"No! I conned you into it with the hope you'd be one of our dancers. We're going to need someone strong enough to do a couple of lifts. But if you think you're up to building sets, well, we can use that help too."

Jack couldn't help but laugh at her audacity. "You are something else, Catherine Henry."

"You agreed with me that you need some work-life balance, remember? You said you needed more joy in your life. You can't be about death all the time."

"First, you did all the talking, not me. Second, I am not about death all the time, and third, I am not a dancer. Or a set builder. This is all beyond my skill set, Catherine. And anyway, why didn't you just come out and ask?"

"If I had said, 'Please come be in a musical with me and my elderly friends,' would you have agreed?"

He frowned. "No. I've been to one musical in my entire life, and that was in high school."

She stood up from her chair, put her hands on her hips. "You are what is wrong with America."

He rolled his eyes. "I thought what was wrong with America was people who didn't take care of their garden plots."

"You're both what's wrong with America. You never have to think about anyone but yourself. You, you, *you*. There are at least eleven of us who will be out on the street if we don't do something. That means me, Jack. But if you're too busy taking care of dead people, then by all means—"

"They are not dead people. They are dying, and someday we'll be doing the same, so stop acting like they aren't worth my time."

"Stop acting like this isn't worth mine," she shot back.

They glared at each other for one intense moment.

"Fine," Jack finally muttered, and Catherine smiled.

Chapter 20

At the Stinking Iris, Nick eyed Nora's tomato plants with an expression of either severe disdain or abject awe. It was hard to tell with him. He slipped his pinky under one tiny leaf and bent down, peering closely at it.

"What?" Nora demanded. "What is it? Is something wrong? I did everything you said."

"Don't get your panties in a bunch," he said gruffly. He straightened up, then stalked off, disappearing into the back room. He returned moments later with some sort of meat thermometer–looking thing and thrust it at Nora.

"What's this?"

"It's to check the pH balance of your soil."

"My what?"

"Listen closely now. You won't have a snowball's chance in hell of growing tomatoes if the pH balance is too high. This is mine, aye? Bring it back." He thrust it at her again, forcing her to take it.

"Gee, Nick, you're trusting me with your plant-o-meter?"

"It's a pH meter. Know your tools." He muttered something under his breath, walked over to a display, and picked up a pair of knee pads. "I'll give you the garden club price. But you'll need to join the Green Thumb Club if you want the 10 percent discount. Gloves are on sale next week."

Nora was delighted by the prospect of joining a garden club. "You'd let me join?"

"We'll discuss it. It might be your only hope."

She smiled and put the pH meter in one of the tote pockets. "Thanks again, Nick. I'll bring it back, I promise, when I come to get my gloves. There's something else I want to show you." She reached into the interior of her bag and pulled out three bulbs wrapped in newsprint. She placed the bundle on the counter.

He unwrapped it. "Where'd you get these?" He turned one particularly muddy specimen over.

"My parents' house. While they were playing tennis, I snuck in and dug them up. Do you know what they are?"

He gave her a withering look. "Calla lilies."

"They were my grandmother's favorite, and my grandfather always had a patch of them."

"Trying to make amends, are you?"

Amends.

"Nothing wrong with making amends," Nick said. "Just a little tougher when the affected party is no longer with us. These need loose soil. And lots of water. You can't drown a calla lily."

Couldn't drown Nora November either, apparently.

That thought suddenly sent her soaring back to the beach at Surfside, standing there in the cold wind, her feet sinking into wet sand. The water had been so choppy—little whitecaps everywhere, the clouds purple and gray on the horizon. *You're a calla lily*, the buzz whispered.

"They're like everything else," Nick continued. "They're self-sufficient to a point, but you can't neglect them. Everything withers with neglect."

The buzz grew. Somewhere in Nick's garden lecture, an internal whisper was growing—if she neglected herself, she would wither.

It was as simple as that, and yet it was as hard as bringing Grandpa's garden back to life.

He reached under the counter and produced a mesh bag. He put her bulbs in them. "Loose soil. Plenty of moisture. You got that?"

"I've got it." She picked up her flat of tomatoes and the mesh bag.

"By the way, I've got some dahlia tubers coming later this week that you might like. Come back when you can. And take some pictures," he commanded as she went out.

......

The first thing Nora noticed when she walked through the gates of the Goodfellow Community Garden was the birdsong. *Optimism.* It was astonishing how quickly the sounds of the city could fade from her consciousness. She'd been coming every chance she could get, even cutting out of work early when James told her the coast was clear. She felt she was in a whole other universe in here, especially on a gorgeous spring day.

She surveyed other plots as she passed through, muttering her congratulations on jobs well done. When she reached her plot, she took a moment to appreciate what she'd accomplished thus far. She'd successfully removed most of the weeds. She still had to trim some mystery plants that looked like they might come back to life. At least they weren't yet dead, so there was that.

She placed her flat of tomato plants on the ground and took out her pH meter. She thrust the needle into the soil and watched the digital display race up to number eight. She realized instantly that she'd failed to ask a very important question, because she didn't know what that number meant. She took a picture of the reading with her phone to show Nick. He'd act like he was perturbed that she didn't know, but privately he'd delight in explaining it and instructing her what to do next.

She took a spade from her garden tote and her new knee pads, pulling them up over the legs of her thrift store overalls, then set to work digging holes for the tomato plants. She liked the feel of pushing her fingers into the soft earth—the same earth her grandfather had dug—and the slightly pungent smell of soil that had been lovingly cared for by her grandfather over the last years of his life. It felt good and natural to her. However, she could see the utility of gloves, given how dirty her hands were.

She moved easily down the row, planting her seedlings. She knew how to do this part—it came back to her like waking from a dream. She was back on the ranch, on her knees beside Grandpa, digging her hole a foot from his. He'd shown her how to tap the seedling from the flat, how to settle it squarely in the hole and softly tamp the earth in around it.

Before she put each seedling into its hole, she dropped in a penny. Grandpa always added a penny to each new planting. *"Make a wish, kid,"* he'd say jovially, and she'd think of one, *really* think of one, then blow it onto the penny. She wondered how many pennies were buried at the ranch. He'd promised her that those wishes were the best wishes and they would all come true.

None of them did. Her dad was still her dad. Her mother was still her mother. She was not a princess or a pirate or any of the other things she'd wished to be.

Still, traditions ran deep. With each tomato seedling she planted, she took out a penny, made a wish, blew on it, and dropped it in the hole. Planted the seedling. Went to the next.

Her wishes were much simpler now. She wished for a burrito and beer later (she couldn't be *all* about personal growth). She wished the buzziness would disappear. She wished the plants would grow. She wished she'd find the corner store guy. She wished she could feel it again, that emotional connection, that heady, sizzling sensation of knowing that the man standing in front of you could be the one. That light that sparked in the heart when the rest of the soul felt dark.

She wished, she wished, she wished.

When she'd finished planting all twelve, she found a spot and planted the calla lily bulbs. In loose soil, as instructed. She brushed dirt off her knee pads and began to return things to her garden tote. When she had everything packed up, she looked at her plot. "I'll be back in a couple of days to check on all of you."

A breeze rustled through the plot, making it look like the seedlings were waving at her.

She made sure the footlocker was locked, and the rusted chair was tucked behind it, then hoisted the garden tote on her shoulder and started out. On her way to the main gates, a shadow swept past her peripheral vision and she turned her head, trying to catch it, always expecting Grandpa. He wasn't there, of course; he never was—but her gaze landed on some beautiful tomatoes. She halted.

Those were awe-inspiring tomatoes in Plot Seven. The closest thing she'd seen to the tomatoes in Grandpa's celestial garden. She shivered—she was almost convinced that Grandpa had sent those tomatoes to remind her, to remind her that she could do this. She could grow this garden.

She stepped into Plot Seven. The tomatoes weren't as big or as perfect as Grandpa's, but they were ripe. She touched one, her fingers brushing against the firm, fireplug-red skin.

"Get out of there!" She heard a shout and something hit Nora square in the back, then fell with a dull *thud*. She whipped around and looked down to see a broken clump of dried clay at her feet. Someone had thrown clay at her.

That someone was Catherine Henry, star of the stage. She was standing beside her wheelchair looking murderous. "What in the hell do you think you're doing? Do you think that's any way to fit into this group?" She swept her arm to indicate the community garden.

Nora looked around them—several of the other gardeners had turned toward the commotion.

"Don't you *want* to fit in?"

That question sank its talons into Nora. *Yes.* She wanted to fit in. All she had ever wanted in her entire life was to fit in. She glanced down at the tomato she'd come so close to pulling from the vine, like she was entitled to it. Just like David November would have done. She looked back at Catherine. "Yes, I want to fit in here more than you know."

"You damn sure don't act like it," Catherine said. "That's the worst offense you could commit, taking from another plot without permission. I can't believe you even tried."

"Me either," Nora said. "I'm usually a big rule follower." *Understatement.* "But they're amazing, and I—"

"He's been working hard on this plot, long hours, and you think you can waltz in here and take one."

"I wasn't thinking," Nora said. "They looked . . ." *Like Grandpa's tomatoes in the sky? Good grief.* She pressed her fingertips to her temple. She imagined someone else's grandpa working in this plot, taking excellent care of his plants, growing killer tomatoes and boasting about them to his friends. Hell, this grandpa had probably planted pennies here too. "I'm so sorry. I don't know what came over me."

"Just . . . keep your hands to yourself," Catherine warned her. She sat heavily in her chair and heel-toed back to where Walter was pruning the Venus flytraps. Nora could still hear Catherine over the breeze. "You wouldn't believe . . . That little chit . . ."

Nora turned and walked out of the community garden. All her buoyant feelings were sunk by the shame that seemed to live like a permafrost on her soul. Would it ever melt? What would it take?

She shook her head as she put her things in her car. Speaking of shame . . . she couldn't get all woozy now. She had that damn Sunday dinner tonight.

Chapter 21

N*ora had a new outfit from a little boutique where the* salesgirl guaranteed she would look bohemian chic. Nora wasn't sure that was the aesthetic she was going for, but it sounded fun and different. In the Before, she dressed for these dinners like she was headed to a funeral. In the After, she wanted a completely different vibe. Something that made her feel joyful. *"It's in the little things,"* Grandpa had said.

Her outfit was mostly pink silk, with a filmy, blousy top that featured full-length, off-the-shoulder sleeves. The skirt was a slim-fitting brocade made from different fabric designs and colors, almost as if someone had gone into the remnants bin and created it from scraps of cloth. It was all very *I Dream of Jeannie*, and Nora loved it.

She added some dangly gold loop earrings and a small pink bag she'd picked up at the thrift store. She put the finishing touches on her makeup—the blue eye shadow was a definite first—and headed for her parents' house.

Her parents had bought their mansion after a successful suit against Amtrak. A train had derailed the day before Thanksgiving and four people had died; the suit November and Sons won had made her father rich.

"Or so he claims," Lacey had once muttered ominously under her breath. *"They could be up to their eyeballs in debt for all we know."*

The ten-thousand-square-foot house had more baths than bedrooms and a room with an en suite bathroom for Sharon, the housekeeper, next to the kitchen. Tonight, the Novembers had arranged for valet parking, borrowing a neighbor's ridiculously long private drive for the occasion.

Sharon answered the door in her formal uniform. She was holding a silver tray featuring a selection of wines in crystal goblets. Her untamed eyebrows rose nearly to her graying hairline as she took in Nora's outfit.

"Hi, Sharon."

Her mother swanned up behind Sharon, a cocktail in hand, all smiles. She was wearing a white Chanel dress—classic, simple, and boring. She was about to speak . . . but then she noticed Nora's clothing and her smile faded. "What in the world? Are you trying to embarrass us?"

"No. I love it. It's different. Artistic."

Roberta sighed. "Oh, honey. Why can't you just act normal? It's been weeks now since the accident—can you really not shake it off?"

And there it was, the crux of the problem. All her life Nora had wanted a relationship with her mom that went deeper than appearances, but she never could seem to get there. Wasn't a mother's love supposed to be unconditional? But Nora upset her mother in every conceivable way, was unable to be tolerated, was made to feel contemptible for not fitting the ideal her mother wanted for her.

Tonight, however, she felt righteously indignant that she had to work so hard for her mother's love.

A little colony of buzzing bees began to wake in her chest. This house, and her mother's reproachful expression, was firmly in the oppressive Before, where Nora no longer resided nor had any desire to be.

"All I'm saying is that you didn't dress like this before the accident, so I can't help but think you're trying to make some point."

How had she tolerated this treatment for so long? She was a grown woman; she ought to be able to wear what she liked. "The only point I'm trying to make is that I like color and a different look from you."

"Here we go," her mother said with a slight roll of her eyes. "Why won't you let me send over my stylist to help? She's a genius when it comes to hiding hips."

"I'm good," Nora said curtly.

"Wine, Miss Nora?" Sharon asked, practiced in the art of heading off a family argument.

"Thank you." Nora picked up a glass of wine and walked away from her judgmental mother. She set the wine on the first table she came to, knowing it would soon be whisked away.

One look around and she could see that Important People packed the living room, all of them holding wine goblets or cocktail glasses. She spotted Lacey speaking to an unfamiliar man. She walked over to say hello.

"Hey, there you are!" Lacey said brightly. "You remember Ted Norgren?"

Not even vaguely. "Hi, Ted."

"Glad you're back to health, Nora. I'm going to get a refill." He did a little tick-tock with his empty glass and sauntered away.

"Who was that?" Nora asked.

"No idea. Not that it matters." Lacey was dressed appropriately in a dark tailored suit. She always wore tailored suits to these dinners—it was her concession for refusing to ever wear a dress. "Look at you," she said, taking in Nora's clothing. "So subdued!"

"It's called bohemian chic and Mom hates it."

"Well, sure. It's splashy and draws attention to you, and you know Dad's supposed to have all the air in the room."

Nora would have laughed, but they both knew it was not a joke, and it made Nora feel even angrier.

"There she is. Nora, darling, let me introduce you," Roberta November's voice trilled.

"Uh-oh," Lacey muttered. "Incoming."

Nora braced herself and turned. Her mother was clinging to another unfamiliar man's arm. "This is Trystan Russell. He's one of the VPs at Dell, and he's considering a run for agriculture commissioner."

Nora forced a smile. "Pleasure to meet you."

"You two have something in common," her mother chirped. "You both attended Rice University."

Nora looked at him with renewed interest. "You're an Owl?"

"Yep." Trystan was checking out her outfit, and a lopsided smile turned up one corner of his mouth. His phone rang and he glanced at the screen. "I'm sorry, I really need to get this." He held up one finger and stepped away from them.

"What an ass," Lacey whispered loudly. "He didn't even speak to me."

"He didn't actually speak to me either," Nora pointed out.

"Because he was so confused by your clown outfit," her mother complained. "Lacey, Claudia Wainwright is driving me insane. Go talk to her."

"About what?"

"I don't know—use some of those brains we paid a fortune to educate." Her mother tugged Nora's arm and made her walk with her. "You need to make a point of saying hello to everyone so they can see that you're fine."

Nora snorted. "I don't care if—"

"Nora, please," her mother said curtly. "Don't make a scene."

Good Lord, how she hated this. All she wanted was to be who she was, not the person her mother wanted her to pretend to be. But Nora dutifully carried on. She knew her part—she was to say a polite hello to all the Important People. Hardly any of them were actual friends of the family (did the family have actual friends?), but all of them had something to offer. Or exploit. She greeted people whose names she didn't catch or didn't remember, agreed that yes, the weather was finally warm, and no, she hadn't had a chance to see any of the bands during the SXSW Music Festival. This was not the new her—this was the ghost of Nora, performing her role.

Two servers dressed in ubiquitous black pants and white shirts moved through with cocktails and single-bite appetizers. Her mother picked one cocktail off the tray and handed it to Nora. Nora turned and handed it to another server.

Her mom's tennis partner, Patti Michaels, was excited to tell Nora that her son, Kellen, was heading up the commodities department in some Wall Street firm now. Nora was nodding along to the news when she felt her father enter the room. She didn't see him, but she could sense the distinct deadening to the air. She glanced over her shoulder, and there he was, speaking with a couple who gazed adoringly at him. He had that effect on people—he was handsome and confident, and absolutely brimming with magnetism.

Her father noticed her too. His gaze flicked over her, and his expression briefly soured before he turned back to his guests.

This room suddenly felt too warm, too crowded, too suffocating. The Before was squeezing the breath from her.

And if there was any hope of escape, her mother dashed it by pulling Nora away from Patti and back around to Trystan.

Trystan asked what her plans were now that she was home. She briefly debated explaining that she was busy creating her After, but said simply, "Oh, pursuing new interests. I'm thinking of taking one of those painting classes."

"A painting class," he repeated slowly. "What . . . you mean one of those paint-by-number things?"

"I don't think numbers are involved. But snacks and wine are." She chuckled.

He glanced away, disinterested. "I think my mom did one of those with her book club. It's for women, right?"

Sexist Puritan. "Actually, they're for anyone who has an interest in art." She silently dared him to say something derogatory about women or painting—she was ready. She had so much rage bubbling in her that she was itching for a reason to lop off his head.

Trystan wasn't a fool, apparently. He said, "Well . . . enjoy." And his gaze went back to his phone.

Whatever. She had more in common with the kid from the cooking class than this guy.

She made another circuit of the room, avoiding conversation, but was intercepted by her mother once again, and this time she looked furious.

"What?" Nora asked.

Her mom glanced around to make sure no one was close enough to hear. "Do you think you're funny?"

"Sometimes," Nora admitted.

"Did you really tell Trystan you're going to a paint-by-numbers class?"

Nora was so surprised, she laughed. "Did he tell on me?"

"For God's sake, Nora. That man is a great catch. Could you just maybe act like a normal young woman?"

Nora's brain was suddenly filled with flashes of memory from her childhood and the many times she'd been made to feel too ugly, too awkward to be loved. "Could you stop asking me to be normal, Mom? I *am* normal."

Her mother snorted her exasperation. "You know what I mean."

"Yeah, I know. You want me to be the version of me you wish I was. But I'm not her, Mom. I never have been, although for some weird reason, I damn sure tried. But I'm not trying to fit into your mold anymore, okay? I'm going to be me now. The *real* me. Take it or leave it."

Her mother's mouth gaped open with shock. "How dare you speak to me that way. And what are you talking about? There is no mold. I love you, Nora! All I ever do is work hard to help you be the best that you can be."

Nora's rage soared so high that she felt lightheaded. It was sheer arrogance that her mother could believe she knew better than Nora what was best for her. A lifetime of secret grievances and hurts began to gnaw away at her. "That's my point—you don't love me; you love your version of me. Don't help me, Mom. I've got this."

Her mother looked thunderstruck. Nora expected fat pinot grigio tears to spill at any moment, but her mother suddenly caught her elbow and squeezed hard as she pulled her close. "You haven't *got* anything, Nora—you never have. Stop this 'I'm so different' charade before you ruin the evening." With that, she let go and walked away.

Nora's heart was pounding. She felt ill with fury, ill with grief. Not for her mother but for herself. For the ghost of Nora. What a sad life that poor woman had led.

Lacey caught her eye, looking a little panicked, and gestured Nora toward the dining room along with everyone else. She resentfully followed the herd.

The dining room had a view of the hills and river below. David November directed the seating, because something as simple as suggesting who sat where gave him power, and he never missed an opportunity to wield it. Tonight, there were sixteen of them seated around the dining room table.

As beautiful and stylish as this room was, it made Nora sad. She remembered so many wretched holiday dinners here, especially when Gus's parents had been alive. She could picture her father making his way through half a bottle of scotch as he belittled everyone around him. Her mother desperate to keep the peace by urging everyone to conform. One Christmas Eve, her dad and Gus's dad had such a horrific argument that he'd thrown the whole family out. With a roar of angry vitriol, he'd called his sister-in-law a bitch and Gus's father a douche.

She'd thought that was it, that she'd never see Gus again. But, as was so often the case where her dad was concerned, after a week or so it was as if the fight had never happened. She and Gus were allowed to go for ice cream again. The four adults went out to dinner.

Those nerve-racking dinners had taught the ghost of Nora her place. She'd felt small and buried under the weight of being inconsequential. And even now that she was an adult, the little bees of anxiety that seemed to have permanently lodged in her chest woke up from their nap and started sniffing around as she took her seat.

She was seated next to Mr. Donaldson, who was hard of hearing but whose deep pockets for her father's End SIDS foundation made up for that flaw. To her right was Mason Livingston, who had recently been made partner at November and Sons. Like most people at the firm, he had no use for Nora and kept his attention on guests at her father's end of the table. Mason's wife, wearing a shimmering blue dress, sat across from him. She was blonde and pretty, and she kept looking down the table at Nora's dad with a sultry little smile on her lips. Did no one else see this?

The servers stood against the wall, each of them holding two salad plates, and at her mother's nod, they moved to place the salads before the guests with the precision of a royal palace service. A shadow slipped by Nora's peripheral vision when a server put a Caesar salad in front of her. The same boring salad they had every Sunday.

"Nora?"

She glanced up—Claudia Wainwright was seated across from her. She was smiling, amazingly, given how tight the skin was on her resurfaced face. She hadn't yet picked up a fork. "I've been thinking a lot about you. How are you feeling after your terrible accident?"

"Oh." Nora sat up a little straighter. "Pretty good, thanks. I have a couple of memory problems, but I'm good."

"Your mother said you were clinically *dead.*" Claudia whispered that word as if it were a curse word.

"I was. For several minutes."

"It's a miracle! What happened?"

"Claudia, I already told you. It was a surfing accident," her mother interjected. "They never should have let her try to surf on that beach. I'm sure Nora doesn't want to relive the whole terrible ordeal again."

"I don't mind," Nora said. "Unfortunately, I don't remember much of it."

"That's probably best," Claudia said. She eased back and picked up her fork.

Nora had no appetite for this boring salad and left her fork on the table.

At the end of the table, her father was talking about the upcoming elections and how important it was to keep people hostile to Wall Street out of office. Nora's untouched salad was removed and her wineglass refreshed, even though she hadn't taken a sip. Trystan, seated next to Lacey, was talking about something that required the extensive use of his hands. Mason's wife—what was her name?—kept smiling at Nora's dad. The light caught Mr. Donaldson's heavy gold and crystal watch and created a spark.

She felt as if something were sitting on her chest. She desperately needed some air.

As the main course was served, a man emerged from the kitchen and introduced himself as Chef Adnan. He said they would be dining on Dover sole, zucchini squash blossoms, and a fennel mousseline.

"Chef Adnan recently cooked for Sandra Bullock," her mother proudly announced.

Lacey met Nora's gaze and rolled her eyes.

Nora was studying the fish before her when Claudia Wainwright leaned over her plate again. "Nora? I'm so sorry if I made you feel uncomfortable."

Did she look uncomfortable? "Not at all."

"I don't know how someone comes back from that, you know? It must have been such a profound experience."

"It truly was."

"I had an uncle who had a near-death experience. Afterward, he abandoned his medical practice and moved to New Mexico to live in a yurt."

"Oh my God," Trystan said with a snort. He was listening. So was Lacey.

"I understand," Nora said. "I don't mean the yurt part, but the need for change. For me, things that had seemed unimportant before the accident are so important now. Mostly things I regretted not doing."

"Really?" Claudia Wainwright asked excitedly. "Like what?"

"Like . . . painting," she said, looking at Trystan. "I always wanted to learn to paint, but never attempted it. So I've signed up for a painting class. And I've taken over my grandfather's garden plot. Oh, and I'm finally learning how to cook." A nervous laugh escaped her. "I don't know, but I have this strong sense of urgency now to do all the things I wanted to do but never got around to."

"Don't forget the corner store guy, Nora," Lacey reminded her.

"What's that?" her father asked.

"You probably don't remember, Dad," Nora said. Although it was unclear to her why he wouldn't—it had been kind of a big deal in her life. "Several months ago I was in a corner store when a man tried to rob it. He held me and two other customers hostage."

There were audible gasps from around the room. She had everyone's attention now.

"What does that have to do with your accident?" her father asked with undisguised impatience.

"Nothing, really. But one of the other hostages and I had this . . . insane connection." She unthinkingly smiled as she recalled it. "I want to find him and thank him for getting me through that terrible night."

Her father signaled a server to top off the wineglasses. "You've always had a fanciful imagination, Nora. You're in a great position with the firm, in an office with one hundred and fifty lawyers, with some very important cases on your desk. And yet here you are, entertaining a fantasy of finding some bystander from a robbery?" He chuckled.

The bees in Nora got into attack formation. Instead of mentally curling into a ball as she would have done in the Before, she surprised herself by smiling down the table at her father. "Exactly right, Dad. I am entertaining that fantasy."

The awkward silence that followed assured her that everyone in this dining room could feel the tension rising from her parents like smoke signals.

Nora looked at her plate. She could feel her dad's eyes burning through her. She was not being the model obedient daughter, and he didn't like it. Well, she didn't care. *Put that in your uncle's NDE pipe and smoke it, Claudia.*

"I posted about him on a missed connections site," she announced, because now that she'd crossed the line, she was going all in. "And I posted it on some other social media sites too."

"That is so awesome," Lacey said at the same time her mother hissed, "You did what?"

"What a wonderful idea," Claudia Wainwright chimed in.

"Unfortunately, I can't remember that night as clearly as I would like. But I do remember it was raining heavily—downtown flooded. And it was the night of some protests."

"I remember that," Trystan said.

"Your feel-good project sounds delightful, but perhaps we might turn the conversation to something else," her father announced grandly from his end of the table. "Roberta?"

"Nora," her mother cooed obediently. "I don't think our guests really want to hear about this."

"I do," Claudia said. "I'm fascinated. Aren't you, Roberta?"

"It's just that she's been through so much, and as her mother, I would prefer Nora get on with her normal life."

Which was the last place Nora wanted to be. She smiled across the table at Claudia. "I'll keep you posted."

"Never mind all that," her mother said. "I have an announcement to make!" She picked up her wineglass and held it up, smiling down the table at her husband. "David has received some wonderful news. He is to be honored with the American Philanthropy Foundation's top award for all his work to end SIDS."

Nora turned her attention to her meal, and her father turned attention back to himself, accepting the congratulations from around the table, talking about his passion for understanding SIDS, saying that even after thirty years, the loss of a child was keen and he couldn't bear for it to happen to another parent.

There was no more inappropriate talk from Nora November, no sir. In fact, her parents' vexation with her was so great that neither one tried to stop her when she claimed another engagement after dinner. Her father didn't acknowledge her exit. Her mother whispered hotly that they would speak later.

"Okey dokey," Nora said as she walked out into the spring night air, because the new Nora understood they wouldn't really speak later, and she was fine with that.

Once she was outside of that stifling house, she felt great. Like she'd picked up a heavy gauntlet and could run with it.

Chapter 22

Jack

M*r. Jaisal Hamdy's mother visited him every day in* the last week of his life. The day before he died, he told Jack she was taking him somewhere. He seemed excited. Interested. His eyes were shining with a different sort of light than Jack had seen in the last few days.

"That's awesome," Jack said.

"Yeah," Faisal croaked. He looked like a grinning skeleton, his teeth starkly white against his gray pallor and grayer hair. When he'd first come into hospice, he'd been tormented by the cancer that had eaten away at him, as well as all the things he'd left undone. But once his mother started visiting, that all changed. He seemed at peace. He seemed ready.

Jack never saw Faisal's mother, of course, because she'd died several years ago. She'd come back across the divide to escort her son to wherever they were going, and sometime between Jack's last shift and today, away they'd gone.

It truly was incredible how the dying generally found their peace with it. Sandra said that was the only reason she'd been able to do this job all these years. *"If they were going any other way,*

I don't think I could handle it. Gives me hope my husband will be there when it's my time."

Jack hoped his mother would be there when it was his time too. It had been more than fifteen years.

Before she got sick, she used to take him to Lake Austin on summer afternoons. They would lie on the grass and eat bologna sandwiches she'd made from the box she got at the local food pantry. Jack would ask about his dad, and she would say he was the captain of a ship. They'd make boats from twigs and leaves and grass and push them into the water. *"Bye, Dad,"* he'd say.

If he had a chance to meet his mom again, he'd ask who his dad was.

He'd never had any sort of father figure. No grandfather, no uncle, no male acquaintance who ever stuck around long. Jack had sometimes imagined he'd have three kids, just in case something happened to him. There was nothing lonelier than being an only child and losing your only parent at the age of fifteen.

But he was beginning to doubt he'd ever find his life partner. He'd gone on a date last week, one Tracy had set up for him. Lucinda was pretty, and she had a good job at Google. He liked her—she was personable. But there was something that didn't quite click for him. She didn't laugh at the same things he laughed at.

Just for grins, he'd asked Lucinda what her biggest childhood fear had been.

"Hmm . . . I guess getting separated from my parents. Isn't that every kid's nightmare? What was yours?"

"Spontaneous combustion," he said.

She frowned. *"That's not real."*

She didn't get the game, and maybe he was being finicky, but there was no chemistry. He couldn't have babies with someone who didn't understand the childhood fear of spontaneous combustion.

He was thinking about Faisal Hamdy when he got to the Goodfellow Community Garden. Catherine was incensed by an attempt at tomato thievery—she rolled over to him on hot wheels and without preamble launched into her account of the event. "Plot Nine was helping herself! She was standing right where you are now with her fingers on a tomato. I stopped her. I told her we don't do that around here." Honestly, he never would have noticed if a tomato was missing—he was going to have a bucket of them as it was.

"Plot Nine?" He had to think a minute. "The lady with the twins?"

"That's Plot Two. Her husband is having an affair, by the way. You can take that to the bank."

Jack looked curiously at Catherine. "She told you that?"

"She didn't have to tell me anything. That man is always away on 'business trips,'" she said, making air quotes. "He missed the twins' birthday party too. Anyway, this isn't about them; it's about someone with the gall to steal."

Jack looked across the garden to Plot Nine. It didn't look quite as ragged as it had, and it was clear the new person had put in some work. It wasn't exactly blooming, however.

"You should put up a sign that says 'No picking allowed.' Once that kind of thing starts, where does it end?"

Jack was not putting up a sign.

"You're coming to the theater today, aren't you?" Catherine's tone had changed from angry to excited. "Big meeting, and I'm going to need some backup. Meredith thinks we can bake sale our way out of this."

Meredith thought a lot of things Catherine didn't agree with, and the fact that Jack even knew that surprised him. He was in the thick of it, wasn't he? Last week he'd told Byron and Clark he would have to skip a trip to a new club that had just opened.

"What? You don't want to miss this. I've got a reserved table, thanks to my boss," Clark had said.

Jack was tempted. *"I can't, sorry. I promised Catherine and the crew I'd help out that night."*

Byron stared at Jack like he had a cat on his head. "Are you, like, dating her?"

Jack had laughed. *"She's seventy-six, Byron."* Frankly, he wasn't sure if Byron thought he was dating her anyway.

"I'll be there," he assured Catherine. "Just have to do some work here first."

"Catherine! Let's go," Walter was calling from their plot.

"He's so snippy," Catherine said. She stood up from her wheelchair and grabbed the handles. "See you later."

Jack watched her push the chair back to their plot. He waved to Walter, who waved back. He was discovering that geriatric thespians were a big-time commitment. Between repairs, set construction, learning the two dance routines he guessed he'd agreed to do, and breaking up arguments between Meredith and Catherine . . . it was a lot.

When he finished what he'd come to do, he looked again at Plot Nine. He walked over to have a closer look.

The soil had been turned, which was good, and most of the weeds were gone. But there were a couple of leggy plants in the back that looked like bindweed. Interestingly, the bindweed looked pruned. Next to that were some cucumber vines that had crept over from Plot Eight. And there was a row of neatly planted tomato seedlings. He thought it might be too late in the season to plant them, but A for effort.

He noticed a boot print in the soil. He imagined an older woman in a utility apron with big pockets and a beat-up sun hat. He'd seen a couple of that type in here.

He walked back to his plot and opened his footlocker, rummaging around until he found a used plastic baggie. He dumped some of Mr. Hauser's supersecret tomato food into it. Next, he opened his backpack and took out a small notebook and a pen and jotted down a note:

My friend Ron Hauser gifted me with a secret formula to growing tomatoes. I have extra and thought you might like some too. Good luck with your seedlings. And help yourself to a tomato in Plot Seven anytime.

He left the baggie on top of the Plot Nine footlocker and anchored it with some rocks.

******

The gang was all present at the theater. Meredith and Doralee had mounted an effort to hook new seat cushions, but so far they had covered only ten of three hundred. At this rate, Jack calculated it would take them about four years to finish.

When the thespians noticed him approaching the stage, they shouted, "Jack!" in unison. It was like coming home at Christmas to a room full of grandparents.

Jerry, the dance instructor, was the first to reach him. "So glad someone with sense has arrived."

Doralee put out her hand to stop Jack from advancing any farther down the aisle. She was in charge of costumes. "What are you, a 34, or maybe 36?"

"Doralee, that can wait," Catherine said.

"Can it wait, though? We haven't as much time as you think."

"Let him pass," said Walter. He was sitting on the edge of the stage, a tool belt beside him. Walter had been a decorated set designer, Jack had been told, but Jack had never seen him do any actual set construction—generally he left that to Jack, Mr. Carlton, and Martin. Walter was the de facto director of this entire project. "We were about to review the chores for the day," Walter informed him. "But true to form, Annabeth claims to have a conflict."

"What do you mean, 'true to form'?" Annabeth demanded.

"I mean, every weekend when we try to tackle some tasks, you're indisposed."

"I can't help it that I have a more interesting life than any of you."

Jack took a seat next to Martin, who was married to Mary. Martin handed him a red Solo cup. The cups, and their contents, were standard fare at these meetings. Mary picked up a shaker, opened the top, and poured something into Jack's cup. The smell of alcohol wafted up; they liked their drinks strong.

Walter was still arguing with Annabeth, who was trying to convince him that she'd had this "thing" scheduled for weeks. Walter wanted to know what "thing."

"At the . . . Oh, I can't remember the name of the place. You know, in Montopolis. Everyone knows what I'm talking about."

"I don't," said Catherine. "If it's not within six blocks of here, I don't know it."

"What's that like, Cat, to be a shut-in?" Annabeth asked, and Meredith laughed too loud and too long.

"Okay, okay, let's get back to business," Walter said gruffly. "Let's start with the chore list." He held up a honey-do list of repairs. The thespians raised a hand if they thought they could tackle one. Some of them had their hands shouted down, given past performances with similar tasks. The shaker of booze kept going around. At one point they were derailed from the agenda by a lively debate about performances that had been robbed of Tony Awards, stretching back to nearly the Pleistocene era.

Whatever the boozy concoction was, it was excellent.

When the chores were finally divvied up, Jack laughed at something Catherine said, which, it turned out, was a line from a performance. She made Walter haul her up onto the stage and proceeded to reenact the entire scene, everyone laughing, Jack included.

In the end, when Walter asked if there were any comments, Jack suggested they adopt a no-booze rule for meetings so they could make some progress. He was roundly booed.

It remained to be seen if this group could pull off the impossible, but in the meantime, Jack was having a great time.

Chapter 23

That *feeling of liberation Nora had felt leaving her* parents' house Sunday evening did not follow her into Monday morning. She entered the office like a golem slogging into the Before.

She was desperate to move on from her job, but her medical bills were piling up—she'd received one for "pulmonary services" that was eleven thousand dollars, of which her insurance had agreed to pay five. Until she found another job, she had to face the fact that real-world constraints meant she was stuck. Worse, the deposition for the bus case loomed, adding to her sense of urgency to find another job before she had to litigate it.

At the initial client meeting for the case, one of the kids had sat on the edge of the conference table as if he paid the bills in their offices, his thumbs moving over his phone. He was trim and cocky, like his parents. Nora's dad joked about how hard it was to find decent charters these days, and the kid had said, without a breath of knowledge or empathy or culpability, without even looking up from his phone, "He's probably illegal. You should look into that too."

That was the world she inhabited as a November—a privileged, can't-touch-this world where the less fortunate were looked upon with disdain, or worse, indifference. She wanted no part of it.

She perfected her procrastination each morning by reading the comments on her social media search for the corner store guy. The trolls came out at night, anonymous posters who declared her stupid in not-very-nice terms. Sometimes people had an idea of where she should look—usually something she'd already thought of, but she appreciated the attempt to help. Mostly, people saw her posts as an opportunity to tell their meet-cute story. Still, the shares were growing.

Her favorite part of the day was stopping at the garden on the way to work. On Monday, she intended it to be a quick stop, but she found the tomato food and the note left for her by the old man in Plot Seven. The find charmed her; she left a note thanking him and gifted an overgrown cucumber she'd found lurking in the back of her plot. She'd taken care to write in clear block letters like she used to do for Grandpa, so that he'd have no trouble deciphering her handwriting. She wrote that she now had every confidence her tomatoes would grow to be big and beautiful, thanks to his gift of supersecret food.

But her tomato plants were worrying her. They weren't growing, and the tiny leaves were beginning to brown around the edges. She watered them until she feared the Goodfellow Community Garden board would send her a bill.

By midweek, they had not improved, even after the application of the tomato food. She snapped some pictures of the plants for Nick, as well as the empty space where she'd planted the calla lilies. Nick said she couldn't drown them, so she watered them more—but she had to be doing something wrong.

She dragged the hose back to the spigot, turned off the water, then noticed Catherine standing in the middle of the path, as still as a statue, her arms akimbo, staring at a clump of beautiful rhododendrons. Walter, her constant companion, was nowhere to be seen.

There was something off about the way Catherine was standing, like she wasn't really there. A stroke, maybe? Nora strode down the crushed granite path toward Catherine.

Catherine turned when she heard Nora's approach. "Oh," she said. "It's you."

So, no stroke, apparently. "And a jolly good afternoon to you too, Catherine. Is everything okay?"

Catherine sighed heavily. "Nothing that you would understand. I wish Jim were still here. He had a good ear. I sure miss him."

"I do too," Nora said. More than she could ever convey. "Maybe I could help?"

Catherine looked at her sharply. "Help? I don't even know if I'm talking to you yet."

"Because I wasn't here for Grandpa?" Surprisingly, Nora asked this without emotion. Nothing Catherine could say to her would make her feel worse than she already did, or would erase the image of him lying on the kitchen floor that was burned into her brain.

"Well." Catherine touched the edge of one of the rhododendrons. "You *have* put in a lot of work to make up for it. He'd be happy about that."

"Do you think so?" Nora asked hopefully. Her tomatoes had given her confidence the old heave-ho.

"Look, I know I shouldn't take it out on you," Catherine said. "I always felt like I was in control of my life, but I wasn't. Same for you, right?"

Nora flushed with the truth of that. Was she so transparent? "I'm really trying to change that."

"Well, if you figure it out, let me know, because I could use some tips."

Nora laughed. "Really? Because you seem like someone who has life by the balls, if you don't mind me saying."

One of Catherine's brows arched. "Thank you. Unfortunately, lately it feels like everything is spinning out of my control and there is nothing I can do to save it."

"Save what?"

"The theater."

"What theater?"

"The Triangle Theater. Just up the street from here."

Nora didn't know of a theater nearby and shook her head.

Catherine groaned. "Are you kidding me? Is there any arts education in schools these days? The Triangle Theater. Home to retired thespians."

As far as Nora knew, the Triangle was the name of an area in central Austin. "What happened to it?"

"Happening," Catherine said. She reiterated that Nora wouldn't understand, but then proceeded to tell her about some financial troubles that sounded dire, including a tax lien and a developer intent on throwing the retirees off the property. She said they didn't have the money to pay the arrears, but nevertheless, they were going to try to raise money by staging what Catherine called a "brilliant" production of *A Streetcar Named Desire: The Musical.*

"How big of a debt are we talking?" Nora asked.

"Oh, thousands," Catherine said. "I spoke to a lawyer and he wanted a ten-thousand-dollar retainer to help. Now, where are we going to get ten thousand dollars when we can't even pay the arrears? We're opening in a few weeks, and we still haven't sold a third of the seats."

Nora felt a shift, the seed of an idea taking root. It felt almost like kismet, like Grandpa had made her look up to see Catherine, because this was something she could do. "Who's trying to get you thrown out?"

"Some guy named Brad Sachs."

A bolt of lightning went straight through Nora—Brad Sachs had been to her parents' home on many occasions, was one of her father's closest friends. He was a shark too, just like good ol' Dad. "I'll do it," she blurted. "Pro bono."

The words were hardly out of her mouth before the ghost of Nora frantically tried to claw them back. What did she know about taxes or tax law? Nothing!

The ghost of Nora begged her to say she would *find* someone to do it pro bono, but the new Nora thought maybe this was what it was all about. *Could* she start her own practice? Well, here was a case landing in her lap. Granted, she'd offered her services pro bono and hadn't yet told Catherine she knew nothing about tax law. But she realized, as Catherine began to sputter her *ohmygods* and *areyousures* and *wecan'tpayyous*, that Grandpa had kicked this problem out of his celestial garden and right into her lap.

......

Nora was a full hour late into the office after talking with Catherine but still called out her greetings as she walked down the long row of cubicles. Yet again, she had no takers. *Assholes.*

James hopped up from his desk, striding into her office ahead of her. When she came in, he closed the door behind her.

"Hey, look at this," she said and pulled two cucumbers out of her bag.

James looked at the vegetables. Then at her. "You're, like, really into this gardening thing."

"I am."

"And you're really into a job search too."

Her smile faded. "How do you know that?"

"Because a Ms. Paula Ranstein from Maxwell and Graeber called to set up an interview. I made some assumptions. Why didn't you tell me?"

Nora gasped with elation. She had all but given up hope. "I have an interview?"

"Thursday at four. Nora, are you really doing this?"

She nodded.

"Wow. Does your dad know?"

"Not yet."

He gaped at her, shocked. "But . . . you're taking me with you, right?"

"If I can, absolutely."

"You'd better." He handed her a file. "Here are some notes on the bus case. For your meeting with Andrea to game-plan the deposition."

"You did that for me?"

"Shut up, it's my job."

"It's not your job."

"Whatever."

She smiled gratefully. "Who's out of the pool today?"

James consulted his phone. "Tamara in billing."

"She could use the money, right?"

"Definitely. She's the one whose baby has spina bifida. You have Andrea in thirty," he said, consulting his watch. "She's coming in hot. Like, literally—she gets all sweaty when she comes to ask me where you are, and then I get all sweaty."

Nora nodded.

When James left, Nora opened the file he'd prepared and began to read. The heat of disgrace climbed up her neck—this case would ruin the small family-owned-and-operated bus company. Where was the good in that? What problem did it solve? Personal injury law was supposed to protect people, not hurt them.

She felt weird, the way she'd felt in the beginning of the After, when her body didn't quite fit her skin and her thoughts felt as if they were about to go off the rails. This case had left the station, and there was nothing she could do about it—there was no way that November and Sons wouldn't move forward with it. But the idea of *her* trying the case sickened her. She wasn't the ghost of Nora anymore, wasn't trying desperately to be the lawyer her father wanted her to be. She was the new Nora, the *real* Nora. The Nora who didn't believe in cases like this and wouldn't be party to them anymore.

She pushed James's notes away from her.

She thought of the job interview she had later this week. It was the only one she'd managed out of twenty résumés thus far. She thought of Tamara in billing and how unfair life could be. She thought of Catherine and her gaggle of senior thespians who lived on Social Security without a safety net. She thought of her bills and her anemic savings (where had all her money gone?), and Lacey, and Gus, and her parents, and how cold and choppy the water had been at Surfside.

When Andrea came in, she was, predictably, all business. She had a game plan for the deposition. Andrea was a type A personality, well-suited to this type of work. She would go far. Maybe even make partner someday.

"The deposition is all yours," Nora announced.

"What do you mean, all mine?"

"I mean, I'm not going."

Andrea seemed confused. "Wait . . . what are you doing?"

Nora stood up and started putting things in her garden tote. "An excellent question, Andrea. I don't know yet, but I do know that I am not representing these clients on this case. It's a horrible, awful case—don't you think so?"

James got up from his desk and came inside. "Everything okay?"

"What does it matter what I think?" Andrea responded to Nora. "It's our job to look at the facts and make sure the full remedy afforded by law is made available to the client. That's what I think."

Nora sighed. "If only it was that simple."

Andrea helplessly watched Nora clear out her desk. "Is this because of what happened before? The thing in court? Kate told me about that."

Ugh, the wrongful death case. Nora had gotten heart-poundingly sick as she'd stood to present, and the judge had to recess court. Kate was the one who'd followed her into the bathroom and begged her to pull it together.

For the record, Nora did not pull it together that day. She had a full-on panic attack and a paramedic told her to put her head between her knees next time. Mason had to step in and take over for her.

"No. It's because I find what I do intolerable, so I am leaving this case to you. Take your shot."

"You can't do that," Andrea protested.

"I can, because I quit."

James gasped.

"No," Andrea said, violently shaking her head. "There must be a supervising attorney, Nora! I'm not a supervising attorney."

"Right." Nora scratched her shoulder. "Then I guess you'll have to reschedule until you get one."

"It's this afternoon!"

"Then you'd better make a call."

"Nora, what are you doing?" James asked frantically. "Your dad—"

"Is going to be pissed. Don't I know it." She had to gear up for that, but first things first. "Look, you guys, I'm doing what I should have done a long time ago. James, will you call Paula

Ranstein and give her my cell phone number?" She stuffed her cucumbers into her bag. Then a picture of her, Lacey, Gus, and Grandpa. It was the only picture in her office.

"This is bullshit." Andrea picked up her things and walked out of her office, headed, presumably, for David November.

"Oh my God," James whispered.

"You must think I'm crazy," Nora said.

"Nora . . . no. No. I think, in the long run, you won't survive if you don't get out of here. Just remember you promised to take me with you." He hurried out of the office.

Nora figured she had only a few moments to compose herself. Curiously, she wasn't hyperventilating or feeling panicked. A peacefulness settled on her in these last moments alone in her office. She had not a single doubt that what she was doing was the right thing. It was going to be hard, and she couldn't think of money right now or she'd lose her resolve. This was a scary, huge risk. But she had to remember she'd been given a brand-new world and a brand-new chance at life. She had to take it or lose herself completely.

When her father walked in a few minutes later, she was sitting calmly, her garden tote packed and ready to go.

He looked at her, his jaw working. He folded his arms across his chest and walked to the window to look out. He was wearing a tailored blue suit with a checked tie, and his scruff of beard was neatly trimmed. She absently wondered if maybe he really did have a girlfriend. Mason's wife, perhaps? Nothing would surprise her.

He turned from the window. "I need to know, are you having another episode?"

Why did he have to make her panic attacks sound like temper tantrums? "Nope. I'm feeling pretty good." A little buzzy, but good. Strong.

"Any sort of mental health crisis?"

Nora smiled. "No, Dad."

He moved to the conference table and settled one hip onto it. "I spoke to Andrea."

"I figured. She's good, you know. And she's put a lot of work into this case."

"I don't need you to tell me who is good on my staff," he said quietly. "My question is, why haven't you put a lot of work into it? This is your job, Nora. You're supposed to do the leading around here—not be led."

"Right." She braced her hands against her knees. "Except that I'm being led by you, Dad. I told you I had reservations about this case. I don't like that you're going to bleed that company dry just to show your friends you can do it. Those kids didn't have the kind of injuries that require a lawsuit."

"Are you a doctor now?"

"No. But I know a stubbed toe when I see it."

His exasperation was evident in the glint of his eye. "Honestly, Nora? I've had enough. I've put up with your moping, and your accident, and your stupendous lack of motivation. I don't know what issue you're having now, but I would really like you to work on being present."

Her resolve expanded into her lungs and gave her wings. "Funny you should say that. Because at this moment, I'm more present than I've ever been. My issue is that this is who I am, Dad. I'm not the Nora who inhabited this office before. I'm a completely different person now."

His gaze turned thunderous. He stood up, shifting closer to her, glaring down at her from his superior height. "You sound like a lunatic. Who do you think you're talking to? I've done everything for you. Everything! I took my father's two-bit operation and turned it into one of the largest firms in this city. I created a kingdom so that you wouldn't have to lift much more than a finger. You've had your little seaside jaunt and your time off, so now I ask that you be a November like you were raised to be and stop embarrassing us."

The force of his words, and the unmitigated disdain, stirred up the bees, causing the humming to crescendo to the point it felt a little like her father was talking to her from the other side of a glass wall. "My seaside jaunt?" She laughed bitterly.

His nostrils flared. "Get your shit together," he snapped. "And grow up. Not everything has to have some noble cause behind it. Not everything in life has to make sense to you. Do your job and stop making me look bad. I'm out of patience."

She would have been smart to leave it there, but the bees had begun to swarm, and she couldn't help herself. "You think I'm making *you* look bad? I'm listening to my conscience. I'm thinking about what we do here and how oily it is sometimes. That's what makes you look bad—not me."

"You're pathetic," he snarled. "You're weaker than I ever imagined."

She'd always suspected he couldn't abide her, but now she could feel it coming off him in waves. And although it was devastating that her father didn't like her, she was relieved that, for once, she could face it headlong. "I never should have come to work here. You wanted Nathan, and I wanted to be him for you. We both tried so hard to make that happen. But, Dad . . . Nathan is dead. I'm Nora. And I'm done here. Consider this my resignation."

Her father was uncharacteristically speechless, his mouth gaping at her like a fish seeking air. "What in the hell are you talking about? After all I've done for you? After all I've given you? Where is your gratitude?"

Gratitude. She didn't feel grateful; she felt like she was swimming against a tide, to escape a father and a twin she never knew.

Dad shifted closer, his presence bearing down on her. "You listen to me, you ungrateful little bitch," he said with such iciness that a shiver ran down her spine. She could feel herself wanting to curl into a ball, to hide, just like she had as a girl. "I don't give a damn about your conscience. I risked a lot to put you in a plum position, and this is how you repay me?"

She was shaking internally, and she hoped to high heaven that he didn't see it. "You haven't done as much for me as you think you have. Don't get me wrong—I'm beyond grateful for the education and the opportunity. But you know this work doesn't suit me. And like you said, you took a small firm and turned it into a juggernaut. Why would you want weak, pathetic me at the helm of that? Just let me go be me."

"And just who are you? A cook? A gardener?" he snarled. "This has been your problem from day one—you act like a child, and I must care for you like a child. I'm preparing to file suit against the resort so you can pay your medical bills. How does your conscience feel about that?"

Her conscience couldn't let that happen. "You can't sue them!" Her temples began to throb. "I don't want to sue them!"

"Shut up," he snapped. "Go on, go see if you can find a touchy-feely job that will pay you enough to live on. You're a selfish, entitled brat, and I'm sick of it."

In the Before, that proclamation would have put her on the floor. Nora slowly drew a breath. It was astonishing to realize she wasn't entirely cowed by his anger. He suddenly seemed like a very small man. She felt almost indifferent to the heat rolling off him. It occurred to her that for most of her life, she'd thought she was the unlovable one—but it wasn't her. It was him.

His disdain couldn't touch her right now, and that was amazing. "That's okay," she said after a moment. "Because I'm pretty sick of you too."

She picked up her tote, stepped around him, and, putting one foot in front of the other, began to leave.

"Don't walk out that door, Nora. If you go, don't come back."

Nora paused, then looked at him over her shoulder.

His expression was thunderous. "You have no clue how much you will live to regret this."

"I'm pretty sure I won't," she said confidently and walked out.

Her breath had deserted her. Her heart was racing as she anticipated the moment he would grab her hair and yank her back like he had when she was a teen. But he didn't. And Nora kept walking, feeling freer and more buoyant with each step.

Chapter 24

T*he problem with bursts of confidence, Nora discovered,* was that they were like a bungee jumping cord. There is a brief but powerful swell of certainty that the bungee cord will hold you when you step off the bridge or the crane. But in the next breath, as you hurtle toward a spectacular splat, you sincerely hope your confidence wasn't misplaced.

By the time Nora walked into her apartment, she was anticipating a full splat or, at the very least, a monstrous panic attack. She was terrified of what she'd just done. She couldn't just change overnight. But neither could she stay in that toxic job. She dropped down onto the used IKEA couch she'd gotten off the building bulletin board and covered her face with her hands. She was going to either vomit or laugh hysterically—her mind hadn't settled on which way to go.

"Okay. All right," she breathed. "No crying. Grandpa said to believe in yourself." She thought back to the eighth grade, when she'd tried out for the lead part in the school play. She'd practiced for it every day—Grandpa would swing by the house to help her, playing the other parts in the script. On the day she found out she didn't get the part, she'd called Grandpa in tears. He'd come straightaway, making the forty-five-minute drive from the ranch to pick her up and take her for ice cream. On the way, she tearfully told him she'd sucked at the audition.

"That's a disappointment, to be sure," he'd said after he'd gotten her some ice cream. He stroked her head as she toyed with her cup. *"Sometimes other people don't believe in you. That's why it's so important for you to believe in yourself, Nora. You did the absolute best you could, but you didn't persuade them this time. That's okay—you'll persuade them the next time. I have every faith in you—you can be whatever you want to be if you believe you can. And you don't suck at anything. You're pretty damn near perfect."*

She smiled at the memory. Okay. She'd believe in herself. And grow her garden. She dug her reverse bucket list out of her garden tote. She smoothed the paper and ran her fingers over the eight items on her list to remind herself that quitting her job wasn't the end of the world—it was the beginning.

Reverse Bucket List (in no particular order):
Learn to cook
Grandpa's garden
Corner store guy (??)
Make art
Be a better sister to Lacey
Support Gus
Play basketball
Get a new job

Her breathing calmed. She was making progress. She'd started her cooking class, an important first step. And while she hadn't shown much talent, she was trying. She'd never promised herself she'd be an excellent cook (even if that certainly had been the hope).

She'd cleaned out Grandpa's garden and started planting new, and sure, the tomato plants weren't shooting up like she thought they would, but she'd found Nick, and she had to believe something would grow.

She was supporting Gus, at least as much as he would let her, and she'd taken a step toward making art by signing them up for their first paint class, which, okay, was not a perfect plan, but she had to start somewhere.

Lacey. She was working on being a better sister, but she had a long way to go. She'd called Lacey yesterday, and it had rolled to voice mail. Still, Nora had a plan. She was going to make dinner for her and prepare the garlic sauce she'd learned to make in cooking class. Baby steps.

New job? Well, she'd quit the horrible one and she had a job interview this week. She had yet to play basketball, but she had ordered sneakers and a ball online and they'd shown up yesterday.

And no one could say she hadn't tried to find the corner store guy.

Speaking of which . . . she picked up her laptop and navigated to her main post about him to check for new activity. The views and shares were still growing, but there were only a couple of new comments. One said her post sounded like a scam and everyone should be careful. Another one suggested that she post a place and time for a meet-up.

She'd thought about that idea before but had dismissed it, afraid of the trolls who might show up. But she was running out of options, and besides, she'd allowed fear to rule her for thirty-one years. If she could quit her job, she could try a meet-up. What did she really have to lose?

Maybe don't think about that right now. Nothing could instill fear quite like making a list of all the things she stood to lose.

She leaned back and closed her eyes, and when she did, she was transported again to that night at the corner store.

They'd been waiting for hours for the police to take their statements, watching the rain come down and talking. Nora could still picture him so clearly, how his eyes shimmered in the fluorescent light of the store. How warmly he'd smiled when he said he'd never met anyone quite like her. How secure she'd felt with him, unapologetically herself. She'd felt interesting. She'd felt wanted. She'd felt like a different person.

When the detectives finally arrived at the tail end of the storm, they'd taken Juanita's statement first, sitting her down in the single red plastic booth near the desiccated weenies, which had continued their slow turns on the warming rack all night.

When they finished with Juanita, a burly policeman came for Nora. *"Okay, young lady, you're next."*

She followed the policeman back to the red plastic booth. A man in shirtsleeves with a badge and a gun at his waist was gripping a Styrofoam cup of coffee. He invited Nora to sit, then asked her a few questions. No, she didn't see Darth come in. No, he didn't threaten her. No, he didn't point the gun *at* her, exactly, more like in the vicinity of her. What was she doing in the store? She glanced to her right and her gaze fell on a damp, wilted Cobb salad. *"What does anyone do at a corner store?"* she'd asked. She was there to pick up a few things.

When she was done, the plainclothes policeman said she was free to go. He said someone would be in touch if they needed more information. She waited at the front of the store near the lottery tickets case until the corner store guy finished his interview.

He smiled like he'd hoped she'd be there. It was the strangest thing—she'd just been through such a harrowing experience that would have undone her on any other day. But she felt great. Fizzy with exhaustion but buoyant. This man, this handsome, charming man, liked her. She was convinced she was feeling true kismet.

It was four o'clock in the morning—Nora had entered this store shortly after six the previous evening.

"Aren't you going to offer us something?" the guy asked the clerk.

"Like what?"

"Like, I don't know . . . a sandwich?"

"What . . . for free?" the clerk asked, his tone relaying his clear opposition to the idea.

Nora and the corner store guy looked at each other and laughed. Then they linked arms and walked outside. They stood on the sidewalk in the freezing temps, exhausted and hungry, mist dampening their hair and clothes, giddy with mutual attraction.

He pulled his scarf up around his nose. Then he pulled Nora's collar tighter around her neck. "I don't think we discussed our jobs."

"Or hobbies."

"Or favorite travel destinations."

"Or our favorite colors. How did we miss that? We literally started by listing our favorite Starbursts—seems color would naturally roll right out of that."

"Not knowing your favorite color may be my biggest regret," he said, his smile charmingly lopsided. "Maybe we should get together for a drink to cover all the bases."

"I don't think we have any other choice," Nora said.

They stood a moment more. He touched her cheek and said, "So . . . I guess this is hello?"

She'd laughed with happy relief. She grabbed a handful of his scarf and pulled his head down. He slid his hands into her hair, which had long since come out of its proper bun, and kissed her. Or she kissed him. They kissed like two people who had been looking for each other for a very long time. They kissed until they were soaked through, and then he said it was the most outstanding first date he'd ever had, and she said that was the first time she'd ever kissed a guy on the first date.

They traded phone numbers. He wrote his on her hand. She wrote hers on the back of a receipt. They said good night, and he went south and she went north.

She looked back once, and he was looking back at her. "My favorite color is red!" he shouted.

"Green!" she shouted back.

Christmas colors, which seemed fitting, because she felt sparkly and excited and full of breathless anticipation.

But then she'd gone home and fallen into a deep sleep, and when she awoke, the darkness had already started to creep in. Her depression was like a flu—she'd go for days thinking maybe she was coming down with something, but maybe not, and then one day she'd wake up feeling so bad that she didn't care if she lived or died. She convinced herself in that darkness that she'd imagined everything with him. That it hadn't been as strong of a connection as she had felt in the moment. That she wasn't worthy and didn't deserve a guy like him. Her internal dialogue turned nasty, hurling self-loathing insults. She washed her hands.

And let him slip through her fingers.

It wasn't until she died that she truly understood what she'd let go. She'd lost a pivotal piece to the puzzle that was her life, and now the picture could not be completed without him.

Nora opened her eyes. "His name was Jack." *Jack.* Not John, not Jake. *Jack.* She sat up, picked up her laptop, and posted a note to Jack on the "Lost and Found in the ATX" page.

Your name was Jack. You didn't believe I would eat Takis. I accused you of hoarding the pink Starbursts. We both like basketball and think Sixth Street is overhyped and our favorite place to swim is Deep Eddy, but only in the winter because it's less crowded. I miss you. Meet me in front of the corner store on Duval and 45th Friday at 6?

It was a shot in the dark, but it was all she had.

••••••

Chef Bernice was setting out blenders and butternut squashes when Nora arrived at the Saucepot Kitchen Classroom. "We're making pasta and a butternut Parmesan sauce tonight," she announced as Nora settled in next to Willow and her mother.

"This looks fun," Nora said, determined that tonight would be better than the last class.

Willow, with her chin propped in her hand and her basketball in her lap, shrugged.

"Are you okay?" Nora asked.

Willow didn't answer.

"Apparently spending time with her mother and learning to cook is not her idea of a good time," Tanya said over her head.

"I didn't say that, Mom."

Nora pulled her notebook out of her garden tote bag. "Basketball is obviously better than cooking, right? I think so."

Willow rolled her eyes.

"Wanna play sometime?" The question gushed without conscious thought, surprising her. It seemed her inner athlete was eager to get going.

Willow's head came up out of her palm. "Are you for real right now?"

"I feel more real right now than I have in years."

"I need everyone's attention," Chef Bernice announced.

"I'm serious," Nora whispered.

Willow ignored her.

Chef Bernice took them through the motions of making pasta, which was easy enough until Nora managed to screw up the settings on the pasta-cutting machine. The result was some fat, worm-like noodles. Bernice said it was a good first effort.

Bernice showed them how to cut butternut squash. Nora made a mental note not to grow any of these puppies, as they were not an easy gourd to work with. The chef then produced the butternuts she'd already baked, and they proceeded to the sauce portion of the evening, which entailed sautéing garlic and shallots in olive oil and butter, all of it to be pureed with the squash and spices.

The spices were on a revolving rack, one rack to three cooks. As Nora dumped in her spices and added her mixture to the blender, Derek—one of the guys from the cute guy couple—brought a spoonful of his puree to Bernice to sample. Bernice was putting the spoon to her lips when Nora switched on the blender—but she had forgotten to attach the lid, and butternut puree flew out and onto Derek and Bernice.

Nora shrieked and frantically reached to stop the blender, but her foot slipped in the sauce splattered on the floor, and when she tried to regain her balance, her arm knocked into the stack of plates next to her station. The whole stack crashed loudly onto the concrete floor.

Blenders switched off. There was a momentary silence as everyone stared at the carnage.

"Bro, look what you did!" Willow crowed.

"I'm so sorry," Nora said. "I don't . . . I'm not sure what happened."

"You didn't put the lid on the blender. And you knocked all the plates off the counter," Willow unhelpfully pointed out.

"I'll clean it up." Nora anxiously looked around for a broom and a dustpan. How much more of a disaster could she be? All the time she'd spent wishing she could cook, she'd never once dreamed she'd be so inept at every single aspect of it.

Bernice seemed to be in a bit of shock as she stared at the mess. "Are any of the plates salvageable? I have another class after this."

Unfortunately, the answer was no.

Nora tried to quietly clean up the mess while the rest of the class performed the taste test . . . but picking up pieces of broken plates and dumping them into the trash was loud work, and every time Nora did it, the rest of the class jumped.

She was the class pariah. An idiot who didn't think to put a lid on a blender. It was hard not to feel defeated.

By the time she'd finished cleaning up—and googling how much it would cost to replace twenty plates—Tanya and Willow's pasta dish had been voted the best.

"We didn't taste hers," Willow said, pointing at Nora. "Look how fat her noodles are."

Chef Bernice smiled sympathetically. "You'll get the hang of it," she said to Nora as she handed out containers for everyone to take their dishes home. "Next week we move to France and tackle a béchamel lasagna. Nora, why don't you plan on assisting me?"

Great. She'd been demoted to teacher's aide. She stared into the abyss of the trash can and the mess she'd left there.

"Do we have to come next week?" Willow whined to her mother as everyone began to filter out of the room with their containers, Nora bringing up the rear.

"Yes, we do," Tanya said. "I paid a lot of money for this class."

Nora's inner athlete kicked her pathetic inner chef out of the way. "Hey, Willow," she said. "I was serious—would you be up for playing basketball with me?"

Tanya instantly stopped walking and turned around to Nora. "I'm sorry, but why do you want to hang out with a girl you hardly know? It's a little creepy."

"Creepy?" Nora was horrified.

Tanya shook her head and wrapped her arm around Willow's shoulder, intending to walk on, but Nora couldn't let her go thinking she was some sort of pervert. "You want to know why?" she blurted. "Because when I was her age, I wanted to play ball more than anything and I wasn't allowed."

Willow, with that ball tucked under her arm, glanced back.

"That's right," Nora said. "My dad wouldn't let me. He . . . he thought it wasn't ladylike."

Willow snorted.

"I had a dream of playing in the WNBA—"

"Me too." Willow looked up at her mother. "And I would, too, if Mom would ever let me play."

"We've been over this," her mother said. "I don't have time. You know that. I've got three kids and two jobs. *This* was our compromise, Willow. Something we could do together, once a week."

"Just a pickup game," Nora pleaded. "For me, it's a way to get back on the court, and for Willow, it's a chance to play. Is that creepy?"

"I'm supposed to hand my daughter over to you?"

"No. I'll come to her, meet her, wherever you say."

"I'm sorry, but this is weird." Tanya tried to move Willow along again, but Nora's inner athlete was in beast mode after her cooking defeat. *No pain, no gain.* "At least hear me out," Nora pleaded, and surprisingly, Tanya paused. "I'm at this place in my life where I'm trying to do things I let go because . . . because life got in the way. Like this class. I always wanted to know how to cook, and now I'm learning. I really do love basketball and being active. I just want to play, I swear it."

Tanya looked dubious.

"Please, Mom?" Willow asked. "I have to have an adult."

Tanya looked at Nora. It was hard to say if she was annoyed or resigned. "She can't use the court without an adult present."

Nora perked up. Her inner athlete was cheering. "See? Win-win. I could be the adult."

"Mom," Willow pleaded.

Tanya sighed loudly, then took her daughter's hand. "Tomorrow after school. Five o'clock at the Delores Duffie Recreation Center. And don't be weird about it."

"Um . . . how about I promise to do my best?" Nora said with a nervous laugh. "Seriously, thank you, Tanya. And you, Willow."

"Okay," Tanya said and led Willow away.

Nora glanced skyward and silently thanked Grandpa. She was pretty sure he'd had a hand in getting Tanya to say yes. Nothing else would explain it.

Chapter 25

The *next morning Nora called Lacey and caught her on* the way to work. "Hey! Got a minute?"

"Not really." Lacey was driving; her voice sounded like it was coming from a can.

"Okay . . . but I wanted to tell you that I quit my job."

"I heard," Lacey said instantly. "And I'd love to chat, but I have a staff meeting in ten minutes and I won't get to the office for at least fifteen minutes. I'm sorry, I can't deal with this right now, Nora."

It hurt that her sister thought that she had to "deal" with her. And that she couldn't trust Nora to be truly okay. "Oh. Well, I—"

"Oops, I've got another call. I'll talk to you later." Lacey clicked off.

Nora tossed down her phone. It was mortifying to be reminded of how utterly worthless she'd been in the Before.

When the phone rang again, Nora assumed it was Lacey, calling to say she'd forgotten to say something, or maybe to apologize for being so short with her. Alas, it was not Lacey—it was Mom.

Or rather, Mom's eye, the phone too close to her face again. "Nora, what the hell have you done now?"

"I resigned."

"Now you listen to me. You get up and get dressed and get to work. We are not going through this depression thing again."

"'This depression thing'? For the record, depression isn't a weird phase, Mom. Anyway, I'm not depressed. I actually feel great. So great that I don't want to be in a job I hate."

"Hate? How can you say that? It's your legacy."

"I really wish you and Dad would stop saying that. It's not my legacy—it's your pipe dream."

Her mother gasped. "I don't know what's gotten into you. Are you taking your medicine? Are you going to your therapy sessions?"

"Mom, stop."

"I don't think you realize what you've done. I don't know if I can fix it for you this time."

Fix it for her? Her mother had never fixed one damn thing for her. She'd never intervened, had never done anything but shore up the impossible standard by which Nora and Lacey had to live, and then demand they be thinner and prettier while they did it. She had never been on Nora's side.

"I'm not asking you to do anything for me, Mom. I don't want your help. I'm doing what is best for me."

"Best for you? How selfish. What about your father?"

Nora was incensed. "You must be joking," she said hotly. "Mom . . . you know how he is."

There was a long pause. "I know that everyone has more than one side, Nora. Your father is a good man. Look how much money he's raised in Nathan's name."

"Yeah . . . for a son he lost thirty years ago."

"It doesn't matter how long ago it was," her mother snapped. "The death of a child is a grief you can never overcome. You have no idea, Nora."

It was true she had no idea what it was like to lose a child, but she knew what it was like to lose a twin. She'd longed to know him. She'd felt his presence missing in her life even though she never knew him. "Maybe not," Nora said. "But meanwhile, I'm still here."

"I can't have this conversation right now." The screen went black. Her mother had hung up on her. Nora regretted she hadn't done it first.

She spent the rest of the day trying to stay out of her head, researching the property tax issue with Catherine's theater. She texted Gus a couple of times, first asking him to weigh in on which jersey she should wear to play basketball. Spurs or Mavs?

His response was a thumbs-up.

Paint class this week! Want me to pick you up?

Gus texted a simple C U there.

She groaned and texted him the time and place. Her attempt to engage him wasn't going as well as she'd hoped.

James called midafternoon. "How's life without a job?"

"It's like that feeling you get when you eat so much Mexican food that you can't even breathe." Her gaze meandered over to the pile of bills on her kitchen bar. No wonder.

"Regretting it?"

"Not for a minute," Nora said firmly. "How is it there?"

"Awful. Everyone is walking on eggshells. Charles and Melinda came into your office and looked around like a pair of vultures. Nora, if I'm forced to work for them—"

"As soon as I get a job, I'll send for you."

"Right." He sighed wearily. "That's why I'm calling. Maxwell and Graeber canceled the interview."

And just like that, it felt as if the air had been sucked from the room. "What?"

"I called to give them your personal cell, and I was informed by Ms. Ranstein that they had filled the position from within."

"But they just called me," Nora said and sank down onto her bed.

"Firms do that all the time. You have other résumés out, right?"

"Two dozen at least."

"Someone will want you."

Her confidence bubble began to leak—would anyone want her before she was tossed out of her apartment? Before she was hauled off to debtors' prison or whatever they did in the twenty-first century?

Nora promised James that she'd call the moment she had a job lead. When she hung up, she gripped both hands into tight fists and pressed them against her knees to keep the buzz from rising into her chest.

She'd spent exactly one day unemployed so far. *One. Day.*

Believe, she told herself. Dr. Cass said it would all fall into place. She had no choice but to trust that.

At five minutes to five o'clock, she was standing outside the Delores Duffie Recreation Center wearing a vintage Nike T-shirt emblazoned with the "Do it!" slogan, a find at Goodwill. She peered longingly through the clouded windows of the doors to the basketball courts.

At ten past five, just when she'd begun to think Willow had stood her up, a minivan pulled up, the side panel door slid open, and Willow hopped out with her ball. Three girls followed. The four of them walked to the entrance loose-limbed, tall, and exuding youth. They came to a halt where Nora was standing and eyed her curiously.

"An audience," Nora said. "I like it. Are you sure you want them to see me slaughter you on the court?"

"Whoooоaaaa," one of the girls said with a laugh.

"She's like that," Willow said to her friends. "She talks a lot."

"I'm Nora. I'm here to play some hoops."

"Don't try to be, like, fly," Willow warned her. "No one says that."

"Noted." She was dying to ask what they did say.

"Are we going in or what?" Willow asked.

Inside, Nora reserved a block of time, handed over her driver's license, then followed the girls. It had been a lifetime since she'd stepped on a court, but the excitement for it was still there, the desire to play still pumping.

The gym was full—a kids' basketball clinic was underway at one end, and kids were gathered in groups on the bleachers, waiting their turn.

When their time came, Nora discovered instantly that whatever skill she might have thought she possessed remained in the Before. Willow's first pass of the ball to her was so hard that she was forced back a couple of steps. It went downhill from there. Nora's shots were wide and short. The girls were physical, as was the fashion on the professional circuit these days—they slammed into her when guarding her, knocking her down more than once, then laughing at how gracelessly she got up.

Willow was the hardest on her. She made a quick move around Nora as she went in for a layup, hip checking her, and Nora went flying, landing hard on her back and then sliding into the wall headfirst. Nora's first thought was that the kid was strong. Her second thought was that she didn't know if she could move.

Basketball? Really, Nora?

Sprawled on the floor with the wind knocked out of her, she heard her inner athlete telling her to get up. Had she really believed she could still run circles around everyone on the court? That she was some sort of phenom?

Willow walked over and stared down at her for a long moment. "Her eyes are open," she announced to the other girls. She disappeared, but in her place was a woman with silver glasses, a whistle around her neck, and a name tag that said *Wanda*. Nora recognized her as one of the clinic coaches.

"Don't move," she commanded Nora. "Did you hit your head?"

"Not hard," Nora said. "My butt is the injured part." She tried again to get up, but Wanda put a hand on her shoulder.

"Don't move. You could be seriously injured. You went down hard, and at your age, you have to be especially careful."

"I'm thirty-one," Nora protested. She tried to sit up again but winced at the pain in her lower back.

"Stay still," said a masculine voice.

Now two firefighters were peering down at her. "Really?" she said to Wanda. "You called an ambulance?"

"You can't be too careful with head injuries," Wanda said.

Willow and the girls had gone back to playing, ignoring the triage that was going on at the side of the court.

As it turned out, Nora was no phenom. At least nothing was broken. The thing about sports is, you fall, and you get back up. She imagined Grandpa in the bleachers, encouraging her to find her feet. She finally stood up. Her head throbbed, her ankle throbbed, and she could hardly move her left shoulder. And even though she refused to go to the hospital for a more thorough examination, Wanda—who was also the recreation center manager—put her on concussion protocol.

"Meaning?" Nora asked as Wanda handed her an official-looking piece of paper.

"Meaning you are not allowed on the court for two weeks. After that, we'll need a doctor's note clearing you before you can play here."

"No!" Nora protested. "Come on, I'm fine. You don't understand—I need this."

"Then, honey, you need to get in shape. This was all in the papers you signed."

Nora deflated. So much for her triumphant return to sports—she felt old, puffy, and delusional. She had no job, a mountain of bills, a garden that wasn't growing, two small cuts from picking up all the dishes she'd broken at cooking class, and her inner athlete was sucking wind. Her confidence bubble had completely burst.

Forlorn, she retreated to the bleachers to nurse the tatters of her pride.

When the allotted time was up, Willow and the girls joined Nora. "Are we too much for you, Grandma?" Willow asked jovially.

"Looks like," Nora admitted. "You guys are good. You ought to be in a league."

"Can't," Willow said. "You have to have an adult coach and a sponsor."

"Ask one of your parents."

"Duh. We have."

A shadow slipped past Nora's peripheral vision. She turned; Tanya was standing there, listening. "Girls, get your things."

The girls went courtside to get their discarded bookbags, calling out to the boys playing at the other end of the court.

Tanya took a seat next to Nora. "I thought you said you were good."

"I sincerely thought I was." Nora wiped perspiration from her face. "Willow is really good."

Tanya nodded. "I know."

"Is there really no one who can take them on?"

Tanya turned her gaze to Nora. "What's so hard for you to understand? These girls, all their parents work long hours. No one's got time for this. The league is hours of practice and then games on weekends. What about my other kids?"

Nora felt instantly contrite. "You're right; I don't understand. I don't understand so much we could fill a book."

Tanya gave her a slim smile. "Are you coming again after you're allowed back in? Wanda doesn't kid about a doctor's note. Or have you fulfilled your fantasy?"

Nora rubbed her aching shoulder. "I don't know."

"Well, here's my number just in case," Tanya said and handed her a business card. "See you in cooking class."

"Right. The other place I suck," Nora muttered.

"True . . . but not as bad as you suck on the court." Tanya chuckled at her joke, patted Nora on the shoulder, and went to collect the girls.

Nora grimaced in pain all the way home. She wasn't sure what hurt worse—her ego or her body. When she walked into her apartment, she leaned her back against the door and looked around her apartment, her gaze landing on her bills. Her gardening handbook. Her laptop. Her combat boots.

What the hell was she doing? She wanted desperately to believe that she'd been elementally changed by her NDE and that she could forge a new life. But could she really? The fear of failing and the doubt in her own abilities were rumbling around, trying to gain a foothold.

She needed a lifeline. It was after hours, but Dr. Cass had invited her to call if she needed to. Nora needed to.

"Nora," Dr. Cass trilled when she answered the phone.

"I know I should wait until our next appointment, but I've done something a little scary, and I'm feeling anxious."

"We do need to speak about your next appointment—"

"I quit my job," Nora blurted.

"Goodness," Dr. Cass said.

The story tumbled out of Nora—how she'd felt sick about that terrible bus case and had quit. Just up and walked out. She told Dr. Cass about all the brick walls she was encountering in trying to find Jack, and the job opportunity she'd had and lost within twenty-four hours, and how she was on concussion protocol and was beginning to flounder, scared of what she'd set in motion.

"But look at all the great progress you've made," Dr. Cass said.

"Progress?" Had she heard anything Nora had said? "I have no job or money to pay rent and bills. My dad told me to get it together and grow up, and maybe he's right. Maybe . . ." She sucked in a breath. Fear and doubt clouded out all the sunshine she'd managed to hang on to. "Maybe I'm kidding myself," she admitted. "My medical bills are piling up. I need that job. That's what I mean—I'm paying attention to things that aren't important and completely disregarding the things that are." She could feel the dark side of her brain slowly awakening. "Oh my God, I'm losing it."

"That is self-defeating talk, Nora. You're not losing it. Now, you may have thought you could make a list of regrets and then simply rectify them with no trouble whatsoever, but life rarely works that way. I think it's very encouraging that you stood up to your father and went off to pursue the things you want to pursue. Without a doubt, it will be challenging. There will be setbacks. You'll need to continue to take a hard look at how you got here. But that doesn't mean it wasn't the right thing to do."

"How am I supposed to believe that when I need an income and I'm terrible at the things I thought would make me happy? What if I'm setting myself up for disaster all because I had a stupid accident and think I had some sort of grand epiphany?"

"Be grateful for that epiphany," Dr. Cass said. "You're seeking meaning from your life, and from meaning, your happiness will flow. Don't you think that's what the reverse bucket list is all about? You're doing a complete one-eighty, and that is a significant challenge on the best day. You're not defeated, Nora; you're rebuilding."

Nora wanted to believe her.

"In yoga, students are encouraged to take deep breaths because when you breathe deeply, your body understands that it is safe to open more. Breathe deeply, Nora. Let yourself open to this new life."

Yes, deep breaths. "Right. Okay. Thanks, Dr. Cass. I won't take any more of your time—"

"About our session this week," Dr. Cass said. "Your insurance company denied the claims."

Nora's face turned hot. She felt unsteady, a little nauseous. She needed Dr. Cass. "Are you sure?"

"I spoke to a representative today. Your mental health benefits are extremely limited on your company plan, and you've maxed out the number of outpatient visits for the year. Going forward, you'll need to pay out of pocket."

Nora's breath caught in her throat. How could she pay for therapy on top of everything else?

"Unfortunately, that's the situation. In the meantime, Nora, practice believing in yourself. Nothing worth having ever came easy."

Well, that was painfully obvious.

Chapter 26

Jack

Margarite Espinoza begged her daughter to let her go in the end. "I want to die," she said. But her daughter, Joanna—a slight thing, only twenty-four, and an only child like Jack had been—clung to her mother's hand, begging her to stay.

Jack had seen this play out again and again—the patient made peace with their fate, and either their loved ones accepted it or they didn't. Margarite had been ready for more than a week. But Joanna couldn't get ready, because the idea of a life stretching before her without a mother could not be conceived of in someone so young.

When her mother passed, the poor girl's racking sobs could be heard all the way down the hall. Sandra swept in like a grandmother and let the young woman sob onto her bosom.

Joanna's raw emotions had exhausted Jack, and when he arrived at the garden, he was dragging. These were the moments he wished he had someone in his corner, someone he could go home to, who would hold him the way Sandra had held Joanna.

He was expecting to make quick work of his watering today and get on to the theater and rehearsal, but as he walked up to the garden plot, something caught his eye. Something huge. He squinted, dragged his fingers through his hair, and leaned forward to have a closer look.

It was an exceptionally large cucumber on top of his footlocker. There was a note wedged under it. He pulled it free.

Greetings from Plot Nine. Thank you so much for your generous gift of tomato food. I should like to return the thoughtfulness. I only recently discovered that what I thought was a weed was a vine busy sprouting this monster cucumber. My garden adviser says vegetables that grow too big lack flavor, but maybe I got lucky with this one. Enjoy.

Jack grinned. He tucked the giant cuke into his backpack and set it aside. He harvested a few ripe tomatoes, then got out the radish seeds that Gabe, the janitor at work, had given him. Last week, after Jack had handed out bags of homegrown tomatoes—to say he was producing a bumper crop was an understatement—Gabe had sensed a fellow gardener and had brought him the seeds. *"I grow these every year,"* he said. *"Can't beat 'em for taste. Now, be sure you mix some coffee grounds in the soil. Six inches deep, and keep 'em watered."* He also handed Jack an article that backed up his claims about coffee grounds.

Jack planted the seeds next to his carrots, mixed the soil with the coffee grounds he'd brought from the break room, and watered them. When he got ready to leave, Jack took some of the seeds and found some paper to pen a note to Plot Nine.

Congratulations on single-handedly tackling the food shortage crisis by growing a cucumber big enough to feed an entire city block. I can't wait to try it. In the meantime, my garden adviser said the radishes grown from these seeds are the best in the state. In addition, he is keen on coffee grounds as a soil enhancer. He gave me an article that perhaps you will find interesting.

He placed the seeds and article along with his note beneath a rock on her locker.

From there, he went to the theater. The thespians were already gathered in the auditorium. Doralee was onstage arguing with Jerry about choreography. Mr. Carlton, one of the older thespians with a penchant for bow ties, was napping in the back row, his head tossed back, his mouth open. "Hey," Jack said softly and gave him a nudge.

The old man woke with a sputter and looked up. "Oh. You made it. Some of us were starting to wonder."

"I haven't missed a rehearsal yet," Jack reminded him.

"No, but we keep expecting it. A kid like you must have better things to do than hang out with a bunch of old-timers."

Jack had many things to do, but he didn't know if they were better than this . . . project? Pastime? Craziness? Whatever it was, it was more fun than he would have guessed. It was sort of starting to feel like he had an odd little family.

As he made his way down the center aisle, he noticed more needlepoint seat covers had appeared on various rows with no obvious rhyme or reason as to their placement. Lovebirds Martin and Mary were sitting on two of them. They had their heads together as they pored over a sheet of paper.

Karen was standing below the apron of the stage. "Jack! Thank God. Please come speak to Annabeth." She cast a glare to the wings where Annabeth stood with her arms crossed tightly, her mouth stubbornly pursed. She was in a dressing gown.

"Is something wrong?" he asked.

"Yes, something is wrong, and it starts with an *A* and ends with *beth* and it's her attitude."

"Well, you've got a bad one yourself, Karen," Annabeth shot back. "Is a thank-you so impossible for you to say?"

"What exactly are we arguing about?" Jack asked.

"Costumes, obviously." Karen waved her hand at Annabeth, up and down, Vanna White style. As it turned out, Annabeth had significantly changed the costume Karen had made for her, proclaiming she'd fixed it. Karen, of course, thought she had ruined it.

As that battle wore on (for which there was no real solution, as Annabeth had definitely altered it), at least the debate over who would play Blanche DuBois had been sorted. It came as no surprise to anyone that Catherine had won the plum role. But Meredith did not take defeat quietly and said, loud enough for everyone to hear, that Catherine's version of Blanche was overwrought.

"Well, maybe that's because Blanche is overwrought, Meredith," Catherine shot back. "Remind me, what lead roles have you ever had?"

Meredith gasped. She was winding up to respond, but Catherine spotted Jack. "Oh, hey there, kid. I've got some news to share—"

"It will have to wait," Walter said sternly and lifted a hand in a silent attempt to quell any argument. "Listen up, people. We're all on edge. We've got a lot riding on this and we're running out of time, and these arguments aren't helping. Who can tell me the best thing we can do at this point?"

The seniors looked around at each other. Martin was brave enough to venture a guess. "Give up?"

Walter sighed. "We rehearse! And we rehearse and we rehearse until we can't, and then . . . we rehearse once more and put on a show."

"I don't disagree," Mary said cautiously. "But we have sets to paint."

Walter looked like he might explode. "Yes, Mary, we do. That is my point. There is much to be done. I think you can all trust that this will be a late night. Except for you, Jack. It's not your tush on the line. All right, can we get on with rehearsal? Places, everyone! Act one, opening musical number."

Everyone scrambled onto the stage to take their places for the opening dance, Jack included. He was really nothing more than muscle, and because his dancing skills were so bad, no matter how often Jerry tried to help him "loosen his hips," he was in the very back, next to the crude rendering of a bus stop. Annabeth sat at a piano and began to play; the cast sprang into action, singing and following the choreography they'd learned. Jerry wandered through them as they danced, correcting postures, demonstrating the moves for those who couldn't remember. Mr. Carter sang, "What's the matter, honey, are you lost?" from an original song, "Elysian Fields," written by Doralee and Karen, which, Jack had to admit, was pretty good.

Their collective dancing had improved over the disaster it was last week, and even lifting Meredith was a little easier than it had been, thanks to his hitting the gym this week.

When they had completed the run-through of the opening number, they silently looked around at each other, their faces lit with shock and delight.

"We sort of nailed it," Karen said.

Jack would not have believed it, but this show, this crazy-ass musical, was chaotic and fun and original and interesting and might be worth the price of admission.

But as they found their places to go through the opener again, Jack couldn't help wondering how they could possibly make enough money from it to pay off their debt.

Nevertheless, they were committed. They were still working on the opening number when he ducked out early to meet up with Byron.

Chapter 27

Nora was beginning to panic about her job search. She figured she had about two months of living expenses in the bank before things got dire—as in learn-how-to-be-a-barista dire.

She had an idea, however. After applying to posted job openings for attorney positions around the state through the usual job search sites, she decided she'd start calling people she knew. But when she attempted to log in to work for her contacts list, access was denied.

She called James.

"Please tell me you found a job," James said instantly.

"I wish. I tried to log in for my contacts, but I can't get in."

"Yep, standard procedure. The moment someone leaves the firm, they change all the passwords and lock the doors."

"Hmm. Remember the malware attack we had last year?" she asked. "I printed a list of contacts and kept it with some other papers in the bottom right-hand drawer of my desk just in case. Can you get that for me?"

"Probably. I boxed up your stuff and put it in a storage closet in case people were sniffing around. Let me put you on hold and see if Sally moved it."

James clicked off and the elevator music played for several minutes. When he returned, he sighed into the phone. "Bad news. The box I labeled with your name is gone."

"Gone? Where did it go?"

"According to Sally, it went home with your dad. And get this . . . she said that he isn't assigning your office to anyone. He told her you'd be back."

Nora recoiled. She wasn't entirely surprised that he thought he could wait her out, but the thought of returning made her queasy. She realized her father didn't take her seriously. He probably thought she was having a tantrum and would come crawling back any day. It was infuriating.

"He doesn't believe you quit," James said.

"Yeah," she said with a sigh. "He thinks he can make me change my mind."

"Well, HR is carrying on like you've quit. They told me yesterday that when a new senior attorney is named, I'll have to move offices. To the second floor, Nora."

The second floor was where administration and accounting were housed. Nothing legal existed on that floor.

"So please hurry up and get a job."

"I'm trying," Nora said. "Trust me, I need it worse than you."

"Debatable. Okay, let me see if I can re-create your list from my files." He promised he'd be in touch.

She followed her call to James with a video call to her mother. This morning her mother was dressed in tennis togs.

"Mom . . . did Dad bring a box home with my name on it?" Nora asked.

"I hope the reason you are asking is because, praise God, you've come to your senses." She was walking through her enormous house, presumably on her way to her car.

"I have," Nora said.

Her mother stopped walking. "You're going back to work?"

"Not at November and Sons."

Her mother sighed wearily. She raised her arm to glance at her watch. "I've only got a few minutes, Nora, but really."

"Mom, I seriously quit. That's it. But I need that box."

"It most certainly is *not* it. He's still your father. You'll have to come for dinner Sunday if you want your box."

Nora laughed. "I don't think so."

"Well, I do," her mother said sternly. "Do you intend to never see him again? Or me?"

Nora hadn't thought that far ahead, but maybe. "I need some distance right now. I need to get on my feet, and when I do, maybe I can talk to him then. Mom, I really need what's in that box. Could you drop it off?"

"Absolutely not. I'm not driving through that gauntlet of homeless camps to get to your apartment. If you want it, you can come home and get it. Now listen, Nora—it could take you a very long time to get on your feet. You don't want to burn all your bridges. Come for dinner. You have my word your father won't bring it up. And I want your solemn promise you won't either."

"Who are you kidding?" Nora scoffed.

"I mean it," her mother said and brought the phone close to her face. "This is very important to me. I'm not losing my daughter over this. Dinner will be only family."

"Which I presume means Lacey but not Gus."

Her mother pressed her lips together and neither confirmed nor denied. "I am asking you as the person who gave you life, as the one who loves you, to please come to dinner. I can't bear this."

For God's sake. Nora really needed that box. "Fine."

"Good. And now I'm off." She clicked off before Nora could change her mind.

Since she was tackling family this morning, Nora called Lacey. Surprisingly, Lacey picked up. "Hey!"

"Hey, yourself. Are you going to Sunday dinner with Mom and Dad?"

"As if I would ever hear the end of it if I didn't. Are you?"

"Yeah. Mom is holding my work papers hostage. Anyway, that's not why I'm calling. I wanted to make dinner for you next Tuesday if you're free."

"Dinner," Lacey repeated, as if she'd never heard the word.

"Yes, dinner. Do you have plans?"

"Um . . ."

Lacey sounded like she was trying to think of a plan.

"I'm going to cook for you," Nora said quickly before her sister shut her down. "I'll come to you."

Lacey was silent.

"Hello?"

"Sorry, I'm having trouble wrapping my head around the idea that you're offering to cook."

"Well . . . that's the plan, anyway. You're my little sister and I want to do this for you. But at your house, in a real kitchen."

"Huh."

Nora's hopefulness was beginning to fade. Why did everything have to be so hard right now? "Could you maybe sound a little more excited or something?"

"Okay. I will admit I'm intrigued. But I don't have the stamina right now to get my hopes up that we're going to be friends, only to have you flake on me."

Nora winced. "Okay, that hurts."

"You've done it before."

"For the record, I didn't flake. I battled depression, remember? I'm just asking you to give me a chance." She curled her hand into a fist to keep from buzzing, her nails biting into the skin, waiting for Lacey to answer. She could hear shouting in the background and the wail of traffic and sirens on the street. Then Lacey said, "Sure. I'm being cautious, that's all. I've had enough with the letdowns lately."

"Understood. But, Lacey . . . trust me when I say I'm not the old Nora anymore."

"We'll see," Lacey said. "But I accept your gracious offer. See you Sunday at Mom and Dad's?"

Unfortunately, she would.

••••••

Nora spent the next afternoon at the tax appraiser's office, learning what she could about Catherine's property. She spent another day writing cover letters and sending out résumés. In the evenings, she kept tabs on her social media posts about Jack. And there was the garden, always needing her attention.

Today, after a trip there, she stopped in at Nick's. She showed him some leaves she'd clipped from one of her tomato plants. Nick examined the way the edges of the leaves were curling up. "Too much water," he said immediately. "Better hope you don't have root rot."

"Too much water? But the leaves were turning brown."

"You underwatered, and then you overwatered."

"Oh my God." Nora groaned and sank onto a small barstool he had at the counter. "I'm ruining it."

"You're learning it. No two garden plots are the same." He put two bulbs that looked like potatoes on the counter. "These are dahlia tubers, ready to sprout. Plant them just below the surface."

She looked at the tubers and shook her head. "I'll kill them. I'm a terrible gardener."

He cocked his head and looked at her. "What, you've never done anything hard before?"

"Growing tomatoes is not supposed to be hard."

"You're a novice. You'll learn. And the calla lilies?"

"Nothing."

"You've been keeping the soil moist?"

"I'm trying. But I can't be there every day. I soak it when I am."

"The plot has sun?"

"Plenty," she said morosely.

"Then the only thing you need is patience." He handed the leaf back to her. "And fertilizer. And a couple of dahlias to brighten your day."

"Yeah, well, I'm running a little thin on both these days."

He put a container of fertilizer on the counter between them.

"I let it go too long, Nick," she said and handed him her credit card. "I killed Grandpa's garden and now I can't bring it back." Her remorse for letting her grandfather down would never leave her—she'd regret it all her life.

Nick rang up the sale. "You remind me of the elephant with the rope."

She looked at him—was it a joke?

"Never heard that story? A long time ago, before people cared much what happened to animals, baby elephants were trained to stay put with a rope around their leg, staked to one spot. Just a thin garden-variety rope holding them to the post. They'd try to get free of it, but they weren't strong enough. The babies grew to adults, and still, all their keepers ever needed to keep them in place was that bit of rope. Because the elephants never believed they could break the rope."

Nora sighed. "Yeah, okay, I get it."

"There you go," he said with a hint of a smile. "You know, I was an elephant once, stuck in a small town with no job. Had no money. Thought I'd never break free."

"Until you believed you could?" She smiled wryly.

"No," he scoffed. "I *knew* I could. I just needed to save up a few hundred bucks and buy a plane ticket. Your card has been declined."

Nora blinked. "What?"

"Declined."

"That can't be right."

Nick ran the card again. And again, it came up as declined.

She'd paid the bill, hadn't she? She'd never had a card declined, couldn't imagine how it had happened. A flutter of fear ran through her—she'd screwed up somewhere. She reached into her wallet for money for the fertilizer as she tried to think.

Nick gave her change, then went into the back while she stared into space trying not to panic. He returned with two small pots. "I cut these bell pepper plants for you. I'm giving you only two, because you can't plant willy-nilly, Nora. Gardens require careful planning. You don't want to find yourself with the same dead spot next spring that you had this spring, do you now?"

Lord help her if she found herself in the same dead spot next year.

He handed her a can of iron supplement. "That's complimentary. If you have time, go now and apply this."

"I will. Thanks, Nick," she said. "I'll pay you back, I promise." Her whole body ached with worry. She gathered her things and started out.

"Read the instructions," Nick called after her. "And don't you dare give up!"

Chapter 28

T*he garden was much busier than it had been earlier* today when she'd come to water. People Nora had never seen before were tending their plots. She almost felt like one of the gang with her garden tote and her pepper plants and her wide-brimmed gardening hat. Or maybe gang-adjacent. She wasn't quite there yet.

"Hello!" she called with a friendly wave to those she passed. "Hey, that's impressive," she said, pointing at a trumpet vine that covered a small arch. "Be careful!" she warned twin girls who were chasing each other among the plots. One of them stuck her tongue out at Nora, the gesture completely missed by her mother, who was digging furiously in the earth like she had a body to bury before sundown.

As she made her way, she noticed a commotion around Catherine and Walter's plot. Walter was on his knees, frantically digging around his Venus flytraps while a man and a woman from neighboring plots watched.

"What's going on?" Nora asked the man.

"Someone drowned his flytraps. They're notoriously susceptible to death by overwatering."

Nora was stunned—his award-winning Venus flytraps? "Who would do that?" She imagined a jealous gardener who resented Walter's success with the finicky plants.

"Someone left the water running," the man said and nodded at the water spigot between her and Walter's plots. Nora's heart plummeted to her toes—she'd been here earlier to water. Surely she hadn't—

"Hey, you were here," the woman said. "Plot Nine, right? You were watering your plants this morning. Did you turn it off?"

Walter's head jerked up. He pushed himself to his feet. "Nora? Were you watering this morning?"

"Yes, but I—"

"And yesterday too," the woman said. "You're overwatering your plot, you know. I reported it to the community board president. We don't allow overwatering in here."

"Did you forget to turn off the water?" Walter asked. "Because the ground is soaked between our plots."

She didn't know, couldn't think. But she felt sick. "Walter . . ." Nora's voice made plain her alarm. She was horrified that she could be so careless. "I was here, and I was watering. But I'm sure I turned it off."

"Don't think so," the man beside her said. "I turned it off when I got here. The hose was on the ground and the water was just pouring out." He made a sweeping gesture with both hands to indicate the flood.

Nora swallowed down a well of nausea. She couldn't recall the act of turning off the spigot. "I . . . don't know," she admitted quietly. "I'm so sorry, Walter. It was an accident."

Walter looked at his Venus flytraps. One had fallen over onto its side. The other was actively wilting.

The woman snorted. "Sorry doesn't do much for his plants. He's won Best Exotic three years in a row now. You can't believe how hard it is to grow Venus flytraps."

"But easy to kill," Walter muttered.

"I'll replace them," Nora said.

The woman laughed. "You think you can just pop into Home Depot and pick up Venus flytraps? First of all, they're rare carnivorous plants. And second, only a certain type will grow outdoors."

"It's fine," Walter said tersely. "They're plants." He turned his back on Nora.

"I'll replace them," she said again. "I know a guy."

Walter didn't respond.

Nora trudged miserably to her plot.

The tomato plants that she'd watered so vigorously were falling against the cages she'd put around them, and there was no sign of the calla lilies.

She dropped her bag and put down her peppers. She sank down onto her knees in the soggy plot and pressed her hands against her thighs, dragging ragged breaths into her lungs. Her After was turning into a huge disaster. All the hope she'd put into this new life was being battered like a seawall every day. What would she do if she truly couldn't make it in the After? Where would she go from here? It was too bleak to even consider.

"Don't you dare give up."

Yeah, okay, but what was she supposed to do, merrily work away as Walter mourned his prized Venus flytraps she'd murdered? With a sigh, she turned to her footlocker. She saw a gift left for her there—a small pot of purple flowers.

She picked up the note.

> *I made cucumber sandwiches for all my friends and still had some left over. That was a cucumber for the ages—thank you for sharing. I am leaving a bit of Jacob's ladder for you. I thought you might like a bit of color. It grows with hardly any assistance! Enjoy. #7*

Nora stared at that pot of little purple flowers. Growing something so pretty felt out of reach for her. Everything was going wrong. *Everything.* Who was she kidding? She was just as inept as she'd always been.

She wished Grandpa hadn't sent her back.

She put aside the little pot to pen a note.

> *The color from the Jacob's ladder will be a welcome addition to my sad little plot. I hope to share some peppers very soon, as my gardening adviser has graced me with two pots that are already blooming. He has advised me to treat my soil, as nothing seems to be growing. Here's some iron for your soil too. #9*

She glanced across to where Walter was digging around his Venus flytraps while the woman from the neighboring plot supervised. "That won't work," Nora could hear her say. "They're done."

Nora glanced up through tears at the blue sky and the clouds drifting lazily overhead. Funny how the brain worked. Or didn't. She'd been so optimistic when she walked out of her office. Now she felt like a helpless idiot.

The Before came tumbling down on her, her shoulders and neck seizing with the weight of it, her body aching with the memory of feeling less-than. That's what depression did to you—it was a cruel master, piling on day after day until it was impossible to see past it.

Through the years, she'd tried various things to free herself when it grabbed her. Medicines that left her feeling like a zombie or deep underwater. Meditation. Creating her own endorphins by running marathons or taking Zumba classes. She'd tried to activate the part of her brain that craved something new, like surfing. Even though there had been periods in her life when she'd felt good and strong, the depression always seemed to come creeping back . . . until she nearly died.

But something had truly shifted that day, and she didn't want to lose it. And even though she felt like crap right now, she couldn't let a few setbacks derail her. Her new outlook was too important to her well-being, wasn't it? No less than her life. She could do it, just like Grandpa had said. She only had to believe she could.

Or am I lying to myself?

Maybe her mother was right. Maybe she had some sort of brain trauma that prevented her from seeing the truth about herself—that she was, at her core, hapless and hopeless and incapable of change.

No. She refused to believe that. She'd felt the power in her—she was capable of great things. Like Dr. Cass said, she just had to dig deep. And if there was one thing she could say with confidence, she was very good at digging.

So she began to dig. The peppers and Jacob's ladder weren't going to plant themselves.

Chapter 29

Gus *was not answering Nora's texts. It didn't take a* genius to figure out why, but stupidly, she had not scheduled time in her day to pick him up. She'd assumed he would meet her at the art studio like he'd said he would, but now she wasn't so sure.

Her anxiety prompted her to fly home from the garden to shower and dress quickly, then speed across town to his apartment.

It took several knocks on his door before Gus finally answered, reeking of alcohol and sweat. His hair stood on end, and his T-shirt hadn't been changed in what looked like weeks. "We have a painting class, remember?"

He blinked, his eyes going wide. "Sure, I remember. But man, I thought you said . . . eight."

She shook her head at his lie. "You can't go like this."

His smile faded. "Give me a few minutes."

"Gus—"

"Give me five minutes. Just wait."

She waited, taking stock of his pitiful living conditions. It seemed the bottles had only multiplied since she was last here. When he came stumbling out of his bedroom, he still looked a wreck. "Let's go paint," he said, trying to sound cheerful.

They loaded into her car. As she pulled away from his apartment complex, she asked, "Did you find a meeting?"

He kept his gaze straight ahead. "I was going to, but . . ." He rubbed one big hand over his face. "It's the darkness, Nora. It, like, edges in, and everything feels bleak, so . . ." He shrugged.

She understood deeply what he meant, and it filled her with sorrow. "You know what's not bleak? Painting."

"You know what else isn't bleak? Your T-shirt."

Nora laughed. She was wearing a T-shirt she'd found at the thrift store. The graphic was a grid made up of nine Darth Vaders, all identical. The caption above the grid read "The Expressions of Darth Vader." She thought Jack would appreciate it if she ever saw him again.

"Remember that time we took Aunt Roberta's tablecloths and made capes?" Gus asked.

Nora instantly recalled that cold winter day. They'd been around eight years old—too young to resist impulses, but old enough to know better. "And painted them with the symbols of our make-believe space tribes?"

"She was so mad." Gus laughed.

"Furious!" The tablecloths had come from Harrods in London, which had somehow infused them with Great Importance. "I was grounded for two weeks—in my room."

Gus laughed and inadvertently belched. "But it was fun, right?"

"It was so much fun. I mean . . . until it wasn't."

"Like most things. Let's have some fun, Nora. Until we don't."

••••••

The studio was tucked behind a salon in South Austin. It was on the second floor, and Gus labored up the steps. The room was small and packed with aspiring artists. Nora and Gus squeezed into the last row, their easels so close they were touching. Nora could smell the sour mix of Gus's body odor and liquor. The poor guy literally reeked of loneliness.

The instructor—a young, wiry man with dark corkscrew curls—introduced himself and directed them to sketch pads at their places. He said the first exercise was a simple one. "It's a quick five minutes, so don't overthink it. I want you to imagine one shape that represents your life and sketch it. For example, my shape is a door." He held up a drawing of a simple door, shaded red. "I feel like I am always going through one, you know? This exercise doesn't have to be complicated—it's all about getting you to think in terms of shapes. Art is shapes. *Life* is shapes. Life and art intersect."

Gus immediately bent over his sketchbook. Nora stared at hers. A rush of images flew at her. She remembered lying in the golden field after she'd died and all the things that had come to her then. What was the shape of regret? Gus lifted his head. He smiled at Nora and held up his sketch pad: a bottle.

"Oh," she said weakly.

"I'm sure there are other things, but that . . . that is the shape of my life."

The man next to Nora had drawn a prism. Someone in the row ahead of her had drawn a tree.

"Time," the instructor said.

Nora quickly drew the shape of her life. A circle. Flat. Uninspired. A blank space to be filled. It was the shape of the ghost of Nora, which was no shape at all.

The instructor went on to talk about how the exercise would play into the first lesson—how their shapes would form the cactus they would attempt to paint tonight. He held up a finished version of the cactus. But Nora hardly heard a word he said—she'd drawn a hole where a life should have been.

At the end of class, she and Gus each had small paintings of a cactus—round petals in little red pots. Gus had decorated his pot. Nora had left hers blank. They agreed they hoped that they would improve and looked forward to the class next week when, the instructor said, they would begin with an exercise that captured their mood before painting that class's picture.

Gus seemed happy on the ride back to his apartment. "That was fun. I'm going to hang mine."

Where? Behind all those empty cans and bottles? Nora loved Gus so much, but how was this helping him? Someone had once told her that the way you supported an alcoholic was to be there for them. Did this count as being there? Or was this merely pretending it could all be fixed by calling him more and taking him to painting classes and attending AA meetings with him? What he needed was treatment. What he lacked was money. And maybe a desire to be sober. She didn't know.

What he really needed was someone to care about him enough to make him care about himself.

When they reached his apartment, Gus started to get out of her car, but Nora stopped him with a hand to his arm. "Gus . . . I'm sorry."

He looked confused. "For what?"

"I think I've really let you down."

He seemed even more confused. "No, you haven't."

She squeezed his thick forearm. "Do you know what Grandpa would have said?"

"About our paintings?" He sounded nervous. "That mine is better than yours."

"Not that."

Gus sagged against the passenger seat. He swallowed hard. He gripped his hand into a fist to keep it from shaking. "I don't want to do this right now, Nora. I had a good time tonight. Can't we leave it at that?"

"Sure. But when are we going to talk?"

He looked out the passenger window for a long moment. "What would he have said?"

"That you can't do this alone. And that he was there for you."

Gus snorted.

"He's not here, but I am. You really can't do this alone, Gus. Let me help you."

He chuckled darkly. "Thanks, but no thanks. No offense, but this is what you do—you say you're going to help, and then you don't. And come on, it's not like you don't have your own problems. You can't just wave a magic wand and—voilà—no more depression."

His words stung as much as Lacey's had. It was so difficult to acknowledge the truth of how she'd checked out the last couple of years. "I know. But I'm different now, Gus."

He laughed darkly. "Because of your near-death, yada, yada."

That stung too. "Exactly because of it. Just . . . just give me a chance." She was saying that a lot these days.

Gus sighed and rubbed his forehead. "But how can you be so sure that you won't disappear again?" He dropped his hand and looked at her. "How? You're acting like you're cured."

"I'm *not* cured. Depression is a lifelong battle, I know that. Still, this time it's different. I don't know how to explain it, but it just is."

"Yeah," he said. "Forgive me if I'm a little skeptical." He gave her a thin smile. "I gotta go. I'll talk to you later." He got out of the car and took his cactus painting with him.

She had a feeling that regaining Gus's and Lacey's trust was going to be one of the hardest things she'd ever done. Ranking right up there with learning to trust herself.

Chapter 30

Jack

D*amonte Granger's adult children took turns sitting* with him in his final days. When they were all gathered, the reminiscing of their childhood would flow, and invariably, one of them would lay a hand on their father's leg and say, "Remember that, Dad?" Even though he was heavily sedated most of the time.

The skin of Damonte's feet began to mottle, and that mottling began to march up his skinny legs, a sure sign death was approaching. One day he asked his kids to give him some space, that he wanted to rest. Jack suspected he was asking them to leave so he could die. Some people were funny that way—they wanted to be alone when they went.

The four adult children and their spouses and a couple of grandchildren shuffled out of the room and went off to lunch at a place Sandra recommended.

Jack gave Sandra a sidelong look as the family walked down the hall. "The Blackbird is notoriously slow."

"I know." She looked through the door to Damonte. "We can wait in the staff break room."

Together they retreated and sat, looking away from each other, both of them lost in thought. After a time, Jack said, "I'll go."

"Thanks," Sandra said. She looked particularly exhausted today. Sometimes this job could get to even a stalwart like her.

When Damonte had first come in, he'd told Jack about a near-death experience he'd once had. *"Died on the operating table,"* he'd said, sounding almost proud of it. *"I rose out of my body and was watching them below me, trying to save me. You know, it was beautiful in a way. I felt so easy."* He'd looked at Jack. *"I'm not afraid."*

When Jack walked into Damonte's room, the air had changed, had already gone stiff and lifeless. Damonte had slipped away, unafraid, and when his kids got back from the Blackbird and said their final goodbyes, Jack would prepare his body for transit.

Today, Jack was so thankful to Mr. Hauser for giving him his garden to go to. Nothing was quite like it for renewing his spirit.

As he walked toward the community garden entrance, thinking about Damonte, he noticed a woman in green overalls, carrying a garden tote, walk out of the gates and down the street in the opposite direction. His people. He smiled to himself and went in.

The Jacob's ladder was already planted in Plot Nine, along with some pepper plants. The plot was progressing from the overgrown weed lot it had been when he'd first started coming here. It still needed work—there was some sort of problem with the tomatoes. A blight, perhaps? But there was a freshly turned space and some new plants.

Next to Plot Nine, he noticed something else—Walter's award-winning Venus flytraps were gone. That was odd.

At his plot, Jack found a can of iron and a note. He was going to meet this kindly old lady someday. And when he did, maybe he could convince her to join a senior thespian group.

Chapter 31

On *the day Nora had posted the invitation for Jack to* meet her, her hope and anxiety were painfully balled up in the pit of her stomach.

She checked her social media post that morning as she always did, expecting nothing. But to her surprise, something had happened, seemingly overnight—the shares had almost doubled on her posts. She didn't know what to make of it. What did that mean? What if Jack appeared today? What if he didn't? But Nora couldn't obsess about it, because if she did, she would convince herself of the worst—she was a master at that.

At some point during the day, James texted her to say he'd made some discreet inquiries around the office and had a few leads for her.

At twenty to six, dressed in her Darth Vader T-shirt and jeans for the meet-up, Nora pulled up outside the November and Sons offices and texted James to come down. He appeared a few minutes later with his satchel slung over his shoulder. He leaned down and propped his arms on the open passenger side window and handed her a yellow piece of paper. "Not much there, I'm afraid."

Of course not. Her luck had not been trending toward the positive. She tucked the paper into her garden tote. "Thank you. Hey, you want to go see if the corner store guy shows at my meet-up?"

James's eyes lit up. "That's today?"

"In, like, twenty minutes."

"Hell yes. Are you kidding?" He opened the door and got in.

The neighborhood around the corner store was notorious for a lack of parking, and they ended up about four blocks away. James linked his arm through Nora's and they pretended to skip à la Dorothy and the Tin Man in *The Wizard of Oz* . . . until they rounded the corner and saw the crowd of people in the store parking lot.

"Damn," James said.

"Could they be here for something else?" Nora asked. "I thought there'd be a couple of trolls, but this is crazy."

"Here for what, a barbecue? A concert? It's the parking lot of a corner store, Nora. They're here for your meet-up. There are at least thirty people."

Her anxiety immediately shot up. That was thirty people to watch her crumble if Jack didn't come. Her instinct for flight had always been much stronger than her instinct for fight, and she thought about turning back, but what if by some miracle he was here? Was she really going to let her anxiety take this chance from her? *No.* The new Nora didn't have time for anxiety. "Okay," she said, ignoring the slight tremble in her voice. "Okay. We're doing this."

"Correction. *You're* doing it. I'm only here for moral support."

"Right." Nora turned to James and clamped her hand on his arm, holding tight. "How do I look?"

His gaze moved over her body. "You look great. Healthy. I'm going to say it—you even look sane."

She smiled. "Finally!" She pressed a hand to her belly in a vain attempt to contain her nerves. And then somehow she made herself turn toward the crowd and begin to move. James had her flank.

No one noticed them at first. But as they neared the front door, someone recognized her. "I think that's her!"

The crowd turned like a single organism toward her. Most, she was relieved to see, were beaming at her, apparently excited about the possibility of witnessing a reunion.

James gave her a not-too-gentle push forward into their midst.

"Um . . . hi," she said nervously to the eager faces. She didn't see Jack in the crowd. But the clerk—the *same* clerk—was standing in the doorway, his shoulder against the frame, scowling. He'd put up orange cones to keep the crowd from mobbing the store entrance. Behind him, curled on a stack of water flats, was the cat.

"Is he here?" someone shouted at Nora.

"I don't . . . I don't know," Nora stammered. The buzz began to bubble up her throat and she coughed. The crowd moved closer. There were so many people. A woman with a mic shoved her way to the front, followed by a guy with a camera mounted on his shoulder. The light shone directly in Nora's face, forcing her to blink. "Oh," she said and put up a hand to shield her eyes. "What . . ."

"Hi there," the woman said. "I'm Megan Sommers from KXAN. And you're . . ." The woman thrust her microphone into Nora's face.

"Nora."

The woman nodded, apparently waiting for the rest of her name.

"November."

"Nora November. Any relation to the November and Sons law firm?"

"Um . . . yes."

Again, Megan waited.

"That's my father."

Someone in the crowd gasped. A murmur started, people repeating, "November and Sons."

"Oh my God, your dad will not be happy," James muttered behind her.

Nora could only nod—she was trying desperately to fill her lungs.

"Nora, according to your original 'Lost and Found in the ATX' post, you were in this store when it was robbed last winter, is that correct?"

Nora sincerely hoped the lump in her throat didn't turn into projectile vomit. A shadow slipped behind the reporter, and she thought of Jack, his eyes and his smile. He would have loved this. They would have laughed about it. "Yes. I was."

"Can you tell us what happened?"

Probably not without a lot of stammering and perspiring, but with a steady hand from James on her arm, Nora managed to find her bearings. She began to talk. Someone shouted at her to speak up. She raised her voice, told Megan, and by association the crowd, about Darth Vader, and how they'd been ushered to the storeroom, and how they couldn't help but laugh at Darth Vader's attempt to rob the store because they'd never imagined anyone could be so bad at it. Someone in the crowd pointed at her shirt. She said she thought Jack would find it amusing. Everyone laughed.

She told them they'd talked all night and how she'd felt a connection to Jack like she'd never felt before.

"Can you elaborate on that?" Megan asked.

"Not very well," Nora admitted. "It was like . . . finding a ray of light when everything else feels dark. Like some ancient wisdom was revealed and I just knew."

"That is so awesome," a girl said. "You can't get that connection on dating apps."

"Well, I wouldn't recommend a hostage situation either," Nora said.

Everyone laughed again. But *with* her. That was new, and it emboldened her.

"It's really hard to meet people," another man said. "It's luck, that's all—you have to be in the right place at the right time." His remark was met with murmurs of agreement. "He could be here now."

People in the crowd began to look around, presumably for Jack.

"I don't see him," Nora admitted, and the disappointment felt heavy on her heart. She'd known this was a shot in the dark, but she'd clung to hope.

"Didn't you exchange numbers?" Megan asked. "Why didn't you get together after that harrowing event?"

"Why?" Nora repeated. "Well . . . you know how it is. After something like that happens, you wake up, and you hope you didn't dream it because it was so remarkable, and then you get busy with your job and your life, and you think, *I'm going to call him tomorrow*, but then again, he hasn't called, and you start to question yourself, and maybe it was just you who felt that thing, and maybe he was just relieved we weren't killed, and maybe you don't really deserve that sort of connection, you know? And time marches on, and you lose the number, and another month goes by, and then you start to think, *No, it was real*, and *Girl, you are so dumb, you let him get away*. And you know you let him get away because you were afraid, and you should have called, but you didn't, and now it's too late. And then something miraculous happens, something that makes you rethink everything you ever thought you knew about life, and you discover that you have these terrible regrets. At first, they seem so small, but then they become really big, like, so big that you know you have to do something about them or you'll lose your mind. Because you finally understand that happiness and joy are what matters in life, and it's not the best job or making the most money or having the most things. It's really the small things, like a cool guy in a corner store. So you decide, I'm not going to be afraid anymore, and I'm going to find him, and I'm going to say thank you and tell him, 'Wow, I think you might have been the one.'"

At that point, Nora stopped allowing every thought in her head to tumble out of her mouth so she could drag breath into her lungs.

At first, no one said a word, and she supposed they thought she was ridiculous, and honestly, she was thinking that herself. She didn't know if what she'd said had made sense or sounded deranged. She looked to James for help.

But then someone clapped. Others joined in.

"Why are they clapping?" she asked James.

"I'm not sure," James whispered in return.

"What was his name?" Megan asked.

"Jack. His name was Jack."

"It doesn't appear that Jack is here," Megan said. "Are you going to continue your search for him?"

"Yes. I have no choice—he's where my heart is, and I have to find him." Okay, she wasn't sure where that had come from. But it was the truth, wasn't it? She wouldn't rest until she found him.

Someone *awww*ed in the crowd.

Megan lowered her mic and the cameraman turned off the light. "I wish you luck, Nora. I still think about the guy I let get away fifteen years ago." She began to put things away. "This will be on our website tomorrow. Maybe it will help you find him."

More people came forward to share their own experiences with her, or to offer their advice on where to look next, or to wish her luck. The buzz slowly faded. No one outwardly seemed to think what she was doing was dumb or a waste of time. Everyone seemed to be rooting for her.

It felt wonderful to have people on her side in this way.

The crowd stood around until the clerk yelled at them for blocking the entrance to the store. People moved on to a nearby bar or headed inside to pick up a few things.

Nora turned to James. He was staring at her like he was seeing her for the first time. "That was . . . I mean, I never knew . . ."

"I know." She smiled sadly. "Should we get a drink or something?"

"We absolutely should." He grinned. "You are full of surprises, Nora November."

James chattered all the way back to her car. Nora was grateful that he had come. His presence helped her, for the space of the next couple of hours, anyway, to avoid the hard truth.

Jack hadn't come.

And she'd run out of ideas for finding him.

She'd blown her real opportunity all those months ago, and now the haystack with her needle kept getting bigger and bigger. She could feel the sink of despair in her chest, a hole that grew when she lost hope. She tried to focus on James, but she could feel that hole burning in the center of her chest.

Chapter 32

Nora slept restlessly—she dreamed she was chasing Jack, but he was always out of reach and moving so fast she couldn't catch him.

She woke feeling grumpy and lumpy.

Over coffee, she viewed the video from last night on the news website. It was just a clip: "With her hair swept over one eye, she said he had her heart." A paragraph below explained more.

Nora felt so sad for the woman in the Darth Vader T-shirt.

She took her coffee to the balcony that overlooked the parking lot. She couldn't hear the birds this morning—the sound of traffic drowned them out. She could feel the ghost of Nora hauling her gloom around like a heavy backpack as she Eeyored her way into Nora's brain. She couldn't blame her ghost—everything was feeling futile this morning. Her dead end with Jack, her dead garden, Walter's dead plants, her empty job search, her inability to really help Gus or bridge the gap with Lacey. She couldn't even shoot from the free throw line or blend a sauce. Plus, she was getting notices from her credit card company.

When she'd believed everything was different, she'd thought her life was better. Now she wasn't so sure. "Where are you, Grandpa?" she murmured.

The dark creep was real—if she marinated in negative thoughts, she'd drown in them for days. She forced herself to get up and do something before she couldn't and spent the weekend researching treatment options for Gus (expensive) and Brad Sachs (shark), the man who wanted Catherine's theater.

Brad Sachs had made a business of doing complete teardowns and building high-end apartments. His method was to buy tax deeds on foreclosed buildings and then evict residents as soon as the required grace period of around a year was up. He left people no option, which was what Catherine had hinted at—he'd initially try to buy them out for a few pennies on the dollar, and when they wouldn't or couldn't budge, he bought the deed from the taxing authority and started the countdown immediately. Catherine's countdown had begun months ago. She had less than forty days to get the arrears paid.

Nora needed to consult with a tax attorney. She didn't know any off the top of her head, but she'd graduated law school with a guy named Terrell Carter-Smith who'd gone into tax law. She would give him a call this week. In the meantime, she'd try to think of some roadblocks to buy the residents more time.

When the time came Sunday evening to make the dreaded trip to her parents' house in Rob Roy, Nora changed into a sunny yellow dress splashed with tiny white ducks and held up by two thin spaghetti straps. She styled her hair into a messy bun at her nape. Her dad hated messy buns. *"One should take the time to groom oneself,"* she'd once heard him say to an associate. That young woman had disappeared into her cubicle with apple-red cheeks.

There was no valet at her parents' house tonight, but there was a car in the circular drive she didn't recognize. *Only family, huh, Mom?*

Sharon answered the door with a tray of drinks. "Hello, Sharon," Nora said cheerily. She declined the offer of a drink and went into the living room. The big French doors were open to the mild spring temperatures, and Cynthia and Drew Firestone, her parents' oldest friends from the club, were outside admiring the view.

Cynthia brightened when she saw Nora and came forward with arms wide. "Look at you, hon. You're looking very well, all things considered."

"Thank you, all things considered," said Nora.

"Do you have a scar? I don't see it if you do."

"A scar?"

"From the head injury," Cynthia said and touched two fingers to her own forehead. "Do you get headaches? Drew says that can be a sign of damage."

"Nora, darling, there you are," her mother trilled, emerging from the hallway to the right. She peered closely at Nora's dress.

"They're ducks," Nora said.

"I see that. I also see you're putting a bit of the weight back on." She playfully pinched Nora's waist.

Nora had not thought once about her weight in the After, and that was one small but powerful bit of change from the Before. She wanted to gain total liberation from her mother's view of her. "You mean the weight I lost when I was in a coma?" she asked cheerfully.

Her mother blinked, surprised by her cheek. "That's not even remotely funny."

"Oh, sure it was, Roberta," Cynthia said, laughing. "Well, I think you look wonderful, Nora. Healthier than I expected. Drew had a patient who was in a coma, and it took him two years to fully recover. Most people don't recover at all, you know. What's the statistic, something like 10 percent?"

"Well, that's sobering," Nora said. "I guess I'm one of the lucky ones." In a manner of speaking, she supposed, given her run of bad luck. "Mom? Where's my box?"

"By the door." Her mother pointed to a small box. "Look, here comes Lacey."

Thank God. Nora excused herself and went to her sister.

Lacey's smile was wan and there were dark circles under bloodshot eyes. "You look exhausted, Lace."

"I haven't been sleeping well."

"Is everything okay?"

Lacey shrugged. "Hannah. Hey! Your page is really blowing up."

It was a valiant effort to change the subject, and Nora let her. "I had the meet-up Friday night."

Lacey grabbed her arm. "Already? I missed it. What happened?"

"He didn't show. But I—"

"Nora."

The disembodied voice of her father startled her. She preferred to see his approach so she could get her game face on. She steeled herself and turned. "Hi, Dad."

He was nattily dressed in a button-down shirt ironed within an inch of its life, the cuffs turned up revealing colorful paisleys, and dark trousers. His gaze flicked over her. "How are you?"

She thought it might be the first time he'd asked since her accident. "Great! And you?"

"What do you think?"

"I think dinner's ready," Lacey blurted. "I think Mom is trying to get everyone to the table."

Without a word, Nora's father turned and walked to the dining room.

Nora and Lacey exchanged a look. "He's in his usual cheerful mood," Lacey muttered.

Her mother had taken charge of the seating tonight ("Sit here, Drew, so you can see the river."), and as a result, Nora ended up next to her father. *Thanks, Mom.*

The caterer served a Caesar salad to begin. What was with this family and Caesar salads? Nora didn't touch it—it seemed blasphemous to her now. Not that anyone noticed; Dad was holding to his end of the truce by ignoring her completely. He was engrossed in his conversation with Drew, a neurologist who had a former patient who'd filed a malpractice suit over a lumbar puncture that had gone wrong. Nora's dad was suggesting they go after the maker of the puncture tool Drew had used. Nora's stomach clenched just listening to them.

When the main meal of trout and potato soufflé had been served, Cynthia asked about Nora's search for Jack. "I read about it on the KXAN website," she said.

"Read about what?" her father asked.

"Um . . . the corner store guy, Dad. I told you about him the last time I was here." She turned her attention to Cynthia. "No luck so far."

"Your daughter is very clever," Cynthia said. "She posted on social media asking him to meet her at the corner store where they were held hostage. The article said dozens showed up in hopes of seeing a reunion."

Nora's scalp began to tingle. She could feel her father's displeasure dripping down her spine. But she had too much to lose now and would not give in to the fear of his wrath like she would have in the Before. She decided to roll with it—her life couldn't get any worse. "Yep, thirty to forty people."

"What are you talking about?" Mom sounded frantic.

"Nora," her father said, smooth as ice, "let's not have the evening hijacked by your—"

"I'm looking for the corner store guy, Mom," Nora continued, boldly ignoring her father in a way she'd never had the guts to do in the Before. "He's one of the regrets."

"What are the regrets?" Cynthia asked.

"When I recovered from my NDE, I had some strong regrets about things I hadn't done before I almost died. Like interests I wanted to pursue. Since I have a new lease on life, I'm doing them now. I call it my reverse bucket list—all the things I mean to do after I died."

"Wait," Drew said. "How does this corner store person fit in?"

"His name is Jack. He was a fellow hostage, and I really connected with him. I regret that I never saw him again, and I want to find him to say thanks."

Her dad laughed coldly. "I don't see how this man can be a sincere regret, sweetie."

"Sweetie?" Lacey whispered with revulsion under her breath.

"Makes sense to me," Drew said. "It's not unreasonable to experience something traumatic and be drawn to someone you went through the experience with."

"Trauma drama," Cynthia said with a laugh.

"I think it's exciting," Lacey defiantly chimed in. "It's very cool that you're at least trying, Nora."

"I'm sorry, but I can't condone this sort of thing," Nora's mother said. "Drew, you're a neurologist. Didn't you say Nora was possibly brain damaged?"

"Whoa, whoa." Drew instantly threw up his hands, his face reddening. "I said it wouldn't be unheard of for an experience like Nora's to result in brain damage. I didn't say *she* had damage."

"But how do we know that she hasn't hallucinated this man? I mean, when one's brain completely shuts down for several minutes, isn't it possible?"

It was both alarming and hideous that Nora's own mother was so casually hypothesizing about the possibility of her brain damage. "I don't have brain damage, and I'm not hallucinating, Mom. I had a life-altering experience."

"There is a more practical reason why you shouldn't publicly chase this fantasy," her father said, quite matter-of-factly, as if it were up to him. As if she'd asked.

"Not a fantasy," Nora said curtly. But wasn't it? How in the hell would she ever find Jack? Her father was saying aloud what she feared deep down. As usual.

"Because of the lawsuit I have filed on your behalf against the resort for negligence," he blithely continued. "You don't want to generate any publicity that could harm that suit."

The old, familiar quake of anxiety came back with a vengeance, rocking Nora's belly. "You did what? I specifically asked you not to do that."

Her father smiled indulgently, as if she were a precocious child. "I told you I took care of everything. You shouldn't have been on that beach that day, plain and simple."

This news was infuriating. Her father expected her to back down, to not cause a scene in front of guests. But he'd underestimated the new Nora. "You know we have no business suing them, Dad. It wasn't their fault; it was—" She had to swallow down a lump that suddenly lodged in her throat. She wanted to say exactly what it was, but the words wouldn't come. Something was blocking her, a memory not fully realized.

"It was a result of their negligence."

"No," she said. "That's not—"

"Can we talk about this later?" her mother interjected.

Nora ignored her. "You can't sue them if I don't want to. That's unethical."

Her father's eyes narrowed dangerously. "Are you telling me, David November, what is ethical?"

"David!" her mother all but shouted. "Did I tell you? Cynthia is on the board of the Austin Ballet and she was telling me about the upcoming programs."

There was a moment of silence before Cynthia dutifully picked up the baton. "It's going to be a delicious year," she said and began to talk about the planned performances.

Nora's skin was crawling with anxiety and alarm about what her father had done. But there was something more, a feeling or a thought that wanted to be set free. Part of a memory squeezing her throat, making it difficult to breathe.

And yet it was also strengthening her resolve that her father would not railroad her into this lawsuit.

She looked at Lacey, who was staring back at her, wide-eyed.

Nora needed to get her box and get the hell out of here. She needed to breathe, to go back to her apartment where she could be anyone but a November.

Chapter 33

Nora had hoped for vindication in the box of papers James had grabbed from her office, or maybe for a job lead she hadn't thought of. But there was nothing useful other than the paper copy of her contacts.

She went over the list several times, wondering how exactly she was going to call these people to ask them to hire her. The very idea filled her with fear, as if she was exposing some major flaw in her character—an inability to abide her father and a weakness in litigation. She wished she could talk to Dr. Cass—she was always so encouraging, pointing out things Nora maybe hadn't considered. But her rate was three hundred dollars an hour, and there was no way Nora could afford that right now.

She told herself to put on her big girl panties, ate several cookies for sugary carb courage, and then started making calls.

Most of them rolled to voice mail. Those who answered listened to the spiel she'd prepared about looking for a new opportunity, a chance to spread her wings, *blah, blah, blah*. They said, sure, if something came up, they'd give her a call.

Fisher Franks, an attorney she knew with the Loewe firm, answered on the first ring. He was a rancher-turned-lawyer, a good ol' boy with a decidedly Texas swagger. After she'd given her spiel, he asked her about her accident. "I hear you had some sort of weird surfing accident."

Nora was taken aback. "I did."

"And you almost drowned?"

"Um . . . yes."

"I've never surfed that part of the coast."

He'd probably never surfed at all on a cold, wet, and wintry day just to push himself to the limit to see what he could feel. Well, Nora had. She'd been so numbed by bouts of depression, she'd wanted to feel *anything*.

"Anyway, why would you want to leave your dad's firm? You won't get a better deal anywhere else."

"I need a change of pace."

"Interesting," he drawled, clearly not believing a word she'd said. "I don't know of anything off the top of my head, but I'll let you know if anything opens up."

"I'd appreciate it." Nora was gripping her phone so tightly it was a wonder it didn't break. She said goodbye and clicked off, then tossed her phone across the room as if it had burned her.

She got up and went to the window and stared out. Surfside Beach came roaring back to her mind's eye. The cold and the wind. The spray in her face. The water so dark and choppy. She could see herself on the beach . . . but then what?

It wouldn't come. She shook her head and turned back to her task.

••••••

After the better part of two days spent calling people on her contact list with nothing to show for it, Nora texted Gus to remind him about the painting class later in the week and to tell him she'd found a rehab ranch in Smithville, men only, and potentially affordable. Gus apparently listened to her message because later that afternoon he texted her a thumbs-up.

Tonight she was cooking for Lacey. She stopped on the way to Lacey's house to get the ingredients for the chicken dish and garlic sauce that she planned to make. Surely she could bake chicken without screwing it up. She picked up a cake mix and those ingredients too. If all else went to hell, at least there would be cake. Now, that was something she knew how to do—no one who'd ever suffered from depression avoided carbs. Nora knew better than most—her mother had kept a running tally of her carb intake in the Before.

Lacey wasn't home when Nora arrived, so she let herself in. The kitchen was still cluttered with boxes, dishes, pots, pans, and lots of paper for packing, and even a dried flower wreath. Nora pushed it all aside to make the cake.

Lacey arrived a half hour after Nora, looking exhausted, and headed for the fridge.

"What's new?" Nora asked as Lacey poured a healthy glass of white wine.

"The same," she said wearily and filled Nora in on the latest round of fighting with Hannah. She said it was truly over, and they were selling the house.

"But you worked so hard on it," Nora said.

"Yeah," Lacey said sadly. "You're lucky you've never had any long-term relationships. Because when they end, it sucks."

It wasn't that Nora hadn't wanted relationships—she just wasn't any good at them. The few times she managed to get out of her own head and date, something inevitably would get in the way: work, her family, her depression, her anxiety.

"Speaking of which, I really hope you find Jack," Lacey said. "Did you see the comment suggesting you buy a billboard on I-35?"

"If I had the money, I'd try it."

The cake came out of the oven, and as Nora iced it, she told Lacey about the art class with Gus and that she'd found a potential treatment facility.

Lacey groaned. "Treatment again? Why bother? Gus is going to drink himself to death."

"Lacey!"

"Am I wrong? Sorry, but I had to get off that roller coaster. Treatment never works for him."

A heat crept into Nora's cheeks. They'd all leaned on Lacey too much. That's what happened to smart, capable women—everyone needed them. "Anyway, it's a ranch near Smithville. Men only."

"How much?"

Nora sighed. "Thousands." She set the finished cake aside.

"Dad won't pay, you know. He and Mom have written Gus off."

"I know." It hurt Nora's heart that they'd given up on him.

"And I won't pay. I took money out of my savings the last time. And you don't have a job. I don't know what Gus's financial situation is, but given where he's living and that he can't hold down a job, I'm guessing he doesn't have anything."

"Right . . . but I'll figure something out," Nora said.

Lacey snorted. "Yep. Good luck with that."

Tears burned the back of Nora's eyes as she prepped the ingredients for the garlic sauce. Gus needed her more than ever.

"So, for real," Lacey said. "Have you thought about going back to the firm?"

Nora looked up, stunned. "Are you kidding? I finally have the balls to leave and you want me to go back?"

Lacey shrugged. "Dad is never going to let you go, Nora. Who will be his son? I think it puts you in a position to bargain."

Nora's gut twisted with revulsion. "I don't want to bargain. And it won't matter—I'll never be Nathan."

"But you're the next best thing, and he's not going to let you screw that up. He's got this perverse sense of legacy."

"That's just it—I'm *not* the next best thing. I'm not the prettiest, or the smartest, or the most accomplished, or funny or droll or anything. I'm average, and that won't work for him. Anyway, why is it so important to him to have a son?"

"Who knows," Lacey said through a yawn.

It should have been you, the ghost of Nora whispered. She tried to ignore her.

"How's the job search going, anyway?" Lacey asked.

Nora's first instinct was to unload on her sister, but that wasn't why she was here—that was the exact opposite reason of why she was here. "No one is biting. But I took a case pro bono. It's a geriatric thespian group. They own a small theater and got behind on taxes, and there's a lien. You'll never guess who holds the lien."

"Who?"

"Brad Sachs."

"Seriously?" Lacey laughed with surprise. "What a coincidence." She polished off the last of her wine. "What are we having?"

"Chicken in garlic sauce. Grandma would be proud, right? Remember all the hours she and I watched those tapes of Julia Child?"

"I'm so glad she taught you how to bake, because that cake smells delicious." Lacey grinned. "It reminds me of the cupcakes you stole in the Cayman Islands."

The comment pricked Nora. "I didn't steal them."

All of them—Gus and his parents, Lacey and Nora, Mom and Dad, and even Grandma and Grandpa—had vacationed at a swank resort in the Caymans when Cancún became too pedestrian for her mother. They'd worn sun hats, and Grandma stuck paper flowers in the ribbons around the crowns of the hats. *"It's a fiesta,"* Grandpa had said.

"That was the best trip until you met that guy on the beach," Lacey said.

"Winston," Nora said. Winston was sixteen, local, and sold water and snacks on the beach. He had dark skin, a mass of dark curly hair, light brown eyes, and a luscious smile. He could cast off a boat as confidently as he walked on sand. Nora had developed a massive crush on him. "He taught me how to gut a fish."

"Gross," Lacey said.

"But useful," Nora countered.

She'd spent as much time with Winston on the beach as she could, following him around, laughing at his jokes. There had been a molten kiss under the pier. She could still recall how his hand felt against her skin, sliding up under her shirt. His body, warm and firm like the sand, fragrant like the island.

"He was cute," Lacey said. "Then Dad found out."

The memory of that confrontation stabbed so hard at Nora that she was tempted to press a hand to her rib cage to contain the invisible bleeding. Dad's rage was potent—he'd grabbed her by the ponytail and yanked her backward as she'd tried to flee the suite. *"Who the hell do you think you are?"* He'd banished her, and Lacey and Gus by association, from the sunset dinner cruise. He'd left them behind in their luxury suite with no food as punishment and commanded Lacey and Gus to call immediately if she tried to leave the hotel. But they were hungry, so Nora had snuck into the concierge suite and brought back cupcakes and orange juice.

She suddenly recalled it all—the shame, the guilt, the uncertainty. The terrible feeling of needing to warn Winston but not knowing how to reach him. The humiliation of being locked away like a leper. How her insides had felt ripped to shreds when she realized she would not see Winston again, and then the torture of imagining what he would think of her when she disappeared.

"Are you all right?" Lacey asked. "Do you need me to push your head between your knees?"

Nora shook her head. "I'm good." She wasn't hyperventilating, but she could feel herself gearing up for it. That was the problem with anxiety—sometimes it crept in before you knew it was there. She rubbed her forehead. "Why was Dad so mad? That's what happens when you're seventeen and on vacation—you meet a cute boy, you develop a crush, and it's over when you get on the plane. It's not like I came home pregnant."

Lacey snorted. "Why is Dad ever anything? He's a racist and a misogynist, and I'm like ninety-nine percent sure he's an adulterer. And a narcissist, we mustn't forget that."

Nothing about dear old Dad surprised Nora, but to hear Lacey put it all together was sort of startling in its obvious truth.

"Do I have time to shower?" Lacey asked.

"Yep," Nora said. "I'm going to make the sauce and then cook the chicken."

"Great, I'm starving," Lacey said. She topped off her wine and left the kitchen.

Nora got out a pan to make the sauce and checked Bernice's recipe. She put the required amount of oil into the pan and turned on the gas burner, then went back to her phone on the counter to read the next steps. But she got distracted by the memory of how Grandpa had come to her rescue that awful summer in the Caymans. He claimed he and Grandma wanted to go home and took her with them. But Nora knew her father had sent her away. While the rest of the family remained in the Caymans for the next ten days, Nora was curled on the window seat in Grandma's kitchen on the farm, mourning Winston.

An acrid smell filled her nose. Nora glanced over her shoulder—the dish towel she'd tossed down had caught the flame under her pan. Nora dove for it, knocking it away from the flame, and accidentally sent the pan flying. Sizzling oil landed on her hand as the pan clattered to the tile floor. She shrieked at the resulting burn on her hand and looked for something to put on it—but the towel had landed on the dried flower wreath, which caught fire. "Lacey!" she shouted and frantically looked for a fire extinguisher as the flames spread to the stack of papers.

Not finding one, she grabbed her phone and called 911.

Later, when the firefighters had gone, Nora and her bandaged hand stood next to Lacey in her bathrobe, her hair still wet. Nora felt physically ill at what she'd done, at what could have happened. She kept swallowing down waves of nausea.

Lacey looked at the fire damage to the counter and the wall in her renovated kitchen, then at Nora. "What the hell?"

"The towel—"

"No, I mean, what the actual hell, Nora? I have to sell a house that I love, and now I have to deal with this?" She gestured wildly at the damage. "I don't have money to fix this."

"I'm so sorry," Nora tried.

"Sorry," Lacey repeated darkly, her voice dripping with derision. "You're always so *sorry*!"

The adrenaline Nora had experienced while the firefighters had put out the fire turned into nausea. "I'll fix it—"

"No, you won't," Lacey said, seething. "I'm the one who will fix it. I'm *always* the one who has to fix it." She looked around the kitchen again. "I can't deal with you right now."

Nora stared at her. Her sister sounded exhausted and resigned. "Lacey, I—"

"Seriously, Nora. I can't deal with you, okay? It's always something with you! I don't want to see you. I don't want to talk to you. I need a break. Can you just . . . go home now?" She picked up the cake, yanked open a drawer and grabbed a fork, and marched out of the kitchen with both.

"I'll fix it!" Nora shouted after her. But her gut was already churning with pessimism. Why did she think that after thirty-one years of being a loser, she could fix anything? How had she let herself buy the notion that she was different? She wasn't different—she was still the same old Nora, disappointing everyone.

Gone was all the euphoric certainty of life she'd felt after her NDE. Gone was all hope. She couldn't cut it, she couldn't fix it, she couldn't seem to do anything right but take up space.

Nice work, Nora November.

Chapter 34

Nora felt dead inside, like she was a heavy bag of wet sand. Immovable.

She couldn't sleep. She sat on her used couch in the dark, reviewing all her missteps, and especially Lacey's burned kitchen. How had everything gone to hell so fast? All she'd wanted in the After was to get her life together and live on her own terms. Was that asking too much? The hope and euphoria that had come with her NDE had now given way to the terror that maybe she was incapable of change. That maybe the only thing she was good at was screwing everything up.

She couldn't stop seeing the look on Lacey's face when she'd said she didn't want to see her or talk to her. She'd looked so tired and disappointed and so over it all. Nora needed Lacey; she needed her sister in her life for friendship, for support, for solidarity. But she'd burned down any hope of Lacey trusting her again. Literally. She'd felt Lacey's fatigue and disappointment to her core—hell, she'd been living with it most of her adult life. Had she really believed her NDE had changed her? What a joke. She was still the same miserable waste of skin and bone she'd always been.

At some point she found herself on the floor. She sobbed at the memory of how freeing it felt to write the reverse bucket list after she came home from the hospital. She'd felt so hopeful, and she was learning how to tame that awful inner voice, the hyper-critical one. The new Nora was starting to believe she could be anything she wanted to be.

That stupid, misguided Nora. Nothing had changed—her reverse bucket list hadn't magically transformed her into some sort of superwoman. She was still unforgivable and unlovable. Still making life hard for the people she loved.

When the sun began to rise, Nora was sitting on her balcony overlooking the parking lot, completely numb. As the first rays of light appeared over Riverside Drive, her numbness turned to grief again. Surely it hadn't all been in vain? Surely she hadn't nearly died only to come back and be worse than she was before? Surely she hadn't lived just so she could hate herself for the rest of her life?

Come on, Nora. You can't give up.

She tried to motivate herself. She went back inside and spent time checking on applications she'd submitted for jobs. Unfortunately, calling large firms that only accepted applications online was akin to calling outer space—no one answered, and if they did, they didn't know anything.

Her hopelessness began to turn derisive. She knew herself, knew that if she stayed in her apartment, her thoughts would get even darker.

She managed to get herself dressed and made a trip to the garden.

She expected some sort of divine transformation when she walked through the gates, but nothing happened.

Her tomato plants had died. The calla lilies were refusing to grow. The bell peppers were freakishly small.

Her failure at the garden was particularly soul-crushing. It didn't make sense. Yes, she'd neglected the garden after Grandpa's death, but she wasn't neglecting it now. She was furiously tending it, and her garden was not growing.

The metaphor for her life could not have been more obvious.

She sank down into the dirt next to her dead tomato plants, killed by too much water along with the Venus flytraps next door. She'd failed at reviving her inner athlete and had managed to get herself barred from the basketball court in the process. She couldn't cook without breaking something or starting a fire, had alienated Lacey, and for God's sake, she was useless to Gus—what was a painting class to him?

Her phone pinged. She pulled it out of her pocket—it was a text notification that her credit card payment was past due again. A tear slid down her cheek.

It was official—she was falling apart. "Why did you have to leave?" she whispered to Grandpa. Why hadn't she gone to see him when she said she would? Why couldn't she have stayed with him in his celestial garden?

The tears came in a torrent, sliding down her face and her nose, carrying her last gasp of optimism and hope with them. And on her ragged breaths, self-loathing rose like a phoenix to spread its wings and thrive.

There was only one real solution to her troubles. One she'd been trying to ignore for days.

She had to go crawling back to November and Sons.

What else could she do? She needed to pay her bills and her rent, to fix Lacey's kitchen, to get Gus into treatment . . . The list went on. She'd been lying to herself all this time. She wasn't different after her NDE—she was delusional. The person she believed herself to be at her core had been buried under reality. She was no more capable of recovering the girl she'd been than she was cooking, or painting, or anything else.

Her dad was going to make her grovel. Then he would make sure that she never again stepped out of the lines he'd painted for her. She would not be able to bear it.

She could hardly see through her tears. She slid down onto the earth and rolled onto her back, the sky a blurry, watery blue above her.

She needed a lifeline. Someone to help her, someone who could promise her it would be all right. What would Dr. Cass say? That transformation was hard and there would be setbacks. But did everything have to be a setback? What would Grandpa say? Nora moaned and closed her eyes. He would tell her she was perfect the way she was, that God didn't make mistakes, that she had to keep going. *Grow your garden.* He would tell her that she would find her way, because he believed in her. *You have to believe in yourself.*

"I'm trying, Grandpa," she whispered. "I'm trying so hard." But the thought of having to return to the Before was so excruciatingly painful, like tiny daggers stabbing her over and over. It would be so much worse. She truly didn't understand the point of life right now.

"Are you all right?" a woman called to her.

"Yep. Fine," Nora said, waving her off. With a sigh, she forced herself to sit up. She wiped her face with her fingertips, probably smearing dirt on her cheeks. *You have to believe in yourself.* The weak thought whispered across her mind. "I do," she muttered. "I believe I can screw things up better than anyone." She stood up. She dusted off her pants. She took a few deep breaths. Okay. She'd go home and figure out how to approach Dad and try not to completely hate herself in the process. She leaned down to pick up her tote, and when she did, her gaze fell on a spot near where she'd planted the calla lilies. A clod of dirt that looked . . . disturbed. She walked to the spot and bent down to have a closer look. There, barely visible under the clod, was the tip of something green. It was impossible to imagine how something so small and tender could be strong enough to push a lump of earth out of its way, but Grandpa's calla lilies were rising up, coming to her rescue.

The cascade of hope that immediately fell over her was so great, Nora burst into tears again.

That was the point—*life* was the point. These calla lilies could not be drowned. They had literally moved earth to breathe and live. She was at least as strong as that, wasn't she? She could not be drowned. Sure, she had some mountains to scale, but they weren't insurmountable, were they? She had to figure out how to get Gus into treatment, to fix Lacey's kitchen, and to pay her bills. Those were not character flaws; those were problems to be solved.

She could do it. She had to change her mindset. She was many things, but she wasn't stupid.

She remembered Grandpa telling her that this was her season.

This was her season, dammit. If the calla lilies could push off the weight of the world to grow, then so could she.

••••••

That afternoon she drove to the Triangle Theater. She'd talked to Terrell Carter-Smith, her former classmate, about the tax lien, and he'd given her a couple of ideas. Which were, he said, "not great." When you owed taxes, the government was pretty good about squeezing and squeezing until they got blood from the proverbial turnip.

At the theater, she was charmed by the pots of fresh flowers at the door of an otherwise nondescript beige building. Inside, the paint was peeling, the box office leaned slightly to the right, and there was a distinct smell that made her think a sewer had malfunctioned.

She could hear music and went into the auditorium where a rehearsal was underway. Catherine was singing—she had a surprisingly delicate voice for a woman who pulled no punches. She and a tall, gangly man whose deep bass voice rattled the rafters sang a duet. Given the state of the theater, Nora feared that such a performance could quite literally bring the place down, curtains and all.

She walked down the aisle, curious about the number of seats that had been covered with needlepoint. It was obvious some work had been done—the new lumber on the apron of the stage indicated the boards had been replaced. There were a few patches in the curtains, detectable by the slightly darker fabric. And the fabricated set of tenement housing was well done.

Nora took a seat in the front row. Catherine spotted her and waved at the end of her number. The director—Walter!—applauded them. "Great job. Take ten!"

Catherine came down off the stage, patting her face with a towel. "Can't we turn on the air-conditioning, Walter? It's boiling in here."

"We can do anything you want with money, Catherine."

Catherine winced. "That, we do not have." She fell into a seat next to Nora with a grunt, then leaned forward and looked behind her. A wire was pressing against the back of the seat. "Another one." She sighed. "We need to replace all the seats, but of course, we have no money." She looked at Nora. "Well, Venus flytrap killer? What do you think?"

Nora winced. "I'm so sorry about the flytraps."

Walter looked up with a frown.

"Hi, Walter," she said sheepishly. "I'm going to get you some more flytraps."

He rolled his eyes.

"What about the theater?" Catherine asked.

"I've consulted with a tax attorney, and it's not good."

Catherine's face fell. "But you'll figure it out, right?"

"I'm going to try, Catherine, but this is not my area of expertise," Nora said. "My friend said you have two options: one, pay the arrears. Or two, declare bankruptcy, which will slow the process. But even then, you'll still have to pay the arrears plus twenty-five percent interest."

Catherine gaped at her. "Well, aren't you Little Miss Sunshine?"

"I've never been accused of that. Look, I have more research to do. But in the meantime, you focus on making as much money as you can from your show to go toward the back taxes. And anything else you can scrape together."

Another member of the troupe took a seat on the edge of the stage.

"Don't sit there, Meredith. We just painted!" another woman shouted.

"Well, excuse me, Annabeth," Meredith said and clambered to her feet. "Do we have a chance?" she asked Nora.

"Like I said, I still have a lot to research. But honestly? Probably not," Nora said with a sympathetic wince.

"Should we be looking for alternative housing?" asked one of the men.

"Don't talk like that, Martin. What is the matter with you?" Catherine groused.

"I'm being realistic, Catherine. Why do we always have to believe?"

"Hey," said another man and pointed at Nora. "You're that girl."

"Excuse me?"

"That girl . . . on the news. We were just talking about it. We saw you on TV looking for a man from that robbery."

"She's *her*?" A woman turned to peer at Nora. Then all of them were staring at her.

"That's me," Nora confirmed.

"What's happening with that?" the first man asked. "Any leads? Speaking of believing, Martin," he added as an aside.

"Not yet," Nora said. "But people are sharing the search, so maybe."

"Sharing what, exactly?" Catherine asked.

Once again, Nora told the story of the robbery and the hostage situation and her connection with a fellow hostage. In the interest of time, she kept the details to a minimum. She summed up by saying the night was kismet.

"Kismet is highly underrated on the whole," mused Walter.

"Why didn't you call him? Why didn't he call you?" Annabeth asked.

"That's what the whole TV thing was about, Annabeth," said Doralee.

Annabeth shrugged. "Seems like one of you would have called the other if you had such a great connection."

"You'll find him," Martin said. "If you believe." He gave Catherine the side-eye.

"Of course she believes," said Walter. "Hope's the only thing she's got."

How was it that all old people said the same things? It was like an auditorium of grandpas in here. And it might seem like all she had was hope on the surface, but Nora had more than that. She had a brain, and like those calla lilies, she had dug down deep enough to discover a will to thrive.

"My husband and I ran this theater on little more than hope for years," Catherine said. "You put hope into the universe and it comes back to you. I read that in a book. What was the name of that book?" Her brow scrunched into a frown as she tried to recall.

"Keep believing, kiddo," Walter advised Nora. "Maybe your luck will change. All right, everyone, we'll talk about this later, but right now we need to rehearse. We have only two weeks until opening night."

"But what about our lawsuit?" Catherine complained, gesturing in Nora's direction.

"Not a lawsuit," Nora corrected her. "How are your ticket sales?"

"Wretched," said Meredith as she began to climb the stairs to the stage. "I said all along we need a marketing strategy, but no one listens to me. Social media, I said. We ought to be on TikTok. That's where they all are now."

"I'll listen to you over cocktails, Meredith," Catherine said as she got up. "But I'm not doing the Tik."

"It's not called that," Meredith complained as they found their places. "Nobody calls it the Tik."

Nora watched them rehearse the first act. Catherine was a wonder as Blanche DuBois. Grandpa would have loved this so much. He would be buying a block of theater seats, determined to fill them with his friends. Hey . . . she could do that. Okay, yes, she was feeling a huge financial strain, and she had only one friend . . . but surely she had enough money to buy a block of seats as a contribution to a worthy cause. She sincerely wanted to help them.

Because they weren't giving up, and neither was she.

Chapter 35

N*ora's despair didn't miraculously disappear. Darkness,* her old friend, was still lurking around the edges, making various attempts to shove her under. She made a point of rising before dawn every morning to walk along the lake and listen to the birdsong. Grandpa was right—it was a very optimistic sound. So optimistic that she had started to believe in herself again. She wasn't quite ready to make that phone call to Dad, wasn't ready to throw in the towel today.

She was on the way out the door to the cooking class when she decided to check her social media posts.

And there it was—another tiny miracle.

Oh, it wasn't Jack—that kind of luck seemed to be avoiding her. But it was possibly the next best thing. Megan from KXAN had direct messaged, asking her to call. Nora's heart began to pound—maybe Jack had gotten in touch after seeing the story on the website.

She dialed Megan's number.

"Hey," Megan said. "Did you see the piece?"

"I did. Did you hear from Jack?"

"What? Oh . . . no. I'm sorry, I didn't mean to get your hopes up. But I do think I can help. We'd like to have you on our morning show. Your story has resonated with viewers—the whole the-one-who-got-away trope."

Nora didn't view her life as a trope, but okay.

"And maybe it will get your search out to more people. I mean, someone is bound to know this guy, right?"

Nora's brain was suddenly spinning like a top. Television? She hadn't even thought to try it. "Right," she said.

"You'll do it?"

"Are you kidding?" Nora laughed. Hope, man. She was brimming with it these days.

They wanted her tomorrow.

******

At cooking class, Willow proved that not only could she play basketball, she could cook. Her béchamel lasagna was voted the best. Tanya swore she'd given her daughter the reins and had acted as her sous chef.

Nora didn't have a dish for tasting because she was Bernice's assistant. All that was missing was her dunce cap. But Nora wasn't quitting. She paid careful attention to everything Bernice did. She'd paid for this damn class, and she would finish it being able to cook something.

Chef Bernice took photos of Willow's lasagna for her website. "You know what's so great about this? It proves that literally anyone can learn how to cook." Her gaze happened to land on Nora. "Just about anyone. Next week we're moving on to Spain." She gave Nora a pat on the shoulder. "I bet you'll do great with Spanish food."

Nora wouldn't be holding her breath, but she'd try her hardest.

She followed Tanya and Willow out, Willow carrying a container with her lasagna. "You did great, Willow. Very tasty."

"Thanks."

"Hey, think we can play again when I'm off restriction?"

Willow sighed. "I don't know. You're not very good. And besides, I really want to be on a team." She sounded resigned to her fate.

Nora felt Willow's hurt—she'd been that kid once. She turned to go to her own car, but a shadow wisp slipped past and Nora's inner athlete suddenly had an idea. Why hadn't she thought of this before?

She turned back. "Hey, Tanya?"

Willow was already in their car. Tanya paused before she got in and looked at Nora.

"I have an idea. What if it was me? I mean, you said you had to have an adult sponsor to have a team in the rec center league. What if I was the coach and sponsor?"

Tanya sighed. "Are you the white savior now? Swooping in to lead our girls to victory? I thought you just wanted to play. I don't understand why you keep pushing to be so involved. Don't you have a job or something?"

Because she'd been Willow once. Because maybe she could make a difference somewhere. "I'm currently between jobs. Listen, Tanya." She stepped closer. "I wasn't kidding when I told you how much I love the sport. And that I wasn't allowed to play. My dad literally stabbed my basketball."

Tanya stared at her. "Excuse me?"

"That's how against it he was. And obviously, my playing days are behind me, a fact that I have reluctantly come to terms with since Willow and her friends destroyed me on the court. Trust me, nothing obliterates one's ego quite like a group of twelve- and thirteen-year-olds taking you down."

Tanya smirked a little. "I hear that."

"The thing is, this would be an opportunity for me as much as it would be for Willow. I would be thrilled to be a sponsor and get to go to the games. I would be ecstatic being on the court and without getting the stuffing beat out of me. Plus, I have the time to do it."

Tanya stared hard, taking Nora's measure. Several moments ticked by before she finally sighed. "You are very weird, Nora."

"I know, right? Sometimes I amaze even myself."

"I guess I can talk to the other parents."

Nora squealed with delight.

"Don't get all goofy on me. They're not going to like that you're kind of a head case. No offense."

"None taken."

"And Wanda's going to want that doctor's note."

Great. Another expense. "Sure," Nora said. "Thank you, Tanya. You won't be sorry."

"Please don't make promises you can't keep," Tanya said as she opened the driver door. "I'll let you know."

Nora's inner athlete lumbered through some victory laps as she watched Tanya and Willow drive away.

It occurred to her that maybe this was how she needed to look at her reverse bucket list—instead of seeing defeat, maybe all she had to do was open her mind to different interpretations.

Chapter 36

Megan had arranged for a driver to pick up Nora at five the next morning. They drove through empty streets to the studio, where a young woman in slim brown pants and a black sweater came out to greet them. "I'm Katie. We're just going to pop you in for makeup."

They primped Nora, then ushered her into the greenroom. Katie offered her a coffee and a scone. Nora felt strangely calm. While she ate her scone, Katie explained how the show would go. Megan would introduce her and her story. A clip would air, taken from Megan's interview of Nora at the corner store. And then Megan would ask Nora a few questions.

Someone came for her and led her down a narrow hall full of TV producing equipment. They put a mic on her. Nora could see Megan behind a plexiglass desk, chatting with the weatherman. And then Megan looked at the camera and said, "Have you ever thought about the one who got away? After the break, we'll be talking to a woman who is trying to find the one who got away from her."

Someone yelled, "Clear!" Nora was hurried out to sit at the desk.

"Hi," Megan chirped. An employee pushed into Megan's view, and there was a whirlwind around them, then someone shouted, "Quiet on the set!" and someone else counted, and then lights were blinding Nora.

Megan began by talking about the way people generally viewed that one love interest who might have gotten away and how hindsight was twenty-twenty. But in Nora's case, that hindsight had come to her in a near-death experience. She gave a brief summary of what a near-death experience was. Then she turned and welcomed Nora to the set.

"Let's start with your near-death experience," Megan suggested. "Tell us a little about that."

Nora was amazed by how calm she was. How well she spoke. There was no uncertainty, no bees swarming in her. She'd told the story so many times now that it felt natural. She said the only thing she remembered about the accident was that it was cold, but that she'd technically drowned. She described the field of gold and her dog and the bright light. She mentioned Grandpa but left out his garden—that felt entirely too personal. She talked about the regrets that had come flying at her, all the things she'd left undone. And that when she recovered, she'd made a list of those regrets to create her reverse bucket list.

"A reverse bucket list. I love that. Can you tell us what's on it?"

Nora told them about cooking, painting, and playing basketball, a game she'd loved as a kid. She told them she had a garden now, and that she really, really wanted to find a guy named Jack.

"Can you tell us what he looks like?"

Nora smiled for the first time since the fire. "He was tall. He had beautiful, warm blue eyes. His hair was darkish, and he wore this adorable hand-knitted scarf."

"What was it about him that makes you think he was the one?" Megan asked.

"Well . . . everything. I felt almost drunk with giddiness. He was so familiar and appealing, and it felt like nothing else in the whole world mattered, not even being held hostage in a robbery. He had this way of looking at me, like . . . he could really see me."

Megan smiled.

"I wanted to know everything about him. I wanted to bask in his smile. It's that feeling of wanting to pinch a baby's cheek because you can't contain your emotions, you know? I didn't want the night to end, if you can believe it." She remembered standing next to him before the policeman came to get them for their statements. She remembered the fondness and attention in his eyes when he touched her face and tucked some hair behind her ear. "*Wow,*" he'd said.

"Is it possible that what you were feeling was adrenaline?" Megan asked.

Nora shook her head. "I wasn't scared. The robber was so inept."

Megan laughed. "If you felt so strongly, why didn't you get in touch with him after the robbery?"

"A great question," Nora said. "I didn't trust what I'd experienced. But I should have." She paused and looked at the camera. "I'm sorry," she said to Jack. "I am so, so sorry. I don't know why I let you get away. But I am so lucky to have a second chance at life, and I want to find you and see if maybe we can have a second chance too. But even if you've moved on, even if it wasn't the same for you, I need to tell you that you mattered to me."

"Well," Megan said. "I think I can hear the *awws* across Austin." She put her hand to her ear, then said, "My producer is telling me that during this segment, Taylor Swift has tweeted about you. She's in town for the F1 concert series, isn't she, Steve? She has over ninety million followers."

The camera crew began to applaud.

"Good luck to you, Nora," Megan said. She turned back to the camera and instructed viewers how to find Nora's social media posts.

Nora smiled at the camera again, willing her message to wing its way through the clouds to Jack.

Chapter 37

M*uch to her surprise, it looked like Nora would be* coaching a girls' basketball team. Tanya had been in touch to let her know that the other parents were okay with her sponsoring and coaching the girls in the rec center league.

"I had to do some persuading," Tanya said. "They're a little suspicious, to say the least. But Willow likes you and she really wants this, and if I don't let her have it, she will pester me to death."

"Tanya—thank you," Nora gushed with surprise and elation. "You won't regret it."

"There you go again, promising something you don't know you can deliver. I'm bringing the girls next Thursday after school. Get your doctor's note, then come and show us what you've got."

"Can't wait," Nora said.

She hung up and danced around her living room with her basketball . . . until it occurred to Nora that she'd never coached anything and wasn't sure how to go about it.

Her law degree came in handy. Over the next twenty-four hours, she filled out the paperwork required to establish the team at the rec center (which she named Hot Shotz in a moment of what she considered inspired brilliance), drew up a proposed practice schedule, and even drafted an agreement for Tanya and the parents of all the girls to acknowledge shared costs.

She arrived at the community center fresh off her visit to the clinic, with her doctor's note, her sponsor credentials, her new sneaks, and her University of Texas women's basketball jersey for inspiration. She had a plan for practice, and had even made peanut butter and jelly sandwiches and sliced up the last cucumber from her garden for snacks.

Her team—five of them—arrived with Tanya shortly after school. Willow led the way, her basketball tucked under her arm. One of the girls, who had not been present the last time Nora met this crew, stared at Nora incredulously. "You play basketball?"

"I do."

"Are you, like . . . good?"

"I used to be. I know the game, though. I think the better question is, are *you* good?"

The girl looked at the others and shrugged.

"Uh-uh," Nora said. "You have to believe you are the best on the court and then play like it." The words tumbled out of her before she recognized them—Grandpa had said those words to her. He'd said it to the skinny girl standing on the edge of the court at the Pflugerville YMCA, afraid to join the others. *"Go on out there,"* he'd said. *"Don't be afraid. You have to believe you are the best on the court and then play like it."*

"Did your dad really stab your basketball?" another one asked. "That's mean."

"So mean," Nora agreed.

Willow began to dribble her ball. "Are we going to stand around talking about your psycho dad or what?"

Nora grinned. "Come with me."

Tanya stuck around to watch, but she spent most of the practice on her phone. Near the end of the hour, a sweaty, exhausted Nora left the girls to work on their layups and climbed up onto the bleachers to sit next to Tanya. Her inner athlete clearly needed to get to the gym.

"Their first game is in a few weeks. Do you have more in your bag of tricks, or are layups all you got?" Tanya asked without taking her eyes off her phone.

"Come on, Tanya, give me some credit—I have a wing and a prayer too. Also, I've been watching some coaching videos on YouTube."

Tanya was silent.

"Are you okay?"

"Got a lot on my mind."

Nora snorted. "Don't we all."

Tanya looked up from her phone. "You want to go toe to toe on who has more on her mind, Miss High and Mighty Lawyer? You have no idea what kind of troubles I have. You *are* a lawyer, right?"

Nora leaned back, propping herself on her elbows against the bench behind them. "I have a law degree, and I am licensed. But let's just say I'm better at writing briefs than actual lawyering."

Tanya sighed and rubbed her forehead. "You're not exactly selling yourself."

Nora gave her a curious look. "Should I be?"

"You know anything about independent contractors?"

Ah, the old hypothetically-speaking-let-me-ask-you routine. People always wanted free legal advice from a lawyer. Hell, Nora wanted free legal advice. "A little."

"My brother, he does home renovations. He's got a client that owes him a lot of money and he's saying he doesn't have to pay for work my brother did."

"I'd have to look at the contract," Nora said. A spark of an idea inserted itself into her brain. "He does home renovation?"

"Yeah. Kitchens, baths . . . that sort of thing."

Kitchens. Nora sat up. The spark was suddenly ablaze. "How much is he owed?"

"Twenty-five thousand."

"Wow." Nora reached into her gardening tote and rummaged around until she found a business card. She handed it to Tanya. "Tell him to call me."

Tanya looked at the card, then at Nora. "For real?"

"For real."

"I don't know if he can pay much."

But maybe he'd be open to some trade in services—like, her legal help in exchange for repairing Lacey's kitchen? Optimism began to bloom. Was it possible that she really could get Lacey's kitchen fixed? She didn't want to get ahead of herself, but she was feeling a little giddy with the possibility. "Don't worry about that," she said to Tanya. "Have him give me a call."

Tanya suddenly beamed. "I still don't understand why you want to get all up in our business, but thank you."

When Nora handed out the bags of sandwiches and cucumbers at the conclusion of practice, Willow said Nora was lame but ate a sandwich anyway, then asked her if they were getting jerseys or what.

Nora and her inner athlete were going to love this.

Chapter 38

Jack did not miraculously appear after Nora's appearance on KXAN's morning show, but every troll in Central Texas did. The comments on the "Lost and Found in the ATX" ranged from You're a fucking moron to Good luck and were sprinkled with more long posts from random people about the ones who'd gotten away from themselves.

Nora fretted that she hadn't described him accurately. Her description of him—tall, dark-haired, blue-eyed—fit a significant number of men in Austin. In the world, for that matter. But surely he'd mentioned his experience to someone, and that someone would recall the conversation.

She was racking her brain for any other clues when James called. "Everyone is talking about you," he said breathlessly.

"Because of the morning show?"

"Exactly. Kevin's theory is that you do have brain damage."

Nora realized she didn't care what they thought. Progress!

"Anyway, some guy named Manuel Cervantes has been calling for you."

"Who's that?"

"Someone who needs to talk to you. He said he had an opportunity he wanted to discuss with you."

She gasped. "A job?"

"Or he knows something about Jack?"

Her breath quickened with excitement. "Did he leave a number?"

"Yep. Texting it to you now. Speaking of jobs . . . any luck?"

"Not really. I'm doing a legal thing pro bono, and I'm going to talk to a man who I am hoping will be willing to repair Lacey's kitchen that I burned down in exchange for some contract work."

"Wait . . . you burned down Lacey's kitchen?"

"Not all the way to the studs," Nora said, a little defensively. "It's fixable." She hoped.

"Oh my God," James muttered disbelievingly.

She filled James in on the kitchen fiasco, then promised she would let him know what Manuel Cervantes wanted. James asked if she needed anything from him. She didn't—November and Sons was a Death Star spinning out of her little planet's orbit, off to menace some other solar system.

She called Manuel Cervantes on her way to the garden, hardly able to contain her eagerness. Her "hello" burst out of her like a rocket.

"Hey, Nora, thanks for calling me back. I saw your spot on the morning news. Fascinating story you've got there."

Nora's heart pounded with anticipation. "Do you know him?"

"Oh . . . no, sorry."

Her eagerness exploded into nothing, and she sank against the driver's seat. "Oh."

"I'm a producer, and I would love to talk to you about capturing your experience on film. Your story is so compelling. Like, everyone understands the concept of the one who got away, but the near-death experience adds the extra pizzazz. The concept would need some tweaks, of course," he said. "You know, a little zhuzhing it up for a larger viewing audience. But I think this would be perfect for HBO. I'd like to offer you an option for development."

Manuel began to describe just how many tweaks her story would need, which, as it turned out, was a lot. Her story of drowning and coming back to life apparently wasn't dramatic enough, and her recovery and search for the man she'd let get away wasn't challenging enough. But with a few changes, he told her, she would be an inspiration to millions.

Hyperbole, much? She had no desire to be an inspiration to millions. Right now it was all she could do to inspire herself on a daily basis. "I need to think about it," she said.

"Sure. How about in a few days we get some coffee and talk it through? Give me a time and place, and I'll be there."

She agreed and promised to text him.

Something felt not quite right to her about his proposal—making her NDE about a woman searching for the one who got away felt wrong. Her story was so much more than that. It was about her figuring out who she was and who she wasn't. It was about the sea of emotions and beliefs in which she'd been treading water for so long that it took her dying to swim out of that sea. It was about discovering herself every day, including all the reasons she never called Jack, or why she didn't take the private cooking lesson, or why she was ever on that beach to begin with. It was about fighting off demons every step of the way.

It was not about the one who got away. It was about how she'd almost gotten away from herself.

••••••

At the garden, Nora found her bell peppers were shriveling. They were not going to get bigger, quite obviously. But her calla lilies were starting to come up, strong and tall, pointing the way for her. She wanted to hug them.

She cleaned out the dead from the cucumber vines, planted the dahlia tubers Nick had given her, and left two tubers and a note for Plot Seven.

> *I have never grown dahlias, have you? My success here has not been great, so I intend to join a garden club. Have a great week. #9*

She was late getting home to change and then late to her painting class. When she'd texted Gus this afternoon to tell him when she'd pick him up, he'd responded, I'll meet you there.

Something about that response didn't feel right, but Nora had pushed the thought down. And then Gus didn't show. She wasn't surprised, but she was disappointed. She had genuinely believed that he would come.

The assignment that evening was to paint a sky that reflected their moods. The mood, the instructor said, could be found in their subconscious minds if they looked hard enough. Nora searched her brain for her mood. What was it? Buoyant. Hopeful. A little scared of her path. In the end, she'd painted a bright light spilling over green, and in the corner, a hint of a shadow, as if someone was standing behind a veil. But this wasn't her interpretation of the Grandpa shadows. This shadow was Jack. Just there, just beyond her reach. Losing him was perhaps the item on her reverse bucket list that she regretted the most.

When class was over, Nora packed up her canvas and headed to Gus's apartment. She was afraid of what she might find, but unlike the ghost of Nora, she would not avoid the chaos and muck. She knocked, unrelenting, until he opened the door. "Yeah," he said, his voice hoarse and groggy.

"I'm here," she said simply. *I'm here for you. I'm here, and I won't leave you again.*

"Oh, shoot. Tonight was . . ." He didn't bother to finish. "I'm sorry."

"We painted moody skies. Anyway, I came over because I think you need me, and I think we need to talk about the place I found."

Gus sagged against the doorframe. "Nora . . . I don't have any money."

"I know. But I truly believe we can make this happen if you want it to. It won't be easy, and I don't know where we'll get the money, but we can figure it out, right? But, Gus . . . you have to want it."

A single tear slipped out of his eye and traced a path over his florid cheek into a week's worth of beard. "I'm scared."

She reached for his hand. "Me too."

"Really?"

"Oh my God, Gus—every day. Can we at least talk about it?"

He let her in.

••••••

Her week continued like that, one thing after the other. She reached out to the treatment facility in Smithville. They said they might have a bed opening. She prepared paperwork for a bankruptcy for Catherine to mull over in the event it came to that. She called Brad Sachs's office to inquire if there was any room to negotiate. The woman she spoke to said she would speak to Mr. Sachs and get back to her. Nora wasn't holding her breath. She bought some canvases and paints with her dwindling funds, paid as much of her credit card bill as she could, and downloaded some Bob Ross videos. She went to see Nick, and they examined her bell pepper closely. *"Not enough sun, then,"* he decreed.

She asked about Venus flytraps. He said he would see if he could find some, but they were tough to locate and transport.

She had coffee with Manuel Cervantes and learned his vision for the limited series he wanted to create. She didn't care for his vision, and she didn't get the sense he had much interest in her take. But she needed to be practical—he was offering a decent amount of money for the rights. Sometimes deals had to be made. She agreed to think about his offer and get back to him.

She met Tanya's brother, Josiah, and struck a tentative deal with him, based on what Lacey had to say about it. She arranged for Josiah and Lacey to meet. Lacey was resistant at first, commanded Nora to stop blowing up her phone . . . until Nora said she'd figured out how to pay for the repairs. Lacey agreed to meet Josiah then, but she made it clear Nora was not invited, as she was still fuming. Baby steps.

Nora stopped taking her mother's video calls. Her mother began to text instead. She didn't respond to those either.

She painted. She wore old jeans and T-shirts and moccasins to the store to run errands. She cooked the paella they made in cooking class and took some to Lacey's house and left it in her fridge with instructions for heating it up and a warning—she'd overdone the cayenne pepper. She left her some cupcakes she'd made too.

She went to the theater twice to review finances with Catherine and Walter. She told Walter she had someone looking for Venus flytraps. He sighed impatiently.

And she kept posting under "Lost and Found in the ATX." Anyone see him?

No one had.

Chapter 39

A*bout a week later, on a Saturday morning, Nora was* still in her pajamas when there was an unexpected knock at her door. She peered out the peephole, and with a groan, she opened the door to her mother. "I'm surprised you actually braved the homeless encampment."

"You left me no choice."

In her tan slacks and twin set, Mom looked Nora up and down, her gaze lingering on her bare feet. And then on her pink poodle pajamas. And the uncombed mess of her hair. "Did your flat iron break?"

"Nope."

"You haven't been returning my calls. You missed last week's dinner."

"I know. Want some coffee? I made cinnamon rolls."

"Why on earth would you make cinnamon rolls? Are you *trying* to put on weight?"

"Don't you miss Grandma's rolls, Mom?"

"No. I don't."

Nora padded into the kitchen to pour coffee. "So . . . did someone die?"

"Very funny. I want to talk to you."

"Cream?"

"Heavens, no. And you shouldn't either."

Nora poured cream into her coffee. She took a fork from her cutlery drawer and cut off a bite of one roll. This batch was excellent—three inches tall and extra gooey. She was pleased. "What did Grandma put in her cinnamon rolls to make them so good?"

"Extra butter," her mother said and pinched off a tiny piece of the roll Nora was eating.

Then she put down her purse and walked into Nora's apartment. "What happened to all the beautiful furnishings I arranged for you?"

"They weren't my vibe, so I got rid of them."

"I see," her mother said primly. "Used IKEA is your vibe?"

Nora laughed. "I'm still figuring it out."

Her mother paused in front of the canvas Nora had up. "What's this? A salad?"

Her work in progress was supposed to be an impressionist view of the Goodfellow Community Garden, but it did look a little like a colorful salad. "I guess it could be."

Her mother turned from the painting. "I want to fix this thing between you and your father. Between you and all of us. Tell me what I need to do."

Nora picked up her cinnamon roll and coffee and headed to her used couch, settling in. "Just curious . . . does Dad want to fix anything?"

Her mother perched daintily on the edge of the bucket chair across from her. "He can be stubborn sometimes, but so can you."

Nora rolled her eyes.

"What did you expect, honey? You walked off the job."

"I had to, Mom. I can never be what Dad needs. You know that."

Her mother looked confused. "What are you talking about?"

"I mean that I can never be Nathan."

The change in her mother's expression at the mention of her dead son was stunning. She gasped and looked as if Nora had struck her. "What would make you say something so vile?"

"Vile? To me, it's simply the truth."

Her mother's lovely porcelain skin, which came at quite a cost, turned splotchy. She pressed a hand to her heart. "You don't know what you're talking about. It was a terrible tragedy, and of course he mourns his son. But he loves you."

"Mom—"

"You listen to me. You two need to patch things up. Forget about the office. What about Christmas and New Year's? What about weddings and funerals and Sunday dinners? I've lost my parents, my sister, and my baby. I will not lose you too. Doesn't family mean anything to you? Because you have a lovely one, and you are throwing it all away."

Nora's heart began to pound. She was not the one who was throwing it away; Dad was. She was the one who was breaking free of the chains. All these years, she'd lived with the idea that she should have been the one to die. But maybe she was supposed to be the one to live. She was the one who could break the cycle of pretending this family dysfunction was something to aspire to. She put aside the cinnamon roll and said calmly, "That's a lie you tell yourself, Mom. We have an extremely dysfunctional family, and I am getting off the train in order to save myself."

Her mother frowned darkly. "That's ridiculous. We have our issues like any family does, but we are not bad people. Your father understands that you are going through a rough time. He's giving you this grace period to think things through. He admits that he wanted you back at work too soon after the accident."

Nora shook her head. "He has completely missed the point. Or willfully ignored it."

"What he's ignored are the horrible things you've said, which is what any father with a heart would do. You're not thinking clearly."

Her mother thought she could gaslight her? "I am thinking very clearly, Mom. But I'm a different person from the one who drowned. I'm not brain damaged; I'm *renewed*. Do you understand? I am not the same Nora. And come on, you know how he is. He's a narcissist."

"He is not a narcissist," her mother said, but she didn't sound completely convinced. "He's different from you. He's driven, he's a good provider, and he has held on to the memory of his son and helped so many others through his foundation. He is, in his way, a good man."

One foundation did not erase the damage he'd done to this family. Nora stared at her mother in disbelief. "Mom," she said quietly. "You don't believe that. You know there is more to it than that."

Roberta November straightened her spine. She looked out the window for a long moment, and Nora wondered if she, too, suspected her husband was a philanderer. She met Nora's gaze. "What I believe is that in life, there are trade-offs. No one situation or person is perfect, and every human being must decide which trade-offs are right for them."

Nora stared at her, comprehending for the first time in her life the sort of trade-offs her mother might have made. She wasn't willing to make the same.

"Come to dinner tomorrow," her mother said.

"No."

"All right. Take some time, think about what I've said, what we've all said, and come to dinner *next* Sunday. Please. For me, Nora. Dad is thinking about it too."

Nora wanted to laugh. She wanted to cry. Actually, she wanted to put her fist through the brick wall. "I have plans. I've taken on a pro bono project with an old theater."

"What?"

"The Triangle Theater. It's run by retired thespians and they're staging a musical, and their first show is next Sunday at five."

Her mother looked confused. "That's a strange time for an opening."

"Well, they're senior citizens. They're banking on getting the predinner crowd, and then they won't be up too late."

Her mother waved a hand, uninterested in the seniors. "Then come to dinner after that."

"No. I can't bear to look at him, and he clearly despises me."

"He doesn't despise you. He—" She pressed her lips together. "What do I have to do to convince you to come?"

"I can't be convinced."

"There must be something."

Nora sighed. "Okay . . . buy a block of seats at the theater and come watch the musical." She almost laughed. There was no possibility her mother would ever agree to that.

"Where is the theater?"

"Just north of the Triangle."

Her mother grimaced. She was probably thinking of the homeless camps there too.

"What's the play?"

"*A Streetcar Named Desire: The Musical.*"

"I wasn't aware that was a musical." Her mother sighed heavily. "Fine. We'll come and have dinner after."

Nora froze with shock. "What?"

"I said, you have a deal."

"Mom, I'm serious. You have to buy a lot of tickets. They're trying to raise money, so you—"

"Nora." Her mother waved a hand at her. "Send me the time and location and how many tickets I have to buy."

Dammit.

Chapter 40

Jack

S*omething unusual happened during Jack's last work* shift for the week—Laurie Milano went home. She was one of their long-haul patients, in for two months with incurable cancer. But, as miracles are sometimes wont to do, one occurred for Laurie. After taking a new, experimental cocktail of drugs and therapies, her cancer slid into remission.

This had happened only three times in Jack's career.

When Laurie had first arrived, so frail no one thought she'd last to the end of the week, she'd vowed she would die at home surrounded by her family and her dogs and cat. *"I just need to get well enough to go home,"* she'd said to Jack. *"Will you help me?"*

Jack would help all he could, but death had a mind of its own. And when it let go of its grip, it was cause for celebration. Even with all the science that surrounded them, death remained unpredictable as hell.

Jack, Sandra, and the rest of the staff pitched in for a cake that Laurie couldn't eat but her family could. They put up streamers and poured punch into paper cups and laughed with glee. The staff waved as her family wheeled her out. The heads of two slobbery dogs craned their necks out the window of the waiting SUV, excited to see her. When Laurie and her family drove away, Jack and the rest of the staff closed the doors and went back inside to administer a round of meds to those who wouldn't be so lucky as to go home again.

Jack left work in fine spirits, thanks to the wellspring of hope Laurie had released into the universe. As he packed his things into his backpack, he said to Sandra, "You're coming, right?"

"To see you dance? Pauline and I wouldn't miss it."

"Tickets are at the box office. But there might not be anyone manning the box office. If there's no one there, the envelope will be on the counter with your name on it."

Sandra frowned. "That doesn't seem very secure."

"Security is not an issue, trust me. We'll be lucky to fill ten seats."

"I still can't believe you're a dancer." She laughed, shaking her head.

"All will be painfully revealed," he said on his way out. "But hey, I did help build the set. Look at that while I'm dancing."

When Sunday rolled around, Jack was surprised by how nervous he felt. He marveled at how he'd gotten completely wrapped up in this geriatric cast and was part of them now. Catherine was right—he really did need more joy in his life.

On opening night—or rather, afternoon—the cast was gathered in Catherine's apartment to dress and apply makeup. Catherine was really in her element—she swanned around in a dressing gown in her star turn as Blanche DuBois. All that was missing was the cigarette holder and the turban. "I'm not a dramatic actress," she said. "It's not really on brand for me. However, I've discovered that I am very good at dramatic acting." She walked past Jack and gave him a friendly slap on the back of his head. "Wouldn't you agree, young man?"

Jack was mindful of Meredith, who still had not gotten over the fact that she wasn't in the starring role. "You're all a showcase of talent."

Catherine clucked her tongue at him. Then suddenly: "I forgot to tell you that I found a lawyer to help us."

From what Jack understood, the only "help" that would make any difference was to pay the back taxes and outrageous interest.

"How'd you manage to hire a lawyer?" he asked as Mary tilted his head up so she could dab eye makeup on him.

"She volunteered. I think she feels guilty for killing Walter's flytraps. She's Plot Nine."

Something slowed way down inside Jack. What the hell? That made no sense. "Plot Nine? I thought Plot Nine was someone's grandma."

Catherine clucked her tongue. "Why would you think that? She's young and pretty and happens to be a lawyer."

"Young and pretty?" he repeated dumbly. He tried to reconcile that with the notes and the references to a garden adviser and dahlia tubers. "We're talking Plot Nine, right? With the enormous cucumbers and dead tomato plants?"

"Yes, Jack, overwatered Plot Nine," Catherine said. "But don't get too excited—she has her heart set on finding a man she met during a corner store robbery."

Now everything turned watery around him. It took a moment before he could move his mouth. "Wh-what?"

"Haven't you seen the story, love?" Jerry asked. "It's everywhere on social media. Except on the Tik. Or maybe it's on the Tik, but I don't go there. No, sir, it's too much work. Give me the 'gram and a good photo—"

"Are you going to tell the story or give us a rundown of your thoughts on Twitter too?" Catherine asked.

"You really haven't seen it?" Jerry asked Jack.

Jack shook his head.

"Don't move!' Mary shouted. "Well, that's just great. Now I have to redo your eyeliner."

"There was a robbery in a corner store," Jerry said. "She was there with another customer, a strapping young man who tried to stop the robbery but couldn't because the robber had a gun. And she wants to find him and thank him. They would have been killed had it not been for him."

That was not what had happened to him and Nora. Jack was confused—could there have been another hostage robbery of a corner store? Austin, man—keeping it weird.

"You've got it wrong, Jerry," Annabeth said. "They got stuck or something."

Jack's pulse began to pound all over again. Was it possible? "When was this robbery?"

"I don't know, two or three years ago?"

"Maybe not," Martin said. "Mary and I were talking about it. It couldn't have been too long ago, because why would she wait so long to find him? It must have happened recently."

"Taylor Swift tweeted about it," Mr. Carlton said casually. "Now everyone is looking for this guy."

Ignoring the fact that Mr. Carlton knew who Taylor Swift was and, more astonishing, what a tweet was, Jack said, "Here? In Austin?"

"Please, everyone," Walter interrupted. "The curtain goes up in thirty minutes."

But a bolt of lightning had slipped down Jack's spine and was sizzling in him. *It can't be Nora.* Except that he was the man from the corner store. *Wait, wait, wait . . . she's Plot Nine?*

His face flushed. He'd thought of that surreal experience so often. He'd felt in tune with Nora, had been excited to have met her even with nearly being killed in the process. He'd really wanted to see her again and had been so confident she'd felt the same way about him, had felt it in his marrow. But he'd lost that slip of paper with her number. And she'd never called him.

"There you go," Mary said and stood back to admire her handiwork.

"Hey . . . about that robbery." Jack was about to tell them all that he thought he was that guy, but Karen came barreling through the door before he could get the words out.

"You're not going to believe it," she said breathlessly. "We're sold out!"

"We're sold out?" Catherine shrieked. "Are you sure?"

"Someone bought the last block of tickets. The whole thing!"

The room was so still for a moment that Jack could hear Mr. Carlton's labored breathing. And then suddenly all of them burst into chatter and dance. It was almost as if their taxes had been fully paid, which, of course, wouldn't happen even if they sold out ten shows.

In all the excitement, Jack lost the conversation about the robbery.

Chapter 41

Nora had finished dressing for the theater when Lacey called. Her sister was slowly beginning to come around, thanks to Josiah, who had helped by getting to work immediately and being very good at what he did. "Don't you dare cancel on me," Nora said, skipping over any greeting.

"Are you kidding, after you made me buy twenty-five tickets? I'm getting my money's worth. Is Gus coming?"

"Um . . ." Nora had gotten a call she almost missed between basketball practice, a trip to the Stinking Iris, and her classes. It was from the treatment facility in Smithville. They had a bed. Everything after that had happened so fast. She'd gone to Gus's apartment and helped him pack. "Actually . . . we drove to Smithville yesterday and checked him in to a thirty-day program."

Lacey was silent. "But . . . wait. Did Mom—"

"Mom and Dad don't know. Gus told me to tell you not to worry, that he's got this."

"He doesn't have any money."

"I do. Not a lot, but I had what we needed to get him in."

"Nora!" Lacey gasped. "You can't. You don't have a job—"

"I've figured something out." Manuel Cervantes's offer for the rights to her story would be enough to pay for Gus and put a serious dent in her medical bills. She'd have to find a way to continue to pay for his treatment until she had that money in hand, but she'd figure out something. "I'll tell you later, but everything happened so quickly, we didn't have time to call."

"Gus agreed to go?"

"He agreed to try." Gus had been a wreck, crying and sweating on the hour drive to Smithville. At one point he begged her to turn around. He said he didn't know if he could quit drinking. But then he'd told her to keep going, that he'd try, and Nora cried for Gus all the way back to Austin.

"Wow, Nora. That's . . . amazing. I can't wait to hear this," Lacey said. "I'll see you in a bit."

Nora hung up. She reached into her closet shelf for a pair of sandals, and her hand brushed against the box of things that had been on the dining room table before her accident. It fell to the floor, scattering the detritus of the Before across the carpet.

Several envelopes and papers lay on the closet floor. She bent down to pick them up. Most were bills, some bank statements . . . but one envelope, made of thick cream stationery, caught her eye. On the envelope, she'd written simply, *From Nora.*

Her brain began to sizzle like fireworks. She slowly picked up the rest of the things and put them back in the box. But the envelope . . . she stared at it, the fireworks blazing, trying to form an image. She suddenly had a vision of herself standing on the beach at Surfside, and the last pieces of the puzzle of her memory of what happened that day began to snap into place.

She knew immediately she didn't want to remember it. She didn't want to recall how cold the water had been, or the terror she'd felt when water was going into her lungs and not coming out. But the memory came crashing back, just like that furious surf had rushed the beach. She'd been wild with hysteria as she'd felt herself sinking into the dark depths of the Gulf, understanding there was no turning back.

Nora stood there in her closet like she was standing on that beach, her eyes closed, and forced herself to open that door, to remember every detail. She could almost feel the cold and the weight of her body as the air had left her. She could still feel the pressing desire not to exist any longer.

It was a relief to know that her heart had moved on from that horrible day, had even tried to hide that day from her because it was so gruesome. But she was stronger now, and Nora never wanted to forget how far she'd sunk into her private anguish that she'd believed death was infinitely better than life. That she needed to deliberately walk into that water to end her pain and suffering once and for all.

She couldn't say how she'd gotten so despondent that she'd decided that was her only option—it was a long accumulation of despair, of feeling worthless, of whispers in her thoughts that she was already dead inside, so what was the point of living? She'd just wanted to stop feeling awful all the time and had lost any will to do anything about it. Existing was hard enough as it was. She'd always heard drowning was a peaceful way to die. She'd had a man from the resort take her to a beach where the warning signs were out for riptide currents. She thought she'd walk into the Gulf and the current would carry her out to a peaceful death, à la Hamlet's Ophelia, and she would no longer feel pain.

Nothing could be further from the truth. It was a truly terrifying experience to realize she wanted to live at the very moment she'd ended any possibility of it.

And then, for some reason, she'd been given a second chance.

Nora opened her eyes. She needed to always remember everything about that day so she could measure how far she'd come. She needed to remember how vicious despair could be if she let it in, and how illuminating and uplifting love could be if she practiced it every day—loving herself, loving her family, loving others, loving life.

She was a calla lily, pushing out of heavy wet sand, growing stronger and taller than she'd ever been. Nothing was going to stop her now.

Nora put the box back on the shelf and carried the envelope across the room and tossed it into the trash can. What was written on the note card in that envelope—the apology to her family, the incoherent explanation of why she'd made that choice—had been penned by the ghost of Nora, and none of it applied to her now. No matter how difficult things would get, those words, and that person, were not who she was anymore.

••••••

Two hours later, she stood on the sidewalk in front of the Triangle Theater awaiting her guests.

James was the first to arrive. He'd brought a date. "I hope you didn't oversell the musical," Nora muttered as his date got out of the other side of the Uber.

"He loves musicals. And he's dying to get a glimpse of you. You're famous now. By the way, I gave my cousin your number. He needs an attorney to help with a workman's comp claim." He waggled his brows at her.

"James! I don't know what I'm doing about work yet."

"Don't be absurd. And you need to make some money, honey, if you're going to employ the best legal assistant in town."

The next guests to arrive were Nick, in the company of two members from his exclusive gardening club, senior citizens wearing matching bucket hats embroidered with a stinking iris.

"You didn't tell me you got a hat if you join the gardening club," she complained, admiring them.

Nick looked at the women. "These ladies belong to the Mighty Girls' Gardening Group. I had in mind the Green Thumb Club for you. The kids' group. They get a discount on gloves too."

Okay, well . . . all gardeners had to start somewhere.

Tanya came with Josiah. But no Willow. "She could not be convinced," Tanya said apologetically.

Nora laughed. "I understand. Senior citizen musical theater is not for everyone."

A group of people walked up from the street. Many of them were dressed in dirty clothes, but a couple of them had tried to clean up. They lived in a homeless encampment a couple of blocks away. Nora had bought the entire premium seat section—thirty dollars a seat. And then she'd walked the tickets down the street to the camp. These tickets hadn't sold, and she didn't want the seats to be empty for Catherine and her friends. Some people at the homeless camp were skeptical. But then she mentioned the air-conditioning.

She'd add the tickets to her growing list of things that she needed to figure out how to pay for.

Last, and almost late, a town car pulled up to the curb. Nora's mother was the first one out. She looked up. "I thought you said it was a theater."

"It is, Mom."

Next was Lacey, who popped out, put her hands to her back and stretched, then looked at Nora and rolled her eyes. *Good luck*, she mouthed.

And then came Nora's father. In all honesty, she hadn't expected him to show. And after one look at him, she wished he hadn't. His jaw was clenched, his gaze hard. He looked agitated as he took in the dilapidated building. For a moment, Nora felt sorry for him. It must be hard work to be a dick all day, every day.

"Thank you for coming," she said. "I know this isn't the sort of philanthropy our family is accustomed to, but sometimes help can take the form of moral support."

Her father slowly turned his head from his study of the theater and pinned her with a dark look. Oh, but that was one that would have slayed her in the Before, making her want to fade into the wallpaper. "Okay!" she said cheerfully. "This way." She led them into the theater.

Their seats, admittedly, were not great. The better seats had gone to friends and family of the cast. Nora's mother was so confused by the needlepointed seat covers that she ended up sitting on her scarf, apparently convinced the yarn was covering something heinous.

Nora's seat was behind a giant column so she could see only half the stage. The place wasn't yet full, but people were trickling in.

"Hey, here's a fun fact—the actress who plays Blanche was a friend of Grandpa's," she said.

"That's nice," her mother said absently.

When the curtain finally came up, it stuck, and Walter had to run out and untangle a cord. Eventually it came all the way up and the cast trickled out onstage for the opening number.

For an amateur show with no stage crew save Walter, it was not half bad. Catherine's talent really shone. The musical numbers were entertaining, though maybe not for the reasons the cast had hoped but because they were drowned out by Annabeth's heavy hand on the piano. The dancing was . . . interesting.

Since Nora could see only part of the stage, much of the performance felt as if someone were delivering lines from the wings. In the end, the musical was surprisingly campy and fun. The cast didn't take themselves too seriously . . . well, except for Catherine.

When it was over, before the curtain call, David November stood from his seat. "Call a car," he said to his wife and began to make his way out of the theater.

"Now you've gone and done it," Lacey whispered. "But it was fun."

"Move, Lacey," their mother said.

Nora caught her mother's arm before she could escape. "I'm just going to congratulate Catherine first and then I'll head over."

Her mother glanced at the stage, where some of the cast was still milling about, and then at her husband's retreating back. "Don't be late and make this any worse. Our guests should be arriving for dinner in a half hour."

Nora said she'd be there, then made her way to the stage. Catherine had an armful of grocery store flowers. She smiled brilliantly. "Nora! You must come up to my apartment—we're having a party."

Nora would have liked nothing better than to ditch her family and go to the party, but she'd made her deal with the devil. "Thanks, but I have a prior commitment. Catherine, you were phenomenal. Grandpa would have loved it so much."

Catherine graciously inclined her head. Someone called Catherine's name, and Nora, conscious of time, waved to her. "I'll talk to you soon."

"If you change your mind, come round," Catherine called after her. "We'll be up until ten or eleven." She then walked grandly to the other end of the stage to speak to a few more admirers, most of them from the homeless camp.

Nora walked outside as her parents and Lacey were getting into a town car. Her father glanced at her across the top of the car, his gaze unreadable before he dipped inside.

Nora felt the buzz begin to build in anticipation of another dinner in Rob Roy. But the buzz felt different this time. Not like it would drown her—but like it could light up the evening sky.

Chapter 42

This was the third time Nora had been to Rob Roy since she'd stood on the beach at Surfside. She thought of the cold wind, the endless, deep horizon. She thought of the anxiety that had made it so difficult to breathe. It was not unlike the anxiety she'd felt for so many years in this very house.

She got out of her car, tossed her key fob to the valet, squared her shoulders, and walked into the house.

A usual assembly of Important People had come. Cynthia and Drew, of course. Saritha and Raghu Kumar—Raghu was a brilliant tech wizard who everyone said would take over Google one day. Also in attendance was Trystan, whom she'd met at the last dinner. He shared a whispered joke with her mother when he spotted Nora. Allison and Jason Bunch had come—Allison was the managing editor at the *Austin American-Statesman*. Lacey, of course. And a couple of other people she didn't recognize and didn't care to know.

One of the servers tried in vain to get Nora to take a glass of wine, but she refused. She skirted around the perimeter of the room, a low hum of anxiety buzzing through her, that terrible feeling of waiting for a hammer to drop—only this time she wanted to be the one to drop it.

She said hello to the Bunches. Allison said she understood they'd just come from the theater, and she was so happy to hear that Nora was getting back into the swing of things again.

Mrs. Kumar said Nora looked almost too trim; what was her secret?

"My secret is not caring," Nora said with a smile.

Trystan asked how she'd been. "Your mom said you were taking a short leave of absence from work."

Nora laughed. "I'm not on leave. I quit."

"Oh." He looked at her strangely. "I must have misunderstood."

"I've no doubt you understood perfectly whatever she said."

"Yeah," he said and moved on.

Lacey told her she really liked Josiah. "Thanks, Nora," she said. "I really didn't think . . ." She shrugged sheepishly.

"I know," Nora said. Earning Lacey's trust would be a slow build, but she was off on the right foot. "It was pure luck that I found him."

"He even worked with my insurance company to get more out of them. Oh, and those cupcakes you made? So good."

Nora beamed. She couldn't cook, but it turned out that she could bake.

When the guests were seated in the dining room, Mr. Kumar asked what show they'd had the pleasure of seeing this afternoon.

Her dad smirked. "It wasn't meant to be a comedy, but that's what we got."

The buzz in Nora zigged and zagged. It was such a callous thing to say given how hard those senior citizens had worked. "It was *A Streetcar Named Desire*," she heard herself say, and rather loudly at that. "The musical."

"One of my favorite Tennessee Williams plays," Mr. Kumar said. "I've never seen it produced as a musical."

"First time," Lacey said. "The performers were mostly senior citizens. I thought it was delightful."

David November chuckled. "And here I'd hoped I'd given my daughters a better appreciation of theater."

The guests tittered politely.

"The cast live on fixed incomes on the same lot as the theater," Nora said. "It's the Triangle Theater. Maybe you know it? Catherine Henry is the owner. She's trying to save it from being torn down."

"Catherine Henry? From Esther's Follies?" Mrs. Kumar asked. "Years ago, Raghu and I used to attend quite often."

"That's a pity about the theater," Cynthia said. "Unfortunately, that sort of thing happens a lot."

"You could make a donation to help them save it," Nora suggested.

"Nora!" Her mother gave a strangled laugh. "I'm so sorry, everyone."

"I'm serious, Mom," Nora said. "They've gotten behind in taxes and staged the show to raise money to pay them. But the person who holds the deed wants to kick them out so he can build luxury apartments. You all know him—Brad Sachs."

"Don't feel too sorry for them," Nora's dad said. "That building is so run-down that Brad's doing them a favor."

Raw anger was growing wildly in her—the bees in her chest could swarm an army. "I don't know, Dad—he won't return my calls. But I think Mr. Sachs could show a little compassion for the seniors in this case." She looked at him. "And so could you."

Everything went perfectly still. Nothing moved—not a server, not a guest, not a wisp of air. Then gazes began to fly between father and daughter. Dad's displeasure burned in his eyes, and he was so intent on Nora that he didn't acknowledge the waiter as he put a Caesar salad before him.

Identical to the one someone put before her. No variety, soggy with dressing, no *life*. How had she lived like this for so long?

"What do you suggest, Nora? That we pass a hat?"

"Do you think that would work?"

The tension was thick enough to strangle the air from the room. The guests began to shift uncomfortably in their seats. *Welcome, everyone, to the life I lived in the Before!*

Dad smiled thinly. "You must all excuse my daughter. Unfortunately, she's a little soft when it comes to bad-luck tales."

Nora's mother put down her fork. "That's enough family talk, please. Our guests don't want to hear our dirty laundry."

But they *did* want to hear it. And oh, was it dirty.

"Speaking of family, we haven't seen your nephew in a while, Roberta," Cynthia said.

"He's been busy," her mother said quickly.

A lifetime of grievances and regrets and secrets was frothing like a stormy sea in Nora. Gus had struggled with his demons, but he was not the blight on an otherwise perfect November family. They said horrible things about him . . . and yet they never acknowledged that there were even bigger blights on the family sitting in plain sight. A dodgy legal practice. Possible extramarital affairs. A genuflection at the throne of appearances. A palpable wish that their daughters were different from who they were. And from at least one member, an unspoken but clearly conveyed desire that Nora had died instead of Nathan. How hard would it have been to be grateful that one twin lived?

She was sick of pretending that all was well in the November snow globe. She wanted to live an authentic life. *Her* life. Not theirs. "Actually, Mom, Gus is at a drug and alcohol treatment facility."

Her mother's fork clanked against her plate. "Pardon?" She laughed. "Nora, stop teasing us. Anyway, I applaud your desire to help the seniors," she blathered, desperate to pull this conversation back from the brink. "Why don't you use some of the settlement you'll get from the suit against the resort to help them?"

And just like that, Nora's buzz turned to unfiltered rage. She looked down at her predictably boring salad, and that last hard nub of compliance shattered. Her utter rebellion came from a place so deep that it very nearly launched her from her seat. She didn't care if she failed at everything on her reverse bucket list, if she was forced to live in her car—failure was more palatable than this life.

She shoved the salad away from her. Some of the lettuce spilled onto the tablecloth. "Because I won't accept a dime of any settlement from the resort."

"Nora, sweetie, calm down," her father said, like she was a petulant child who needed to be put to bed. "It will help to pay your substantial medical expenses. Comas and rehabilitation don't come cheap, so let's not be foolish."

And *that* tipped her right over the edge. "Talk about dirty laundry," Nora said and looked around the table at the uncomfortable guests. No one was eating and all eyes were down, as if they couldn't bear to witness this. Lacey was ashen.

"Dad's right. My medical bills are insanely high. But my family knows that my accident was not the fault of the resort."

Her mother surged to her feet. "Nora? May I have a word with you in the kitchen?"

"No, Mom." She was having the moment that she hadn't known she needed but that was suddenly crystal clear to her—her brain had laid it all out for her to see, her memory of what had happened on that beach finally and fully realized. She thought of the envelope and note she'd tossed in the trash. The one her parents had never mentioned. They all had to have seen it, including Lacey.

"You know, I've been trying to remember exactly what happened that day on the beach, and today, I did. I remember that the resort took me exactly where I wanted to go."

"Nora, please." Her mother's voice was full of terror.

"The so-called accident was literally my fault. I didn't surf. I didn't even attempt it. But what I did do was try to end my life."

The moment Nora said those words aloud, the buzz went out of her in a *whoosh*. Deliverance came by putting words to an event that had taken her weeks to fully remember. But one her family had known about all along.

She looked around the room, at all the faces staring at her with various expressions of concern and alarm. "That's the truth that my parents don't want you to know. I tried to kill myself and I botched it. Can you imagine? I actually drowned . . . but then I lived!" She wanted to laugh at the sheer irony of it.

"Nora, go lie down," her father commanded her. "We know you've been through a lot, but you're not remembering things clearly."

"I was there, Dad. I remember it quite clearly now. You're so ashamed that you'd rather lie about it and let someone else pay for it. Now who's soft?"

The room filled with stunned silence. Her mother looked shell-shocked as she slowly sank into her chair. Her father, on the other hand, looked as if he was working to keep from exploding. He leaned back in his seat, picked up his wineglass and drank, then calmly put it aside. "Are you taking your medicine, sweetie?" her father asked.

How slick of him, to imply she was not taking her medicine and was therefore crazy. "Every day, Dad." She looked around the table. "My struggle with depression didn't fit in with the November narrative. My parents have often advised me that I could snap out of it if only I tried. I did try, but now I understand

I didn't try in the right ways. I'm not ashamed of it anymore. I'm proud of who I've become since I tried to kill myself. I'm proud of me for surviving. The only thing I'm struggling with now is the question of how or why I put up with this charade for as long as I did." She looked at her father. "Dad, I can't be the person you want me to be. I need you to know that I really miss Nathan too. But I need to be true to myself for once in my life."

"Well, Nora, if this is how you feel after all I've done for you, after giving you an impeccable education and a seat at the table of one of the most powerful law firms in the city, then maybe you would be happier in another profession."

He rose out of his seat and braced his hands against the table. "But I won't help you," he added through gritted teeth. "I am done helping you. If this is the gratitude I get, this embarrassing and childish effort to force my hand for whatever it is you're after, you best know I will not budge."

It was astounding to Nora that in this moment, her father still would not acknowledge that she had tried to commit suicide. He was still trying to make this sound like it was a simple argument between them instead of recognizing that she'd been so unhappy she hadn't wanted to live another minute.

Except, as Catherine once said, she *did* want to live. She just hadn't known how.

Well, she had a pretty good idea of how to now. She'd just burned her Before to the ground, and her After stretched before her, yellow-brick-road style. She was setting out on a new adventure. She had new interests, new friends, and hopefully a new purpose. And none of that was here in Rob Roy.

Also, she was late to a party.

"I don't lack gratitude, Dad. If I haven't said it enough, I'll say it again—thank you for everything you've done for me. But this is *my* season now."

She turned to Lacey. "I'll call you." She stood up and stepped away from the table. "Good night, everyone."

"Nora," her mother called after her.

But it was too late. Nora had left the moment she'd walked into the ocean.

Chapter 43

Nora *could hear the laughter and music drifting out of* the last apartment to the right of the run-down apartment building. When she reached the door with the big cardboard star that had *Blanche DuBois* written across it, she knocked. And then a little louder to be heard over the voices inside. A moment later, the door swung open. Catherine stood there in a silk caftan. The bun of her hair looked like it was sliding off one side of her head. She held a martini glass in her hand and had a glassy-eyed look about her. "Look who it is," she crowed when her eyes focused on Nora. "Plot Nine!"

Strange, but Nora smiled. "You said to come by if I could."

"I did indeed. Annabeth! Annabeth, come here! Look who it is!" Catherine shouted over the din.

Annabeth, with pink cheeks and bright eyes, pushed through the small crowd. "Who?"

"Plot Nine, darling. She's here."

Catherine and Annabeth looked at each other, then burst into laughter. "I thought he was drunk and imagining the whole thing," Annabeth crowed.

"Who?" Nora asked.

"Come in, love," Catherine said, sloshing a little of her martini onto the carpet. "We've been talking about you and your man. He's here!"

"What man?" Nora asked, confused as to what these delightfully drunk ladies were talking about.

"Jack." Catherine said it like Nora knew who she was talking about. "Or, I should say, *our* Jack. Whether or not he was ever in a corner store remains up for debate."

Nora's heart began to beat. "What are you talking about?"

"The corner store," Annabeth cried, as if Nora was being willfully ignorant.

And then he appeared. He was just standing there, a martini glass in his hand, looking as stunned as Nora felt.

Nora's breath froze in her throat. Her entire body felt made of lead, and her head was doing a dizzying spin, but this was Jack. Here. It was impossible. There was no conceivable way he could be here, standing before her, after all these months.

"Your hair is shorter," he said.

Nora looked around her—at the apartment filled with people. She was too scared to believe this was real, but . . . it was real. "Oh my God." *Oh my God! Jack?* "How . . ."

"Wait a minute," Catherine said. "Jack really is the guy?"

Jack did not take his eyes from Nora. "That's what I was trying to tell you. I'm the guy. And she's Plot Nine? With the sad tomatoes and giant cucumbers?"

Nora gasped. "How do you know that?"

"Nora . . . I'm Plot Seven." He laughed suddenly, and Nora felt like she was floating above them all, drifting off into space.

"That's impossible."

"I planted the dahlia tubers you left me."

She pressed her hands to her cheeks. "How can this be real? You know Catherine? You're Plot Seven? I thought it was an old guy."

"Yeah," he said with a soft laugh. "This is real."

Grandpa. He'd done this. He'd brought her to Jack. She suddenly surged forward, her eyes glistening with elation, and caught his hand. "I'm so sorry. Oh my God, I've missed you so much, Jack. It felt like I'd lost my best friend, which I know is crazy, because I'd only just met you."

"This is like a movie!" Catherine crowed. "Are you all hearing this? Jack's the corner store guy!"

"What?" Jerry shouted.

"We need a minute," Nora said pleadingly to Catherine.

"The theater," Catherine said grandly. "The place where all great love stories are told. Jerry, I need a refill!"

"But I want to hear this," Annabeth complained.

Nora grabbed Jack's hand before anyone could talk their way into accompanying them and tugged him through the open door and down the stairs. She kept turning around to look at him, unable to fully absorb he was here. He looked just as confused. So many thoughts raced through her head. If this was a dream, she never wanted to wake up.

But first, she had a lot of explaining to do.

The lights were still on in the auditorium, and they sat on the edge of the stage, facing each other. "I can't believe this," she said, her gaze moving over his face. "I can't believe you were right in front of me all along. This is going to sound insane, but I'm pretty sure my grandpa did this. He's dead, but . . . Wait. I'm getting ahead of myself." She took a breath. *Slow down.*

"This is what I remember," Jack said. "This sort of off-kilter conversation. Delightful, but so different from anything I've experienced."

Nora's heart soared. This was the moment she'd dreamed of.

"I have to apologize," he said. "I am so sorry, but I lost your number. You wrote it on that bit of paper, but that night was so crazy, and somehow I lost it. But I thought we had this connection and waited for you to call me. And . . . you never did." He gripped her hand in his, his fingers wrapping around hers.

His eyes were the warm blue she remembered. "Was it because I didn't call you? Did you think I'd ghosted you? Or maybe . . . maybe you didn't feel the attraction between us that night?"

"Oh, I swear I've never felt attraction like that before. Or since," she gushed. Too much? But she was afraid that if she didn't say everything on her heart, he'd disappear again. Sometimes you got another chance at life and maybe love and you had to take a big swing for the fences.

"Then why didn't you call?" he asked. "Did you have a boyfriend? Girlfriend? Second thoughts?"

"No, no, nothing like that." She was trembling. She could feel the weight of the next few moments. Either he'd forgive her or he wouldn't, but she had to go for it. "I wanted to. I left that store on cloud nine. I hadn't been that happy in months. But I'm not going to make up some funny story about why I didn't call."

"Okay," he said uncertainly.

"The thing is, I . . . I was on my way into a deep hole of depression at the time. Like, clinical depression."

"Oh?" He sounded more uncertain.

She feared she would blow this like everything else, but he needed to know the truth. She couldn't hide from who she was for anyone else ever again. *This* was the real Nora. She suffered from depression; she was sometimes funny, sometimes sad. But she wanted love. She wanted life. A real life, of her own making, with love and acceptance and cupcakes and basketball and whatever else made her happy.

"I . . . I sort of spiraled after that night. I was already starting to spiral, really, and then that happened, and the way I felt about you was so real and intense, and I . . . I convinced myself that I didn't deserve you. That it couldn't have been real." She rubbed her forehead. "It went downhill from there. I got worse. I had your number on my hand, but I felt unworthy, and I washed it off. Eventually I couldn't work, and I couldn't eat properly, and then . . . It's a long story, but . . ." She met his gaze. "I tried to kill myself."

Jack's eyes widened with surprise. He pressed his lips together like he was trying to keep from speaking.

Her eyes began to fill with tears. "By drowning, of all things, which statistics will tell you does not have a high success rate. But I did it. I drowned myself. I was technically dead for several minutes until someone pulled me out, and they brought me back to life and when they did . . ." She paused and drew a breath. She realized her hand was trembling in his. "This is so crazy pants, right? The point is, I'm not suicidal now. I had a near-death experience, and it had a profound impact on me in so many ways, and I've had some excellent therapy, and I'm on new antidepressants, and I've made some significant changes in my life. I'm good, Jack. I don't mean cured; I don't know if I will ever be free of it—but I'm better than I've been in years."

"Wow," Jack said quietly. "That's a lot to take in." He looked down at their hands. He had not let hers go.

"So . . . ," Nora said shakily, "I don't know if you're single or—"

"Single," he said. "You?"

"So single. Obviously." She smiled a little. "I don't know if love at first sight is really a thing or if I've read too many rom-coms, but I would love to have dinner sometime and talk, if you're okay with that. And if this sounds like the most absurd thing in the world and you're seeing red flags everywhere, I get it—talking about death and dying is not what normal people do." She wrapped her other hand around his. "I'm just so grateful that I found you and at least have the chance to tell you I'm so sorry I didn't call, and that you really mattered to me, and you still do, and you always will, and I really do think you could be the one. Apparently I think that even when I'm dead."

"This is really so unbelievable," Jack said. Nora's smile began to fade. "You nearly died?"

"I'm sorry about all the death stuff," she said. "You probably thought Darth Vader was the strangest part of our story."

He gave her a lopsided smile. "Yep, it's definitely you—funny, bizarrely interesting, weirdly enchanting Nora. So the first thing you need to know about me is that I happen to be super familiar with death. When we have dinner, I'll tell you about it. But, Nora . . ." He leaned forward, his gaze locking with hers. "That has to be tonight. Because I'm not losing that chance again."

In her head, the heavens opened to the rich, creamy light of a celestial garden. Something settled over her, like peace, or tranquility, or just the full force of optimism. "Really?" She bent over their clasped hands. "One sec—I may need to hyperventilate a little." She straightened up again. "I can't believe you were where I was the whole time. It's a miracle. Oh my God, I have so much to tell you."

"And I want to hear every word. But first—put your number in my phone."

Chapter 44

NINE MONTHS LATER

James, Jack, Byron, and Gus hauled the last of Catherine's many things to the truck. Copper wanted desperately to help, but her idea of helping was to nip at everyone's ankles. Lacey was supposed to arrive at any moment to pick Copper up.

Copper had been one of Nora and Jack's first joint acquisitions as a couple—a rescue mutt with an overly helpful disposition.

Of all the things that had happened to Nora in the last year, the one thing she couldn't quite grasp was that if she had not told the truth at her parents' house that Sunday night, she would not have run into Jack.

What were the odds? They were almost as staggering as surviving her NDE. Almost as staggering as Jack being at Catherine's and being Plot Seven.

She and Jack had been together since that night. They'd both agreed they'd be idiots to ignore fate twice. Nora had moved into his apartment six months ago, shutting the door on the last piece of her Before when she handed over the keys to her apartment.

"Can we move this along any faster?" Catherine shouted from the second floor of the apartment building. "We have rehearsals at five!"

"Oh my God, is she always this bossy?" James complained.

"Always," Jack confirmed.

With the furniture loaded, James hopped down from the truck, wiped his brow, and said to Nora, "This is where my help ends. I can't believe you talked me into manual labor."

"You're the best, James."

James bent down to scratch Copper's head. "I know I am, and you still don't pay me enough. Don't forget you have the meeting with the lady suing the city Monday morning."

Nora's law practice wasn't as robust as she'd like it to be, but she had enough cases to keep James busy. And they were cases she believed in—her clients were people who truly needed her help.

Neither James nor Nora kept up with the gossip of November and Sons, but James had recently heard they were changing the name to the November Law Firm. They'd been awarded a huge settlement in a medical malpractice suit, and everyone was getting a bonus. *"When are we getting bonuses?"* he'd asked.

Nora had laughed so loud that he'd told her to turn it down a notch.

"I'm out of here," James said. He waved to Jack and Byron, then shrieked when Lacey pulled into the parking lot too fast. "What is the matter with you?" he yelled at her when she hopped out.

"Sorry!" she shouted back. She jogged to where Nora was standing with Copper. "How long can I have her?" she asked, bending down to greet the wiggly dog. Lacey, who swore she had no time for pets, came over at least twice a week to take Copper to the Yard Bar, a popular dog park that served adult beverages.

"Just get a dog, Lacey. Can you bring her back tonight? I'll order dinner. I made an Italian cream cake."

"Oh my God, yes," Lacey said. "I love your cream cake. Come on, Copper. Come on, girl, let's go to the dog park!"

Copper was off like a shot to Lacey's car, as familiar to her as Nora's. Marnie—Lacey's girlfriend—waved at Nora from the passenger seat.

"Bring Marnie!" Nora shouted after Lacey.

"I will!" Lacey shouted back.

"Let's go!" Martin joined in the shouting.

Despite their best efforts, Nora and Jack had not been able to save the Triangle Theater. But Nora had found a way to help Catherine. While she couldn't get Brad Sachs to come to an agreement for the seniors to keep the property, she did manage to negotiate enough time for them all to find living arrangements. And with the money she'd been paid by Manuel Cervantes for her story, she'd been able to pay for Gus's treatment, and then used the rest to help Catherine and the senior thespians pay the up-front costs to get into a retirement community. That hadn't left anything for medical bills, which was still a source of worry. But when she got overwhelmed, Jack would wrap his arms around her and rest his chin on top of her head and say, *"We'll figure it out. You have to believe that we will."*

She believed him. He was her beacon in the dark. She tried to be that for him too. She was always there to hold him when his job was too much to bear. It was funny, wasn't it, that they'd been so weirdly connected by death, but united by life?

Catherine and her friends had taken the move in stride. One afternoon, when Nora and Jack had come to help with the packing, Catherine told Nora that they had expected it to happen all along. *"Miracles don't really happen like everyone thinks they will,"* she'd said.

"True. Sometimes you can't see them except in hindsight," Nora had said, watching Jack help Karen. Nora considered herself lucky—she'd found her place with Jack and these wacky seniors. With Copper and Lacey and Gus and James. It was her life, her design, her season, and she loved it.

"We'll be staging The Little Foxes,*"* Catherine had informed her this morning. As luck would have it, there was a theater

group at their new retirement community. *"You won't believe this, but Carol thought she ought to be the lead."*

Carol, Nora had learned, was an upstart already living in the retirement community who had dabbled in theater.

"I don't know who she thinks she is," Meredith said from across the room. *"What person in their right mind would think they could compete with our experience?"*

"Exactly," Catherine had agreed.

Carol had united Catherine and Meredith where so many others had failed.

"Ladies, can we wrap this up?" Walter complained. He waved at Nora. "Did you see my flytraps?" he called to her.

Nora had seen them. Nick had helped her find a variety that Walter could live with, and he'd won Best Exotic again this year. Nora was super careful to turn off the hose every time she used it.

The last things were loaded, and the thespians marched to their cars. Most of them had moved weeks ago. Only Walter, Doralee, and Catherine had remained until the bitter end.

Before they left, Nora made everyone arrange themselves for a photo and darted up the stairs to take it. Her social media exposure had changed to a single Instagram account, where she posted pictures of paintings, most of them pretty bad. And snaps of everything she and Jack ate, and their gardens, and lots of pictures of Copper—on the couch, on her bed, and in Lacey's back seat.

During the basketball season, Nora had posted photos of the Hot Shotz, who, she was proud to say, took third place in their division out of a field of three. The basketball season had come and gone. But Nora was on board to sponsor and coach the team next year. Some of her original girls were returning, and some new . . . including Willow's little sister, Summer.

Nora's shooting was getting better too. She wasn't going to win any tournaments, but she could at least run the court and do a layup.

"Willow's impossible," Tanya complained over coffee last weekend. *"Just eaten up with boys. Nora, this coffee cake is so good. You should open a bakery. The pie you made at Thanksgiving was unbelievable."*

"Thanks!" Nora had not given up on cooking—she'd filled Jack's kitchen with pots and pans. She just happened to be much better at baking, which the few new pounds on her proved.

After she took her group photo, Gus met her at the bottom of the stairs. "I'm going to take off."

"Really? Won't you come to dinner tonight? Lacey and Marnie are coming."

"Nah, I'm going to head back to the ranch. We've got a new guy, and I'm a little worried about him."

Gus and his huge heart. After he completed his program, he'd stayed at the facility to get his counseling credentials. He'd found his calling, a job he could stick with. He'd been sober since entering the treatment program. And he looked good too, strong and healthy. Most important, he looked happy.

"Next weekend?" she asked.

"It's a date." He hugged her, and on his way to the car, he high-fived Jack.

Jack closed the back of the truck and secured it. "Ready, gorgeous?"

"Ready."

"Why does it feel like we're sending the kids off to college?"

"Right? I thought they'd never get out of the house." She slipped an arm around his waist as they walked to the cab of the truck. "What was your worst move ever?"

"Hmm . . . to California when my mom died. Yours?"

"Home after college."

At the driver's door, he pulled her into his chest. "Best move?"

"Into your apartment. Yours?"

"Same." He tipped her Stinking Iris bucket hat back and kissed her. "Let's get this over with. I've already promised Walter I'll be out sometime next week to help build sets and help him transplant those damn Venus flytraps in his new community garden plot."

Nora laughed. For better or worse, they were part of the senior thespian crew.

Catherine was in the passenger seat of her car when Nora got in behind the wheel. "Did anyone tell you?" she asked as Nora started the car. "We're donating the proceeds of the play to that mental health alliance you told us about."

Nora gasped. "Really?" Months ago, she'd texted Dr. Cass for a recommendation for a therapist she could afford. Dr. Cass had sent her some names with some hearts and hand-clapping emojis. The therapist Nora had begun seeing had recommended that in addition to ongoing therapy, Nora attend a support group for mental health sponsored by the National Alliance on Mental Illness in Central Texas. Nora attended once a week.

"It's the least we can do after all you've done for us." Catherine patted Nora's knee as they pulled out of the parking lot. "Jim was right about you."

Nora laughed. Depending on Catherine's mood, what Jim was right about varied.

As for Grandpa's garden, Nora worked in it twice a week without fail. This spring she'd grown spectacular calla lilies of every color. She made cuttings and gifted them to the gardeners in the Stinking Iris Mighty Girls' Gardening Group, to which she finally belonged—she had the bucket hat and everything. Recently Nick had asked her to assist in the Green Thumb Club, where he taught urban kids how to grow their own food.

"You know," Nick had told her recently, *"I had not even a smidge of hope for you in the beginning."*

"Gee, thanks," Nora said.

"Not a sliver. If ever there was someone who could not garden, I thought it was you." He'd wrapped her in a one-armed side hug. *"Nice work, Nora November. Feeling a bit proud, I must admit,"* he'd said as he gazed at her calla lilies.

Nora felt a bit proud of herself.

As she pulled out of the parking lot of the Triangle Theater and headed for Catherine's new life (with Catherine singing a show tune, of course), Nora was a bit overcome with emotion. There had been so many days in her life she'd believed she would never know true happiness. And now she had it in abundance. Every single day.

She hadn't seen her parents since that night in their dining room, but some months later, on a cool autumn afternoon, she saw her mother in the Goodfellow Community Garden. She'd done a double take—it was indeed her mother watching her from afar. Nora waved. Her mother did too. And then she disappeared.

She didn't feel Grandpa around her like she used to, but every so often she'd catch sight of a big tomato or a perfect rose, and she'd imagine him moving down the path of his celestial garden with Roxie. He'd still be there when it was time for her to go.

In the meantime, she would work to make every day better than the last. She now truly believed the best was yet to come.

Life was for the living.

Acknowledgments

I have so many people to thank for the existence of this book. I could not have achieved it without the encouragement and guidance of my longtime agent, the fabulous Jenny Bent of The Bent Agency. She has always been more convinced of my abilities than me, and she does not give up. I am eternally grateful for her and to her—she has been a faithful steward of my career. Plus, she's a lot of fun.

The publishing industry is not without its rewards, but it can also be the hardest thing to navigate. Only a fellow author can truly understand the agony of this life. Teri Wilson has been my sounding board for many years on many topics. She is the BFF who builds me up every time my confidence wavers, who convinces me that the book I am writing is spectacular, and that I really should buy that very expensive handbag. She has bolstered my belief in myself from the moment I had the idea for this book and through its many iterations. Love her.

I would not be able to accomplish much of anything were it not for Linda Walker, who is not only my right hand but my very good friend. She's been making my life easier for years, and I think she would follow me off the edge of a cliff so she could clean up the mess I leave behind. There is no one I'd rather vent to than her about my favorite topics: books, men, children, food, and reality TV. Not necessarily in that order.

My family is just the best, but two of them in particular have helped me get where I am today. My mother, Wanda Keller, who instilled a love of reading and books in me from the very beginning, and who really wishes I'd write a mystery. My earliest of memories is our weekly trip to the library. And my sister, Nancy Vaughan, who started me on the path of published author many moons ago when she, in true big sister fashion, told me to send my first book to publishers or stop talking about it. That remark made me mad enough to do just that, and the rest is history. She is my ride or die, my mentor, and my dearest friend.

I must acknowledge the two teens who live in my house, the J's, from whom I've learned so much. Some of it is even useful. They are entitled to their privacy, and they would probably die if they saw themselves here, so let's just say they have contributed to my understanding of the world in ways I was not on track to learn before they came along.

I wouldn't even be writing this were it not for my editor, Laura Wheeler, who saw the potential in this book from the first read. She is the best of editors—smart, thoughtful, kind, and encouraging. I am excited about what I hope is a long and fruitful collaboration.

I am thankful to Julie Breihan, who got down to the nitty-gritty in my manuscript and uncovered all the bits that needed to be cleaned up before the pages went into production. An intensive read like that is necessary, but it is also a job no one wants. Few can do it as well as Julie.

The team at Harper Muse excited me from the jump. It is evident everyone there is rooting for the home team. Special thanks to Becky Monds and Nekasha Pratt who, along with Laura, left me with all the warm fuzzies after our initial acquisition meeting. The winning atmosphere extends to all parts of the team, and while there is no way for me to know everyone who touches my book, I am indebted to everyone who does. Special thanks to the publisher, Amanda Bostic, for leading Harper Muse in such a collaborative way. To Lizzie Poteet, the editor who stepped in when my editor was on maternity leave. Thanks to Natalie Underwood and Caitlin Halstead, who guided this manuscript through the process of turning pages into an actual book. Thanks to Kerri Potts and Colleen Lacey, who worked with Nekasha Pratt to market this book so that you, the reader, would know it is out there. Thanks to Margaret Kercher and Taylor Ward, who picked up the baton and publicized this book to buyers big and small. Thanks to Jere Warren and Patrick Aprea, who tackled marketing this book in a digital world. It's been a great pleasure to work with everyone.

If you or a loved one is struggling with mental illness, I recommend exploring the website of the National Alliance on Mental Illness (NAMI) or the National Institute of Mental Health (NIMH). Both organizations are a great place to begin a search for support and resources available in your area.

Discussion Questions

1. Nora's NDE is almost whimsical. Have you ever had a near-death experience, or known anyone who has? What do you think the phenomenon is?
2. Nora is aware early on that she wasn't always "there" for her family. Family dynamics are often impacted by misunderstandings and expectations. How do you think Nora's depression fit into the dynamic of her family?
3. Nick at the Stinking Iris garden shop really cares about gardening. What role do you think he played in Nora's recovery?
4. Nora's mother is a distant figure to her daughter. What did you think of Roberta November as a mother? Why do you think she chose to care for her daughter in the way that she did?
5. Nora's sister, Lacey, is a fixer. Every family has a person everyone relies on to get things done. How do you think Lacey found herself in that role? Was she justified in finally drawing a line with Nora?
6. Nora's cousin Gus is an alcoholic. At one point, she realizes that she was ashamed of his alcoholism but that he was never ashamed of her mental health issues. How does society view two very debilitating challenges such as depression and addiction? Should they be treated differently?

7. Grandpa's garden is a central theme in the book. What do you think the garden represented to Nora in her recovery from her NDE?
8. Nora and Jack felt an instant connection when they met in the corner store. Do you believe in love at first sight? Was this a case of love at first sight?
9. Jack is a hospice and palliative care nurse. How do you think his work has informed his outlook on life?
10. Nora's decision to quit her job may have seemed rash in the moment but was a long time coming. Afterward, she experienced some setbacks that could have sent her back to beg for her job. Was she reckless, or did she need to take that leap of faith to move on?
11. Catherine Henry, star of the stage, was a thorn in both Nora and Jack's sides in the beginning. What do you think the two of them learned from Catherine and her crew?
12. What do you think of the title? Does it fit the theme of the book? In what way?

From the Publisher

Help other readers find this one:

- Post a review at your favorite online bookseller
- Post a picture on a social media account and share why you enjoyed it
- Send a note to a friend who would also love it—or better yet, give them a copy

Thanks for reading!

About the Author

Kathy Whitaker Photography

Julia London is the *New York Times* and *USA TODAY* bestselling author of numerous works of romantic fiction and women's fiction. She is the recipient of the RT Bookclub Award for Best Historical Romance and a six-time finalist for the RITA award for excellence in romantic fiction. She lives in Austin, Texas, with two teens, two dogs, and an astonishingly big pile of books.

••••••

Connect with Julia at julialondon.com
Instagram: @julia_f_london
Facebook: @JuliaLondon
Twitter: @JuliaFLondon